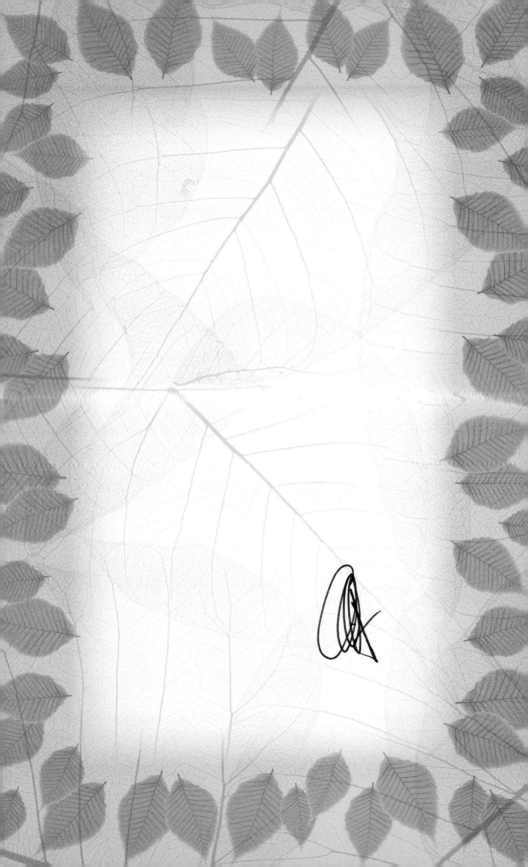

Eyes Like Leaves

Eyes Like Leaves

Charles de Lint

Subterranean Press 2009

Subterranean Press
PO Box 190106
Burton, MI 48519

www.subterraneanpress.com

Contents:

❧Introduction

YES LIKE LEAVES IS an early novel that comes from the same time period as the four collections of short stories that Subterranean Press has published to date.

Why was it never published? Let's go back in time…

I sold my first book in 1983—I sold three of them in the same week, actually. Kay Reynolds at Starblaze Donning bought *The Harp of the Grey Rose*, while Terri Windling, who was with Ace Books at the time, bought *The Riddle of the Wren* and *Moonheart*.

Eyes Like Leaves was my fourth novel, finished sometime in 1980. I was a far more prolific writer back then, and by the time *Moonheart* was published in 1984, I had finished *Yarrow* and was already researching and writing *Mulengro*.

I was fortunate to have found an enthusiastic readership for my work and, when Terri Windling asked for another book, I offered *Eyes Like Leaves* and it was accepted. But before we went to contract, Terri had a cautionary talk with me. She pointed out that at the moment I had two secondary world fantasies published and one contemporary. If we went with yet another secondary world fantasy, that was fine, but it would forever be my brand as a writer.

So I had a decision to make. I was happy with *Eyes Like Leaves*, but I realized that I wanted to take a different direction with my career. *Yarrow* had cemented my love affair with contemporary fantasy and there was no turning back, so I offered it up instead. So *Yarrow* was the book that followed *Moonheart* and, eventually, *Eyes Like Leaves* fell between the cracks like some long-forgotten lover.

REVISITING ALL those old stories for the various short story collections brought *Eyes Like Leaves* back to mind, and I'm happy that the novel will finally see print. I've just spent the past seven months entering it from its typewritten state into my computer. Working on the manuscript was an interesting process. In many ways it was like flipping through old scrapbooks, or high school yearbooks.

I may not remember exactly who I was when I wrote *Eyes Like Leaves*, but there are traces of the influences that got me to write that book on every page. A predominant one is the psych-folk movement that came out of England in the mid-sixties/early seventies—music by groups like Dr. Strangely Strange, Trees, Bread & Dreams, C.O.B., but especially the Incredible String Band and Tyrannosaurus Rex (the early acoustic version of T. Rex), with undoubtedly a hefty dash of Donovan.

I don't know if you'll see it the same way that I do, but I hear a soundtrack that runs from the first page through to the last. That soundtrack has my favourite bits from the artists mentioned above, but also includes traditional Celtic music, German electronic music, and pre-fusion jazz. In other words, the usual stew of influences that most people who work in record stores pick up, by way of osmosis, if nothing else.

For those of you who like to follow continuity threads, the setting is the same as my novel *Into the Green* and some of the pieces that appeared in the previous early story collections. It's just a lot earlier in the time line.

Because the novel had never been published, I was free to edit it as I wished, but I wanted to give due respect to the kid who had this vision of his story some twenty-nine years ago, when high fantasy was in its heyday, and everyone was captivated by the likes of J.R.R. Tolkien, Andre Norton, Roger Zelazny, et al, so most of my changes have been grammatical. I hope I've remained true to the young man that I was, and that this book will stand nicely alongside the classic works of those times.

THANKS AGAIN to all of you who made these books possible. If you hadn't kept buying them, Subterranean Press wouldn't have kept publishing them.

And just for fun, let's pretend this is a DVD, because at the end of the book, when you've finished the story, you'll find a bit of bonus material.

IF ANY of you are on the Internet, come visit my home page at www. charlesdelint.com. I'm also on MySpace and Facebook, so you can drop in and say hello to me there as well.

—Charles de Lint
Ottawa, Winter 2009

for
Robin Williamson
and dedicated to the memory
of Marc Bolan

Eyes Like Leaves

...let us chime in the heather blue of their two-handed harpers
spiralling from red and silver strings
tones of the faces that speak from Jurassic rock
with eyes like leaves
a winding music keen and exultant
through the green drum of the hills

—Robin Williamson,
from "Five Denials on Merlin's Grave"

Part One:

Gathering the Threads

These are the mythic times when sages get their say,
who sing like firebirds from the ash, whose deeds are legendary...

—Robin Williamson
from "Mythic Times"

First

ARN KNEW HIM FOR a wizard, the tall greybeard, calm as a tree, with the wisdom of longyears patterning his sky-blue eyes. They met on the streets of Tallifold, a large port on the south coast of Fairnland, dhruide and streetsinger, Puretongue and Tarn.

"I have been searching for you," Puretongue said. He touched the mark on Tarn's brow that was shaped like a crescent moon. "I need a prentice. I have a task that reaches beyond my lifetime—in you I will see it fulfilled."

Tarn's eyes widened. A tremor of strangeness stole over him, fear mingled with bright wonder.

"Me?" he asked.

"You."

"But, why?"

"The reasons are unimportant. Are you willing to learn what I can teach you? It won't be an easy task."

"I'll try, but..." Tarn met the greybeard's clear-eyed gaze. "Are you sure you haven't mistaken me for someone else?"

"I am sure."

"When will we begin?"

The tree-wizard smiled. "We have already begun."

They left Tallifold that day, journeying north to where autumn touched the summer woods of Avalarn. The wind teased their cloaks with curious fingers. The sky dreamed blue above them. The woods whispered wise about them.

Listening, watching, Tarn began his lessons.

THERE WAS always salt in the air around Codswill, a small town on Cermyn's east coast, even miles inland when the wind was right. Salt and the sharp odours of fish and fish-smoking, the smell of nets drying, for Codswill lived by its fishing trade. Its small boats timed their comings and goings to the tides. They spun and wove a spider's web of nets across the waters of the Channel Sea by day, docking at the wharves at night like moths clustered about a flame.

Tarn Galdmeir stood at the window of his room in The Hart's Inn, his hands on its broad sill as he stared out across the darkened town to the wharves. Beyond the small forest of ships' masts, the restless waters of the Channel Sea shimmered with phosphorus and moonlight. It was almost midnight, in the late spring of the year 526, as reckoned by the Dathenan calendar.

Tarn was exhausted, but sleep eluded him tonight. Snatches of memories flitted like fireflies through the greyness of his fatigue. He listened to the sea murmur against the wooden pilings of the wharves, distant, but clearly audible in the quiet that wrapped the town. Closer, the inn creaked to itself in the darkness.

It was in an inn such as this in Tallifold that he'd lived years ago. He'd been just one more street urchin, eking out a meager living from singing in the streets, sweeping the inn's main room for his board, pick-pocketing at times. But that had been before he met Puretongue.

"I can't do it," Tarn said.

"You can."

Puretongue's voice was firm. His form shimmered in the firelight, grey hair and cloak feathering, shifting, changing...

The raven cawed once, a harsh, impatient sound, then the dhruide faced Tarn once more. His lips curved in a slight smile, eyes a glint in the fire's glow.

Tarn sighed and gathered his thoughts, focusing them as he'd been taught.

Forms are fluid when named, he remembered, so he named it: raven. He drew strength from the hidden places inside, from the dhruide's lessons, from his own deep dreaming. He sought his taw—the inner silence where the power lay hidden. He saw his fingers shimmer, feather. His head ached as he reached for the shape.

Almost he felt the change...so close...

Then it was gone.

Lost.

"I'll never learn," he muttered.

"You will," Puretongue said softly. "You must."

IT WAS a sense of discordance out there in the night that kept Tarn at the window. It was not so much the Saramand, though their viking raids were worse than ever this spring. There was something else abroad in the night, something old and dark. An evil that he couldn't name, and nameless it was a greater threat. He didn't dare wake a seeking-magic to find it for fear that the spell would draw whatever it was to him, as surely as he was already drawn to it. He wasn't about to repeat the wizard Jaal Osser's mistake—seeking a hill mage, but waking instead the dragon-shaper that destroyed him.

He ran his fingers through his dark corkscrew hair and frowned.

TARN LOOKED up. High amidst the interweave of the oak's branches he saw a snug house with a leafed roof and trailing vines that grew from the flower boxes under the windows. He smiled, thinking, where else would a tree-wizard live?

"How do we get up there?" he asked.

He looked for a ladder or a rope. The closest branch was twenty feet from the ground.

"I will have no difficulty," Puretongue said. "But you will have to learn to feather yourself. It's that, or sleep on the ground."

He shapechanged. A raven lifted sloe-black wings, rose to disappear into the house. Tarn sighed and sat down, back against the oak's broad trunk. When the evening deepened into midnight, he stood and called a question up to the silent house.

"How long do you plan to leave me down here?"

There was no answer except for the wind moving through the leaves high above.

Tarn kicked the tree. Cursing the sudden pain in his toe, he sat down again, damning all wizards and their incomprehensible methods of teaching.

THE TEA in the small clay cup on his nightstand was cold when Tarn finally turned to taste it. He returned to the window, sipping, and studied the night. His eyes were round and wide, a strange mingling of gold, grey and mauve. They pierced the darkness with the intensity of a wolf stalking its prey. His gaze roved the streets, searching for something more than the inky spill of long shadows. The buildings were black bulks with light spilling here and there from an unshuttered window. Then, at the end of a cobbled street, he saw movement, furtive and sly.

"I'M TRYING," Tarn protested. "I really am. But everything you teach me just slips away when I finally think I understand it."

"If you want to learn the old magics," Puretongue said, "you must first put away your need to view it as a constant. Stop scribbling every little truth I give you in your notebook. How long is truth true for? The old knowledge is like a bird in winding flight—always in motion, ever changing."

Tarn nodded. He heard in the dhruide's words an echo of something he'd always sensed and had a sudden need to write the words down so that he would remember them. Writing was one thing that had set him apart from the other street urchins and he'd cherished that difference. But writing it down only perpetuated his present problem. He sighed and pushed the need from him—out of his mind, but not forgotten.

"There must be more to it that that," he said. "I know there must be more."

"More?" Puretongue chuckled. "Tarn, O lad. There are worlds within worlds more."

Tarn looked away. As he lifted his gaze to the night skies, the darkness fell back before his eyes, growing ever deeper. The longer he looked, the smaller he felt. The stars loomed huge and brilliant while he diminished. The dark between them was an empty void without end. He shook his head in fearful wonder. He'd been with the tree-wizard for three weeks. Had he learned anything?

"How do I find it?" he asked in a small voice.

"Within yourself. The answers—"

"Lie within myself. I know. But knowing that doesn't help. I've searched and searched till my head aches, but all I find are more riddles."

The dhruide was silent. Then he smiled and laid his thin hand on Tarn's brow, covering the moon-mark.

"There is power in names," he said. "That is the Third Lesson of the Oak. So I will name you Galdmeir—Riddle-well. With the strength of that naming, you can't fail."

"But—"

"Don't try so hard. Learn to be quiet inside. Still your inner conversations, your restless feelings. In your taw, in the heart of that stillness, you will find the answers to your questions."

Tarn nodded. He tasted his new name, thought over what he'd been told.

"What of the First Men?" he asked, changing tack. "Those ancient people who set their mark across the hills. What can you tell me about them?"

Puretongue smiled, knowing where this new line of questioning was leading. "Know this: Those who lived here in the first days knew truth, and never hoarded it."

"But what about their stoneworks? The longstones and towers, henges and roadways? They pattern the land, hinting at wisdoms, and they're more lasting than any words my pen might put to paper, but they hide their secrets."

Puretongue sat quietly, considering.

"They are patterns," he said after a moment. "Storehouses of...power some might say. And now I can see a use for your scribbling as well. Like the stoneworks, your letters can set echoes of those patterns reverberating in the minds of those who might read them."

He regarded Tarn with a new interest, his deep blue gaze piercing through to the youth's heart as though reading all he'd ever written, perhaps all he would ever write.

"And you have used your gift wisely," he added, "I can see now, for all that you scarcely understood what you were writing down half the time. A wise man follows his deepest instincts—that is the First Lesson of the Birch."

"Can you teach me to read the patterns in the stones?"

Puretongue smiled. "Do you have the time to walk the length and breadth of these isles to read them? And then, when we are done, to start all over again, for they will have changed their tale before ever we reached the end." He shook his head. "Listen to the voices of the stones if you must read them. Your taw can hear them speak, though you think you can't." He paused, then added, "These days they speak of things waking."

"The old ways are returning?"

That was one thing Tarn never tired of hearing the dhruide tell—tales of the old days, before the coming of the Dathenan, when the Isles were ruled by wizards, and the Tus and erlkin dwelled in an uneasy balance.

"Something returns," Puretongue said.

"Is it the Summerlord?" Tarn tried, remembering a certain tale.

Something flickered in Puretongue's eyes and for a moment his shoulders seemed to bow under some great weight.

"The Summerlord's kin," he said.
His voice was like the wind hovering on the edge of a storm.

TARN SET the half-empty tea cup down on the windowsill and leaned forward. The moon-mark on his brow pulsed as he gathered his taw. That inner silence cloaked the jumble of his thoughts, clearing his mind. His range of sight deepened, his breathing slowed.

He saw two figures on the cobblestoned street, the first oblivious to the presence of the second. The first was mortal. The other, the stalker...

"A dyorn," he murmured.

His blood chilled.

HIGH ON the downs above Avalarn, with his taw wrapped about him like a mantle, silence inside him like the soundless tread of the night, Tarn stood. His arms were outspread, his face serene, eyes closed. He looked inward. From that silence, he found the name he sought and took it. He shaped it with the power of his taw into a sound like wings the colour of his own dark hair and embraced the sky.

As he spoke the name his body shimmered, feathered. He rose into the air, sailed on the wind with a wild joy pounding in his heart. A dozen yards he winged, then faltered, tumbled down. The wide spread of a juniper broke his fall. He stood in the middle of it, bruised but triumphant, his face flushed with pride, then ran the remaining distance to Puretongue's tree.

"I did it!" he cried, finding the dhruide gathering herbs in his garden. Not even the dull throb of a headache could diminish Tarn's joy. "I did it!"

Puretongue looked up. That slow smile of his spread across his face, crinkling his moustache.

"I knew you would," he said.

TARN STILLED the sudden leap of his pulse. He altered his normal vision into deepsight to pierce the night's shadows and fixed his gaze on the dyorn. Time elongated into slow moments. He took in the misshapen body, powerfully muscled, the white hair that hung in greasy strands from its saurian-shaped skull. Its skin was swarthy, its leather tunic and trousers dirty. But the long length of its curved blade glittered bright and polished in a shaft of moonlight. It glittered menacingly, then disappeared as the dyorn moved into deeper shadows.

Tarn tracked it with his deepsight. With a rush of adrenalin, his first moment of fear shifted into excitement. He wasn't a novice, helpless in the face of his first foe. He knew how to deal with Lothan's stormkin.

He moved to the sill, balanced on the balls of his feet, poised and certain. Waiting a long moment, he loosed his taw. The power enfolded him, changing his flesh and shape. He was airborne, a winged form, swooping downward, the wind of his descent exhilarating as it rushed through his head feathers.

But by using magic, he had warned the dyorn.

Faster that he could have thought possible, the dyorn lifted his blade in a long sweep. Tarn dodged as the sword whistled by his wing, but he lost his balance in the process. His landing was ungainly, losing him precious seconds. Letting the winged shape fall from him, he rolled to his feet, shaping a scabbarded blade at his back. It was a twin to the dyorn's weapon, a two-edged sword, slightly curved, with a guardless hilt. He ripped it from its scabbard, only just catching the dyorn's second blow.

He felt the violence of the impact all along the length of his arm, dodged, then stepped in and to the side. Their blades engaged again in a quick flurry of movement that warned each of the other's skill before they broke apart.

Tarn reached inside himself to shape his taw, but the dyorn charged, denying him the moment's respite he needed to harness his magic. Cursing, he fell back before the creature's onslaught. He could hardly defend himself, much less attack. He'd been too sure of himself, he realized—a lesson he might not live to profit by.

Centering his deepsight on the dyorn's unblinking gaze, he continued to fall back, feigning a weakness in his defense. He let the dyorn almost catch him in a whirling figure-eight weave and took another step back, only to feel the stone wall of a building. The dyorn grinned.

Tarn sidled left, stepping into the dyorn's next attack. They grappled for a moment, the creature's foul breath heavy on Tarn's cheek. Disengaging, he sidestepped, repeating the figure-eight weave, again feigning the weakness, before rolling under the creature's long reach. He felt the sting of a cut along his upper arm as he came to his feet.

Their blades clashed again and he opened his defense a third time. He caught the glitter of anticipation in the dyorn's eye and twisted his blade to meet the expected attack. In and around their swords wove their figure-eight, but Tarn dropped to his knees. His blade became a blur in the shadows as he swept it in, thrust up and forward. The dyorn toppled onto him, the hilt of his blade striking Tarn on the shoulder. Tarn heard the clatter of the sword as it fell to the cobblestones behind him and bowed under the sudden dead weight of his foe.

Rolling free, he pulled out his sword and stood, His breath laboured in heavy rasps and he slowed his pulse with an effort. He stared down at the slain dyorn, and he felt a little weak as the rush of adrenalin evaporated . His eyes misted and a throb began at the back of his head. The shapeshifting took its toll, brief though it had been, and coupled with the way he'd overused his powers these past dayss. He knelt beside the dyorn, cleaned his blade and sheathed it. But he was too weak to unshape it. It hung on his back like a leaden weight. His earlier weariness rushed up to meet the throb in his temples.

Three days ago the summoning had come to him in Tallifold. Expected as it had been, it still took him by surprise. He'd woken from a dream to hear the heavy footsteps of Saramand soldiers thumping on the stairs of the inn where he was staying and known he was discovered. He'd left through the window, a feathered shape winging through dawn's early light, and headed north, as the dream had bid him to.

North...

Leaving Tallifold on swan-wings, watching the fields unfold below, finding the familiar skies above Hemenbrawe Wood, remembering the woods of Avalarn and the times gone...how many years?...hiding from the invader, awaiting the summons Puretongue has said would come... but the dhruide himself was gone...his own youth was gone...and the summons...

Had finally come.

Wings gave way to the sure-footed lope of a wolf's gait, the swift graceful pace of a stag, shapes not lightly taken, but filling the heart with a lawless joy, drawing from the hoarded powers of his taw, replenished when he could...

A day as a drowsy oak, broad leaves taking strength from the sun, tangled roots nourished in the dark rich earth...nearing Codswill...by night now, the white horn gleaming on his brow, sharp hooves cutting the sod... north and north as the miles fell away behind...calm as the moon dreaming silver on high in its web of star...north to Codswill, the unicorn...

Stepping onto the beach this morn, sleek shape falling from him, woods behind...waif-thin now and curls all tangled, hearing the wind in the trees like a tune of old when the longstones were young...and mixed in its measures...the wave-washing harmony of the Channel Sea...

TARN SHOOK his head and looked around. The dyorn's prey had long since fled—if it had even known it was being hunted. But the dyorn's body remained. If he wasn't so tired...

His swift journey north, the years of hiding, had worn him down more than he'd thought. Tempered him, perhaps. Made the magics more ready at hand. But it had done little to curb his impatience. He wanted to be *doing*, not waiting; and now that the time for action had come he moved too quickly, spent his energies when he should have been hoarding them as never before.

Oh, Puretongue, he thought. I've still to learn patience.

Bone-weary, he delved inside himself to find a shape for one more task. Finding it, he named it. His thin shoulders widened, his chest deepened. The ache in his head was a steady pounding as he stooped to lift the dyorn. Slowly he set off with his burden, leaving the town behind. There were enough rumours of stormkin abroad without adding fuel to them by leaving a corpse where anyone could trip over it. Such creatures fed on the fear that such a rumour would generate.

He secreted the corpse in a thorn thicket, far from the town and the roads leading into it. As he pushed the last branch into place, his stomach gave a lurch. Too many shapes, held too long. He pitched forward. The shape he wore fell away like a discarded cloak and he lay as he'd fallen: A slender form, dark like a stain upon the grass.

HE WOKE to find the sun hot on his back. Slowly he rolled over to stare up into a brilliant blue sky. For long moments he simply lay there, letting his mind clear. When he finally sat up, he rubbed the moon-mark on his brow and smiled, feeling rested for the first time in long days. The forced sleep had done much towards making him feel whole again. For awhile he'd been stretched too thin, his life essence elongated, as he drove himself on. But now—

He remembered the previous night in a rush.

The dyorn he'd slain—it had been hunting. What had become of its prey? He turned his thoughts back to that moment before he'd recognized the dyorn for what it was. His deepsight had shown him a young woman, plainly featured but with bright red hair. And there'd been something about her...

He shook his head, recalling again his summoning dream. He was to go north. And in Codswill, just before Beltane, he would find a mage that he must lead to Pelamas Henge. To the Oracle there. Beltane night was less than three days away now. That was the reason, as much as the Saramand pounding on his door, that he'd come north with such speed. But once he'd reached Codswill, he'd not found even the whispered memory of a mage.

Again he thought of the dyorn's prey. Her? Was she the mage? The one he must lead to the Oracle at Pelamas? If she couldn't even fend off a dyorn...

He stood up, still undecided, and returned to the town. He'd left his staff and pack in his room. Hunger rumbled in his belly. He could do with a meal. He would eat, then go ask in the market again today. And if he saw a girl with flame-red hair...well, she wouldn't be too hard to miss in a town of dark-haired Dathenan. And if she *was* the one he sought...

"AYE, I remember her," the old fisherman said. He set his half-mended net aside and took the time to relight his pipe before he went on. "Hard to forget hair that bright. Think she came with the latest landless out of Meirion—docked yestermorn. The ship's long gone back for more." He shook his head and spat on the dock. "Terrible business. They say the invader plans to strike at Cermyn next. What do you think?"

Tarn shrugged, hiding his impatience. It was still before noon and the day was warm. Gulls winged over the wharves, their cries like the sharp haggling of chapmen. Salt was strong in the air, the reek of fish stronger. Danger and talk of war seemed out-of-place.

It was a peaceful scene, Tarn conceded , for all the fisherman's words. But the undercurrent could not be ignored. There were too many refugees, housed wherever there was room—and that was fast coming to a short supply. At one time or another throughout the morning, he'd noticed there were three or four of the landless staring east across the waters to where their lost homes lay. The spectre of war reared its head. And, Tarn thought, remembering his own mission, there was more than the Saramand to contend with. There were stormkin abroad—like last night's stalker.

"The girl..?" he began.

But the fisherman cut him off. "Dath! If the king had any guts he'd have sent men into Fairnland and Gwendellan when the snake-lovers first landed. Then we'd not be overrun with homeless crofters, nor fearing the threat our own selves."

"Do you know where I can find her?" Tarn asked.

"Eh?"

"The girl. With the red hair."

"Her?" The fisherman shrugged. "Left this morn, she did, with a pack of tinkers—least I think it was her I saw on my way down here after breakfast. Had the same hair, sure enough, though it hung down her back in a long braid today. Say." He regarded Tarn curiously. "Why are you looking for her? Are you kin?"

Kin? Tarn remembered kin.

"THE DARKNESS will grow, Tarn," the old wizard said, "before ever it diminishes."

"But why?"

He was close to understanding much, but for every knowledge gained, a new chasm of ignorance opened under his feet.

Puretongue sighed. "Who can say? The weavers weave, Meynbos, the Summerlord's staff, is broken—and with it, his power. Year by year his strength flows from him, like blood from a wound. That wound is almost dry now, Tarn. The summers will grow colder until they fail altogether. And then the Icelord alone will rule the Green Isles."

He made the Sign of Horns as he spoke Lothan's name.

"We do what we can," he continued. "I, and a few others who still have our magics. But we grow thin. We bind the old evils to their prisons and seek to keep the Everwinter at bay. But this is a god's work, and none of us are gods. The time will come—all too soon, I'm afraid—when we will no longer have the strength for our tasks.

"The Woodlords are forgotten and the erlkin no more than a memory. We need to return wizardry to the Isles, we need to wake the sleeping magic of the Summerlord's kin. They wander through their lives, unaware of the Summerblood that sleeps inside them. But they hold the final fate of the Isles in trust, whether they know it or not. Woken, they will either aid Hafarl, or avenge his death."

"What can I do?" Tarn asked.

"Magic is like a fever, Tarn. Each spell you use echoes across the Isles, waking in turn the sleeping taws of the Summerborn—Hafarl's kin."

Tarn met his gaze steadily. "I'm only one person, Master, and a small one at that. Your time might have been better spent opening a school of magic, instead of teaching one streetsinger spells."

The tree-wizard shook his head. "Do you think it will stop with you? Your strengths are growing. Given time, your taw will be as deep and still as your name. The magics will spread from you. Each spell you use affects more than the task at hand—that is why such care is needed when you use magic. Echoes of each spell will ripple like long waves across the land and who knows how many they will wake?"

"And that's all I have to do?"

Puretongue smiled sadly. "There will be another task. I have foreseen that much. But the summons to begin it will come from Hafarl—not from me."

Tarn sat quietly, awaiting more. The dhruide looked away into unseen distances, his eyes bright and shining.

"What will the task be?" Tarn prompted at last.

"You will gather the Summerlord's kin."

THE SUMMONS had come, but it hadn't been clear. The dream had sent him north to find only one mage. Perhaps if the Saramand hadn't come pounding up the stairs, the dream would have told him more.

"Kin?" he said, repeating the fisherman's question. "No. But I think I know her."

"Well, she's travelling with tinkers now, lad. That's all I know."

"Where do you think they were bound?"

The fisherman scratched his chin. "Well, it's late spring, isn't it? Then I'd say north." He pointed with his pipe. "Up into Umbria and Kellmidden for the summer fairs."

HE LEFT Codswill by the north coast road, following the half-day-old trail of a tinker's wagon. The more he considered the red-haired girl, the more certain he became that she was the one he sought. That she hadn't used her powers against the dyorn, that he hadn't even sensed power in her...those were riddles that would remain unanswered until he caught up with her.

Night came when he was miles from town, still walking. His staff made tiny holes in the dirt beside his footprints. He wrapped his cloak around himself to ward off the night's chill. Gathering the endless questions that rose in his mind, he spun them into silence.

He longed to lift above the road in winged flight, or to feel the distance disappear under sharp hooves, but he contented himself with the more mundane mode of transportation that was his own two legs. He needed to conserve his strengths now for the tasks that lay ahead. And if there was one dyorn abroad, there might be more, or other of the Icelord's creatures. Any use he might make of his magics would draw them to him as surely as the moon draws the tides.

There would be time enough for spells when he caught up with the girl. If she was the one he sought, she'd know more than him anyway. He could wait for her guidance. She knew enough to head north, didn't she? And north lay Pelamas Henge and its Oracle.

⚘Second

THE COASTS OF MEIRION were aflame. Towns and small crofts smoldered in ashes, leaving black scars on the coasts. The stench of smoke flowed on the winds, and in it, the unpleasant reek of burnt flesh hovered like a nightmare edging into a dreamless sleep.

The Saramand were raiding.

On a hill overlooking the ruin of Gullysbrow, an old man stood watching the longships pull away from its charred wharves, sailing north along the coast with a strong wind in their red and yellow sails. He watched them with eyes as blue as the skies in summer, tempered with the edge of flashing steel in their depths. He wore a plain woolen tunic and leather breeches, a rough cloak overtop. His hair and beard were long and grey as stone, his frame thin, his features strong and not unhandsome.

He felt like weeping.

He watched the longships until they were only specks on the horizon, then wearily made his way down from the hills to look for survivors.

Gullysbrow had been a small village, its one short street encompassing a market square that ran down to the wharves. It was a pleasant enough place, though plain as most coastal villages were in Meirion. Traders came only twice a year, the tinkers once at Samhain. Mostly the folk eked a sparse living from the sea, trading to the shepherds on the inner downs for wool and leather, harvesting tiny crops from patchy gardens no bigger than their small cots. The soil was poor on Meirion's coasts, rocky as the sullen cliffs that took up most of its shoreline.

The old man made his way through the village, his boots scuffling through ash and dirt. Stone foundations supported smoldering wood frameworks on either side of him. From time to time he bent over a still form, shaking his head as he closed the corpse's eyes and straightened the stiffening limbs. He would go on.

It was worse near the wharves. The wooden docks once white with salt stains, greyed with sea and weathering, were red now with blood, and charred. Ships' masts, the keels and hauls of fishing boats, protruded from the shallow waters near the shore. Bodies were strewn everywhere. It was here that the brave folk of Gullysbrow had made their stand.

The old man's heart beat loudly, tattooing a quick anger in his ears. His hands clenched and formed strange shapes at his side. If only he'd come an hour sooner.

He bowed his head sorrowfully. The raiders would have faced more than peaceful fishermen weaponed with little better than harpoons and gutting knives. Their viking craft would not be the first snake-ship to vanish on the Channel Sea.

But he was only one man, with only so much power in him, and he could not be everywhere.

In his heart he knew the true struggle lay not with the Saramand, but with the Icelord of Damadar whose schemings had made raids such as this possible. Reflexively, his singers shaped the Sign of Horns. He sighed. Not man nor wizard could stay the Mocker's cold plans. For that the balancing strength of the Summerlord was needed. But Hafarl was gone and the Green Isles were at the mercy of the Lord of Winter.

The heap of bodies grew alongside the wharf as he dragged them one by one from where they'd fallen. His back ached and his arms and hands were tacky and red from their lifeless blood. He could have shaped a stronger form for this task, but he was determined to finish it in his own. He owed the dead that much honour.

As he worked, he muttered under his breath, cursing whatever ill-luck had caused the Summerlord's staff to be broken and forced Hafarl to flee before his brother's power.

Why does evil always have so much strength? Why must the meek and gentle fall under its heavy heel, ground into the dirt as though they were less than nothing? The knowledge of longyears, more centuries than one, might be his, but this was a thing he never could fathom.

The weavers wove. They wove an endless tapestry of strife, so that it seemed history repeated itself and merely the players changed.

Dark times had come to the Isles before. The Tus had driven the erlkin from the coasts, north to their final refuge in Ardmeyn. The Dathenan, in their turn, had taken the Isles from the Tus. But it had never been like this. The Tus and Dathenan had been content to take the land and hold it. There had never been a need for kind of genocide.

The old man frowned over the awful word. The Mocker's hand lay heavy on these new raids of the Saramand. But to what purpose? When the Saramand had cleansed the Isles of all life except for their own—what then? Would the Icelord sweep down from his holdings and kill them as well? Could even these mighty gold-haired warriors stand firm against hordes of stormkin—dyorn and ice trolls, dire-wolves and others, unnamable, unimaginable? Or would he simply lock the Isles in an endless Winter?

The bleak possibilities embittered the old man's heart, bringing a sour taste to his throat. He fell to his task with renewed energy. Better to finish this quickly and walk the clean hills once more. Desolate they might be, but at least they were free of this horror. And though the memory of this day, and too many others like it, would return to him again and again, at least there would be a distance to lessen the immediacy of what he felt nowhis feelings.

He bent over a youth. Look at him. No more than seventeen. Such a waste. His tired fingers grasped the neck of the boy's shirt, seeking purchase, and he stared at the lifeless face. A sword of ax had cut across the left side of his face—cut to the bone—and there was another terrible wound along his back. But the youth's limbs were still flaccid and his skin was…warm!

Gently the old man laid him back down and knelt at his side. He could see now the almost imperceptible rise and fall of the boy's chest. Fairlord! By all rights the boy should be dead. But if even a spark of life remained…

Cradling the boy's head between his hands, he took a deep breath. He stilled the murmur of inner conversation and enfolded his anger and bitterness in knots of silence, pushing them away. As his breathing slowed, his taw rose in him—cool and dark and quiet.

He leaned forward. Reaching out with his mind, he sought the boy's fading life essence, looked for a name…and finding it, he loosed his taw. Spells murmured from between his lips to knit the broken bones, smooth and reweave the life essence, heal the flesh. There would be scars. He could not heal the ruin of the boy's eye. But at least he would live.

The old man poured strength into the healing and watched the wounds close and heal. Breath rattled in the boy's chest and he could see movement now. Shock would hold the boy unconscious; his body needed sleep to combat the recent horror and further the healing, but…

The old man sat back and laid the boy's head down. He covered him with his cloak, found another to pillow his head.

Understanding flickered through him as he stared down at the youth. In that moment of soul-sharing that was part of the healing, he had discovered the reason for the boy's survival. There was unused power in him—asleep, it was true—but present all the same.

The old man bent his head as he let his taw recede. A jabble of inner conversation ran through him. His temples ached. There was so much to do—bindings to keep bound, lawless energies to stem. His power was spread throughout the Isles. At times he felt his small efforts were all that kept them from rifting apart in the cold grey seas. If only Hafarl would return.

The ache in his temples grew stronger. Nausea rose to join its discomfort. Perhaps he was growing too old for all of this. If there were others trained, he would gladly give way to them. But the time it would take to train others...

He shook his head. It was an old argument that constantly turned back on itself. It was pointless to bring it up again, even to himself.

If only he wasn't so tired.

Healing always seemed to take the greatest toll on him. It drained his life essence, as though his own body was the one that fought to live. He was weary, more weary than he had a right to be, for there was still so much to do.

He returned to his unpleasant task, pausing from time to time to crouch by the youth before going to fetch a new burden. It was hours before he gathered up the last of his strength and bore the still limp boy out of the village, up into the purple heather of the hills. Behind, a new fire burned in Gullysbrow—a pyre for its slain.

Not until they were out range of the ill-smelling wind, the boy settled in a bed of cut heather, did the old man look back. A thin trail of smoke rose from the village, starkly outlined against the sunset. The waters of the Channel Sea burned red in the west.

"Anann," he said. "O Worldmother. Give them rest. Let their spirits know peace."

He lay down beside the boy and his weariness rushed him into healing oblivion.

Third

ARN HAD BEEN ORPHANED too young to remember his parents, but any regrets he might have nurtured over that fact had been purged by the simple need to survive. Small for his age, he'd had to struggle all the harder against his urchin peers to scrape a living from Tallifold's cold streets. He learned quickly enough the futility of looking to the past. The past was gone. It was in the present that he had to survive.

Even as a child his features had been fine-boned. His high cheekbones and dainty brow, combined with eyes that were round, large, and dark against his pale complexion, soon brought him helpful attention. He became a favourite with the women of the brothels along King's Street and by the time he was ten he had more mothers than most children had aunts.

It was in the brothels that he received his learning—lettering and reading, coaching in manners that were useless on the street but necessary amongst the courtesans and their clients, and misguided attempts to convert him to a dozen different faiths. He soaked up teaching like a sponge, for he meant to rise above the streets to become someone of importance in the world. He'd seen enough of petty thieves, pimps and drunkards to last him a lifetime. Of one thing he was certain: He wouldn't end up like them.

Many and varied were the dreams he had for his future. Learning his letters, he saw himself as a scholar—perhaps in time, an advisor to Fairnland's king. Then, when his singing voice was found to be pleasing, he thought he might become a bard—a great singer like the harpers of old. When Justen, the sallow-faced hostler of The Carle & Queen Inn, showed him swordplay, his dreams took a new turn. Now he could imagine himself as a bold highwayman, or a knight of the king's guard, or the lost son of a high lord who had been spirited away as a child and now must fight his way back to his inheritance against impossible odds.

But for all his ambitious dreams, he never contemplated wizardry or magic. Even so, he devoured legends and folk tales with an appetite that never diminished with the passing of years. He never believed that wizards were real until he met Puretongue and learned that the old legends were true.

Dhruides and dhruidry. They were ill-treated by all the accounts Tarn had read.

The old legends detailed the cruelty of the ancient tree-wizards; but Tarn came to understand that they were written by men as blind to truth as they were to wisdom. The stories recounted the terrors the dhruides woke—of forests that yanked free of their roots to march upon command; of the Wicker Men on high hills, burning with a hundred innocents trapped inside their withy bodies; of seas that drowned fishing thorpes to which the dhruides bore ill-will; of hills that moved to the tree-wizards' summons, swallowing and crushing their foes.

The garbled accounts drifted down through the years, heaping the worst of deeds upon the brown-robed backs of the tree-wizards, never once telling the whole of the tale. For in each such Great Magic, Puretongue explained, was the shadowed hand of the Icelord and his stormkin.

Tarn's mentor knew the history of the Green Isles, from the time the Tus first stared in astonishment at the great stoneworks of the ancients, down through the centuries. Longyears, the dhruide called them, using the erlkin term for the passing of a hundred years.

The Mocker was the root cause of each of those legends. The Great Magics were loosed to stop him, but used sparingly, for their use cost too dearly. They were brought into play by the wise ones of the erlkin, sometimes by mortal wizards, sometimes by dhruides. But not without good cause.

Puretongue told Tarn of the forest that walked at the bidding of Evalarn, when the trolls of Bragdal stole the Erlking's son; of the moors that rose to Kastlwere's call and so ended the Long War between the Upper and Lower Kingdoms of Gwendellan; of the great waves that Feol the Sealking spelled to revenge himself on the coastal town of Brigwin when those fisherfolk sacrificed his daughter to better their sea harvests; of the five hundred rievers that the antlered Woodlord Keelscar burned in cages of wicker and heather for their part in the spoiling of the Seven Earldoms of Rosehorn.

But that was all long ago. Now the erlkin were hidden from men's eyes and magic was faded. And of the old dhruides, only one remained.

From Puretongue Tarn learned his histories and magics: The Lessons of the Trees, as the dhruide called them. He learned the names of more things that dwelled in the Green Isles than he had ever imagined existed. He learned dragonspeech, the language of magic, and windthought, the casting of speech mind to mind without sound. He learned fiercing, the taking of shapes for war, and deepsight, the vision that pierced night and lies. He learned softspells, the healing magics, and erlsongs, the spells that charm men and animals. And most importantly, he learned the strength from which all spells came: His taw.

His taw was the silence inside himself that was an echo of the stillness that underlay the power of the Isles; the power that filled each leaf of each tree, that rounded the hills and raised high the mountains; that flowed through river and stream and lay still in lake and pond, that coursed through the blood of every living thing; that feathered wings, furred limbs, scaled limbs; that rode the winds on high and hummed through the earth below; that bound the Green Isles by moonroad leys connecting longstone to cairn, shore to shore; deep, still, wild; filled with wonder and quiet beauty, but tempest-strong .

As Tarn learned, he saw himself in a new light. He knew himself to be but a small part of a great all. But for all he acquired, the street-urchin in him was hard to humble. He dreamed still, only now he was a great wizard, a master of dhruides who held the balance of the world in his palm, to whom kings and bards came for counsel. He was still small in stature, and couldn't forget the streets where he had survived by his guile and wits. He longed to be looked on with wonder and awe, much as he looked on Puretongue. He worked so hard at his studies in order to prove himself to others as much as to himself. Had he finished his prenticeship, he might have learned to deal with his pride and his need to achieve greatness. As it was...

"THE TIME has come," Puretongue said, "when we must follow our own roads awhile."

Tarn, misunderstanding, felt a hot flush of pride.

"Have I finished my studies?" he asked.

The old wizard shook his head. "Would that you had. No, Tarn, You still have much to learn. If I could, I would help you become complete, but I have other duties to fulfill and they can no longer wait. I thought there was time, but..."

His thin shoulders lifted and fell.

"What should I do? Where can I go?" Tarn asked, panic fluttering in him.

"Remain here, or return to Tallifold. But wherever you go, continue to work. Hone what you have learned. Seek to strengthen and deepen your bond with the dwystaw, the deep silence that binds the Isles, shore to green shore. Remember, there will still be a task for you to do. This summons will come all too soon, I fear."

"Why can't I come with you?"

"The weavers weave, Tarn. We will meet again."

HALF-COMPLETED THOUGH his training might be, the years with Puretongue had still tempered him into a finely-honed mage. What he lacked was practice. Experience. But returning to Tallifold, he was no longer the same youth that had left.

There was no need for him to sing in the streets for his living, but he did. There was no need for him to find lodgings on King's Street, but he did. He returned to await the summoning that Puretongue had spoken of, taking up the reins of his old life as though nothing strange had ever befallen him and he knew no more of the old magics that what he might have read in old tales. He was wise enough to keep his power to himself. In secret, he continued his studies, perfecting and honing his skills, and waiting.

Until the Saramand came into Fairnland.

They ravaged the coasts first, then drove their way inland. The folk of Tallifold fled before them—all except for those who lived on King's Street, for invaders or not, the yellow-haired warriors still had need for entertainment, ale and women. Those of King's Street prospered if they were cautious and luck shone on them. If not, they died quickly.

That last year in Tallifold, Tarn wore a new persona. In the taverns and inns he played the buffoon, the jester, and all the while he waited. He knew he trod a thin line. Unlike the tavern-keepers and courtesans, what he had to offer the invaders was far from indispensable. But they laughed at his jests and taught him their own ribald ballads.

And still he waited.

When the summoning came, he was more than ready. He had a year's worth of bruised pride that demanding reckoning, but the boots on the stairs had spoken more eloquently to him that even the summoning, and he fled.

The summoning. Walking the coast road north from Codswill, he remembered. It came as a dream...

FIRST A keening wind, sharp as a knife, cutting the bone...grey seas and grey hills...waves of wind-lashed waves, speaking in hidden tongues,

gorse and heather bending to the wind's grey voice...a bleak sound... moon above, glittering, silver...a strange music winding across miles of moor and sea...snatches of visions...henges, cold-stoned and towering... grey-stoned like the sea...old towers, overlooking the waves, ancient as unwritten history...bleak...

Taking him...through forests heavy with slow wonder, across lands once ruled by the dark-skinned Tus, once the wild kingdoms of the kowrie and erlkin, north and north...a vision of a place where frozen seas join white island to white island...colourless...evil like seawater clogging a drowned man's lungs...then the music drawing him back...back... to where a cloaked figure spoke voiceless words that echoed in his mind, having never passed through his ears:

Now it comes. A dark time, riddled with uncertainties. And I can do nothing. You, with the name of dark still waters. I give you this task. Gather my kin, those that survive. Gather the Summerborn.

"Where?" Tarn asked. "How will I know them?"

They are few, and fewer still with each passing day. There will be one I need, greatly, in Codswill, just before Beltane night. Bring that one to the henge at Pelamas. The others, those that can, will follow.

"Is it a mage I'm to find?"

If you will it to be so.

"And his name?"

There was no reply. Only the wind and its faint music, threading a melody that wrung a deep sadness from Tarn's heart as it grew fainter.

"The name?" he cried.

He felt himself awakening, heard a cry from the street below:

"Wizards burn the same as men if you bind their voices!"

Footsteps on the stairs...the vision still on him, making it hard to think...wakening...understanding his danger...fleeing...

HE REMEMBERED it well.

Shrugging his thoughts away, he looked for the peace within, in his taw, the inner silence. Searching for it, he found only the face of a red-haired girl, clear and sharp as though she stood before him. Her eyes widened and she gave a sharp cry, then the image was gone.

Tarn shook his head. The roadway was quiet. He listened to the murmur of the sea. The wind ruffled his hair, greeting him like an old friend. It seemed to speak, to ask, *Why do you walk, when you could ride me?*

How far ahead were the tinkers? He longed to answer the call of the wind, to cast this shape from him and ride the skyways, or race across the hills, unfettered and free. It took an effort to shake the desire. He knew he needed to conserve his strength. He would need it soon enough in the days ahead.

He thought of the girl again and was troubled. She seemed too innocent, too unknowing to be the one he sought. What if he was mistaken and the correct mage came to Codswill in his absence, and was gone before Tarn could return? But no. The feeling he got from the girl was too strong. She was the one. Only, if the Summerlord's kin were like her, what hope was there that the Icelord could be stayed? He shaped the Sign of Horns. Or was she hiding her power, aware of the stormkin that might be seeking her?

He cursed the slowness of his pace. What if she got too far ahead? Or if she were attacked while he plodded along here? He tasted his taw, sifted it for weakness. Surely he was strong enough to hold another shape until he found her? Puretongue had said...

"I GROW OLD, Tarn, and my power is spread too thin. If I fail in the days to come, it is you who must carry on."

"If you fail? What could I do then? You're so much stronger than I am."

"Stronger, perhaps, but stretched. My power spans a web touching all of the Isles. Much of it is caught up in bindings and healings and guardings. My taw is bound, Tarn."

"But..."

"You are strong, too, Tarn. Your taw is as deep as your naming. You will have strength enough."

ENOUGH? ENOUGH for what? He would see this task through as best he could, but knowing as little as he did, it was like walking in the dark without nightsight. If he stumbled…

It was worse than frustrating. Why wasn't he trusted with more of an explanation? There were always riddles, things half-said, barely explained. His pride rebelled against what seemed to be the very small part he had to play. Surely there was more he could do than escort some mage to Pelamas?

He knew he was being small-minded, but he couldn't shake the endless conversation from his head. One part of him asked, another answered, a third argued. At last, as though his saliva held all his troubles, he spat on the road and drew on his taw. Staff and pack joined his sword in the unshaping that was necessary if he still wanted them when he returned from—

…swan-shape…white wings cutting the chill night air…

He felt uncertainty burn away inside him as he gloried in the wind rushing through his feathers. Finding an updraft, he rode it north along the coast. Weariness would come later. It didn't matter now. For now he flew as though it was what he was born to do, giving less than half a thought to what perils his magic might call to him.

Were there stormkin abroad? He would deal with them. His confidence was strong. He had already slain a dyorn. He would confront other problems as they came to him, not fret over them like some haggard old priest of Dath worrying over his flock's sins.

The coastline unwound steadily beneath his flight.

Fourth

OT QUITE HALF THE distance between Codswill and Swaston to its north, a tinker wagon stood well off the coast road beneath a canopy of trees. It was sixteen feet long, half that length wide, and about ten feet high from the bottom rim of its large spoked wheels to the brass railed perch on its roof. It was made all of wood, with a leather-covered window on either side, a back door with folding steps and a driver's seat in front, two feet short of the width of the wagon.

The two large Umbrian wagon-horses that normally pulled it had been rubbed down and grained, and now were grazing quietly. A fire flickered behind the wagon, shielded from the road by the wagon's bulk, its light shredding as it disappeared into the leafy boughs of oak, aspen and birch above. A hoot owl called in the distance and Long Tom Turpen smiled.

He sat on the fold-down steps that hung where the wagon's tailgate would have been had it not been a tinker's wagon. He took a sip of his tea, grimaced and reached behind himself for a clay jar. Topping he tea with whiskey, he took another sip and smiled once more, leaning against his wife Megan.

They both had the red-gold hair and honey-brown skin of Fern Isle tinkers. Long Tom wore hunting leathers, dyed red and yellow and green, while Megan wore the traditional garb of a tinker woman: flounced plaid skirt, cotton blouse, low cut and embroidered, a woolen shawl over her shoulders. They were both barefoot, though Long Tom's boots stood by the fire.

Long Tom took another sip of his heady tea and regarded the three adolescents by the fire. Fennel and Kinniken were his own blood, both in their mid-teens, though Fenne was a year older than her brother. They were children to be proud of. Fenne had all her mother's good looks and more of her own besides, while Kinn was tall and straight with a voice that could charm gold from the clutch of the greediest miser, or a kiss from any girl, no matter how disdainfully she first looked upon him. But it was the stranger girl he regarded now, wondering.

Her hair was a tinker red—brighter even. "Fey as a poet," as his dad would say for hair that red. She was a slim girl, not even as tall as Fenne, with intense green eyes and a heart-shaped face. She claimed to be Dathenan, from Meirion, but her complexion was too dark, and where was the Dathenan with hair so red?

"It's quiet Carrie is," he said softly to Megan.

Kinn tucked his fiddle under his chin and began another tune. Fenne plucked a strange harmony on her cittern that, by all rights, should not have fit the old tune Kinn drew from his strings, but its notes slipped snugly into all the right place just the same,

"She has reason enough, Tom," Megan replied. "Poor lass. There's the blood of her family and friends aching in her heart. Aye, and whatever strangeness befell her in Codswill, besides."

Long Tom nodded. Perhaps she was fey. She'd told an odd tale of being followed by a cold shadow and then hearing the clash of a swordfight that brought home all the loss she was trying to forget. A swordfight! Codswill was a fisherman's town, quiet as any you could hope for. And he'd heard no talk of a swordfight, or even a knifefight, before they left. Still...

"I hope she brings no ill-luck," he began.

"Tom! And is that the way your dad brought you up? Speaking ill of guests and—"

"Whisht, whisht, Meg. 'Twas the tea talking, not me. I mean her no harm. She can ride with us until the Mocker speaks a kind word."

"It *is* the whiskey talking," Megan muttered. She made the Sign of Horns, then smiled and kissed him. "Do be still now and listen to the children play."

"Like a mouse I'll be," he promised.

He tried to look serious but his good humour broke through, sparkling in his eyes, spreading over his face.

"Away with you!" Megan said.

She laughed and gave his moustache a tug.

"Do that again, woman, and it's a-field you'll be sleeping tonight."

"Grim you'll never be, Long Tom Turpen." She gave his whiskers another tug. "Now do be still. Ach, listen. You've made me miss that the tune and knowing Kinn, he'll not want to play it again."

"Kinn!" Long Tom called. "You mother'd hear that one again."

His son looked up, teeth flashing in the firelight.

"And will you both be listening this time?" he asked.

Long Tom waved him to continue, then turned back to Megan.

"He grows too bold that one."

"He's your son."

"Oh? And who bore him? The goose in your dad's garden?"

"No. I found him in the back of *your* wagon. Now whisht yourself, Tom."

Long Tom grinned and leaned back, listening to Kinn draw the tune anew from his strings. His gaze met Carrie's and he caught a faltering smile start on her lips before she shyly bent her head.

"She's a good wee lass," he murmured, more to himself, "and bedamned be those that'd harm her."

Carwyn Lorweir watched the fire, felt her cheeks and neck flushing, more from pleasure than the warmth of the flames. She listened to the music, longing to join in, but she didn't know a fret from a string. Still, she knew how to enjoy. As she listened, she could feel her heart loosen its tight hold on memories that seemed more like bad dreams. For what seemed the first time in weeks, she was at ease, not fearing for her life, not reliving the terrors of…

She shook away the memory of the Saramand and their serpent-prowed longships. She could only begin life anew. It was hard to forget, but it was what she must do.

She tapped her fingers against her knee to the rhythm of the music. She felt safe here, enclosed in a small world no larger than the perimeter of the fire's light. The Turpens treated her with kindness and sympathy, but not overbearingly so. They, too, knew she must forget. And they had promised her a place in their wagon for as long as she wanted. A home, though it moved on wheels. Security. Surety that the terrors would not return.

Then she remembered Codswill.

Had that sense of being followed been no more than anxiety on her part? And the clash of weapons? She recalled a glimpse of a face behind her, horribly inhuman. Superimposed over it was something she thought was a bird, then it appeared more like a small man with kowrie features topped by black curls. She wasn't sure which frightened her more. The one changing from creature to man, or the thing that was never a man.

Just remembering brought the tightness back into her chest. She took a long breath, concentrated on the music and the camaraderie of the tinkers that hung like a palpable essence over the camp. The tightness eased and she stole another glance at Long Tom. She was rewarded with one of his brimming smile and felt the flush creep back up her neck. But she smiled back, her lips still stiff, before she looked down once more.

TARN RODE the night winds into dawn. He banked in the pinking air, his swan shape white as sea foam, bright with the sun's whisper upon his wings. He circled the woods above the tinkers' camp and came to earth a half-mile to the east, where the Channel Sea spoke tidal tunes against the lime cliffs. Staggering as he took on his own shape, he reshaped his staff and leaned heavily upon it, pressing the back of his hand against the sudden ache in his temples. It was yet another lapse of wisdom that had him lifting white wings into the sky, but though he was weary and for all the pain of power used, his heart was glad. What was a mage without magics? They were *supposed* to be used. But he was wise enough to approach the tinkers' camp with his magics hidden.

Long Tom looked up from last night's coals, a bundle of brittle kindling in his hands as he heard the footsteps nearing. He turned slowly, saw Kinn melt into the trees on the stranger's blind side, bow in hand, and nodded in approval. Fully turned himself, he laid the kindling down and stood up. He wiped his hands on his trousers.

"It's early you're abroad, stranger," he said in a friendly voice.

Tarn paused at the edge of the camp, leaning on his staff.

"I've come a long way," he replied, "and have a long way yet ahead of me. Day or night..." He shrugged. "The road fares on."

Long Tom took in the dark circles under Tarn's eyes, the tired set of his lips and stooped shoulders.

"So it does. Will you set and eat with us?"

"I would be honoured," Tarn said.

He crossed to the cold fire and lowered himself gratefully down. Laying his staff beside him, he tried a smile.

"My name is Tarn," he added.

"The silent pool, high on a mountain," Long Tom murmured.

"REMEMBER, TARN," *Puretongue said. "The names you keep for yourself are as important as those that others give you. Together those names form the various facets that make up the jewel that each of us is. That is the First Lesson of the Oak."*

Tarn felt the sway of the tree below them, heard the wind rustle leaves like tiny claws scratching against the windowpanes of the tree-house. He looked at the old man, trying to see beyond the salt-grey hair and lined face, remembering that he was a dhruide, a tree-wizard whose blood flowed slow and wise like the sap of the ancient tree under them.

"But..." he began.

Puretongue smiled.

"If it is a talisman you seek," he said, "I will give you one: Your name."

TARN SMILED, remembering, and humour awoke in his eyes.

"Whatever else it may be," he said, "it's a name as well. My name."

"Indeed." The tinker grinned. "And I am Long Tom Turpen, late of Codswill, and Ippswillow before that, for the wagon's my home and the road my only country." He motioned to the wagon where Megan and the two girls now stood. "My wife and daughters and…" He snapped his fingers and Kinn stepped silently from the undergrowth beyond the wagon. "My son."

Tarn nodded, only half-listening. His eyes were on the girl with the redder hair spilling loose across his shoulders and down her breast. His strange eyes brightened with an inner light. But before he could speak, she stepped close to the tinker's wife, her own eyes wide with fear. The blood rushed from her face.

"You," she said in a voice so low it scarce carried to where Tarn sat. "You…you were in Codswill…"

She clutched Megan's sleeve, her knuckles whitening. Tarn made as if to rise, then stopped when he saw Kinn's bowstring taut, an arrow notched. Long Tom looked grimly from Tarn to Carrie.

"Speak, lass," he said softly. Dangerous undercurrents hung in his voice. "What did he do to you in Codswill? How has he harmed you?"

Carrie's throat was tight with fear and she couldn't answer.

"I did no harm," Tarn said carefully. "Rather I did her good. I was sent to Codswill to find her and instead, slew one of the Icelord's stormkin that was stalking her." There was a touch of pride in his voice. He saw Megan make the Sign of Horns and his lips twitched bitterly. "Call not on the Horned One, mistress. It was not his blade that cut down the dyorn."

"Dyorn?" Long Tom repeated in a puzzled voice. "Carrie? Do you know this man?"

Numbly, she shook her head. Long Tom turned back to Tarn.

"Then how did you know to look for her in Codswill, you who name yourself after a mountain's silence?"

"I..."

Tarn met the tinker's gaze and was at a loss for words. His head still ached. For a moment his vision blurred. He reached for his taw to quell the growing fever, knowing that later, when he let it fade once more, he'd regret using it so soon. But now it served to clear his sight and ease the pain in his temples. He found words which he spun out before his listeners.

"I was summoned," he said, "by who, I'm not sure I can explain except to say that it was dhruide who told me to expect the summoning. It came to me in a dream and that dream sent me north to Codswill to find this girl." He nodded in Carrie's direction. "I was waiting in my room at The Hart's End when I finally spied her. She was in the streets below, shadowed by a dyorn—do you know them? Eyes like lizards, pale haired and yellow eyed. Gruesome."

"How can a servant of the Winter Lord be a reptile?" Long Tom asked. "I've seen enough of snakes and such to that know that the cold would freeze them."

"You'll have to find your own explanation for that. I can only tell you what a dyorn is. It is *like* a lizard, Master Turpen, but its blood runs as warm as yours or mine. I know. I slew it. I can show you where I left its—"

Long Tom waved him into silence. "Finish this tale of yours. What were you to do with Carrie? Who do you serve?"

"I serve myself, though in this matter I've been guided by the dhruide I spoke of. I didn't know who I would find in Codswill, only that I should go there to find a mage—a kin of the Summerlord. Once I did, I was to bring him—her—to the Oracle at Pelamas Henge."

Carrie regarded him, sick with terror. Long Tom noted that. He chewed on his moustache as he thought. At length, he sighed.

"It's a good enough tale," he said, "I'll give you that. Only—"

"Do you think I lie?"

Long Tom sighed again. "I mean, I believe you had a dream and I believe you slew, or dreamed you slew, someone or something in Codswill—though with what, I don't know. Your staff, perhaps? No matter. I also believe you were mistaken about who you were meant to meet in Codswill. My daughter is my kin. Not the Summerlord's, not a mage, not some changeling. *My* kin."

Tarn knew he was lying. He knew as well that Long Tom knew that he knew. But there was nothing he could do about it. He shot a glance at the girl and shrank at the terror he saw in her face. He had not meant to cause that. He had only...

He rubbed the moon-mark on his brow. What was he supposed to do? Raise up his magics against innocent tinkers? He had but to speak its name and his sword would reshape on his back. He knew he was quick enough to draw it and fend off the son's first shaft. It would be a near thing, but then what? He shook his head.

"I swear to you," he began again, "that what I say is true."

And the more he looked at the red-haired girl, the more certain he was that she *was* the one he sought. Why she hid her power, why she refused to recognize him, was a riddle for which he had no answer.

"No more," Long Tom told him. "It's my daughter you're frightening with your wild tale. I must ask you to leave. Meg will pack you up a loaf and a small jar of heather ale to take with you, for I'll not have it said that Long Tom sent away a hungry man. But it's go you must."

"But—"

"You're wearing my patience thin. Fenne, ready the horses. Carrie, into the wagon with you."

He stared at Tarn, dark eyes flashing. Tarn nodded. He took up his staff and slowly rose to his feet.

"Save your guesting," he said. "I have no need for it." He reached inside himself, drew more strength from his taw with a roughness born of frustration and anger. "And you, lad," he called to Kinn. "Save your shafts for the stormkin. They have come for her once. Don't be so foolish to think they won't return."

"You—" Kinn began.

The loosened bowstring tightened against his cheek.

"Loose your shaft," Tarn said, "and see if it be as swift as this."

He spoke a name and his form shimmered blindingly. The long white horn thrust from his brow, sharp hooves tore the sod as he bounded away through the trees, white flanks flashing.

Kinn's jaw hung slack. He loosened his bowstring and the arrow dropped from his limp fingers.

"Dad," he said.

He turned to see his father standing as slack-jawed as himself.

Then the fear woke in Long Tom's Heart. He'd been humouring the dark-haired stranger with his talk of stormkin and gods, for where were the magics alive in the world today? Such were fit for tales around the campfire, or when winter-bound in the wagons. But as his gaze followed the dwindling figure of the unicorn, all his mortality rushed over him in a wave of superstitious dread.

If such a thing were possible, man into fabulous beast...

He looked to Carrie.

Her face was buried in Megan's shoulder and both Megan and Fenne stood with the blood drained from their features. Long Tom named the thing Tarn had described to them. A dyorn. Stormkin were chasing Carrie.

Ballan, what had he done? If a man could become a unicorn in the blink of an eye, then surely the Mocker was real and he could send his stormkin.

Long Tom shaped the Sign of Horns, stared at his fingers. What use a warding when—

"The horses!" he cried, his voice brusque as he tried to put his fear from him. "We've miles to go if we mean to reach Swaston by nightfall. Kinn? Fenne?"

As they sprang to obey, Long Tom crossed the camp to where his wife stood. He motioned her away with his eyes and took Carrie in his arms, stroking her hair with an unsteady hand.

"Never fear, lass," he murmured in her ear. "We'll not let anyone harm you, be they spooks or ghosties or what. Be strong, lass. Ah, be strong."

Listening to her weep, he called in his heart to Ballan, the god of the tinkers. Oh, Lord of Broom and Heather. Give me strength to be strong as well.

He held Carrie closer. Over her shoulder he could see the wizard's staff lying where the small man had dropped it. The long length of wood seemed to stare back at him with reproach.

TARN SPED for miles, the wind sharp in his mane until he lost his anger in the four-footed drumming of his hooves. He galloped till the cool hand of reason wiped his anger away. Then he knew shame. He regained his natural shape. Tumbling to his knees from weariness, his head pounding. His hand reached out for his staff before he remembered that in his haste, he'd forgotten to unshape it and so had left it behind.

Fool, he named himself bitterly. Worse than fool. He was a prideful boasting ass with scarcely an ounce left of the sense that Puretongue had instilled in him. Oh, Puretongue. And what would he say to see his prentice now?

His thoughts turned from the dhruide to the girl—Carrie, the tinker had named her. She was like a rowan, he thought, lonely on its hill. And what was the First Lesson of the Rowan? Wisdom and power against spellings. And loneliness.

He was lonely himself. The tinker and his family—he'd felt their unity. Even Carrie, with them for less than a day, was already a part of that unit. It was his own temper that had kept him from enjoying their company. His temper and his pride. He should have realized how they would react to his tale. Tinkers knew some small magics—conjuror's tricks and the like—but the Great Magics were only legends to them. Something to fit into tales and ballads. Something to name a tune after.

Had he not felt the need to boast, had he kept his mouth shut and simply travelled with them—Fairlord! They were even headed north.

Tarn bent his head. He ached in every muscle and the throb in his head grew worse. Still. He would have to watch over them, for more dyorn would return. They'd return and this time they'd be expecting a mage.

Tarn lifted his head to look about himself. He was between the shore cliffs and the coast road. From his vantage point, he could see the wagon coming. He'd wait for them here, then. Gather what rest he could and wait for them. And when they came, he'd follow and ward them as best he could. As things fell now, there was nothing else he could do.

Fifth

WITH HIS ONE EYE, Deren Merewuth stared past the ruins of Gullysbrow, away across the Channel Sea. The salt wind that blew up the long slope of the hill brought a frown to his lips. Salt and sea only served to remind him of the Saramand. Their longships ploughing the waves. The cursed red and yellow sails, and the serpent-prow.

"Why?" he demanded of the wind in an anguished voice. "Why did they spare me? What is there for me now? What hope in the world?"

"You could help me," answered a mild voice from behind him.

"Help you, Gwyryon?" Deren asked without turning. "Are you going to slay snake-lovers? Can I help you in *that*?"

His empty socket seemed to burn as he spoke. He lifted a hand to it, dropped the hand against his thigh, clenched it tightly.

"I heal," the old man said softly. "I don't destroy."

"Then heal my memories as you've healed my body. Heal my soul!" He faced Gwyryon, his single eye blazing with torment. "My kin lie slain below us—all of them. And for what? I ask you, where is the fairness in it? Why should I live and they not?"

"The world is neither fair nor unfair, Deren. It simply is."

"Then use your magics to let me forget."

"I can't do that."

"Then go away—and leave me to my torment."

Deren turned his back on the old man and stared at the sea again, hands opening and closing at his sides.

They stood quietly for a long time. The wind blew the heather against their legs. Gulls cried in the grey clouds above. Deren felt the silence grow between himself and the old man, and he withdrew inside himself to escape it. But there he found only the sight of swords, rising and falling, the helms with the hammer symbol beaten into their metal, the axe that cut down his father. He heard the crunch of metal breaking bone, the screams of women and dying men, the crackle of flames.

He stared seaward, but all he saw was blood, oceans of blood for as far as he could see. He heard again the harsh laughter of the yellow-haired giant whose blade took his lost eye. Felt the wooden docks rush up against his face, felt the second stroke searing into his back muscles.

He turned to Gwyryon, tears streaming from his remaining eye. His legs gave way and he knelt in the purple heather.

"Speak to me," he pleaded in a broken voice. "Help me forget."

The old man lowered himself by Deren's side, his eyes dark with sympathy.

"I will try," he said, "But the only tale I know these days is interwoven with the one that came upon you and your people. Would you still hear it?"

Throat tight, Deren nodded.

"Then I will tell you of gods, Deren. Of the old gods. Not the Skyfather of the Saramand, nor your own Dath, nor the myriad others who each have their own fane or holy place. I will tell you of Hafarl, the Summerlord, and his brother Lothan Icelord, who are two of the three Keepers of the Green Isles. I will tell of treachery and deceit, and the approach of a winter so long that there will be no ending to it."

Gwyryon looked away across the hills, swept his gaze to the sea. When he spoke again, his voice took on the storytelling cadences of a barden, deep and resonating. All it lacked was the accompaniment of a harp's or a cittern's strings.

"The Summerlord has—*had*—a staff and it was named Meynbos. Stonewood, in the old tongue. It was the focus of his power, the symbol of his rule. With it, he guided the Isles through the long days of summer. He wakens the land from winter's iron grip, that the fields and woods might grow fruitful and fair. Not until Samhain does he let go his reins and pass the great steeds of the land into his brother's care. Ah, and then. The wild winds blow down from the north, bearing the stormkin who bring with them ice and snow, month upon month, until all the land is bleak and forlorn.

"In those months, Hafarl seems less than a memory.

"Now, the tale has it that one Samhain the Summerlord misplaced his staff. How you might ask? How could he lose the very symbol of his power? Better riddle logic from the ancients' stoneworks than seek the answer. But stormkin found it. Or perhaps they stole. Perhaps they were dyorn, perhaps frosts. No matter. Found it was, and carried swift as a breath to Lothan. And he, he took his great sword Yaljoryon, the Deathreaper, and shattered Hafarl's staff into innumerable pieces, then scattered those pieces the length and breadth of the Isles. Ah, they were so many, and so dispersed, that Hafarl had never a hope of uniting them again.

"And so, Dark Days returned to these Isles.

"The following Beltane, Lothan gave up his rule—as he must, for the weavers weave, and therein he is without choice—returning the land to Hafarl's care. But with his staff lost and his power unfocused…have you not felt the summer of late, even you with your few years? How the nights are chillier, how they days grow shorter sooner than they should, how the crops are not so hale, the wild harvests less bountiful?"

Deren nodded wordlessly and the old man sighed.

"In time Hafarl will be no more," he said. "Already Lothan's stormkin hound him, smelling out his weakness, mocking his faltering steps. In time the Icelord will rule forever and the Green Isles will be green no more." Gwyryon's gaze pierced his companion. "Not often are good and evil so clear cut. A man might live his life through, struggling to choose between them, worrying that he might err with one action or another, the issues never seeming clear. Now they are.

We stand at a crossroads. We must choose between Hafarl's order of growth, and Lothan's chaos of stasis. Or rather, we must seek an equal balance between the two.

"For it *is* chaos that Lothan brings. We dwell now in a time just before the Everwinter, in the midst of madness. Why else would the Saramand raid in such numbers? They know that our folk grow weaker with each passing year. The heart is gone from them. From Fairnland to Kellmidden, our kings bicker and argue while those same kingdoms fall, one by one. Together, enheartened, those kings might raise an army to drive the Saramand forth. Instead they huddle, each in their individual keep, and wait their doom.

"And the Saramand—poor fools, they. They know nothing of Lothan, yet they do his work for him. They think they will rule the Isles. But they will be White Isles, and only the Mocker's stormkin will dwell in its winter wastes."

Deren looked troubled, but his concern now was for something much larger than himself.

"You paint a bleaker world," he said, "than even I might have imagined it to be."

"Bleak. Aye, that is the word for it. A world without heart. Summerlord waning, the balance tottering, the Everwinter upon us. Time was there was a High King who ruled over all. His High Seat was in Granweir, and he died a longyear a-gone, without heir. Who remembers him now? In the years following his death, the people of the Isles each went their own way. A hundred kingdoms sprang up. And when those new kings died, they divided their rule amongst however many sons they had until..." The old man shrugged. "In time, Deren—if Lothan were to give us time—every small crofter will be a king. Bah!"

Gwyryon spat and looked away. His brow was creased with worry lines and the wind fluttered his beard.

"Is that why you need my aid?" Deren asked. His own hurts were now completely forgotten. "To help you find a new High King?"

The old man shook his head. "No. Would that it were. But that blood is long gone from these Isles, I fear. I found my task in Kellmidden—or rather, I was given it there by Penhallow, the Oracle of Pelamas Henge. He is a priest of Cernunnos, the Horned Lord, who fathered the Keepers of our Isles," Gwyryon added at Deren's blank look. "It was Penhallow who bade me find the Summerlord.

"I have sought him wide and far. I have sought him a-land and under the sea. I sought him through his kin—the Summerborn, those who are touched by his spirit, fey folk but mortal, born unknowing of their own wonder. But never have I found him. I found instead the land empty, the sea silent, and his kin...

"Stormkin haunt the land, Deren. They hound the Summerlord, they slay his kin, and I grow weary. Power I have, but it is bound to the dwystaw, the deepsilence that Cernunnos wrought to give the Isles their wonder that now falters. Each of us has an echo of that silence within himselfourself. The silence of magic—our taw, the source of our power. And it comes from the very soul of the Isles. The deepsilence. Dwystaw. And silence, boy, is the oldest tune of all."

"What will you do? Deren asked. "What can I do?" He touched his empty socket. "By all rights, I should be dead. As dead as my...as my kin. You healed me with your magics. I owe you a debt that I want to repay. Give me a reason to live, Gwyryon."

"Cernunnos healed you," the old man said. "His was the power. I was but the vessel. So the weavers weave."

Deren nodded, though he didn't really understand. Was Cernunnos another name for Dath? Or was one god real, the other not? Were they in conflict over his soul? Or did the Saramand follow the one true god? No, never them, But what of the red-robed monks of Ose? Was their way false? Or those who followed the teachings of the Nameless Lord? If this concerned gods, then...

"How could I ever help?" he asked aloud. "I have a strong back—for all that it still aches—but little else."

Gwyryon smiled. "When I spoke the softspell—the healing magic—over you, it was needful for me to learn your name. Magic needs a name. The taw, the inner silence, provides the power, but the name is the focus—as Hafarl's staff was the focus for his power. Mages hide their names from each other, but yours was there for me to read. When I found it, and through it touched your spirit, I saw that your taw was awake—unlike that of most folk. Untapped, but awake. It was your own taw that kept you alive long enough for me to heal you."

"*My* taw?" Deren stared at him, wide-eyed. "In me?"

"In you."

"You're making fun of me. I have no magics—"

"Did you ever dream, and have the dream come true? Or know what another would say before he spoke it? Or perhaps you have a knack for finding things that are lost? Or you just *know* where the best gulls' eggs lie on a certain day?"

Deren shrugged helplessly. That and more, he thought, but never when he wanted it. It only came at random times.

"He has the gift," his mother would say.

His mother. The ache was still there—bitter, so bitter. Could he ever forget? But he didn't want to forget. Not his parents. Not home and loved ones. Just the pain. The bitter ache and the…loneliness.

"Gwyryon?"

"Aye?"

"I'll help if I can. I don't know how or what I'm to do, but if you'll have me, I'll go with you."

His one eye met the old man's clear gaze. In those blue eyes he saw longyears unspiralling, deep and bright.

"Gwyryon?" he asked again.

"Aye?"

"Where did you come to learn of…of Hafarl and Lothan and all you've told me?"

"I knew the Dark Days were coming," Gwyryon replied. "They were foretold to me. I was there when Meynbos was first shaped. And ten years ago, in a vision, I saw the iron blade of Lothan fall upon it and so end the wonder of the Green Isles."

Sixth

---

*I*T HAD NOT BEEN a day that Long Tom would look back on and smile—if he was even to survive it. The wizard's talk of stormkin and his changing into such an impossible shape, the act of changing itself…it was beyond belief. Broom and heather! It made the danger too real and he had a family to keep safe.

The poor start to the day had left a taste that bittered each following hour, for the more the tinker thought about what he'd been told and what he'd seen, the more he worried. He thought of Carrie, of the wizard's tale. The wizard. Tarn. Whenever he used the wizard's name, he shaped the Sign of Horns, as though Tarn was the Icelord himself. But was the small wizard evil?

Long Tom remembered the weariness on the man, the intensity in his strangely-coloured eyes as he'd put forward his case. Pride had been there, and anger. But not evil. And when he thought of Carrie… the wizard could well be right. She'd seemed fey to Long Tom from the first moment he'd laid eyes on her. Afraid, aye, and shy. But fey.

He shook the worries from him, tried to smile, to no avail. Tension hung like a pall over the wagon, over all of them. There'd not been a song or an unforced laugh the whole day—only worry and fear. And how long would it stay like this?

Ah, Long Tom, he thought. You've always looked to having a part in some grand tale. Now here you are, with the makings all about you, and don't you wish you were a thousand miles away—and that you'd never seen that wizard's face?

The long afternoon dragged by, the horses plodding with the weight of the tinkers' mood as heavy as the wagon they pulled behind them. The coast road ran through land that was moorland, then wood and brush, then moor again. It was slow going uphill, and slower going down, for then Long Tom or Kinn must clamber up beside whoever was driving and push and strain against the brake so that the whole of the wagon didn't bang up against the horses' withers and shove them helter-skelter down the slope.

That it grew overcast after the morning did nothing to help their mood. That the bread and cheese of the mid-day meal tasted stale and too sharp, the ale flat, could only be in their minds.

Aye, Long Tom thought. But the mind's a powerful thing. Where is the man who can't recall a time he'd scared himself witless just thinking of what might—not was, but *might*—be lurking beyond the campfire's glow, within a tin mine, outside a tavern's door. And how could it be anything but worse when you saw a man become something out of a fable before your eyes—a man who no more than five minutes earlier had warned you that the ghosties of your granddad's tales were real and coming for you?

Ballan! How could you *not* believe?

When the skies began their greying march into night the wagon was still a league or so from Swaston. Too long a league, Long Tom thought. His heart quailed to think of what the night might bring and they still on the road, not yet having gained the safety of town. Or was there safety even there? Could men, or the works of men, hold back the—what had the wizard called them? Durn...dwarm..? He settled on the name his granddad had given them: Stormkin. That was a word he knew. From tales. From ballads. The wizard had used it, too.

Ah, the gloaming deepened and still the road ran on. Would the creatures come like silent shadows? Or in a rush, like the howl of a winter wind?

Long Tom was brave enough. He'd fought with other men before, for the life of a tinker, or that of anyone who traveled the roads of the Isles, had its own inherent dangers. A drunk, perhaps. A town that thought itself too fine for gypsy-folk. He was quick with his fists—too quick, Megan said—and quicker with his knives, tinker-made with steel blades twelve inches long, honed as sharp as a whetstone could make them. Not the blades they sold in the fairs and towns, but the ones that the tinkers made and kept for themselves.

No, Long Tom was never a coward when it came to a fight. When it could not be avoided. When it was with men. But what would this night bring? Could good tinker-steel cut a nightmare's flesh? Did they even have flesh? Could—

"Dad?"

Kinn's voice was low, the urgency plain in it. Long Tom moved to walk by his son's side, followed the pointed finger with his gaze to see…in the dusk it was hard to tell…a shape with a loping gait like a wolf's…

"It's a dog," Long Tom said. "A shepherd's dog, no more."

The wagon creaked, the wheels clattered, the horses plodded on, unhappy that there was no stopping for nightfall, worrying after their corn. Long Tom caught his wife's gaze and Megan snapped the reins. Broad shoulders strained harder and the wagon picked up its pace.

The Winter Lord had wolves to command, Long Tom knew. That's what the old tales said. You'd see them when snow cloaked the ground—great grey beasts with red tongues and redder eyes. The old folk named them direwolves. But surely these creatures were no more than beasts? Big though. They stood a half shoulder taller again than a good-sized dog, with deep chests, long mottled hair all grizzled, grey and white and black. Teeth as long as his own middle finger.

How far was the town?

"Dad?"

Long Tom nodded. He saw them, too. There were more now. Pacing the wagon. Keeping their distance. Three, four. Ballan! There were a half-dozen. Keeping pace, their movement as liquid as water.

"Fenne," he said, keeping his voice calm. "Take your bow. You as well, Kinn. Up to the roof with you both. And mind you keep the arrowheads away from the whiskey skins..."

Ah, what was he thinking? What mattered whiskey when the world had gone mad? Better they took care of their own skins. But he could use a drink now, he surely could.

He leapt up the seat beside Megan and strung his own bow.

"Where's Carrie?" he asked.

Foolish question, he thought as soon as he asked it.

"In the back."

Megan's voice was tight with fear.

Long Tom nodded. Aye, where else would the lass be?

"Oh, Tom. What's to become of us?"

"We'll do, Meg. Surely, we'll do."

His bow was strung. He took the reins from her and snapped them against the horses' backs. Startled, they broke into a half-trot. The wagon lurched along behind them.

"Hie!" Long Tom cried. "Move there!"

He wouldn't look to the wolves. He trusted Kinn and Fenne. But they'd need help. A half-dozen of these wolves were too many for two archers without secure footing. Aye, and if the beasts weren't natural...

The wagon began to seesaw back and forth as the horses broke into a rough trot. Long Tom could hear tins and pans clattering in the back, heard a clay jar smash. Better that be broken than us, he thought. Ah, but what if there were more than wolves abroad? What if—

"They're coming!" Kinn shouted.

Long Tom heard their bowstrings hum. He rose to his feet. Tossing Megan the reins, he fought for balance as the wagon swayed and jolted, drew his own bowstring until the feathered end of the shaft was at his cheek. When the first grey shape came rushing into range, he loosed his shaft, drew another.

ON A hill less than a league from Swaston, overlooking the sea, a small thorn tree stirred. It was late in the afternoon, almost dusk. There was no wind. The thorn shivered from root to topmost limb, shimmered, then Tarn knelt where it had stood, his knees and hands against the rough earth, his strange eyes blinking.

Some of his weariness was gone—enough so that his mind was clear. For just as some shapes—moving shapes, breathing shapes—drained the shaper's taw, so did others—stone shapes, and especially tree shapes—replenished it. He could still taste the nourishing power his roots had drawn from the dark earth, and the sun's strength that had burned through an overcast sky.

He looked about himself to see what had drawn him from the slow flow of sap thoughts. When he saw the tinker wagon coming down the coast road, he hugged the ground so that the tinkers would not see him outlined against the sky. He knew all too well what kind of welcome he could expect, and he was not here to greet them, only guard them if need be. And the red-haired girl, this Carrie. Was she still with them? He drew on his taw and reached out to the wagon with his mind to find...

...tension in the air, thick as morning fog on Tallifold's harbour... slow equine thoughts, a pair of them, then the tinkers...and the girl...

Family? He considered, remembering how the tinker had avowed that Carrie was his daughter. Then why was her thinking as different from theirs as a sparrow's was from a flock of gulls? But they shared the same...

...cloak of fear...and then he felt...coming along their backtrail...a cold shadow...a momentary flash of a wolf's sharp thoughts, a crow's red ire...and ice...

He drew back and let the wagon pass, then took a windhover's shape and lifted into the air, sleek and swift. The road below became a small ribbon to his hawk's eyes. Circling, he waited long moments before he saw what he sought. The grey shapes trotted well off the road, ears flattened to their heads, tails pointed straight behind them. They moved quickly, hidden from view. Above them, three crows winged, and behind came something else again...white shapes, angular.

He did not stay to look.

He gave a sharp hawk's cry and speeded after the wagon. How far was Swaston still? The wagon seemed to plod along, getting nowhere, while the day's light drained swiftly from the sky. As the twilight came creeping over the hills, he felt a change in the air. From behind the wagon, the pursuit quickened its pace. He saw the wolves come bounding in, closing on the wagon, saw the tinkers string their bows. The white shapes moved more quickly now as well. They spread to either side of the wagon in a wide-sweeping circle that they began to draw taut. And the crows...

Tarn's deepsight pierced the gloom and he understood. The crows were shape-changed dyorn. And the white shapes—fear cat-walked up his spine. They were frosts. Frosts and dyorn, and he but one mage against them.

The frosts moved swiftly. They were stormkin seldom seen beyond winter's grip. They had awkward, brittle edges to their man-like forms. Hoarfrost crackled and spread under their tread, chill winds awoke at their breath. The crows flew in patterns and using his deepsight, Tarn realized they were shaping runes in the air. He hovered, high above and unseen, uncertain. From this height he could see the glimmer of lights that was Swaston two hills away—a mile and a half, no more. The tinkers were dealing with the direwolves, but the frosts were closing in. Had the tinkers seen them yet? What would they do to defend themselves against such creatures? Fairlord, what could *he* do?

Then Tarn knew. He shrank from the thought of it. He'd held the shape only once before—dire, dire!—and almost died using it. But...

A fourth wolf was down. He deepsaw Long Tom grappling with another on the driver's seat, Megan fighting with the reins to keep the panicked horses in line. The wagon tipped uneasily from side to side.

Tarn drew into the deep well of his taw and formed there the name of the one terror that might stop these stormkin—frosts and dyorn. He drew it from memory, from the time he'd worn it himself—so briefly, but at such a cost. It was the name of a being that had stalked the land and skies when the world was still young, a creature that the dyorn had driven to extinction to lay rest their fear of it.

His drew in his hawk wings and dropped from the sky. As he spoke the name aloud, he changed. His body grew scaled, grew huge. Fires awoke in his belly and he sent out a scalding breath of flames.

In dragon-shape, Tarn attacked the stormkin.

He swept down on the frosts as they neared the wagon. Cries like wailing winter winds tore from the throats of the frosts as they saw the dragon. The crows wove their runes more tightly. The dragon roared. Frosts melted under his burning attack, fell back, were driven to face the monstrous shape once more by the power of the dyorn who ruled them.

The wagon clattered away, horses driven mad by the reptilian reek and flames that cut the night. The dragon swung back to attack once more. The runes of the dyorn, completed now, glimmered weirdly in the night air, entangling the dragon. Ice caked his mighty wings and the heavy beast dropped lower under its added cold weight. The frosts howled and raced for the falling dragon, fleeing in panic as he cast the frost weaving from him and rose into the air once more, breathing fire.

The frosts gathered themselves for another charge. Behind, in the darkness, small black shapes lost their feathers and bulked, grew squat and bow-backed, yellow-pale eyes gleaming. The frosts charged anew. Fiery breath dropped two, three, but a dozen more broke through and leapt onto the beast's back. The dragon threw them off, flaming their ice shapes into steam. But behind, the dyorn edged closer.

A silence fell, sudden and unexpected.

The dragon drew himself up to full height as the frosts circled his giant form once more. Ice caked his limbs too heavily for him to lift into the air. He stored his flames for the dyorn who broke from their distance to approach.

"I know you," the largest of them said. His voice grated on the ear, uncomfortable with the language he used. "We knew you remained when we slew your kin, knew you were hid away in some deep hold in Ardmeyn, cowering under the mountains, afraid of our wrath. Did you think we would forget? We had a stone with each of your kin's names cut into it. A tall stone it was, and many names. Now, dragon-shaper, yours is the only one that remains.

The lead dyorn spoke a name that hummed like fire in Tarn's mind, joining that name to a rune of blue-frost fire. The creature grinned as the rune took shape, cloaking the dragon in a mantle of think ice, chaining the beast with the flesh-numbing power of Damadar's glacial fields. Then the grin slipped, faltered, as they ice crackled and broke, falling from the dragon in large chunks that steamed as they hit the ground.

"Named!" the dyorn cried, stepped back. "We had you named! Lothan's rune and—"

The dragon's laugher thundered. Named! Oh, the dyorn had spoken a name—a name as long as the history of man's first settling in these Green Isles. But it was not Tarn's name. They had named Puretongue. Perhaps he *had* been the last dragon-shaper. The last until he taught his prentice the shape.

Flames erupted along the path of Tarn's laughter and the dyorn fled, the frosts scattered. His power blasted the land for long yards in front of him, to either side as he swept the great dragon head back and forth. The heat of his flames melted the ice that still encased his wings and he rose, spiralling high, before swooping down to strike the largest of the dyorn.

The stormkin stopped his flight, threw himself aside as flames scorched the earth where he'd stood. He rolled clear, leapt to his feet. He drew a cold thought into life and misted. The dragon roared to see his prey disappear. Flames exploded through the mist, but it only steamed, drifted slowly on the wind, dissolving and breaking up, vanishing.

"No!" the dragon bellowed in the ancient speech of his kind.

He lifted higher on his scaled wings, scanned the ground, but they were all gone. Dyorn, frosts. Gone. He faltered, his rage spent. The great shape swept downward and reshaped into the form of a small man. He stared about himself as waves of nausea broke over him.

All about the ground was torn from their struggle. Rocks were slagged, the earth raw and gougedtorn , vegetation charrcd, puddles of dark water steamed. The aftermath of wearing the dragon-shape came rushing over him. He crumpled to the ground, shivering, drawing what strength he could from the earth to lift his head, for he was wary of another attack. But the pain was blinding. If the dyorn returned now, he was a dead man.

He retched, sprawled full length on the dirt. He was alone, a small forlorn shape lying on the coast road, hands opening and closing spasmodically, eyes rolling. Alone. Fairlord, he needed aid. He…the time before…he'd survived…aye…but Puretongue had been there and…

It WAS dead, with a harpoon piercing its side, no more than a child, a small silkie, half seal still, lying on a long beach with its red blood staining the white sand. Tarn winged above it, re-shaped as a man at its side. Sorrow swelled in him to see such a sweet fey thing slain. He knelt, held its frailness in his arms, stared seaward. Half-blinded with tears, he staggered to the water's edge with his burden, found a name for a merman, spoke it into his taw, re-shaped, cut the waves with the grace of one sea-born.

The seal-folk found him, far west of the Green Isles, found him as he sought them. But they saw his strangeness with eyes like dead fish, their anger thrusting aside the luminous warmth that a silkie's gentle gaze more often held. They came at him from all sides, ignored his protests, forced him to drop his burden. The small spiralling bundle of sadness disappeared into the ocean's depths as the seal-folk attacked.

They named him child-slayer, and so named, he could do nothing but flee. They drove him further and further west. They drove him beneath the waves. So swift and relentless was their attack that he could not find the stillness of his taw to shape-change, he could only flee.

Three days from shore, he could go no further. Exhausted, he groped for his taw, ignored the battering of tooth and claw and fin, the strange horror of the silkies' wrath, and found a shape out of his own terror, a shape Puretongue had taught him.

He lifted in dragon-shape from the waters, cutting the air with huge reptilian wings, breathing fire with each ragged breath he exhaled. Airborne, away from his foes, he fell prey to his own anger. He grew blinded by the silkies' injustice and found hatred. The seas boiled with his power, fueled by a twisting darkness inside him that he had never known was there. Many of the sea-folk died. The remainder fled.

Alone, suddenly desperately, he fell into the sea, lost dragon-shape to that of driftwood, lost himself to the horror of his deed, lost his name. The dragon-shape had stolen his power. He would have died had Puretongue not found him.

Weeks later, he found the Seal King ashore on a small strand and offered himself up to the silkies' justice. The old sealord bent eyes deeper than the ocean to him.

"No," he said softly, before he disappeared under the waves once more. "No, you were wronged. We drove you to it and it is we who must bear the burden of that shame."

Along again, where the tide rules the land betimes, Tarn could only bow his head and weep...

TARN LAY as one dead.

Puretongue, he cried in his mind, but the strength of windthinking, sending his thoughts across distance to another's mind, was not there. And Puretongue was gone.

Tarn's eyes stared blankly into the night skies. A limp hand rose once, clawing the air, before it fell to the dirt. Through his agony, he saw a vision of...the slain silkie he'd found...only a child...

It was beckoning to him.

Seventh

THE TINKER WAGON CLATTERED and roared into Swaston as though all the fiends of Damadar were on its heels, which to Long Tom's way of thinking, was too close to the truth for comfort. He drew back on the reins when he saw a torch-lit crowd gathered in the town's square. The light of their torches cast sharp shadows between the two storied buildings. As he brought the wagon to a halt, the horses hung their heads in their braces, sweat-drenched sides heaving, their bits white with froth.

Numbly, Long Tom stared at the crowd and he knew he looked a sight. His shirt torn from the struggle with the last wolf that had leapt onto the driver's seat. His chest and forearms were bloody. They didn't hurt yet, but he knew the pain would come later. Megan sat quietly at his side, her face white, lips taut with worry. On the roof, Kinn and Fenne looked down, wondering whether or not they should notch another arrow.

For the crowd looked in an ugly mood—Long Tom gave them that. Almost a score of Swaston's menfolk were gathered in the square, ranging from a boy of no more than twelve to an old codger in his seventies. The torchlight played on their grim faces, winked on armour that made Long Tom think again. They were well-weaponed for fisherfolk and merchants, these Swastoners. He saw more than one sword and they cost dear. He knew. His uncle, retired from the road now for sixteen years, had a smithy. Most of the men carried axes and iron-tipped spears.

He sensed movement behind his head and turned to see Carrie pushing the leather curtain aside to stare wide-eyed at the crowd. He faced the men again himself, singled out one who stood more to the fore than the rest, and looked him in the eye, matching silent stare for silent stare. The man frowned. He stepped closer, tall and broad-shouldered, a black beard sticking out from cheeks and chin, his hair short.

"Well, you're not Saramand," he said in a gruff voice, "'less they've taken to sailing tinker wagons rather than their snake-ships."

A nervous titter ran through the crowd. Here and there Long Tom could see a man relax his white-knuckled grip on axe handle or sword hilt.

"If it's the yellow hair that makes you nervous," the tinker said, "I can tell you that it's good Fern Isle yellow with more red than gold. Where's the tinker can afford gold hair, I ask you? Too dear, I'm thinking."

"But you can afford a golden tongue, eh?" the big man said from the front of the crowd, though not unkindly. He sheathed his sword. "Step down from your wagon, tinker. We'll not harm you. I'm Lann Dirkrin, warleader—if I can call myself such—of Swaston."

"Long Tom Turpen, at your service." He swung down from the wagon, wincing as he put pressure on his arms. "You've had trouble here? Raiders, or..?"

He left his sentence unfinished as he thought of their narrow escape. How to begin to tell what they'd seen?

Lann nodded glumly. "Aye, raiders. Two longships landed this morn—"

"And if not for our warleader," a young man at Lann's side broke in, "we'd all be dead now. We knew they were coming. All of Meirion's fallen and their ships are raiding our coasts and up into Umbria now. Lann had us put sharpened masts in the harbour—a row of them. The first snake-ship drove right into them and was floundering, the second hove to. Then we came at them from either side in our fishing craft with flame-tipped arrows. And we put them to flight!"

Lann touched the youth's arm. "Aye, Semler. We put them to flight. But they'll be back soon enough—tomorrow or the day after—with more ships than we have men."

Semler nodded and his pleasure ran from him.

"But still you're staying?" Long Tom asked.

"Not by my council," Lann replied. He jerked his thumb over his shoulder to where light spilled from an open door. "I was meeting with the town elders when we heard the clatter of your wagon." He looked over Long Tom's bloody and torn shirt. "Have you news? You've sbeen fighting—and recently."

"But they weren't Saramand."

"Brigands?"

Long Tom met Lann's gaze and slowly shook his head. "I can't put a name to what attacked us. They were shaped from bad dreams."

"But those cuts..."

"Wolves. Mostly, we fought wolves."

Lann's features clouded. "Wolves?" His fingers shaped the Sign of Horns. "In springtime..?"

Long Tom nodded. "Aye, you'd do well to call on the Horned One for luck. We fought wolves and there were worse than wolves abroad. We escaped, but only because..."

He floundered, uncertain of how much to tell. Surely they'd think him mad.

"You should tell them, Tom," Megan said from the wagon's seat.

Long Tom sighed. "Whatever followed the wolves—we saw them only in bits and pieces through the trees, but they were driven off from us by a dragon."

Lann stared at him, his eyes narrowed and questioning. Throughout the crowd, men shifted nervously. They muttered and shaped wardings, looking upward as though expecting a great winged shape to block out the stars.

"A dragon," Lann repeated, plainly disbelieving.

"I've no cause to lie."

"Aye, but..." Lann shook his head.

"It's a long tale," Long Tom said. "It began this morn when the wizard came to our camp. He—"

"A minute!" Lann broke in. "The town elders await me and this is a tale they should hear, I'm thinking. If you'd come..?"

"Aye. Only—"

"We can see to the wagon and horses," Megan said.

Something in her voice made the tinker turn. His gaze met his wife's, then shifted to Carrie. He nodded, knowing what she meant. Best not tell too much about their newfound daughter. With Saramand and wolves abroad, and tales of wizardry being told, the last thing they needed was a witch-hunt.

Megan watched him go with the tall Swastoner, then shook out the reins. Wearily, the horses lifted their heads and the wagon creaked into motion. She steered them across the square, around the back of The Rose's Thorn Inn where there was a wagon camp for merchants, tinkers, and other travelling folk. When she brought the wagon to a halt, Fenne and Kinn clambered down from the roof.

"If you'd see to the horses, Kinn," Megan said, "Fenne and Carrie can start us a fire and meal. I've sweethallow poultices to ready, for by the time your dad's back from yon' meeting, his wounds'll be worrying him something fierce."

IT WAS well after midnight before they were all bedded down. Carrie lay awake by the door feeling closed in, her mind churning with too many thoughts for her to find sleep. She remembered Long Tom coming back from the meeting with the town elders and Megan asking how it had gone.

"No worse than you'd expect," he'd replied. "They listened, but— Broom and heather! They weren't *there*. They didn't see the wizard become a unicorn. They didn't see those creatures running with the wolves, nor the dragon—Ballan take me! The dragon."

He kicked at the fire with his boot sending sparks flying.

"Sit still, Tom," Megan said, "or I'll never get these cuts cleaned."

"They didn't believe me," Long Tom said. He had a fierce frown, but he sat obediently still. "Ah, and why should they? They've troubles enough of their own and such a pack of fools I've not seen gathered together for many a year. Save for Lann, they're all mad. They're planning to stay here and meet the Saramand again. 'We drove them off once,' they're saying, 'and we'll drive off any more than come.'"

Long Tom sighed and looked at his family.

"Come first light, we'll leave them to their business."

"But, Tom," Megan said. "If we're alone in the hills again..."

"Aye, aye. The creatures could well return. But it's certain death to stay here, Megan. I've none of the Swastoners' faith in their prowess. And who knows? Our dragon might return to help us."

As he said the last part, Long Tom stared helplessly about the fire. One by one, the others nodded. It looked bad no matter what they chose.

The dragon, Carrie thought as she lay now in the dark wagon. She listened to the sounds of breathing about her. Ever since this morning when the small wizard had come to their fire, her mind had experienced an upheaval of conflicting thoughts. Though she denied every thing he said about her, she could not forget the intensity with which he spoke. He was wrong, but he *believed*. And what if he was right?

She shrank from the thought, but couldn't keep it at bay. All day it had nagged at the back of her mind and when the wolves attacked, something had unlocked inside her. She'd felt an evil gather—a tangible sense of evil, beating at her, wave upon terrifying wave, gathering and growing in strength until...

She'd seen it arrive through the back window of the wagon, the huge winged shape dropping from the greying skies, scattering the white figures that trailed the wolves, scalding them with its flaming breath.

If such was real, might not the rest be real as well? For all that she denied it, could she be wrong? She wasn't certain, for there were times when...*odd* things happened to her—like the dreams she'd had before the raiders came to destroy her kith and kin. She shivered and tears brimmed her eyes as she remembered all she'd lost. And there'd been other times, other dreams.

Was that what the wizard meant? Because she sometimes dreamed things before they happened? Because she'd seen the Saramand come, before the longships landed? Did this make her related to—she stumbled over the name—the Summerlord?

What was this Summerlord, anyway? The priests of Dath taught that he was no more than an outworn symbol of the summer, that the earlier people—the Tus who held the Isles before the Dathenan's coming—had worshipped sun and trees and stones, and the Summerlord was no more than another heathen deity in their vast pantheon of gods. She wished Tarn was here now so that she could ask him. For if it was all true, that meant that the...the creatures would return... again and again, until...

She couldn't bear to have the Turpens hurt because of her. But die they surely might

Tarn.

She turned his name over in her mind, tasting the strange wonder of it. He didn't frighten her now—not as he had this morning. His tiny stature and fine-boned features put her in mind of the erlkin—or at least the way she imaged a kowrie man would look. She remembered his eyes most of all, the curious mingling of gold and grey and mauve, deep with secrets that vibrated to his every word and motion, strained to be loosed, yet held back by a hidden strength. The strange-coloured eyes were those of a mage, it couldn't be denied. A curly-haired wooderl with a mage's eyes.

She remembered the sleek beauty of the unicorn and the deep power of the dragon. Surely this was magic—but did it mean he was right? Was she related to some heathen god? Were strange creatures truly seeking her life? How could any of it possibly be real?

She repeated his name again, her thoughts spinning, and saw a vision of the small man that brought her heart to her throat. He lay in the middle of the road by a ruined field, earth torn and raw all around him. And he—he was so white and still. Lying like one dead. Small hands clenched into fists at his side as though he'd died in agony.

It seemed that she hovered over him, could reach out and touch him, she was so close. And in the vision, she sensed life still inside him—faint and swiftly fading. His life essence was like a small amber glow, flickering before the dark winds of his coming death. Softly, she heard music...

Music? No, it was more a stillness. A quiet that was like music in its measures, though how that was possible, she wasn't sure. In dreams, she supposed...

She sat up with a start, staring about the darkened wagon, Tarn's image burned in her memory. Dreams. She had fallen asleep and dreamed of him, but oh, was it true? She had to know.

In her visions she'd seen him lying where they'd been attacked, no more than a mile or so from town. She could go...

But what if those creatures were still abroad? How could she face them, small and powerless as she was?

She saw again the dragon dropping from the sky, remembered Tarn coming to the camp this morning to warn them, to offer his aid. Could she do less for him?

But I'm so afraid, she thought. I...

She stood and unlatched the back door of the wagon with trembling fingers. It creaked open and she paused, listening to the breathing of the Turpens. No one stirred. She nodded to herself. Dath knew what they'd think if they woke to find her creeping from the wagon.

She reached the ground and stood chilled, wishing she wasn't alone. The cold came mostly from inside her, born of fear. She tried to put it aside. Which way had they come into the town? She heard the sea to her right, waves lapping against the wooden pilings of the wharf. The town was otherwise silent.

Taking her direction from the sea, she set off down the dark street, her own soft footfalls echoing loud in her ears. Shivering both from her fear and the chill in the night air, she made her way, looking neither left nor right as she went. So she never saw the shadowed figure detach itself from a darkened doorway to follow her.

ON THE outskirts of Swaston she paused again, staring into the hills. They were dark for the night was moonless and the sky had clouded again. Standing alone, with the grass swaying against her legs, she wondered at her folly. If magic was real, then she was in more danger now than she'd ever been before. Anything could be out there, waiting for her. But she thought of Tarn—his white face in her vision—and moved to step forward.

A hand landed on her shoulder and a gruff voice spoke in her ear.

"Late to be wandering the hills, lass."

A scream shivered up her throat, but before she could loose it, a large hand clapped over her mouth and she was turned around. She stared wide-eyed into the shadowed features of the man Long Tom had been talking to in the village square. He shook his head from side to side, eased his hand from her mouth.

"No need to cry out," he said. "I've not come to harm you. Only my curiosity got the better of me when I saw you slipping from your wagon in the middle of the night. I thought to myself, Now what could be in the hills at this time of night to draw a tinker girl from her wagon?"

He stared at her intently, trying to read the expression in her eyes, but the light was too poor.

"And you know what came to my mind?" he went on. "That perhaps the red-gold hair of the Fern Isle tinkers is but a shade of Saramand yellow. What do you say to that, lass?"

Carrie's tongue felt thick in her mouth and she swallowed hard. Surely he didn't think that she—

"Where are you to meet them?" Lann demanded, all softness gone from his voice. "Did we damage them so much that they must send children to sneak them past our harbour's feeble defenses?"

"N-no," Carrie managed.

"Then tell me: Who do you go to meet?"

Carrie swallowed again, fighting back tears. Lann's hands hurt her shoulders where his fingers gripped her tightly enough to raise marks on her flesh. She shook her head.

"Not them," she said. "Never them. It's Tarn. He's hurt, perhaps dying..."

Lann stared at her, then gave her a rough shake.

"Don't lie to me! Do you think for a moment that we believed your father's faery tales? Who are you to meet? Where will they be waiting? How strong are they?"

The cloud cover broke and dim starlight washed the hills. Lann studied his captive's frightened features. He loosed one hand and drew a long knife from his belt.

"Then take me to them, if you'll not speak," he said, brandishing the blade. "And give but the smallest outcry…"

He shoved her ahead of him and she stumbled to her knees. A rough hand pulled her to her feet and pushed her forward again.

"You can die here, spy, or you can lead me to your meeting place. Obey me, and perhaps you'll yet live to see the dawn. If not…well, there's no need for your death to be quick. Do you understand?"

Heart pounding, Carrie stared at the big man. Numbly, she nodded her head. She looked away, down the coast road. Had it been one hill or two? Was Tarn even there? Oh, Dath! What if he wasn't? What would the warleader think then? She shot a glance at Lann and shivered. She didn't want to die. She—

Lann pushed her again.

"Move," he said, his voice deadly soft.

She set out, stumbling along the roadway, very aware of the long blade in her captor's hand.

THE SKY was still cloudless when they reached the scene of the wolves' attack. As they topped the last hill, Lann stopped, gripping Carrie's arm, and stared at the unnatural destruction that lay below. All along the roadway for a half mile the earth was torn and pushed into huge piles of raw earth. Boulders were slagged. Lann's features paled and the knife in his hand was suddenly a heavy weight for fingers gone numb.

"Seas preserve us!" he murmured. "It was all true…"

Beside him, Carrie caught sight of a small form—no more than a shadow on the road. She tensed, then broke from Lann's grip to run headlong down the road.

"Hey!" he cried after her. "Hold!"

He sprang after her, nervous, his gaze sweeping left and right, looking skyward as thought he expected the dragon to reappear.

Then he saw the small, still form she was running to. She dropped by her knees beside it, looking at the still features with a sense of complete helplessness.

"Who was he?" Lann asked when he reached her side.

"His name was Tarn," she said in a soft voice.

The Swastoner's hand fell to her shoulder, but the touch was gentle now, almost apologetic.

"There's nothing you can do for him, lass."

She shook her head. "He's alive. I *know* he is. But he needs care. Meg could help him with her herbs and...and..." Her voice broke. "Why must everybody die?"

She saw the Saramand storming the shore, her father dying, her mother, her brother. She remembered a hand pulling her roughly into a hidey-hole, and they cowered in the darkness, the invisible stranger and herself, listening to the clash of arms, smelling the blood in the air...

Lann knelt beside her.

"I'm sorry," he said.

She shook his arm from her shoulder and wouldn't look at him.

"Think, lass. How could we know? The tale your dad told was impossible to believe and so we could only assume the worst of you. We...." He looked at the ruin surrounding them, his gaze landing on the corpse of a supernaturally large dead wolf. A feathered shaft stood out from its chest. "*How* could we know?"

Carrie turned to face him. Her cheeks were glistening in the starlight.

"You couldn't be expected to, I suppose," she said . "I— everything's gone wrong for me. My...my family were slain by the Saramand...in our whole village, only ten survived to flee to Cermyn. The Turpens were the first good thing to happen to me, and now they're in danger because...because of me. Did Long Tom tell you what Tarn said about me?"

Lann shook his head. "Only that a wizard came to your camp and...and about this..."

"*I* don't believe it," Carrie said. "And yet..."

Lann looked around them again.

"And yet the evidence is overwhelming." He sighed. "To my thinking, the whole of the Isles are in for a bad time. The snake-lovers are bad enough. I thought I could convince the townsfolk to leave, but they've had one victory now. How can they be expected to understand that when the Saramand do return, they will have no hope of surviving a second battle? And now, with this as well...this wizardry..." He shook his head. "What will you do, lass?"

She looked into his face. Stroking Tarn's curls, she shrugged.

"I don't know. If you could carry him..?"

"That I can do. Your mum—ah, I mean the tinker's wife—she'll be able to help him?"

Carrie made no reply. She didn't know the answer.

"Well, we can only see," Lann said.

He went to pick up Tarn, paused when he saw the knife, forgotten in his fist. Biting at his lip, he thrust it back into its sheath, and lifted the small form in his arms.

"Come, lass. Time we were going."

Carrie nodded. She rose and fell in step with him. Her heart was chilled, her mind blank. All she could think of was the power that had been expended to cause such havoc as lay about them. Dath help them all, it was real. And with that terrible knowledge, she could only ask herself what hope there was for any of them now?

Eighth

’VE DONE WHAT I can," Megan said.

She turned from the bed where Tarn lay to face Long Tom and Carrie. Her shoulders sagged from weariness and her eyes were red-rimmed from the haleweed smoke that still clouded the inside of the wagon. Tarn's cuts had been bathed and cleaned with crushed morningmoon, then bandaged with sweethallow poultices. Sighing, Megan gathered up her medicine sack, leaving a bowl of cool deepcress broth by the bed.

"He's regained some colour," she added. "Later we can try to give him some of that broth, but..." She shrugged. "This is beyond my skill. His wounds are not so sore—it's more as though the will to live has fled him. We'd do better to pray to the Seawife and ask her to gift us with a seaerl healer."

"You've done what you could," Long Tom said. "No one could ask for more."

Carrie nodded in agreement, her gaze fixed on Tarn's still features. She traced the small moon-mark on his brow with a finger, wondering anew at the curious emotions that ran through her when she looked at the mage. She was both attracted and repelled by him... by what he stood for.

"He's still alive, though?" she asked.

It was so hard to tell—he didn't seem to breathe—though he was no longer so ashen pale as he'd been before.

"Alive," Megan murmured, "but I'll not swear that he'll live." She touched Carrie's shoulder in sympathy. "The life is faint in him."

"Can we travel?" Long Tom asked.

"Aye. But give it an hour or so before we go."

"An hour then. But I'll ready the horses now. The sooner we're away from the falsehearts in this town, the better I'll feel. Broom and heather! To think we'd ever be leagued with the Saramand…"

"Whisht, Tom. Give it a rest."

Megan led the way to the door, shooing Long Tom out before she turned back to Carrie.

"Come and get some air, dear. Fenne can look on him for now and you can sit with him while we're on the road."

Carried nodded and joined her on the wagon's back steps. She saw Fenne and Kinn, bows strung and arrows notched, where they waited by the door. Long Tom was arguing with Lann Dirkrin again while a half-dozen Swastoners looked on.

"Aye, glare all you will," Long Tom was saying, "with us out-numbered and your men at hand. *We* never broke *our* trust, Master Warleader. Now give us another hour's peace and we'll be away from your damned town. The place has a stink of doom about it that sickens me anyway."

"These are hard times," Lann began.

"Aye, and you make them harder. It's honest tinkerfolk we are—not spies, not Saramand."

"We know that now, but—"

"Broom and heather, man! Get it through your skull. You're not welcome at this wagon. Now can you leave us be?"

"I am trying to make amends," Lann replied, his own voice rising in anger. "Will you look beyond your nose and see *that*? There was no harm done."

"Aye, no thanks to you. And what if you'd not seen our innocence, eh? What then? Would we be strung up from your hanging tree now, and you apologizing to our corpses? Ballan! You've terrorized my daughter, spat on our honour, and you expect—"

Carrie stayed to hear no more. She wished she'd never gone into the hills last night. Then this whole business would never have—

She shook her head. But then they'd still be guilty in the Swastoners' eyes, and Tarn would still be lying there, perhaps dead by now. She sighed. It was a useless argument that, if she let it, would go round and round in a circle.

She scuffed her feet along the street that led to the wharves. The few townsfolk she met averted their eyes when she looked in their direction, and she wished she were a thousand miles away.

When she reached the waterfront, she sat down on the docks, trailing her feet in the water. She looked away across the waves, beyond the wreckage of the Saramand ship that jutted bow-foremost from the water. Dim in the distance she could imagine the far shores of Gwendellan, and a more personal sorrow reached for her.

Wet-eyed, she stared seaward, wishing with all her heart that she *did* have magical powers like Tarn seemed to think she did, and that she could use them to make things better. If the small wizard was not lying near death, *he'd* do something. Long Tom wouldn't be arguing with the Swastoners, and perhaps the Saramand could be made to pay for what they'd done.

"Tarn."

She whispered his name in the still morning air. He frightened her so, and yet...

The sea lapped at the pilings under the docks and she wished a third time, for a—what had Meg said?—a seaerl healer. Pray to Morennen, the Seawife. Carrie shook her head. Morennen was but another heathen god that the priests of Dath taught was no more than a folk tale. But if she was real, if she could help—please, please, wouldn't she? Carrie squeezed her eyes shut and prayed to the Seawife, but old teachings rose to confuse her. Surely she should pray to Dath, for he was the One Lord over all, the Bright God she'd been raised to worship and—

No. If these were times of wizardry, then it was better to pray to the old gods of the Tus. Tarn would belong to them.

Ah, Morennen, she said into the darkness before her closed eyes. Send us a healer. He helped us, won't you help him? I—

"Carrie! Carrie!"

Her eyes blinked open and for a moment the sharp cry appeared to be an answer to her prayer. Then she turned to see Kinn pelting down the street towards her.

She looked away, back across the waters, trying to recapture the mood she'd now lost. The sea was green-grey in the early light, the waves lapping steadily shoreward, gulls wheeling above. If there had been an answer to her prayer, there was no sign of it. Had she really expected one? There might be magic abroad in the Isles, but it wasn't in *her*—or if it was, as Tarn avowed, then it wasn't there for her to summon up at will.

Disappointment cut like a keen knife through her hopes, foolish though they might have been.

"Come on, Carrie," Kinn said at her side. "Dad and the Swastoner've been at it with their fists and Mum says if we don't go now, there'll be blood spilled for sure."

"What happened?" she asked as she scrambled to her feet.

Kinn was plainly unhappy.

"Ah, he got so mad at the one named Lann that he began to call down the Hundred Curses of Thern. They begin with 'May your loins e're be seedless' and—well, by the time he got to the fourth, Lann took a swing at him and they were at it. Dad'll have a swollen eye and a crooked jaw, I'm thinking. Mum took away his blades to forestall any blood-letting, but the crowd's getting bigger and it's turning ugly."

Carrie listened with only half an ear as she trotted to keep up with Kinn's long stride. The sooner they were gone from Swaston, the better it would be for all of them.

"CAN YOU travel?" Gwyryon asked Deren.

The youth flexed his back muscles, wincing as the flesh tightened across his still-healing wound. The day had dawned with a clear sky, the sunlight gleaming on the waves. His one-eyed gaze fixed on the blackened ruins of Gullysbrow. Memories rose to cloud his brow.

"I can travel," he replied. "Where are we bound?"

Gwyryon shaded his eyes to look up the coast. "North, I think—at least until we can find passage to Kellmidden."

"You think we'll find him there—the Summerlord?"

"Would that we could. No, I sensed magics loosed in Dathen last night—as though some old and ancient wonder trod the land. It's time I returned to Pelamas Henge and spoke again with Penhallow. If the fey things of the Isles are waking, perhaps we can gather and harness them to further our own needs."

Deren nodded though he didn't really understand this talk of fey things and magics. What he did understand, however, was the need for passage across the Channel Sea. He pursed his lips as he looked down to Gullysbrow.

"The Saramand," he said. "Did they leave us anything that would float?"

"Nothing with a sail and 'less you'd row the thirty or so leagues..?"

Deren shook his head. "No need. See, if we float ourselves around Elding's Arm there—" He pointed to the tip of the peninsula that could be seen some ten miles or so west of the fishing thorp. "—with a little luck, we could flag down a fisherman from Morennen's Isle. It's that, or fare up north into Jevan, and that's a good week's trek on foot."

Gwyryon nodded. "A good plan, except if we meet the raiders at sea."

"It's a chance," Deren agreed, "but a slim enough one. I think..." He swallowed, pushing aside a sudden rush of emotion. "I think they're done...about here. If you're game..?"

Gwyryon regarded his companion curiously, wondering not for the first time what manner of youth he'd been before the Saramand had sorrowed all his joys. The leather patch over his eye and the red-white scar that ran down his cheek from under it gave the boy a grim look far beyond his years. Gwyryon sighed.

"The weavers weave," he said. "Let's see what we can salvage."

He led the way down the slope to what remained of Gullysbrow.

GWYRYON LENT what aid he could, but mostly he stood aside and watched as Deren patched the small boat, no larger than a coracle. The lad had studiously ignored the blackened buildings, walking with a straight back and his one eye fixed on the waterfront, looking neither left nor right. The boat they found under a collapsed piling needed little in the way of repairs save for some caulking to make it seaworthy.

Before noon, Deren fitted the charred oars into place and tested the boat in the waters near Gullysbrow's small natural harbour. A lop-sided grin tugged at his stiff features when the craft proved worthy. He rowed back to shore to let Gwyryon embark, then they set off across the waves to Elding's Arm.

"How fares your back?" Gwyryon asked when they'd covered some half the distance.

"Looser now," Deren replied. "But it'll stiffen up again tonight, I'm thinking, when I'm trying to sleep."

He rested the oars a moment and studied his companion.

"If you can work magic," he asked, "why don't you simply spell us to Kellmidden?"

He spoke half in jest, but Gwyryon answered him seriously.

"I must conserve my strengths," he explained. "The longstep—the spell I would use for a magic such as that—draws deeply on my power. It would take time to recover, time better spent awakening your own dormant taw. For we will need all the magics we can gather, I fear, even from those as ignorant of their powers as you." He shook his head. "You are young yet, and for you there is still hope. It is for the old magics that I worry the most…"

He sighed and fell silent, lost in thought as he stared over Deren's shoulder to the tip of Elding's Arm and the waves washing its rocky shores.

Deren shook his head and took up the oars once more. Awake his…the word Gwyryon had used wouldn't come to mind. His magics. Could the old healer do that? How old was Gwyryon anyway? He spoke of longyears as though they were no more than seasons and—but so they would seem to one who lived centuries, he supposed. But how was that even possible? And how much would Gwyryon have seen and done through all that time? How could he remember it all? The joys and wonders, the sorrows...oh, the sorrows...

Deren's own grief tugged at his heart—memories rising that were too fresh to simply put aside. He bent his back to the job at hand, concentrating on the steady sweep of the oars. But under its leather covering, his empty eye socket began to ache once more.

Part Two:

Weaving

Seeing the thickness of the thick black night
Forests and centaurs and gods of the night...

—Robin Williamson,
from "The Iron Stone"

First

THE TINKER WAGON WAS ten miles north of Swaston by nightfall. Plainly worried at what new perils the night might bring, Long Tom and Kinn scouted to either side of the coast road, looking for a defendable campsite. It was Kinn who finally found it—a long cleft that pointed to the sea, stone walls rearing a hundred feet high on either side, leaning outward with enough room under their overhang to protect the wagon from an aerial attack. There was only one entrance, choked with dead brush and rubble.

Kinn and Long Tom cleared a way for the wagon, pulling the brush back across the entranceway once the wagon was inside. To force a way through it now would raise such a racket that the camp would be quickly roused.

"We couldn't have found a better hidey-hole," Long Tom said, biting tiny thorns from his palm, "if we'd carved it out of the hills ourselves. You'd think it'd been prepared for us."

"Or for someone else," Fenne said.

"Eh?"

She pointed to the end of the cleft where a rock fall rose some ten feet up from the ground. Long Tom took a few steps closer, peering through the gathering gloom, and saw what she meant. It was a cairn rather than a rock fall. His uneasiness returned as he looked above the piled stones. There were marks on the cliff face, too regular to be caused by erosion.

"Runes," Fenne said of her discovery. "Can you read them, Dad?"

He shook his head. "No, But they're writings, sure enough. This'll be some old lord's burial plot, I'm thinking. That, or the work of the First Men, though their cairns usually top a hill or some high ground."

Did that make this haunted ground? he asked himself. If other legends were real, what was to say that the dead might not rise from their graves? He shaped the Sign of Horns and shook the thought from him.

"Tom?" Megan's voice was uncertain as she watched the movement of his fingers. "Are we staying, then?"

Long Tom nodded. "Aye. Cairn or no, this place has an honest feel to it."

Looking in her direction, he worked a smile through his swollen lips.

Damn that Dirkrin. The Swastoner had strength behind his blows, sure enough. Long Tom's right eye was blackened and half-closed too. Ah well. Looking back, he was glad Megan had taken his knives from him. Bladework would have served none of them well. And now, having had the time to think it all over, he couldn't honestly blame the Swastoners. In their position, he'd have done the same—aye, and been hastier in the doing of it when all was said and done. But right or wrong, it still galled Long Tom.

The tinkerfolk had thin skins when it came to questioning their loyalties and honour. There were the old lies of horse-stealing and quick-tongued cheating, the stealing of babes...

And now to be named the spies.

Long Tom fumed. Tinkers were freeborn men, giving allegiance to none but their own. The clan came first. What cared a tinker for Saramand of Dathenan? The wagon-tales of the old tinker greybeards had it that the tinkerfolk were here when the Tus ruled—perhaps even before. Just leave us the Fern Isles and our wagons, Long Tom thought. Give us the freedom of the roads.

Ah, but that was it, wasn't it? The Swastoners—no matter that their forefathers had driven out the Tus before them—fought only to hold their own.

Long Tom sighed, then realized his family was staring at him.

"Away with you," he cried. "You've faces longer than billygoats. Broom and heather! Are we pausing here for the view, or setting up a camp? Kinn, we'll move the wagon closer to the wall under yon' overhang, and bed the horses down by those stones where there's some grass. Now if we could get a fire started and a meal in us..."

As Long Tom ordered the camp with good-humoured severity, his family relaxed and went about their familiar tasks. It was not the first time that trouble had come calling on the Turpens, though never before had it come calling in such a strange fashion. Hearing the old lilt back in Long Tom's voice, the others smiled and forgot their worries for the moment. Kinn and Long Tom saw to the wagon and horses while Megan and the girls readied a meal. Soon the camp was organized and they were sitting around a crackling fire, with stew bubbling and a pot of tea steeping on a flat stone by the flames.

But for all that Long Tom kept the smile on his face, he was worried. All his fears came back into sharp focus when he saw Carrie rise from her place by the fire to go into the wagon where the stricken wizard lay. Aye, the Saramand posed no real threat to the tinkers— did they not have kin themselves in the Saramand's homeland? Who ruled the Green Isles was not a tinker concern, so long as the travelling folk retained their freedom of the roads. That was something the Saramand were unlikely to take from them. But this other matter...

Thinking of last night's battle with the wolves and worse left Long Tom apprehensive. How could they hope to deal with things not of this world? A man was one thing—some creature out of legend was another entirely. Oh, the wolves had died as natural creatures might. He'd seen them fall as the arrows pierced their hides, aye, and the one he'd grappled with had expended its life on his blade as any beast would. It was the others, the half-seen shapes behind the wolves that the dragon—the *dragon*!—had driven off.

Long Tom looked at the wagon. Aye, and if those fell things returned this eve...

Their dragon had become no more than a small wizard near death's door. They could not look for aid from him. They could only look to themselves. It was not a comforting thought.

"Kinn," Long Tom said suddenly. "Can you and your sister not coax out a few tunes for us?"

His son nodded, drawing his fiddle from the cloth bag at his side. Fenne took out her cittern and they spent a few moments matching the tunings of their many strings, each to the other.

They struck up an old jig, Fenne following Kinn's fiddling with the doubled melody strings of her own instrument, her fingers dancing along its slender neck. Long Tom sighed, nodding his head in time to the music. He looked to Megan—radiant in the firelight, her red-gold hair spilling down long and full, her eyes shining. She was a better woman than he deserved, he thought as he searched out her hand. Squeezing her fingers, he smiled, the music sweet on his ears, and put aside his fears as best he could.

The enemy might lie just beyond the light of the fire, but bedamned if he was going to sit in fear of them like some simple crofter. There was enough bitterness in the world without allowing it to sour the whole of one's life.

The music played on.

IN THE wagon, Carrie heard Kinn and Fenne strike up the first tune. She looked down at Tarn's face—did it seem more peaceful now?—and the tightness inside her eased its dark grip for a moment. She let the music draw her thoughts out of their gloom to spiral above the dance tune, a faint smile on her lips like an echoing harmony. Then she remembered Tarn, remembered as well the silence that was somehow like music. As though following her thoughts, the tinkers' music slowed—Kinn drawing long sweet notes from his fiddle while his sister's cittern rang with slow full chords.

Not for the first time, Carrie wished she could play an instrument. Though she felt the dexterity and skill required was beyond her, she couldn't help but feel that given the right instrument, she could somehow loose the melodies inside her that longed to be freed. She listened now and her heart ached for the simple beauty. If last night the darkness was filled with terrors, tonight it held an inner peace.

She smiled deeper and breathed the crisp air that came in through the wagon's open door and windows—sweet air touched with just a memory of salt. Beneath the sound of the instrument, she heard the wind rouse to mingle with music she imagined as grassy—those were the frail notes that unclouded above the main melody—and resonant—those were the bass chords, the song of the hills about them. Hoary sounds, deep with rooty thoughts, rich smells, tingling currents…

As wind and earth and music mixed, Carrie let her fears fade. At that moment wonder came to her like an enchantment and she knew those things for which there are no words but dhruide words, runed like tree-thoughts, knowledges that could never be hoarded, spoken, or even fully understood for they changed from moment to moment with a glimmerquick fluidity that was baffling even as it brought its own strange peace. She no longer heard the music—only the silence like music—and hearing it, she could only wonder how she'd never known it before.

Somewhere between that thought and another, she realized that the music had indeed stopped. Her gaze returned to Tarn's still features. The small moon-mark on his brow glimmered amber in the darkness. There was just an echo of music in her ears now. The wind had died down. It held that that echo of quivering echo notes for a moment longer, then it too was gone. The night was still.

Carrie's gaze was drawn from Tarn's features to the door of the wagon and beyond. She found herself rising, stepping to the door and looking out. The tinkers sat quietly around the fire. Beyond them and fire's glow a dim shape stood, a tall shadow adrift in a sea of deeper shadows. Carrie took a deep breath and tried to still the sudden thunder of her heart. That shape…

She sensed no danger, only wonder. Enchantment lay like a dream upon her and slowly she moved to the fire to stand beside Long Tom, waiting, expectant.

When the figure stepped closer, she stirred involuntarily and threw a glance to those around the fire. But the tinkers gave no sign that they saw their night guest. They sat where they were, the firelight gleaming in their unfocused eyes. Carrie moved a hand to touch Long Tom's shoulder, to understand what bound him so still, when the stranger spoke, forestalling the motion.

"Greetings, young mistress."

The voice was deep and resonating, drawing her gaze, sharpening the tension that trembled through her. But it calmed her as well. A figure moved into the light, tall, with the features of a king. The firelight appeared to pass through him, yet twinkled on reed-thin limbs. Ragged hair streamed down the sides of a once-proud face, pinched features formed a crooked smile. An iron crown encircled his brow.

"I heard your call," the fey stranger went on. "I saw through your eyes the swanmage laid low from his dragoning."

He pause, gold eyes flickering, gaze going to hers as though seeking something.

"Will you not give me welcome?" he added.

"I..."

Words tumbled through Carrie's mind, only to catch in her throat. Her eyes were wide with fearful wonder, her legs shaking.

The stranger like an old king shook his head. "Surely you do not fear me?"

As he said that, uncertainties dissolved in a rush. She cleared her throat.

"Who...who are you?" she asked.

"I am Padhain," he replied. "I heard your call—shy as a riddle that would never know its answer. And the music showed me the way—quicksilver sweet it came to me, a sound both pale and mighty, distant and near, stilling only when I found this holy place." His gaze remained on her, searching. "You are new to the silence, are you not?"

Carrie gave a slow nod as she understood. The silence. Like music. And the magic. Oh, Dath, help her.

Her gaze dropped from his, rose again to look for a threat, but she could see none. There was only peace, troubled in part, but peace. Her thoughts swirled, then dropped like a hawk.

"*I* called you? How could I—" She shook her head. "I couldn't have called you. I don't know any magics."

"Whether you know them or not, still they are there, inside you. You called. Not for me, but you called with the sea in your heart and I heard. I am—was a king of the seaerl, young mistress. A silkie who died a-land. This shape I wear is but a memory of part of what I was."

Carrie's eyes widened more than ever. Oh, Dath. She was talking to a dead spirit.

Oh, she wished she understood better what magic was, what it could do. Wished she could be calm and knowing instead of shaking like a leaf in front of this unnatural being. Tarn. If he were well, he could—

Tarn.

"You've come to help him? Tarn?"

The old king's shoulders lifted and fell. "If I can. If you will aid me."

"Me? You want my help?"

Carrie shot a glance to the Turpens, looking for their support, but they still sat silent, unaware.

"What's wrong with them?" she asked, emboldened with the need to know. "What have you done to them?"

"I didn't wish to alarm them when I came. They are...like sleepers. I laid a silence over them to keep them so. They are not harmed."

"But—"

"It is better so. They are mortal, and mortals become unreasonable when faced with the unknown. They—"

"*I'm* mortal," Carrie cried. "I'm..."

Her voice trailed off as the king's gold-eyed gaze met hers, weighty with the wisdom of ages past.

"Never mortal," he said. "On my name, I swear it."

"But I am. I have to be." Carrie's voice was low and frightened. "My parents—they *were* my parents? I—oh, Dath, what am I then?"

"Your dame and sire I do not know, but I know your kind. The Summerborn. They are every kindred, mortal and fey, but one thing they have in common: They share, in part, the soul of Hafarl, the Summerlord. So to him, you are kin, young mistress, no matter what woman bore you, what man sired you. You are theirs, but you are his, too. So it is that you have the silence in you. So it is that *you* will aid your friend. I will show you how if you will but let me."

Carried shivered under the king's ghostly gaze. Protests died still-born on her lips, for what she heard rang too true. This new knowledge fueled the twinned flicker of hope and fear inside her. Could she…was she…did she dare believe..? She remembered that soft touch of the silence like music, dreams that sometimes came true, a small wizard's intense words. So she finally met the old king's gaze with her own steady, for all that her body trembled.

"What must I do?" she asked.

The king's proud features softened into a smile.

"Believe," he said. "First you must truly believe. And this is a place of power, young mistress. Yonder cairn was raised to mark the place of an old wizard's dying. Though he is gone, the power remains here. You can use it."

"This old wizard," Carrie said. "Was he you?"

The question made her feel queasy again, for she couldn't get used to the idea that she was speaking with a ghost.

"No. His name was Wenys, and he died here in peace—of age, not the violence that has slain too many good souls. This small canyon takes its name from him: Wenys Hollow." He lifted his gaze skyward as he spoke. "The night presses on and there is still much to be done—if you would aid your friend. Bring him to the cairn and we will begin."

"You mean carry him? I don't know that I'm strong enough. Can't you..?"

The old king Padhain shrugged helplessly. "This body is born of mist and wind, young mistress. You can see it, but not touch it."

"What must I do in return for your help?" Carrie asked.

She was remembering something from an old tale now—how any dealings with those of the Middle Kingdom, the faery realms, were dangerous. The mortal's side of the bargain was often impossible to fulfill.

"My bones," the ghost began.

Carrie nodded, understanding at once. "They are..?"

"On the moors, under hill."

"And you'd have them..?"

"In the sea."

"In the sea," she repeated.

Of course. What could be simpler?

The whole of this experience had taken on a strange sense of distance, as though it were happening to someone else, and she was merely observing it from far away, as though she were only listening to an old tale. That was why she could be so casual with this—oh, Dath!—this ghost.

She shivered again.

"But first Tarn?" she asked.

"Oh, aye," Padhain replied. "First the mage. I have waited many years, young mistress. A few hours more will make little difference."

TARN WAS easier to handle than she'd expected. The slim wizard seemed to weigh next to nothing. Taking him by the shoulders, she managed to drag him to the cairn, his boot heels carving two trails in the dirt behind them. She knelt by him now, the cairn towering above, the dead king at her side. She brushed a dark curl from Tarn's pale brow. The moon-mark seemed to glimmer brighter here—though whether the illuminations of it came from the moonlight, or the wizard himself, she couldn't say.

"What am I supposed to do?" she asked.

"Open yourself to the silence of Wenys Hollow. Let it wake your own, mingling and growing until it fills you. Then give of that strength to your friend. It is lifestrength he needs now, not medicines."

"But *how*?"

"You have the power, young mistress, not I. I am but the shade of a dead silkie king, not a wizard."

"But—"

"The silence," Padhain repeated firmly. "You must use the silence."

The silence. The silence like music. The magic. The thing that set her apart from others and made her kin to...to the Summerlord.

Carrie shook her head and sighed. Was it the silence that kept her so calm right now? Here she sat with a wounded wizard, a ghost by her side, as far from home as the Channel Sea was wide. Sorrow came welling up behind her eyes as she remembered home and family—kin she could understand, kin that were lost to her forever. All she had now was herself and some impossible magic…

No, she had more than that. She had the Turpens who treated her as though she were their own daughter and sister. And if she had this magic, for all that Tarn had brought words of it to her, it wasn't his fault that she had it. He'd come to help her—he *had* helped when those…those awful things attacked last night.

She suppressed a shudder and stared down at Tarn's still features. The silence. Like music.

She tried to relax, to remember the sensation when Kinn and Fenne had been playing their music, tried to recapture that instant when the music had changed into something different, deeper. Still music, still present, but quiet as an in-held breath, expectant, interwoven with wonder. She strained to recall it flawlessly, bent her head low over the wizard's still form. The moonlight gleamed about her, the night was dark with shadowed pockets.

Her thoughts began to drift. She caught a vague recollection of the tinkers' tune and hummed it softly under her breath, but her thoughts were no longer on the task at hand. So it was that the silence crept upon her unawares. It came and was about her, inside her, before she even knew it had come. She started, drew a quick breath, then it was thick upon her, a magic-filled quickening of her senses, a deep stillness, old and rounded, sharply new.

She focused on Tarn's features and saw his weakness with a piercing insight. It was though she could see through the pale flesh to the spirit inside—a spirit thinned and weakened, bruised and weary. It was her first deepseeing and though she didn't have a name for what she was doing, she understood how it worked. She leaned closer still, cupped Tarn's face in her hands, and breathed his name into the silence.

Second

IS SHAPE WAS MANLIKE—PERHAPS too much so for the creature he was—limbs perfectly proportioned, torso lean and muscular, head aristocratic, features a mix of all things familiar, except for the eyes. They were a colour no man's had ever been—the whites discoloured and bluish, the irises alabastrine. He was clad all in black—tunic, trousers, boots and cloak. And on his brow, whiter still against the deathly pale skin, was a sword-shaped symbol—a scar, perhaps, or a brand.

This was Fergun, the last of Lothan's Field Captains, the Captains. Once there had been three. But Dwar died in the dragon wars, a victim of his own cunning, and Stest had vanished longyears past, before the Dathenan took the Green Isles, and was presumed dead. So Fergun alone remained. Ice-hearted Fergun, the last Captain.

He held council now on a hilltop less than a mile west of Wenys Hollow, where the moors lift from their sea of hills to provide a vantage point overlooking the land for leagues in every direction. He stood by the ruins of a broken longstone, its rough edge jutting up through the gorse and heather. The other half of the longstone lay at the bottom of the hill where the nearby coast road made a wide sweep to avoid Wenys Hollow.

And where Fergun held his council, the stormkin gathered.

Direwolves and frosts prowled the hill's approaches. Lizard-like dyorn, squat and bent-backed, stood with slope-shouldered traal and shadow-like skes, listening. The traal were a foot taller than a tall man, grey-limbed for they were stone trolls, and even featured, with oversized hands and feet. The skes were almost invisible, even in the moonlight. They were masters of shadow, illusionists, assassins of the highest caliber.

Fergun held council and the stormkin listened.

From their vantage point a mortal, looking east to Wenys Hollow, would see nothing out of the ordinary. But to those with deepsight, the whole of the canyon was bathed in a faint shimmer of light— green-gold and dark amber. Fergun, understanding what that light meant, regarded it with distaste.

"The place is still hallowed," the dyorn Galag said. He spat on the longstone and grimaced. "Still guarded by the old mage's spells."

"I weary of your excuses." The Captain's voice was cold. "The Icelord wearies of your excuses."

"But—"

The Captain cut him off. His fingers slashed the night air as he pointed east.

"Yonder lies the dragon-shaper—he who slew a brother of yours in Codswill, and two more on the road to Swaston. He was near death, but now? Now the very child you were sent to slay heals him. We weary, Galag, weary to death. Your death."

The dyorn shivered.

"We are not many…" he began.

The Captain gave an icy laugh and the moors themselves seemed to shrink back from the rasp of his humour. He looked beyond Galag to the others. Five more dyorn. Three traal. The skes numbered three. And below, a half-score direwolves prowled, and the frosts waited.

"Not many?" Fergun repeated. "Not enough for a mage, a waif, and a handful of tinkers? Not *enough*?"

"But she is Summerborn," Galag muttered.

"Aye, and you will be summer-slain do you not fulfill my wishes."

"The Captain speaks," the dyorn said, his voice mournful.

"We have more than these few to worry over, our Master and I. Can you not taste the air, stormkin? There is magic brewing. The Isles stir to the Summerlord's defence. So we must be swifter. North lies the heart of the struggle, and north I will fare. To Ardmeyn where the Everwinter already begins. He is there—Hafarl, the Summerlord. He must be there. And we will find him. And when we do..." The Captain made a slicing motion with his hand. "He will die, too."

Fergun looked again to where the light shimmered in Wenys Hollow. Had he the time, he would place Lothan's seal upon it and so desecrate another hallowed place. But the taw was strong there, and he must conserve his own for the battle that was soon to come. North would the final reckoning come. Not here. And though he knew the stormkin could not enter the hollow, he knew as well that those within must have it if they are to be of any use to the coming struggle. If they remained...He shrugged, smiling to himself. Then they could cause no harm and would die in the long run—die when Hafarl fell and the Everwinter came.

He returned his gaze to the gathered stormkin.

"Slay them," he said. "Slay them, or keep them penned, or by Lothan's Sword, I'll slay you myself."

"The Captain speaks," Galag said. "His will be done."

"Aye, see that it is."

Fergun turned. He drew on his taw and the dark savage silence rushed to fill him. For as the Summerlord and his silences waned, so did Lothan's grow stronger. The Captain's taw flashed through him and he grinned fiercely, took a black-winged shape, and lifted into the air. He left the hill further behind as each long stroke of his leather wings beat against the night air.

Galag scowled, angry fires kindling in his eyes.

"His will be done," he repeated.

He spat on the longstone and turned to his companions. They regarded him with careful gazes. He cut a dark rune in the night air with his fingers—a foul thing that made them grin.

"The Captain has spoken," he said. "Slay them, or pen them in. And so we shall."

And perhaps one day, he added to himself, we will see the colour of a Captain's blood. But that day had not yet come, and he could be patient, patient as stone. He grinned and spat again on the broken longstone.

"Come!" he cried and set off.

The skes melted into the shadows, seemed to vanish. The dire-wolves and frosts sped ahead, dyorn pacing them, traal bringing up the rear. Their stony faces wore the shallow smiles that passed for laughter among their kind. They tasted the blood that would soon be spilled, tasted it and grinned.

DEREN SQUINTED, checking their boat's position for the hundredth time that night. They were anchored in the shallows that lay off Elding's Arm and though he had no reason to distrust his anchoring, still he looked. It helped to take his mind from his pains. His back ached, from shoulder to shoulder, from the knotted muscles in his neck to the small of his back. His eye socket burned, and his temples throbbed as though someone was pounding a drum in the back of his head.

Magic. He snorted, tried to return to the exercises Gwyryon had given him, then gave up in disgust. Better they found passage with some fisherman soon, before the Saramand discovered them conveniently waiting for them here. Better that than sitting here on the dark water, head aching from wizard-lessons he was no longer sure he wanted to learn.

If they couldn't use magic to spell themselves away from a dangerous position such as this, then what use was wizardry? For parlour tricks to amuse children? To earn a few pennies at hiring fares and market places? What benefit this power if it cost so much to use? He peered at Gwyryon, saw that the healer was still awake, and asked him as much.

Gwyryon shifted his legs into a more comfortable position and cleared his throat, but said nothing. He remained silent for so long that Deren was sure he wasn't going to answer. He began to feel guilty for his outburst. He remembered that this magic had healed him. He lived because of it. And Gwyryon had been kind enough to—

He started self-consciously as Gwyryon suddenly spoke.

"Its cost is dear because it is not so easily replenished, Deren. But it was not always so.

"Long ago the First Men patterned the land with stoneworks. The henges and cairns and such were storehouses for power; the leys that connect them form a replenishing rune. So. In those days the Isles were filled with power and mages could call upon it, using their own taw as no more than a catalyst. Then the cost was small.

"But time has passed since those far-off days—for good or ill, who can say? The world changes, the weavers weave. Much of the First Men's work has fallen into disrepair and with it, the replenishing power. Oh, there are still hallowed places, but they are few and far between—few, or good only for small spells. In these days a mage must draw on what lies within himself to work a spell. And the cost?

"He draws on his own taw. He takes from himself, from his very essence, and must give himself time to grow strong again. For his taw to grow strong again. And yes, the greater the spell, the higher the magic, the dearer the cost. But remember this, Deren: Magery is more than the working of spells. It is a discipline that puts one in touch with the heart of the world. The spellings and shape-changings are joys in themselves—I will not deny that—but they are almost frivolous when it comes to true magery.

"It is the peace in here—" Gwyryon tapped his heart. "—to know the silence of the world, the balanced peace and wonder of it, the resonance that underlies all that is. So even though the power of the Isles—its dwystaw, its deep silence—fades and wonders grow less common, there can still be mages. Not so great as they were in days of yore, but mages who still know the inner peace and yearn to share it with others."

"You sound like a priest," Deren said.

Gwyryon nodded. "It *is* a priesthood, and the Summerlord is its High Priest. He is the silence of growth, or orderly change. To know his silence is to know the Green Isles. But now..."

"Now?" Deren asked when the old man's voice trailed off.

"Now we are experiencing another silence—a way of chaos and savage darkness. It disrupts our peace. I speak of dyorn and other stormkin. And the Mocker himself."

The old healer shaped the Sign of Horns.

"But," Deren said, "you told me that the Green Isles were his in winter. That it was a balance."

"Aye, it *should* be a balance. A time of growth, a time of rest. But now that balance swings too far to Lothan's side. Everwinter draws near, and that means doom for these Isles." He looked away across the water, through the darkness, his deepsight cutting the distance. "Magic wakes on Dathenan Isle, Deren. Fair magic. But so does the dark, and it is stronger. So long as Hafarl is hunted like a stag before the Mocker's hounds, it will be stronger."

"What can we do to stop it?" Deren asked. "If he's grown so powerful?"

"For now we can get some sleep so that we will be fresh on the morrow."

Deren nodded, watching Gwyryon settled himself in the aft of the boat once more, cloak wrapped about him against the sea wind. But Deren didn't sleep yet. Head still aching, he thought long and hard over what Gwyryon had said. He had no choice, he realized. Not if he was to be of any use.

He practiced his lessons until he was too weary to concentrate, then fell into a deep, dreamless sleep.

Third

ꝒN THE DEEPEST HOLDS of Tarn's taw, he was all the shapes he had ever worn. He was a multitude of configurations that watched each other with eyes of gold and grey and mauve—those that had eyes. They were distanced, one from the other, but in that distancing, there was a sense of elusive oneness, a unity that drifted just beyond remembrance, beyond recognition.

They were each Tarn, but each was unconscious of their former unity.

They fell, shapes of wing and air, through multi-hued skies. They knew seas both salt and sweet in shapes of scale and fur. They prowled the earth's hoary depths, flickered in flames, were mist, were stone, were tree, were light, were shadow. And those eyes watched, each the other, watched, seeking the memory of that forgotten singleness, watched with eyes familiar, eyes that echoed the struggle to remember, eyes like the autumn leaves of the mythic stonewood tree—gold and grey and mauve.

There was a jammer of sound, a cacophony of cries and voices, growls and leaf-rustles, yelps and earthy groans. There was a babble of phonics, a rush of intimate reverberations and noisy intonations, the rush of water, the crash of waves, the pounding of hooves, the thundering of dragonspeech...

Tarn.

The name fell into the clamoring din, lost like the speck of the tiniest star in the seas of the night, a mere ripple in a raging torrent. The hundred varied shapes heard it, not clearly in that hubbub of sound, but like a bittersweet memory that quickly faded, forgotten almost immediately except for the intimacy it evoked. The shapes watched each other more closely, grew quieter as they concentrated, heard it come again, hushed, fleeting.

Tarn.

Here and there the babble stilled. The name was so familiar it could be tasted. A crow hovered on an updraft, remembering. An antlered head lifted to listen closer, a scaled face, neck gills fluttering, peered through green-blue waves, searching for the source of that voice. A fox cocked its head, a mole trembled. A badger poked its striped face from its sett, fresh earth on its muzzle.

Tarn.

The stillness spread from shape to shape. An old oak ignored the wind in its leaves. A silkie rested its head on a sun-bleached stone.

Tarn.

The named echoed from mind to mind, from shape to shape, leaving a strange quietness in its wake. And in that stillness, a sense of strength grew. A raven settled its ruffled feathers. A unicorn ceased its pawing of the earth and lay down, horned head upon the deep thick grass.

Tarn.

A swan lifted noiselessly into the air, its white shape glimmering in the sky. The stillness took on a mythic quality, an otherworldliness, a depth that held music that was no music, a tune that was silence.

Tarn.

In a shadowed place, a small form lifted his head, dark curls tangled across his brow, moon-mark shimmering there, eyes that were gold and grey and mauve coming alive with comprehension. He stood with a liquid grace.

Tarn.

He nodded, remembering. That name. He knew it. It was *his* name. His talisman. And remembering, he let the silence fill him.

It moved through him like music, hallowed and old, carrying both a wild joy and a gentle sadness in its measures. He let it fill him and he could feel his hurts heal, his strength replenish their lost stores, his taw become so still that all he could do was rise from it, surface from its deep secret place into consciousness.

He met another presence in his mind.

Who? he asked, shaping the word with his thoughts, wrapping it in warm gratitude.

But the stranger who had named him so boldly, returning his strength to him, was suddenly shy and withdrew .

CARRIE SAT back on her haunches. She placed her hands on her lap and watched for the telltale flutter of Tarn's eyelids. The moon mark on his brow glowed bright and even. Around them the sky was paling into dawn.

Her knees were sore from the pressure of the rough shale under them, but though she'd spent half the night crouched over the small wizard, she wasn't tired. The power of Wenys Hollow—that deep silence like music—still hummed in her every pore. She glanced at the ghost of the old king and smiled. Only the faintest trace of her earlier fear was still present on her serene features.

"I feel very strong," she said, her voice soft. "As though I could face anything. Even…"

Even a ghost, she realized. The revelation sent thoughts scurrying through her mind in search of some reassurance that she was still herself. That she hadn't become a complete stranger.

The dead king met her gaze with clear eyes.

"You *are* very strong," he said with grave simplicity. "And the power of this holy place adds to your strength. Beyond this hollow, who can say? You will have your own strengths, but will they be enough?"

"Enough for what?"

Padhain pointed to the cliffs about them. "There and there and there. Stormkin are gathering. The old bindings still hold here in the hollow, but beyond it, on the moors, there is nothing to stop those stormkin except for what you can summon from within yourself. And so I ask, will it be enough?"

Carrie followed Padhain's gaze and found that she could sense the stormkin he spoke of. Her fear—eased insofar as the ghost was concerned—arose again.

"No," she said, her voice a murmur. "It's not enough at all. Whatever's inside me is still too new for me to use when I want to. It—the silence seems familiar, but I don't really understand it."

She looked at Tarn again. The glow was fading from his moon-mark and he began to stir.

She shook her head. "How could I have healed him?"

Her gaze went to the ghost then back to Tarn again, confusion welling up inside her. Tarn's eyes were open—those strange eyes she remembered from…was it only two mornings ago?

The small wizard studied her for a moment, face puzzled until he suddenly smiled.

"You," he said. "You've changed. The last time I saw you, you were as shy as a wren, but now…" He lifted a hand to touch her cheek. "Summerborn. There can be no doubt. How else could you work a spell so quickly? Oh, I thank you and—"

His gaze went over her shoulder to see Padhain who was becoming more insubstantial in the growing light of the dawn. His smiled widened and he sat up.

Carrie frowned. "You shouldn't be moving. You've been on death's door for a day and more and—"

Tarn laughed. "And now I'm well. I've never felt better."

He shook her hand from his shoulder and danced to his feet, balancing lightly on the tips of his toes. When he snapped his fingers, tiny sparks blossomed in the palms of his hands.

"I'm like someone new-born," he said, "and the old tune's so strong in me I could move those cliffs if I felt the urge…"

His voice trailed off and he paused, stared upward, poised and still.

"Stormkin," he said.

His good humour fled. His eyes flashed with anger and his fine features hardened.

"Where are we?" he asked.

"In a place called Wenys Hollow," Carrie replied. "It's north of Swaston."

Tarn imagined a map of Cermyn in his head and got his bearings. Then he turned his attention to Padhain.

"And you?" he asked. "Was it you who woke her taw and showed her the spell to call me back?"

Padhain nodded. "We struck a bargain, the young mistress and I. First we would heal you, and then...then we would see to the sea-sending of my bones."

Tarn's eyes hooded with thought. Dawn pinked the eastern skies. The soft greys of the morning dissolved the night and sharpened the shadows in the hollow. He felt the presence of the stormkin—so many of them. Deep in his taw he was still giddy with the thrumming of the hollow's power that Carrie had given him. He knew what they had to do. Go north to Pelamas. But there were the stormkin to consider, and Carrie's bargain, and—he looked over the cold fire—the tinkers.

"Your bones are here?" he asked Padhain.

As the morning grew brighter he could hardly make out the dead king's gossamer shape. He called up his deepsight until Padhain's form sharpened and grew clear again.

"No. They are on the moors. Under hill."

Tarn sighed, wishing he could pluck a course of action from the ever-increasing jumble of his thoughts. Fulfilling Carrie's bargain complicated matters too much. It would be difficult enough to get her to Pelamas through a land besieged with stormkin. But if they could just go—

He shook his head. They couldn't add to their bad luck by turning their back on a bargain fairly made.

"How far away are they from here?"

"Not far."

Tarn turned to Carrie. "Can you shapechange?"

She looked at him blankly, then understood and shook her head.

Tarn gave her a rueful smile. "No, of course not. How could you? Just two days ago you couldn't even accept what you are and you certainly couldn't work a spell. But..."

They couldn't simply stay here, he finished silently. What they needed was a diversion.

"Don't the stormkin only come out at night?" Carrie asked.

She was remembering the attack on the tinker wagon that had come only at the end of the day.

"They are stronger at night," Tarn said, "and more so in the winter. The sun hurts them a little, but it's more of a mild discomfort than anything serious." He nodded to himself. "But you're partly right. It does slow them down." He turned to Padhain again. "Exactly how far must we go?"

"Walking?"

"Winging."

"Half an hour, perhaps less."

Tarn looked from Padhain to Carrie as he considered their options. The sudden responsibility of having more lives than his own resting on his slim shoulders was an unfamiliar burden. Carrie. The four tinkers. The bargain to fulfill with Padhain. The gauntlet they'd have to run as they headed north.

Thinking of the tinkers, he glanced in their direction.

"A sleep spell?" he asked Padhain.

The dead king nodded. "Harmless," he assured them, more for Carrie's sake than Tarn's. "They—the younger pair—raised the magic with their own music. I merely gave it a different direction. They'll be no worse for the wear. I can wake—"

Tarn shook his head. "Let me."

He walked slowly to where the tinkers sat. He had a two-fold reason for wishing to do it himself. He would ease their cramped limbs—something a bodiless ghost might well neglect—and he planned to gather more of the taw of Wenys Hollow to himself at the same time. In the hours to come he would need that strength and more.

Standing by the tinkers, he began to sing. From where she watched, Carrie felt the hairs on the nape of her neck prickle. She listened to the wizard sing and sensed the power building up again—much more quickly this time; for she had fumbled along as best she could, but Tarn knew exactly what he was doing. Would she ever become that adept? she wondered. Did she even want to?

Tarn's singing rose and fell with a strange lilt. It was a wordless song that reminded her of that moment between music and the silence that was like music.

As that strange silence filled her again, Carrie knew that there was no question about it—she *had* to learn more. Having tasted the wonder of it now, the world would seem far too empty without it.

She sensed, rather than saw, the Turpens stirring. Kinn and Fenne blinking in the bright morning light, Megan pushing away from Long Tom's shoulder and Long Tom himself arching his back, a yawn stretching his mouth wide. Carrie smiled seeing them with her deep-sight. Their kindly warmth was an aura that she detected very plainly as a golden glow.

Tarn appeared at her side, his movements urgent. She met his gaze and saw the power crackling in his eyes.

"We'll go now," he said. "The ghost and I. When you see the storm-kin follow us, gather the Turpens and leave this place immediately. Go north and stop for nothing. I'll join you when I can."

"But—" she began, then shut the thought away. But what if he couldn't find her? she wanted to ask.

"I'll find you," Tarn said, answering the unspoken question.

"I—I'll do my part as best I can."

"I know you will."

He gave her a reassuring smile, then made a motion to Padhain. He drew on his taw, marvelling at its deepness. This must be what it had been like for the wizards of old. The power of Wenys Hollow was a steady undercurrent of strength that swelled, building inside him layer upon layer of the power he needed. And he would need all he could take with him.

Stooping, he picked up a handful of pebbles and tossed them high into the air.

"Go!" he said to Padhain. "I'll follow."

The dead king misted and vanished. Tarn spoke a word and the pebbles became a flock of gulls, filling the air with wings and sharp cries. Then he was amongst them, one more grey and white shape in the circling flock. The gulls rose from the hollow and streamed off in every direction, the sun bright on their wings.

Carrie shaded her eyes to watch them go. She tried to pick Tarn out from the other birds but they were moving too fast, darting in and out and changing positions, and she gave up. Then her throat tightened and fear clawed its way up her spine. Five dark shapes rose in the sky behind the gulls.

Stormkin. She named them silently to herself. Shapeshifting dyorn. And there were others. She sensed their confusion, sensed them leave their watchful positions. Tall stony shapes. Direwolves. The Frosts, all angular and cold. And there were some that seemed to be no more than shadows—moving shadows for all that the sun was bright up there on the moors. The proximity of so many of the creatures chilled her blood.

She wished there was something she could do to help Tarn, then remembered his instructions. She turned back to see that the Turpens were up and about. Kinn was returning his fiddle to its cloth sack. Megan had kindled a new fire in the cold coals. Fenne was looking after the horses.

"Such a sleep," Long Tom said. "I feel as rested as if I'd spent a hundred years enchanted in some kowrie's magical glen."

Well, it was something like that, Carrie thought. Though not quite a hundred years.

She shot one last longing look to the skies above the cliffs—empty now except for a scattering of puffy clouds in the morning blue—then ran to join the Turpens.

But as she shared her tale, nursing a welcome cup of tea in a trembling hand, she outlined a slightly different plan. She cared for the Turpens—never mind that she'd just met them—and she didn't want to take the chance that they might be hurt in the coming struggle. She made a decision to leave alone, and it frightened her more than anything ever had before; but she knew it was the right thing to do, and she wouldn't change her mind—or tell the Turpens about the change of plans.

"That's fool's talk," Long Tom protested. "Broom and heather, lass. We can't let you go out where these damned creatures are while we're sitting here, safe as you please."

"But Tarn's joining me," she said. "We'll be able to go so much quicker than the wagon, and this way Tarn won't have to worry about protecting you as well as me."

"Long Tom can take care of his own well enough, thank you kindly," Long Tom began, but Megan cut him off.

"Oh, and you're a wizard yourself now, are you, Tom? You'll just wave your hand and all the beasties will cower before you? Ach, talk sense yourself or you'll have me thinking the Swastoners did more to your head than the bruises I can see."

Long Tom gave her a hard stare, a quick retort on the tip of his tongue. But then he remembered the attack, two nights past, and the helplessness he'd felt. If the wizard hadn't come...

"It's the lass I'm worrying about," he said. "It's Carrie alone in the hills waiting for the little wizard to join her."

"And well you might worry," Megan said. "My own heart's cold with fear."

"Tarn can't come back here," Carrie told them. "We'll just be surrounded by stormkin again, and the same trick won't work twice. I have to go ahead without you. I *have* to. And knowing you're safe here will set my mind at ease."

"But what of us, lass?" Long Tom asked. "What of our worry? I know it was for convenience's sake that we named you daughter, but surely after all we've been through together, you're as good as kin now. What other to do you have?"

"The...the Summerlord," she replied in a soft voice, her eyes brimming with tears.

The Summerlord. What was he to her except a name? But the kinship was there—she couldn't deny it. No matter how much she might want to protest, she'd discovered something inside herself that wasn't normal, that didn't belong in the world of men. And as long as she stayed with the Turpens, death would be their travelling companion. At least Tarn could deal with those stormkin where ordinary people couldn't.

"I don't want to go on alone," she said, "but I have to. You can follow, once you've given us a day or two of a head start. You were going north anyway—to Kellmidden, wasn't it? We could meet in that place Tarn spoke of. Palm...um..."

"Pelamas Henge," Long Tom said.

Carrie nodded. "Yes, you could meet us there."

He met her gaze for a long moment, then sighed in unwilling agreement.

"So be it," he said. "How will you go?"

"I'll follow the road, I suppose. Until Tarn joins me. After that..." She shrugged. "He'll be the guide."

They fell silent for a time, sipping their tea, eating the cornbread that Fenne had baked in a covered pan by the fire. When she was done eating, Megan arose and began to fill a journeysack for Carrie, her eyes shiny with unshed tears. Long Tom cleared his throat once or twice, but found himself lost for words whenever Carrie looked at him. He wondered how she'd become like a daughter to him so quickly. It was as though she had always travelled beside them.

He stood abruptly and crossed over to the wagon, stomping up the stairs and disappearing inside. When he returned, he carried a belt with double sheaths hanging from it. In each sheath was a long tinker-blade. He sat down beside Carrie and drew the blades out, letting the sunlight wink on their silvery edges.

"These were my great gran'dad's," he said. "There's not a tinker I know can put a name to the metal in them. But they're sharper than razors and never lose their edge, and see here, along these ridges? Those are runes. For luck, gran'dad said. The tale has it that his dad got this metal from the erlkin—for some favour he did the kowrie folk. He's said to have been the finest smith our family ever had and whether or not the tale's true, they're still the finest blades I've ever seen. I want you to take them."

She looked down at the knives with a numb expression. She hated weapons. But they gleamed in the sunlight like no sword nor knife she'd ever seen. Hesitantly, she took one in hand. It seemed light for its size. It didn't feel wrong, either—like she'd thought it would—to hold a weapon. But these were the Turpens' heirlooms.

"I couldn't," she said. "They're too fine. Why don't you wear them yourself?"

"A tinker wears his own blades, lass—ones he's smithed himself. That's the way of it. These old blades, they're passed through the family until someone gives them away—out of the clan. And only to the most loved of friends."

"But—"

"Broom and heather, girl. If you'll not take these blades, bedamned if I'll let you leave this camp!" He caught himself. When he continued, he lowered his voice and it had grown husky. "Take them for luck, please?"

"I...thank you, Long Tom."

Silently, he took the blade from her and sheathed them both before handing her the belt. She fitted it snugly around her waist and stood, feeling a sense of confidence with their weight on either hip. Not that she knew the first thing about using them. Still...

Megan handed her the brimming journeysack and embraced her.

"There's food for a week in there, Carrie. And you'll take that cloak of Fenne's you've been wearing. It's warmer and a tighter weave than the one you had on when you first came to us."

Carrie nodded and hugged her in return. She said her goodbyes to Kinn and Fenne, and then it was time to be going. For if the stormkin returned before she was gone...

She shuddered to think of it.

"It's not for forever," she said. "We'll be together again...in Kellmidden."

"In Kellmidden," Long Tom repeated. "Though all the creatures of the Mocker stand between us."

He shaped the Sign of Horns.

They watched her go, a small figure trudging bravely out of the hollow, the tall cliffs rearing up on either side of her. Long Tom put his arms around Megan's shoulders and held her tight. Kinn and Fenne stared, standing awkwardly to either side of their parents. Long Tom made a gruff motion and they moved closer so that the four of them stood with their arms around each other.

"Two days we'll give them," Long Tom said in a dangerously soft voice, "and no more. Then we'll follow. And Ballan damn any that'd do her harm."

They watched until she was out of sight, then slowly returned to sit around the fire. An oppressiveness hung over the camp now and Long Tom knew it wouldn't be gone until they saw her again.

"Ah, damn all wizards and their magics," he muttered. "Ballan damn them all."

All but one, he amended. Give the best of heather-luck to Tarn, the small man with his tangled hair and strange eyes. For Carrie was under his protection now.

Fourth

O NE DYORN FOLLOWED THE gull that was Tarn. It lifted dark wings in pursuit and Tarn fled before him while he concentrated on strengthening his illusions—the crowd of gulls…and below…Wenys Hollow, by now surely deserted of tinkers and wagon, in accordance with his instructions.

When he was sure that all the other stormkin had dispersed, chasing his phantom flock, he bent his will into putting as much distance as possible between himself and Wenys Hollow. The lone dyorn hung on his trail, gaining. Far ahead, Padhain sped—a glimmer of mist on the morninged hills.

The dyorn drew closer, moment-by-moment, seeing through all Tarn's evasions and illusions until Tarn knew he had to meet it in combat. The name for a battle between wizards was *fiercing*, and that's what this would be—for the dyorn were wizards too, though their taws were dark and strange to a dhruide-trained mage like Tarn.

He banked steeply, shaped from gull to hawk, and dropped like a stone in the windless air. The dyorn retained its shape—black as the heart of a shadow, but white-eyed. A sharp keening came from it, a weird high-pitched sound that sent shivers of expectation running up Tarn's spine. He banked again, under the dyorn now, waiting for its attack. When the dyorn dropped, Tarn spun with a powerful sweep of his wings, up and around. His claws raked the dyorn's back and black feathers choked the air.

Then the dyorn became an enormous snake. With blinding speed, it shot a sinuous coil for the hawk. Tarn dropped under it, but the coil followed quickly to loop twice around him and locking into place. They fell together in a sudden spiral.

But Tarn was prepared for this battle. His mind was as sharp as a tinker's honed blade, and his taw was brimming with the power he'd borrowed from Wenys Hollow. He found a name in his silence and voiced it. He misted and the dyorn dropped away, the ground rushing up to meet him. The dyorn changed shape again—so fast that Tarn's senses reeled at the creature's power. He felt a buffet against his mind. Thoughts struck him like solid blows. Despite his mist shape, the dyorn had still found a way carry the battle back to him.

Tarn held his own for long moments, then opened himself up, drawing the dyorn into his mind.

The act almost cost him his life.

Immediately, Tarn was drowning in a mind so alien, so thick with evil strength, that he floundered. As he fought to regain his inner balance, he caught his first real glimpse of a dyorn's taw and understood why the Mocker's minions had such great strength. The dark chaos of their taws gave them added power. Tarn had to consider his actions, fit them into a certain balance and order so that his surroundings maintained their equilibrium; but the stormkin drew their added strength by ignoring the same. Their power was born in chaos, so in chaos it grew more potent. The danger to Tarn now—as he Tarn fought to break free, to remember his name. But the danger now was that while the dyorn's taw repelled him. But, having tasted its dark power, a part of him longed to be that strong.

A certain pride in his power lay inside him—the desire to be without peer, to wield power without stopping to consider its every ramification. If he let his mage-training go, set that dark power free inside himself, he knew he could—

As soon as he realized what he was considering, he fought against it. It shocked him to realize how attractive that dark alternative to

Puretongue's teachings could be. But he threw the full strength of his taw against this foe. The added power of Wenys Hollow doubled, tripled its potency. The dyorn raised defensive shields that Tarn shredded as soon as they were erected. The swanmage narrowed his attack into one piercing spear of power that broke through the dyorn's defenses like a bolt of lightning.

The creature gave a piercing wail, reverting to its natural shape as it plummeted to the rocky hills below. Tarn continued to drift in mist shape, studying the slain dyorn with his deepsight. He calmed the adrenaline-swift racing of his thoughts.

More than luck had been with him today. Without the added power from Wenys Hollow, this fiercing might have had a far different result. And if he ever let himself be drawn into the darkness that echoed the dyorn's taw...

He composed himself, watching for the approach of other stormkin as he did. When he was satisfied that only one of them had followed him, he searched for Padhain with his deepsight. Locating the dead king, he took winged shape once more.

"**SHOW ME** where I must dig."

The old king nodded. His face was gossamer in the light of day, his body more hinting at his presence than actually present. Tarn shook a vague disquiet from him, concentrating instead on what Padhain was saying. But it was strange listening to a voice that was so strong and hale, while the body it came from was less than mist.

"They wore away my strength," the old king said, "those land lords. Harried me like a thief across the hills. For a week—a month? I can no longer remember."

"Why did they do it?"

"I am of the sea."

Tarn nodded. It was answer enough. Even these days the legends of silkies and other seaerls brought a chill to landsfolk that never a land lake could. Morennen's waters were deep and fey, with a will of their own, and no man could master them. They fished and sailed the waves by sufferance only. And many, many were the ships that failed to return to their harbours.

"And here they caught me," Padhain continued. "In sight of the sea, but too distant to allow me rescue. The hounds penned me and the land lords loosed their spears and arrows. I..." The ghostly head shook slowly back and forth. "I haven't the strength to hate them anymore. All I want is to know peace again. The sighing of deep waters— far from these Isles where chaos stalks the green silences."

The hilltop was quiet as swanmage and ghost each kept their own council. Tarn sensed the old bones underhill. He would fulfill Carrie's bargain. But thinking of her brought up another question that troubled him.

"Why did you choose her," he asked, "when you've had the choice of years? You could have asked another to help at any time. Surely she and I aren't the first mages to walk these hills?"

The old king nodded. "I had the opportunity to choose as the years went by—true enough. But I was here so long. At first I actively sought a mage, but as time passed, I became too much like the hill. I lost my need in the slow confusion of earth and stone. I was troubled, I knew patterns so far from sea-peace that I could never describe them to my people, but..." The gossamer shoulders lifted and fell. "Until I heard your companion call to the Seawife, I'd forgotten who I was. However, upon hearing the sound of waves in her voice, remembering at last, all I could do was come. I did not know she was a novice then, but knowing...remembering...how could I not ask her to ease my torment?"

"I understand," Tarn said.

He found a name and spoke it to his taw, then took a badger's shape.

WHEN THE first grey chords of twilight rang across the hills, the last yellowed bone was unearthed. Tarn wrapped them in his cloak and bore them to the sea's edge. He stared across its grey reaches, gathering silences. The sun set in the hills behind him, taking the last red light from the water. As night came on, he stirred.

"Where shall I take your bones?" he asked.

The old king stared across the water, too. With the coming of night, his body appeared more solid. Tarn could think of him as a man now, or rather a silkie in man's shape—alive, for all that he'd died so long ago.

"Where?" Padhain said, "Far enough that the tides don't return me to these shores. Deep enough to a place where the struggle of Winter and Summer will not disturb my peace."

Tarn nodded. He gathered his burden and took mershape.

As the waters closed overhead, he swam to where the sea was as deep and still as his own inner silence. The old king drifted at his side, pale and green in the dark depths. Here, where the day never ruled, his pale shape was even more pronounced.

Silent as thoughts, they travelled on until they came to a place where the water had never touched Cermyn's shores. The ocean's floor was still and silent. Midway between Cermyn and Morennen's Isle, they found a cavern that cut deep into the ocean's bottom. They went inside, down and deeper still, to where the cavern finally ended.

Tarn laid the old king's bones on the floor of the cavern and built a small cairn over them. The stones he lifted floated strangely in the silent water. As he raised the cairn, he spoke a blessing over each stone, then a binding spell, and a final spell that promised peace.

I am in your debt, the old king said when he was done.

His words rumbled in Tarn's mind.

No, Tarn replied. *I've simply fulfilled the bargain you made with Carrie.*

Padhain ignored his protest. *All I have left is my name*, he said. *On it I will swear: When you have need of sea-aid, you have but to call to me. Call out in my name.*

Our debt—Carrie's debt—is finished. You owe us nothing more.

Is that how you see it? I see it differently. You have fulfilled the debt, yes, but your reverence to those old bones of mine awake a new one. There was no need for you to speak the blessings, but you did. This might seem a small thing to you, but to me, it's as though my own kin have laid me to my rest. This I do not accept lightly. So I say again: if you have need, call me. On my name.

Tarn bowed his head. *I don't foresee such a need*, he said, *but I will remember.*

Where do you go now? Padhain asked.

North. To Pelamas, and then, if the Oracle wills it, Ardmeyn.

The Everwinter is in Ardmeyn.

Padhain's voice echoed in Tarn's mind, the import of the old king's words sending a cold chill through him.

Are we already too late? he asked. *Have they already slain the Summerlord?*

But no. He would have felt that death. The whole of the Isles would have shivered and wept with Hafarl's passing.

Not yet, Padhain said. *But they have him trapped in Ardmeyn and the Everwinter was loosed to bind him there.*

Will the enemy prevail?

The future is not for me to see. But if anyone would know, surely it would be you, Tarn Swanmage.

Tarn gave him a startled look. Swanmage was the third name that Puretongue had given him—one that few knew. How then..?

It is there, the old kind said. *On your brow, winging across your moon-mark. I will hoard its secret like it was my own and never speak it again. But I will cherish it...and the memory of your aid.*

How would I know if we prevail or not? Tarn asked, going back to what Padhain had said earlier.

Tarn, Padhain said. *It is a name of silence—one a mage Summerborn might wear. And would not Hafarl's own kin have some sense of their fate? At least more than one such as I, sea-born.*

That was not an answer Tarn had expected. He weighed it in his mind, testing it for truth. *Was* he one of the Summerborn? If so, why hadn't he known it? Why had Puretongue never told him? Then he remembered that Carrie hadn't known until he'd told her. Perhaps Puretongue hadn't known either.

Will your companions be safe? Padhain asked.

The question was enough to distract Tarn. A shadow crossed his face, then he grinned, lips tugging at the water.

If they followed my plan, they should be. I laid a glamour in Wenys Hollow. When the gulls left, we all disappeared—at least to the stormkin's eyes. Tinkers and wagon, Carrie, you and me. I told them to take the coast road, for the stormkin won't be on it. They'll be following my gulls and I didn't send a single one along the road.

And after? Padhain asked. *When the glamour fades?*

The stormkin will return to Wenys Hollow to find another spell waiting for them. This glamour will make them see the tinker's wagon still there, with the tinkers going about their usual business.

That illusion will hold?

Tarn smiled. *Why not? The stormkin can't descend into the hollow to investigate it, and so long as there is power in Wenys Hollow, the glamour will hold.*

Padhain shook his head. *I have misgivings about this plan of yours. You should return to your companions and go quickly. Leave me to sleep a deep sea-sleep. Leave me to my peace. But I won't sleep so deeply that I will forget you if you should call my name.*

There's no need for you to—

Farewell, Tarn.

The old king's shape dissolved into the water and he was gone. Tarn sighed.

Farewell, he finally said.

He took a sleeker shape and made his way back to the entrance of the cavern. There he swam upwards until his head broke above the waves and could lift as a swan into the air. With the night air on his feathers, he flew with strong even strokes, enjoying the freedom of flight. But Padhain's warning came back to trouble him. Might the glamour in Wenys Hollow fail? If it did, then Carrie and the tinkers would need his help—especially if they'd followed his plan and fared forth from its safety.

The responsibility he felt for them spoiled the joy of his flight. Looking landward, he sought out the coast road with his deepsight, wondering how much distance they'd put between themselves and the hollow, but it was still too far for him to see. He could only hope that they hadn't done something foolish such as staying in the hollow. They'd be safe enough—so long as its protection held—but they would be trapped. The stormkin wouldn't fall for the same trick twice and he wasn't powerful enough to face them all of them on his own.

Other thoughts rose to trouble him—the Everwinter in Ardmeyn and Padhain's claim that Tarn was one of the Summerborn—but at length he shook the riddles from his mind and concentrated on his flight. There'd be time enough for worry at riddles when he'd joined the tinkers on the coast road.

The moon was high above him, gleaming on the waves below. There were winds in the night air now and he rode their currents, adding speed to his flight when he could. The strength he'd borrowed from Wenys Hollow was beginning to fade when he finally caught sight of land. He let his deepsight range up the coast road and was troubled when he couldn't spy the wagon.

With worry mounting, he sped north, searching.

Fifth

As THE DAY DIED in the skies above Wenys Hollow, Long Tom watched the shadows stretch from the cliffs until the campfire gave off more light than the last trace of sun. Fenne hobbled the horses near fresh grazing. Kinn helped his mother with supper. Long Tom sighed, adding more wood to the fire. He felt the eyes of the stormkin upon them once more and it worried him. But at least, he thought, if they're come back, then Carrie and the wizard must be safe. He sighed again. Safe, aye, with leagues to fare and the land crawling with enemies—like fleas on a dog. Broom and heather! He should never have—

His thoughts came to an abrupt halt. He stared at the wagon, at his family, and rubbed his eyes. Ballan! He was seeing double. Either he was more tired than he'd thought, or the strain of these past days was getting to him. But when he took his hands away from his eyes the doubling effect was still there—sharper now.

A scream of rage rang from the clifftops above the hollow. Stormkin. They were…

Then Long Tom understood something, and he cursed himself for a fool.

They weren't supposed to be here.

This was wizard's work—Tarn's wizardry. Tarn had meant for them all—wagon and horses, Carrie and tinkers—to be hieing it north, while he'd left behind an illusion to spell the stormkin. Long Tom knew why Carrie had lied. It was to keep him and his own safe. But his heart quaked at the thought of her out on the coast road alone.

Suppose Tarn hadn't reached her yet? It was bad enough that she might be alone out there when the stormkin were gathered above, watching the hollow. But, broom and heather! They'd now know the trick that had been played on them—the same as he did. They'd be after her for sure now.

"Dad?" Kinn called, his voice nervous.

Long Tom turned to his family. He crossed the distance between the fire and the wagon, put his arm around Kinn's shoulders.

"It's an illusion," he said, his gaze meeting Megan's. "Nothing More." He ruffled Kinn's hair and stepped back from him. "Fenne, ready the horses."

They would leave as soon as the horses were hitched. With heather-luck, they'd soon catch up to Carrie and Tarn and then they could all—

"Long Tom Turpen!"

Long Tom started at Megan's voice. He turned. For a moment he was confused. He saw Megan bending over a pot by the fire, but at the same time she was standing in front of him, hands on her hips. He looked more closely. The woman at the cooking pot moved a little stiffly, her face slack and without expression, whereas the Megan in front of him had a glitter in her eyes that he knew too well.

He shook his head. This was a strange thing. Why he—

He saw himself then, cutting wood, and the blood drained from his face. His fingers shaped the Sign of Horns.

"Tom!" Megan cried again.

"Aye?"

Long Tom tore his gaze away from his double. The other Tom's face held a weird fascination for him. It was him, but not him. A soulless Long Tom that—

"We can't leave," Megan said firmly.

That brought Long Tom around.

"Woman, are you mad? Look around you. It's the Mocker's own work and you'd stay here in the middle of it? It's go we must, and go we will. Carrie will be needing us."

"But she won't need us dead."

"Meg..."

"Use your head, Tom. She left us behind for a good reason. Did you ever think that we might slow her down and bring her more danger than we might protect her from? What will you use to defend us against those creatures? Arrows and tinker-blades? A golden tongue?"

"Mum's right," Kinn said. "There's not much we can do now."

"We'd hinder more 'n help," Fenne added.

"But..."

Long Tom shook his head, looking away from the gazes of his family. He saw that they too were remembering that night in the hills outside Swaston. Coldness filled the pit of his belly. They were right. He knew that. But, Ballan! It irked him something fierce to be so helpless. And these soulless illusions, these mimicries of themselves... they made things no better.

He drew a ragged breath, calming his quickening heartbeat.

"We'll wait the two days," he said. "But we'll move camp—deeper into the hollow by the cairn. Away from those...things."

There was no disagreement in the white features of his family. With trembling hands they broke camp and moved further down the hollow, away from the eerie duplicates of themselves that were now sitting around a phantom fire, eating their evening meal. Long Tom and Kinn eased the wagon into a position that hid the strange sight from their view, building a support of stone and earth under one wheel to keep the wagon level.

They made a new fire between the wagon and the cairn. But for all that Tarn's illusions were hidden from their sight, the tinkers were still all too aware of their presence . They ate their own meal in an uneasy silence. When strains of music came from the other camp, not one of them could suppress a shudder.

Long Tom sat listening to that music. It was very much like the music that his children played, except it lacked the lift that made it their own. It lacked a soul.

He gritted his teeth and stared into the darkness beyond the fire, away from the illusions on the other side of the wagon. The storm-kin were long gone from their earlier vantage points. Was Carrie still safe? he wondered for the hundredth time, unable to stop torment-ing himself with questions to which he had no answer. Had Tarn found her?

He looked to Megan and read the worry in her eyes. Trying on a lop-sided smile that faltered too much before it stayed in place, he reached to her, wishing he felt the confidence he was trying to inspire. She was just a wee lass, this Carrie they'd known for only a few days, though it seemed so much longer. And when he thought of the stormkin, he worried all the more.

LEAVING BEHIND the safety of Wenys Hollow and the warm com-pany of the Turpen family was the bravest thing Carrie had ever done. But she didn't feel very brave when she reached the entrance to the hollow. She paused there, uncertain. Already her pack and cloak were heavy on her back and she'd barely walked a half mile. How was she going to feel at the end of the day? And these knifes...

She shivered.

This was the moment, she realized. Once she left the shelter of the hollow, there would be no turning back. Not with the stormkin returning. Shading her eyes, she searched the skies, then the hills. At last she could put the moment off no longer. Breathing a small prayer to Dath—oh, would he even remember her now, changed as she was?—she set off.

She followed the coast road, keeping to its leeward side. Time and again she stopped to scan the surrounding terrain and sky. At the first telltale sign of danger, she'd plotted out where she would scurry into the undergrowth. There were bushes and briars, tall clumps of gold-topped weeds and scraggly cedar clumps. But the sky and hills were clear each time she looked and she could only plod on.

By mid-day she could no longer see the hill that stood across from the entrance to Wenys Hollow. The road dipped and rose as it followed the coastal hills. Her nervousness grew until she fancied a threat behind every stand of briar or tree, on every hilltop, hidden among the stone outcrops. The nervousness thrummed inside her; it changed to a fear so strong that she could go no further. Shaking like a new-born lamb, she hid in a cluster of mountain ash and lay under the bright green leaves, where she stayed as motionless as the granite outcrops that dotted the hills.

The sun sank steadily and still she hid. Fear grasped her heart in a grip she couldn't break. Above, in the sky, she heard the raucous cries of the stormkin returning to Wenys Hollow and she burrowed her face against the ground, wishing she could dig into the hill and bury herself out of sight. Trembling and weak, she cowered there, listening to the cries grow louder until the creatures were directly above her. Her heart beat like a drum that she was sure could be heard all the way back to Wenys Hollow and beyond. She was certain that the stormkin would hear it, would sense her presence, would come for her.

But the cries vanished into the distance. Carrie stayed in her hiding place, peering up. She didn't dare move yet—not while she was still shaking so much—but she had to see more than the leaves and dirt. She'd seen nothing else for what seemed like forever. The sun was lower now, just a sliver showing above the hills. Cautiously, she sat up.

When the sun sank at last, she rose and stepped back onto the road. She walked slowly at first, twisting her head in every direction, certain she would find a grinning stormkin just a few feet away, but she was always alone. She walked faster, her nervousness getting the better of her again, then jogged. Then ran.

She pelted down the road until her breath came in ragged gasps and pain stitched her side, until she could run no more. Collapsing on the grassy roadside, she stared up into the night skies. She was hungry, but afraid to eat. Her stomach was too queasy and she wasn't sure she'd be able to keep the food down. But she did take a few sips from her watersack. When that stayed in her stomach, she tried some food.

She felt better after eating. Her fears felt more manageable. But worries rose to take their place. Where was Tarn? Shouldn't he have found her by now?

A thought cut sharply through her, a thought so terrifying that she could barely give it shape. It grew nevertheless, monstrous and huge, filling her mind.

What if he never came?

What if she was alone for good? Could she find her own way to this henge and the Oracle like he'd said she was supposed to? Dath! That couldn't happen. She *couldn't* do it on her own.

The darkness closed in on her from all sides. She hugged her knees and rocked back and forth by the roadside, a small, forlorn figure. Her senses—those senses so recently awoken when she'd healed Tarn—reached out into the night. She searched for some trace of the wizard, for any kind of hope, and found nothing.

Then she heard a sound.

It came from the south and she heard it less with her ears than with those inner senses that the silence of Wenys Hollow had opened inside her. It was a sound of anger and rage that summoned such despair that her earlier fears paled in comparison.

She knew what made it.

Stormkin.

Somehow, she'd been discovered. Somehow, those creatures knew that she'd fled the hollow. They were coming for her now. Coming for *her*.

She felt the weight of Long Tom's knives on either hip, but they gave her no comfort. They were useless to her. She'd more likely cut herself then fend off an attacker.

Oh, Tarn, she thought. Where are you? Dath speed him to her.

No, that was wrong. She shouldn't be calling to Dath. She should be calling to the other one—the light in the stormkin's dark. The Summerlord.

Thinking his name, her heart called out to him. Help me, she pleaded. Help me.

For she knew the stormkin were abroad and on her trail.

The stormkin.

Hunting.

Sixth

DEREN SAW THE SHIP before its sailors spied their
own small craft. He nudged Gwyryon awake with
a toe of his boot and stared one-eyed across the
water, trying to make out its colours. Excitement danced inside him.
The Sails were a plain off-white—not the cursed red and yellow of
the Saramand. And though the spiralled prow rode high in the
water, there was a bear's head, rather than a serpent's, carved in its
wooden turnings. A blue flag fluttered on the topmast—blue with a
splotch of yellow in the center. The yellow was a shape he couldn't
quite make out. There seemed to be lines on it, or in it...a triangular
shape that...

"So your plan proved the best after all," Gwyryon said from his
position in the rear of their own craft. He straightened his back, pulling his cloak's hood up so that it fell across his forehead to shade his
eyes. "The weavers weave. We could not hope for a better ship."

"You know it?"

"Not that one in particular, perhaps, but I know its style. That
ship harbours in Kellmidden, Deren—ah! And see the flag?"

Deren nodded. It was easy to make out now. A golden harp on a
field of blue. Harper's blue.

A man on the harper's craft spied them and the vessel turned, its bearhead prow cutting the waves to where they waited. Deren marvelled at the ship's sleek, clean lines as it drew nearer. Here was a craft built by a shipwright who loved his work, he thought. Sweet and lean, built for both beauty and speed.

"It's *The Ardweir*," Gwyryon said, reading the runes on its side. "Briarsen's ship. Now what would he be doing so far from Traws?"

"Briarsen?" Deren asked.

"He's a—"

"Ho! The rowboat!"

The rough voice interrupted any further conversation. Deren looked up to the bearded man who had hailed them and waved. He was a big man with the sea in his face, greying his beard and hair, lining brow and cheek. His nose was like a great crag lifting from the waves—in this case, the waves being the sweep of his moustache.

A few more sailors joined him at the rail, each as burly as the first, their clothing bright and gaudy in the morning light. The men then gave way to a new arrival—a tall, even-featured man. He was lean as a mast, with red-gold hair that fell to his shoulders in a cascade of untidy curls. He wore the harper's blue, and it was his voice they heard next.

"Can we be of help?"

Deren glanced at Gwyryon who nodded for him to speak.

"Depends on where you're bound," Deren called back.

"That I'm not sure of," the harper replied. "Here, catch!" He threw down a rope. "We're looking for a man. We had word he would be found along this coast somewhere, but…" The lean shoulders lifted and fell. "There's not much left now, is there?"

"We're from Gullysbrow."

"Were you attacked by the Saramand as well?"

Deren nodded. "Two days past. What's the name of the man you're looking for?"

"Puretongue."

Deren busied himself with the rope, securing their boat to *The Ardweir*. Beside him, Gwyryon stirred.

"Throw down a ladder," the old healer called up. "I know where this Puretongue is to be found. I will guide you to him."

The harper smiled.

"A ladder!" he called over his shoulder, then turned back to Gwyryon. "Where is he?"

"Not far, harper. Not far."

"WHY DO you seek Puretongue?" Gwyryon asked.

The Ardweir was sailing up the coast under the old healer's direction. He stood with Deren and the harper on the foredeck, gazing seaward.

"A private matter."

The harper smiled. They'd exchanged names—his was Wren Briarsen—but little else.

Gwyryon shrugged. "Your business is your own, of course. But I find it odd that a harper's craft should sail out of Traws on such a matter. Puretongue never had a great deal to do with the kings of Kellmidden. You *are* in a king's service?"

"Yorin's. At least I was. We...argued. And though I winter *The Ardweir* in Traws, we sailed from Twellen."

Deren watched them Gwyryon and the harper, and was puzzled at the strange undercurrent he sensed between them.

"Do you know him?" Gwyryon asked. "This Puretongue?"

"No."

"Then how will you know him?"

"I..." Wren frowned. "Why do you ask so many questions?"

He turned to regard Gwyryon, his deep grey-blue eyes hard and piercing as he searched the old healer's features.

Gwyryon shrugged. "To hear the answers, why else?"

"That is not—"

"An answer," Gwyryon agreed. "I will strike a bargain with you, Harper Wren. Tell me why you, a kingless harper, seeks the dhruide Puretongue. Tell me why, and for whom, and I will tell you why I ask."

Wren made no reply. He leaned on the rail, staring down at the water streaming by the bows. Deren shuffled his feet and both men turned to face him.

"I thought I'd go below," he said.

He felt increasingly uncomfortable in the presence of these two men. They seemed to speak on different levels, all at the same time, and he found it hard to follow the conversation. It also seemed less and less his business to hear any of it.

"There's no need," Wren said.

"Stay," Gwyryon added. Then to Wren he added, "Why is it so difficult for you to speak with me? Have you pledged silence to someone?"

"No."

"You trust me enough to lead you to him."

"That's not such a hard thing to understand. With the coast ravaged by the Saramand and the people either dead or fled, you're all I have. At least you know the name."

He looked away again. When he turned back, there was a troubled look in his eyes. He sighed.

"I will tell you," he said finally. "Are you at all familiar with King Yorin? His holdings are the Dales of Heatherby—along Kellmidden's east coast. I have been his harper ever since I took the blue cloak. I've tutored his children, hallowed his festivals, played for his court, have written up the genealogies of all his kin...well, you would know a harper's duties as well as anyone, I suppose. You *are* a healer?"

"But not guilded."

"No matter. You know what's involved."

Gwyryon nodded.

"I have good memories of those years," Wren continued. "I roadwended less than many of my craft might have, but what need had I for travel? I loved it there in Heatherby. Or at least I did until this trouble came."

"The Saramand," Gwyryon said.

Wren nodded. "At first it drew the kings of Kellmidden together—uniting them against a common foe. Not one of them ignored Caill's summoning to the High King's seat in Traws. But there was no quick solution except to join the rest of Dathenan—Umbria, Cermyn, and the rest—and that meant forsaking the old ways. Well, the kings bickered like errant children, but in the end—oh, it pains me say this. In the end my liege withdrew from the gathering of Kellmidden's kings and joined his fate to that of the lord of Umbria.

"Do you know what this means?"

"Tell me," Gwyryon said, though Deren got the sense that he already knew.

"The new religion is coming into the Dales of Heatherby—Dath, and those loud-mouthed priests of his. I could not abide it, and so Yorin and I bickered in our own turn, and I left his service."

Wren fell quiet. They listened to the wind in the rigging, the flapping of the sails, the water on the boughs, the sound of the sailors joking amongst each other. Deren watched his companions, oddly moved by the harper's tale for all that he had been raised on the teachings of Dath himself.

Then Gwyryon finally broke the silence. "And whose service are you in now, Harper Wren?"

"That of Penhallow—the Oracle of Pelamas Henge."

Gwyryon nodded. "I see now. And he told you to seek out the dhruide Puretongue, to tell him that the Everwinter has come into Ardmeyn. That time has run out on us again."

"I...How could you know?" Wren faced the old healer, his brow furrowed with a frown. "Only Puretongue could..."

"I have been named Puretongue," Gwyryon said.

Wren stared at him, comprehension dawning in his eyes.

"Gwyryon," he said in a soft voice. "Which means 'Truth' in the old tongue. I should have seen that."

The old dhruide shrugged. "Sometimes it seems we only know what's needful at the time it is needful. The weavers weave."

"Why didn't you tell me sooner?"

Deren wondered the same.

"These are dangerous times that we live in, Harper Wren. I wanted to know who sought me, before I answered to that name."

"So you already knew of the Everwinter coming into Ardmeyn? Penhallow said you might."

Puretongue nodded. "It's the reason that Deren and I are bound for Pelamas ourselves. We were hoping for a ship, you see—one from Morennen's Isle seemed most likely—for the time has come for speed. Dathen—the whole of the Isles—are astir with strangeness. Stormkin walk the land, elder magics wake against them, and who knows what else has been set loose upon the world these days? If we don't set right the balance and reinstate the Summerlord, then the Everwinter will spread south and the whole of the Isles will lie under the Mocker's hand."

Wren shaped the Sign of Horns.

"Has that foretold time truly come?" he asked.

"Dhruidic or bardic, the lore is the same. The time is upon us. Either the balance sways to the Icelord, or we stop him."

"What about the Summerlord?" Deren asked. "This is his battle, isn't it? Why doesn't he do something about it?"

"Were you not listening to me when first I spoke of him?" Puretongue asked. "The Choice was taken from him. Without Meynbos, his power has no focus. It is we—his followers—who must provide succor. That, or fail along with him."

Silence fell after the dhruide spoke, and each fell into their own thoughts. Wren left them to give the captain a new course. The ship turned west, away from Gwendellan, then north to follow the Channel Sea to Becks Bay and Twellen. At length the dhruide turned to Deren.

"Gwyryon is gone now," he said.

"What do you mean?"

Puretongue smiled. "There is power in names, Deren. I've already taught you that. I am known as Puretongue where we are going, so Puretongue I'll be."

Deren shook his head. "Didn't you trust Wren? Do you even trust these people that'll be where we're going?"

"I trust them well enough. But even the wind has ears in times such as these, and I'd rather not give my enemies more information than they already have."

"But who are you really?" Deren asked.

"No one knows all my names," the dhruide replied, "but there are some who know too many."

THEY WERE well north of the Isle of Morennen by the time the sun was westering low in the sky. Deren blinked his eye open, then rose and stretched. He'd been practicing his lessons again and felt stiff all over. It was hard to sit still for so long. He rubbed his backside. *The Ardweir* was a beautiful ship, but its planking was as unyielding as the poorest fishing trawler. He went looking for Puretongue and found him leaning on the port rail, his face pale and strained.

"Gwyr—I mean, Puretongue," he said. "What's the matter?"

The dhruide turned a grave gaze in his direction. "The stormkin are hunting."

"Hunting? Who are they hunting?"

"Our last hope."

Puretongue looked away. When he spoke again, his voice was so low that Deren had to lean closer to hear him.

"Ah, Tarn," the old dhruide murmured. "Don't prove me wrong."

Deren shook his head. He was understanding less and less the more he learned.

"Who's Tarn?" he asked.

Puretongue didn't appear to hear him. At length, Deren sighed and went to find a place to sleep. He wasn't sure what the next day would bring, but he planned to be well-rested to meet its challenge. In the end, he curled up in a corner of Wren's cabin, listening to the wind and sea, and the quiet murmur of Puretongue and Wren's voices. When he finally slept, his dreams kept him on the borderland between sleep and waking, and gave him no real rest.

Seventh

HE CRABBERS' CAMP WAS only a few leagues north of Wenys Hollow. Three older men and a boy of seventeen sat finishing their evening meal around a small campfire of driftwood and debris. The white sands of the beach were strewn with their belongings and crabbing gear. On the water-line, two small crabbing boats were beached. Tin pails hung from the rear of each craft, half-filled with crabs. The pails were perforated with dozens of tiny holes to let in the seawater. There was a market for fresh crabs north in Yellfennie, not for dead ones.

"'Twas madness to come this far south," the oldest of the men said, "and don't you know it, Jember Slan. Dath! The catch's so poor we'll be lucky to pay our expenses—that's if we're not hung up by our heels by the snake-lovers. Old Dan Poole told me they're been sighted 'long the coasts—an' not just come a-spying."

The old man cast a baleful gaze seaward, then turned back to scowl at his comrades.

"I've got an ill feel 'bout this night," he added. "Like a cold hand's got me by the knackers."

"An' your trouble, Kenneg," Jember replied, "is that you're too old for man's work." He grinned at the other two. "Come the morrow's nooning an' those pails'll be full. *An'* we'll be stopping in the cove for eggs. The cliffs are riddled with nests. There'll be expenses paid and good profit to boot, mark my words."

"Ah, but it's a bad night, I tell you," Kenneg told him. "An' if it makes me less of a man for fearing what it might bring, then so be it."

Jember shook his head. "Best you see a priest when we get back. Or get a witchwife to give you a charm."

The third man and the boy listened to the exchange but took no part in it. Kenneg repeated his warning and the man frowned, looking to the boy who sat wide-eyed and staring, taking in every word. The third man's name was Hasen and the more Kenneg spoke, the more he worried. For all the old man's bluster, he had an uncanny knack about him—almost a second sight. It gave Hasen a chill.

What if the old man was right? The raiders *had* been sighted along these coasts a few times too often for comfort, and with a fire burning, its light reflecting on the water...

He shook his head and reached to touch the boy's arm.

"Don't you go paying Kenneg too much mind, Bell. He likes to talk is all, an' if he puts the fear in us—well, it's all the better joke on us when we get home."

Bell nodded and smiled, but he still looked nervous.

Hasen frowned again. The lad half-believed the old man, and damned if he didn't feel a little queer about it himself.

"Hey, Kenneg!" he called across the fire. "Give it a rest, would you. We're not all—"

The manlike shape seemed to rise from the very sand, black as a shadow, directly behind Kenneg. A flash of silver caught in the firelight as the blade whispered from a hidden sheath on its back. Hasen half-rose, a cry of warning on his lips, but the sword was already arcing down. There came a terrible sound as it cut through flesh and bone. Hasen was on his feet now, but it was far too late. The shadow shape was already gone, melting soundlessly into the darkness behind the fire, while Kenneg...

Hasen pulled the old man's face from the fire and his stomach gave a lurch. He heard Bell retching. Jember moaned. The killer's sword had cut through the old man's shoulder, slicing as far as his stomach, and as Hasen pulled it back, the body flopped in two directions.

"Why?" he choked, stepping back from the corpse.

Jember stood at his side and handed him a length of driftwood that was suitable for a club, but the beach was empty. They stared about themselves, clubs in hand, with Kenneg's dead body at their feet and nothing to strike out against.

"Oh, Dath," Hasen repeated. "Why?"

THE SKES San Oll slipped back from the beach with the same secret, liquid grace he used in his approach. His feet moved without sound over the broken ground beyond the dunes. A man watching for him would have needed keen sight indeed to catch his motion. He was like a shadow, invisible in the night.

San Oll cleaned his blade as he retreated, smiling to himself. The sword slipped back into its lacquered wooden sheath with a bare whisper . When he was far enough away from the crabbers' camp, he paused, head lifted in the air as he sent his mind out seeking...

"Kill any with the green silence in them," Galag had roared when they'd discovered the trick in Wenys Hollow. "The length and breadth of this land—let none escape. If they have the barest hint of magic in their souls, slay them."

The dyorn's eyes had blazed with anger—and perhaps a little fear as well, San Oll had thought.

He shrugged now. It wasn't his concern. The failure of their task was between Galag and the Captain. He had other work to do. For there, not far from where he stood, he sensed another mind, and in it, another green silence.

Still smiling, he set off in its direction. It was a good night for thirsty blades. Such work had been few and far between of late. But Lothan had promised—had promised them all. There were blood times coming and it would be a long time before his blade would be thirsty again.

BENJAMEN LIFTED his head from his makeshift pillow and peered into the darkness. There was a smell in the air...

Wolves, he would have thought, if it was winter.

His fire had burned to coals that smoldered like red eyes a half-dozen paces from where he lay, head propped up against his peddler's pack. Sitting up, he looked around. The hills were dark, the coast road a ribbon of pale tan in the moonlight. It was a quiet night. Only the wind and the sound of waves coming from the shore disturbed the stillness.

Quiet. Too quiet.

His knife was in his hand and he was rolling free of his blankets when the attack came. Grey direwolves—two, no, three. And something else. A manshape.

The first of the direwolves lunged, its teeth tearing away the padded shoulder of his jacket. He struck it between the eyes with his blade, pulled the knife free, wet and glistening, then sidestepped the next beast's rush. He saw a glimmer of light near the manshape—ochre flickers of light between the fingers of upraised hands.

Benjamen grunted as the third direwolf struck him. The peddler brought his knife down in a glancing blow across the beast's muzzle, and slashed up for the jugular. The second wolf leapt onto his back, knocking him to the ground. They rolled towards the fire. Benjamen locked his legs around the creature's torso and forced its head into the coals. It broke his grip, yelping with pain.

The peddler came to his feet with a dancer's grace and his knife left his hand. The manshape staggered as the blade found its mark, the strange lights about its fingers snuffed out as it pitched backward. Benjamen turned to meet the remaining wolf's attack with his bare hands. He caught it by the throat and bent all his powerful muscles to tighten his grip. The direwolf's claws tore at the padding of his jacket, cutting through the cloth to leave long furrows on the peddler's chest. But Benjamen hung on with grim determination until the beast hung limp in his hands.

He dropped the wolf and stood shaking and weak, drawing long, ragged breathes until his heart stopped hammering in his chest. Finally he blew his coals awake and added fuel. Taking a long burning brand from the fire, he held it over the manshape, staring at the strange creature he had slain.

Had the world gone mad? he wondered . Wolves in summer and...this?

His strange foe had features that were more reptilian than manlike, a squat powerful body that now lay with its limbs twisted in odd angles.

No highwayman, this. Not even human.

As he stared at it, a name came up from his memory, from the old tales he'd heard at his grandsire's knee.

Dyorn. Stormkin. A creature of the Icelord.

Benjamen shook his head. He bent and retrieved his knife, cleaned it on the grass, then backed towards his pack. His chest stung from the direwolf's claws, but the cuts weren't deep. They'd barely broken the skin. Time enough to see about them later.

He shouldered his pack, every sense alert to judge whether more of these things were abroad. The prickle along his spine that had warned him of danger a few moments ago was stronger than ever. He knew better than to ignore it. Pausing for a last look at his campsite, he turned and fled into the night, leaving his campfire blazing and his slain foes where they had fallen.

SKELD HROLFFSSON stared from the bow of the serpent-prowed longship towards the shore. The Green Isles. Here he was, a viking at last, in his seventeenth year and come to this shore. Dathen Isle. He regarded the land with a curious gaze for, although his father was been a rover of Saramand, his mother had come from this very shore. His father had stolen her from a small holding just before the place was put to the torch.

Skeld wondered if he'd have as much luck. He was a handsome youth for all that his hair was a shade darker than his comrades' and his frame leaner. But he wore a man's sword belted at his side and had the three scars of a warrior on his back, and while he'd no lack of interested girls in the homeland, he'd always found them somewhat coarse for his taste. He remembered his mother's dark looks and slender grace, the strange light in her eyes when she spoke of Dathen Isle.

Here his destiny was to be found. A mate, perhaps. Glory, surely. Hadn't his dreams told him so, time and time again?

He shook his head at the turn of his thoughts and concentrated on the task at hand. He took his watch seriously, as well he might. They were in enemy waters and for all that the Islanders fell like chaff before the raiders' blades, they were capable of doing considerable damage given half a chance. They were driven to desperation from the losses already suffered in Fairnland and Gwendellan. If they ever united…

Skeld smiled. Then there would be warriors' work, indeed.

But for all his watchfulness, he never saw the black figure that rose from the water to climb silently up the anchor rope. The first awareness Skeld had of his enemy was the whisper of steel leaving a lacquered wooden sheath—just before the blade bit deeply into his throat. He was dead before his body hit the water.

The skes San Oll cocked his head as he listened to the other Saramand sleeping. When he was certain no one had heard him he left the ship as silently as he had boarded it. There was still more work to do tonight and it grew late.

THE DYORN Galag dropped from the sky in a winged shape, honing in on the small, two-storied building in Yellfennie that had drawn him. He landed silently on a windowsill. The shutter opened with the probe of a claw and he slipped inside, taking his own shape. He formed his blade in his right fist, but the room was empty. There was nothing here that could have drawn him—no mage, no red-haired Summerborn.

His gaze fell on a wooden crib in the room's far corner. He unshaped his blade and strode across to the crib. There his heavy hand lifted and fell once before he returned to the window. It hadn't been the ones he sought, but the green silence had been there all the same—that damned Summerborn silence.

At the window, he looked down the street, grinning without real mirth. There were more here, in this thorpe, more minds with that silence, however faint and untapped. With luck he'd find the ones he sought. But if he didn't, the other stormkin would. They must.

Galag tried not to think of the Captain as he took winged shape again and lifted from the window to seep silently down the street.

CARRIE FOUGHT for courage. When she'd understood that the stormkin were on her trail, hunting her, fear had left her numb. She wasn't sure how long she'd been caught in the grip of her terror. But now...

She lifted her head, heart still drumming, and drew on the power of her taw to give her strength. It was an unfamiliar action. She fumbled—her fear almost driving the calmness away—but she followed the tune into her own inner strength, gathered her taw. Finally, it rose inside her—not majestic and powerful as it had been in Wenys Hollow, but small. Small and flickering. She tried not to be disappointed. At least it was there, and it gave her some measure of calm.

She sat stiff and upright in the quiet darkness, listening and watching. Around her a different silence held sway—ominous, filled with danger and death. One by one she drew the tinker blades from their sheaths and laid them on her lap. She clutched the hilts so hard that her knuckles were white. And then she heard—no, sensed—them coming. Shadow shapes on the edge of her awareness, moving relentlessly towards her.

Her calm fled as she stood. The knives dropped from nerveless fingers and she stared into the darkness, knowing the death she'd escaped in Meirion had now found her. Paralyzed with fear, she simply stood and called to Tarn with her mind, over and over.

Come.

Help me, Tarn.

Please.

Help me.

But the only reply was the approach of black-clad skes with the promise of death in their smiling cold eyes, and the means of death in the lacquered wooden sheaths upon their backs.

Eighth

ARN SAILED THE NIGHT skies above the coast road, the wind thrumming through his head feathers, his wings pale shimmers in the moonlight. His gaze pierced the darkness below. Worry, first a small, nagging thing, swelled in him now. Could they have already come this far? Perhaps, with the horses at a half-trot for most of the day. But it didn't feel right. The land below appeared empty to his deepsight—empty, but waiting. The night itself seemed tense and expectant.

When the sound came—from the south, from Wenys Hollow, from the throats of the stormkin—Tarn's worry sharpened into a keen blade of fear. Discovered! He heard the stormkin's rage in that cry and knew they'd be hunting now.

But where were the tinkers and their wagon?

He dropped from the sky and took his own shape on the road, staggering in the darkness, weary and weak, with the dull throb of that too-familiar pain starting up behind his temples. He took a deep breath to still the pounding of his heart. The pain he ignored. Slowly he quieted his jangle of nerves and bent his inner ear to listen to the world around him.

The night that had seemed so still and expectant hummed now like taut harp strings, plucked and vibrating. Under the earth, the slow rumbling voices of the stone that was the backbone of the hills echoed the sounds of the night. Hill and wind and heather and then...

He could sense the stormkin on the move, dark-shaped and hunting. Winged dyorn. Grey loping direwolves. Stone traals, shadow skes and the frosts. Beyond them he could sense the tinkers in Wenys Hollow and his heart sank. They were all supposed to be gone, on the road. What were they still doing there? And Carrie...

He searched for a trace of her thoughts amongst those of the tinkers, but there was nothing.

She was gone. She must have gone on alone.

Tarn lifted his head, sniffing the wind like a wolf himself. Drawing on his weakened taw, he rose again into the air to sweep in ever-widening circles. How far had she gone? Did she know that the stormkin were abroad and hunting her? If they reached her before he did...

She was untrained and new to her power. She had as much chance against them as a field mouse trapped in the talons of an owl.

Tarn tried to put aside his fear for her so he could concentrate on the task at hand, but her troubled features arose again and again in his mind's eye. He imagined the stormkin falling upon with flashing claws and silver-bright swords, and knew he *had* to find her first.

For more than an hour he flew back towards Wenys Hollow, following the winding turns of the road below. She would be on it, or near it, and with the Fairlord's luck, he would find her first. But the route he followed was deserted. She wasn't there—nor was anyone else. Had he missed her? If she'd cut across the hills she could be anywhere and he'd never reach her in time.

He widened his deepsight, cast his thoughts further and further afield, searching for some—any—trace of her. When he sense the crabber die on the beach, the green silence snuffed out like a blown candle, hope shriveled in him. The stormkin were abroad and slaying. He shivered as he caught their thoughts: Any with even a trace of the Summerlord's blood in them must die. A bleak helplessness settled in him, but he continued his search.

He coasted above a strip of white beach and saw the old man that he'd felt die a few moments ago. The dead body lay in the light of a bright campfire. Three men stood about it and their confusion reached up to Tarn. The memory of their friend's death blazed in their minds. He could see the skes's blade in their thoughts—the suddenness, the senselessness of the attack—then he was past them. He saw moving shapes below him now. The hills were alive with prowling direwolves and the ice-white glitter of frosts. The skes he sensed, but could not see.

He reached out with his thoughts once more, sifting the information that his weary taw drew from the night. The men on the beach, the hunting stormkin. The hills resounded with the heavy tread of a stone traal. And then he caught what he'd missed earlier. It was north along the road and he'd passed it by once already. A small pocket of green silence. A secret glimmer of a familiar taw.

Tarn whirled in the air, his sleek shape riding the wind north, wings beating as he put on speed. It was her. Alone. As he drew near, the cloak of her green silence gave her away as might the brightest fire on a hilltop. He sped towards her and thought his heart would burst from the effort. Then her cry for help came to him, and he knew they'd found her. Skes. A pair of them. Shadow assassins. Almost upon her while he—

An extra burst of speed, and then he dropped from the sky, silent and deadly as the skes themselves, with death riding on the tips of his talons.

The skes heard him, for all his silence. He caught a glimpse of Carrie, ash-white and trembling, then he was twisting under a skes's silver blade, taking a new shape. A storm of feathers erupted from the skes's attack, then Tarn's own blade was in his hand, his cloak hanging in tatters around him. He pivoted, leg rising behind him, heel striking the second skes on the side of the head as his sword met the shining silver of the first one's blade.

The clang of metal upon metal was loud in the still night air. In the distance, Tarn heard direwolves howling, felt the chill of approaching frosts. He twisted his blade, turned the assassin's blow, feinted. They drew back for a moment, then leapt at each other once more , their blades a blinding whirl and clamour in the darkness.

The skes reached into his belt and whipped a small throwing star into Tarn's face. The swanmage twisted his head, felt a sting at his neck as a sharp edge broke his skin. He leapt aside and in, his blade licking ahead of him like the darting of a snake's tongue. The movement saved his life. The skes he fought met his blade while, from behind, the second assassin's sword cut only through the tatters of Tarn's cloak.

Tarn tucked his head close to his chest and rolled between his opponents. He came up on his own left, feinted a blow at the skes there, and followed it through with a slash to the right that bit into flesh. He ignored the desire to see what damage he'd done. Continuing the same movement, he rolled with his cut and came up with his sword holding the two skes at bay. They circled outward, taking up positions on either side of him. One favoured his right leg.

Tarn backed up to keep them both in view. When they were a dozen paces apart, they both reached into their belts. Small five-pointed stars glimmered bright in their hands. Tarn drew a quick breath, steadying himself. As the throwing stars left their hands, he held his sword with both hands on its hilt. He snapped his wrists—right, left. The throwing stars went skittering into the undergrowth as he struck them from the air and charged the pair.

He met the one on the right with a feint of steel against steel, rolled his sword around the other's blade. Holding the skes's sword for a long moment, he waited until the second assassin was almost upon them, then sidestepped and half-turned. His blade flashed in an arc, cut through his first opponent's shoulder, kissed the second's blade with a sliding slash, and then cut through that one's defenses to pierce him through the heart.

His blade went in halfway to its hilt and he struck the skes's sword aside with a blow from his free hand. In and out the sword went, then he reversed his grip, stabbed into the enemy behind him, and stepped free. He whirled to face his two stricken foes and watched them die. Then his own knees buckled under him and he was flooded with waves of pain. His sword fell from limp fingers and he bent his face to the ground.

His fatigue was the aftereffect of drawing too much from his taw in too short a time. He willed the torment away and cradled his head as new agonies rocked through his body. A great blackness welled up before his eyes, and the need to simply fall into it was almost more than he could bear. But to give in now was to deliver both Carrie and himself to the approaching stormkin.

He could feel them coming. Brittle cold frosted the air. The heavy tramp of a traal was loud and near. Direwolf's howl and—

Tarn fumbled for his sword, willing it to his hand. His fingers caught in a tangle of thorns and the sharp prick of their bite helped clear his mind. He retrieved his weapon, closing his fingers about the hilt. Slowly, he lifted his head. Tears streaked down his cheeks at the effort. The pain between his temples was blinding. Slower still, he turned to face Carrie. He could hardly see her through the blurring of his vision.

"C-Carrie...?"

He focused on her, biting back a new wash of pain. She stood like a statue carved from stone. Her eyes were wide with shock. But there was no time for this—neither his pain nor what held her. The other stormkin were drawing steadily closer.

"Carrie!"

The sound of his own voice exploded in his ears. All his senses were overextended, overloading his mind with too much information. He shook his head, then thought better of it...but it was too late. Red agony lanced through his skull at the movement. If he hadn't borrowed so much power from Wenys Hollow, he'd already be unconscious—as he'd been the other night after wearing the dragonshape. But those extra reserves were spent now, as were most of his own.

But they couldn't stay here like this. Not when the hills were alive with enemies. He reached out with his mind, bracing himself as he reinforced the mental call with his voice.

"Carrie!"

She blinked and appeared to notice him for the first time.

The moment froze for Tarn. Despite the imminent danger, the approaching stormkin no longer seemed like a threat. His own pain faded as he stared at her. Her lips were trembling. Across the pallor of her face a flush of blood rushed to her cheeks. Her mind met his; her green silence mingled with his.

In that sudden joining of taws, Tarn glimpsed such depth inside her that he was stunned. An impossible beauty drew the pattern of his identity into the pattern of hers. He heard a sound like the drumming of hooves on long green hills. He heard a strange music born of harp and wind and water, of deep stone and fire. Then her strength flooded him and his pain was gone. There was only the peace with which she filled him, the deep silence she lent him to replenish what he had used up.

Their gazes locked and he saw in hers a reflection of his own eyes—a mingling of colours like autumn woods ablaze with the leaf-fall, veined with mauves and blues and colours for which he had no name.

And the moment was gone.

Her legs crumpled and she fell to her knees, her hair a wash of dark red across her face. The moon chose that moment to disappear behind a cloud. Tarn's pain dissolved into the nameless peace she'd woken in him, but he had no time to riddle its depth. Again he sensed the approaching stormkin, the urgency of the moment. He swept his sword into its hidden sheath and stood, his head clear, his thoughts shining.

He ran to Carrie. Glinting by her feet were two long knives that he replaced in their sheaths at her belt. He drew her up to her feet, while his neck hairs prickled with the impending crisis. His breath and Carrie's were visible now and it was cold enough to rattle their bones.

Frosts were coming. Frost and direwolves and elder stormkin. More skes, a dyorn, the stone traal with his eyes like dark thunder.

"Can you hold on?" he asked.

"I—can I what?"

"Can you hold tightly to me?"

She blinked, staring at him with a strange expression. "I was inside you…wasn't I? We were inside each other. I heard such music…"

"We were. But Carrie…"

"And there was pain. A great deal of pain. Was it yours or mine?"

"Mine," Tarn said. "I don't know how you did it, but you lent me the strength to fight it."

"I did?"

"Carrie, we've no time to talk."

He heard the crackle of branches breaking under heavy feet, of undergrowth catching and snagging on furred hides.

Catching up her journeysack, he slung it around her neck and shoulder. Then he crouched at her feet and helped her straddle his back.

"Hold tightly," he said and drew on his replenished taw.

He found the name he needed and spoke it into his silence. Under Carrie, a white sleek form took shape. Hooves pawed the ground, a white mane shook itself into her hands. And obeying a voice that seemed to speak inside her head, she wound her fingers into it. Then the white horn dipped once to catch a grey direwolf's attack. The unicorn tossed the creature aside and leapt over the heads of three more. On his back, Carrie tightened her grip on his mane, and clamped her knees against his sides. Another wolf leapt for them, and missed as it retreated from the unicorn's horn.

And then they were away.

The stormkin followed but they were no match for the speed of Tarn's shape. The white hooves bit into the earth of the hills, scattering it behind. The direwolves howled as they gave chase; the frosts wailed their frustration with higher-pitched cries. Circling, Tarn made his way back to the coast road. He followed its winding turns, gained still more speed on its hardened surface where his hooves could find better purchase than in the dark soil.

He kept his mind open for danger, sweeping his thoughts back and forth along their way. Once he sensed a dyorn and some direwolves, but they were hours dead, lying by the coals of a campfire. Again he sense a skes, but it was too far off to do them harm. Then ahead of them, a mile or so away, he sensed the closing of a net. Frosts and direwolves, skes and dyorn were gathered to form a long line that stretched from the sea to deep in the hills.

Tarn wondered at their numbers. He'd thought their foes were only a score or so, and that they'd left most of them behind.

He stopped their flight, pawed at the dirt road as he tried to clear his head. The enemy was ahead and behind them. They were in the hills and cut them off from the sea.

"Tarn?" Carrie's voice was more her own—fearful, but not the voice of the shocked young woman he'd first met. "Why have we stopped?"

He spoke his own name into his taw and returned the familiar shape she knew, crouching on the road with her standing over him. He stood with a quick motion.

"They've got us well and truly trapped," he said.

Her eyes widened and she stared up the road.

"They're not in sight yet, but they're close—if not as close as those coming up behind."

"What can we do?"

"Can you raise your taw again?" he asked.

"I think so." She looked at him. "Tarn, what happened back there? I remember those shadow things coming at me and then the next thing I remember is you being there on your hands and knees, and beside you were—*what* were they?"

"Skes. Carrie, time's pressing. Raise your taw."

"Why?"

"We're going to shapechange. It's our only chance."

"But I *can't*."

"Raise your taw, I'll speak the name you'll need into it."

He could sense the stormkin behind them drawing close. Tension crackled in the air. Gathering his taw, he reached out to help Carrie. Her mouth shaped an "O" at the suddenness with which her taw rose up in her. Then Tarn spoke the name into her, spoke another for himself, and they wore new forms.

Tarn gathered black cloak of a skes about his lean form, straightened the lacquered wooden sheath on his back. He glanced down at the direwolf beside him—the wolf with Carrie's eyes. He drew his black hood down over his brow, throwing his own eyes in shadow.

"Don't let them look into your eyes," he said.

His voice held a hiss now and was lower-pitched.

He slipped into the shadows alongside the road, soft-footed and silent, then all but disappeared. On the road, the wolf whined before it followed the barely visible shape into the undergrowth.

Ninth

THE ARDWEIR **RODE NORTH**, its bear's prow ploughing the foam back waves of the Channel Sea with the sleek grace of a dolphin. At midnight, Captain Ander gave up his watch. First mate Irwin, as wide-shouldered and burly as the captain or any of *The Ardweir*'s crew, manned the helm with an easy familiarity, one meaty hand resting on the oakwood wheel, the other hooked in his belt by the thumb. The moon was high above the ship's mainmast. Irwin sailed by the Tather—the North Star, the Fisher's Star. He hummed Harper Briarsen's most recent tune softly to himself and wished Wren would play another.

But in his cabin, Wren did little more than pluck idle chords from his harp, stopping from time to time to adjust a string that was discordant to no one's ear but his. In a corner Deren slept, wrapped in his cloak and an old blanket. Across from Wren, his clear eyes hooded with thought, sat Puretongue. A small brazier glowed warmly between them and the dhruide stared into the flicker of its flames. He thought of the long coasts of Dathen Isle that could only be seen from the decks by day. He thought of Tarn and the stormkin and new worry lines gathered on a brow that was already lined with a webwork of creases.

Wren, his instrument in tune once more, began another air, then paused. The tune hung unfinished between them. When Wren broke the silence again, it was to ask a question.

"Are you always so thoughtful, Master Puretongue?"

The dhruide drew himself from his thoughts. There was a curious distance in his eyes when he regarded Wren. Then he sighed, the moment was gone, and a weary smile tugged at the corners of his mouth.

"Not always. I've too much on my mind these days, Harper Wren. And I grow too old for adventuring."

His eyes clouded again. Adventuring. Fairlord! He saw again the dead in Gullysbrow—those dead and so many others—and in some of the faces of the slain he recognized the Summerlord's blood. It hadn't been an adventure for any of *them*.

"I'm tired," he said. "A war lasting only one day is too long, and this war we have now—we have had a thousand years of it. If the Isles survive, will it only be to see another thousand? The weavers weave, and no one knows what is woven in their threads, but I tire of it."

"But there has been peace for many years," Wren said.

"Peace." Puretongue repeated the word and made it sound alien. "Has there ever been peace?"

Wren regarded his companion and knew again that feeling that men—whether they were harpers or not—were not the same as dhruides. The tree-wizards bore the shapes of men, but they lived more in a shadow realm beyond the here and now, that twilight place of which harpers merely sang, while the dhruides knew it firsthand. And Puretongue himself...there were tales told about him. That he was as old as the Isles themselves. That he had founded the order of dhruides in the dawn mists before even the First Men had come to the Isles.

Wren often wondered whether "Puretongue" was a title—*the* Puretongue, as one might say *the* King—or whether the founder of the dhruides had been an ancestor of the fellow who sat with him now. For in all the old tales and ballads handed down over the years, there *always* seemed to have been a Puretongue.

"I have known peace," Wren said. He let his fingers run along his harp's strings to draw forth a waterfall of notes. "But I have never seen *beyond*, into the Otherworld. Except, perhaps, in dreams. It must be a terrible burden to bear."

"A burden," Puretongue agreed, "but not always such a heavy one, for there is great beauty beyond in the other realms. I remember…" But then he shrugged. "I have known peace as well, Wren. Perhaps that's why the lack of it is so bitter to me."

They were quiet then, keeping their own council, feeling the roll of *The Ardweir* as it cut through the waves. Puretongue raised his taw and let its deep green silence wash through him. The days to come promised to bind him. They wound sorrow and death into an inescapable thread that he must follow. The weavers weave, he thought. But what hope did the Isles have when the Summerborn were so few and the Icelord's army so many?

Wren began another tune and Puretongue sighed, letting the music soak into him. When the tune was done, he met Wren's gaze and drew up a question prompted by their earlier conversation.

"What have you seen in your dreams?" he asked.

Wren said nothing for a long moment.

"You and Penhallow," he said at last, "you are much the same. You always cut to the heart of a matter."

He was silent again, then set his harp down upon the carpet and drew a strip of leather from his pocket. He handed it to the dhruide.

"Have you seen this symbol before?" he asked.

Puretongue studied the leather strip. Burnt into it was a curious design that appeared to shift and change the closer he examined it. At length he focused his taw and the shifting lines settled into shapes he could read. They were runes—three entwined runes.

"Moon," he said, tracing the first. "A waning quarter, but with a hint of…what? Flight? The second is the symbol for a half. And the third…" He pulled at his beard . "The third is a bastardization of two runes—the ones for shadow, and way or path." He shook his head and looked up. "Where did you find this?"

"I made it," Wren replied. "At Penhallow's urging. So that I might remember. But the symbols—they came to me from the Otherworld. From a dream."

"Can you—will you tell me of it?"

Wren picked up his harp and played a few notes.

"I've dreamt this three times now," he said. He began to play his instrument, the music making a backdrop to his voice. "First there comes a sound like rain drumming on a window ledge, or a horse's hooves on a green sward. It comes from a distance—a cluttered sound that becomes rhythmical as it nears me. Or grows louder. I'm not sure which. And then I see…"

Puretongue's taw merged with the harping. He closed his eyes. The music and Wren's voice faded, dissolving into a vision of the harper's dream. Puretongue heard the drumming now from Wren's perspective and saw distant hills as though from a great height. He felt himself being drawn closer to one hill, a high craggy tor that rose steep and tall from the green hills. A path wound around it, spiralling up to where longstones were gathered in a rough circle.

The hoof beats sound like drums now and harp music followed their rhythm. He could hear voices in the music, deep, resonating voices as though the hills themselves were speaking.

The dream drew him on.

In the middle of the stone circle was a smaller longstone lying on its side in the grass—blue and grey, riddled with silver and red veins. He saw the symbols from Wren's strip of leather on it, not so much etched into the stone as emanating from it in a shimmer of amber and gold and green, and seeing that symbol, in that place, Puretongue remembered—

He opened his eyes with a snap and the vision was gone. Wren's harp was silent and the harper was watching him. The dhruide shook his head slowly.

"I know that place," he said, "though that symbol—that stone—was never there."

"Where is it?" Wren asked, his voice eager.

"In Ardmeyn. The vision you showed me was of Taynbell Peak in Ardmeyn."

"So Penhallow thought."

Wren seemed about to say more, but then remained silent.

"Taynbell," Puretongue replied.

"And the symbol?" Wren asked. "Can you riddle its meaning?"

The dhruide shook his head. "Is there more to this dream? Can you show me more?"

"That is all. But...there have been others who dreamed this alsoas well. I had it the first night I reached Pelamas Henge. And twice since. Do you think it's a sending?"

Puretongue nodded. He looked away from the harper, his mind a-brew with possibilities. Then his gaze fell on Deren. Deren's one eye watched the dhruide closely.

"You were awake?" Puretongue asked. "You saw?"

"The harping woke me," Deren said, "Then I felt your silence and raised my own. And Gwyr—I mean, Puretongue. I saw the peak, too. It seemed so familiar, but how can that be?" He paused when he saw Puretongue frown. "Did I do something wrong?"

"What? Oh, no. I was thinking, Deren. Just thinking."

He said no more. After a moment, Deren turned over again, rolling himself more tightly in his blankets. Wren regarded the two of them, then rose and put away his harp. When he turned back from his harpcase, Puretongue stood up and crossed the room to the door.

"I need some air," the dhruide said and left.

Wren frowned, then shrugged his shoulders. Penhallow had told him to tell the dream if he was asked. He hadn't expected the dhruide—nor his young companion—to be able to share what he had seen in such a direct fashion. Had it been something in his harping, or some spell of the dhruide's? And what had Puretongue made of it?

At last, Wren turned to his own bed. As he lay there he remembered an old saying of his Harpmaster: *The minds of wizards thrive on riddles.* Wren smiled. He'd leave the dhruide to make sense out of it.

On deck, Puretongue paced the length and breadth of *The Ardweir*, stopping at last by the bear's head prow to stare northward. In his mind's eye he saw a heart-shaped face, framed with dark curls, and on its brow, the shape of a crescent moon.

"Flight," he said softly into the night. "That first rune was flight. White like a swan's wing."

Then beside Tarn's face, he put Deren's. He was the runic symbol for "the half." His missing eye had brought the thought home to the dhruide, but it was not the lack of it that made up the half. It was the half-woken power. And the third part of Harper Wren's symbol? It could only be the Summerborn that Hafarl—through Puretongue—had sent Tarn to find in Codswill. But…shadow path…or shadow way…

The meaning of it all was so close he could almost taste it. Then it was gone and he was left holding only the pieces once more. Taynbell Peak. He must take the three of them there. But the Everwinter already lay across Ardmeyn and…

Puretongue shook his head. Time was hurrying by. He had to speak with Penhallow and it need to be soon. Until then—perhaps not until they stood on Taynbell Peak—he could only guess.

He turned away and made his way back to Wren's cabin to find his own blankets. There he lay awake a long while waiting for sleep. He listened to the easy breathing of his companions, to the sound of the waves against the ship and the wind in the rigging. And he wondered about Wren's dream.

Tenth

ORNING CAME TO THE Kingdoms of the Green Isles and along the coasts, from Cermyn to Ardmeyn, the weavers wove.

IN WENYS Hollow, Long Tom Turpen roused himself from a fitful sleep and got up to blow the fire aflame, adding wood as the kindling caught. There were dark rings under his eyes and worry haunted him like the nagging memory of a bad dream. His family still slept, as did their copies on the other side of the wagon. Crouching by the fire, Long Tom's gaze went to the ridges on either side of the hollow. The stormkin had abandoned their posts during the night, no doubt to concentrate their search for Carrie and the wizard.

One more day, Long Tom told himself. And then they would follow. And after that? Would there be anyone left to find when they finally took to the road?

He made a noise in the back of his throat and stalked off to give the horses some exercise.

FURTHER NORTH, in the crabbers' camp, the three survivors of last night's sudden moment of horror wrapped their slain companion in a blanket and pushed their boats from shore. In the pails trailing behind the boats' frothy wake, yesterday's catch was forgotten. Hasen and young Bell were numb with shock and even Jembar Slan had nothing to say this morning. He raised his sail, trying not to look at the stiff bundle amidships, and steered out of the small harbour. The wind caught his sail and the tiny craft leapt forward. Hasen and Bell kept pace in their own boat as they sped homeward to Yellfennie.

WELL OFF the coast road, the peddler Benjamen crawled out from his hiding place under a stand of prickly thorn trees. He'd spent a sleepless night, listening to the stormkin prowling in the hills, thankful that they'd been hunting other prey. But he'd known a stab of pity for whoever they sought.

Now he stood quietly in the morning light. He pulled thorns from his coat and stared off into the distance, undecided. The road was empty as far as he could see in either direction, which wasn't odd in itself. The threat of the Saramand kept many a tramp and hawker from travelling this year. And now, with this new threat…these stormkin…

He led his thoughts back to the need to make a decision. Southward lay lands that had already fallen to the Saramand. Only Umbria and Kellmidden remained free—at least they were free of snake-lovers, though they seemed to be waging an even stranger war than most might imagine.

Benjamen frowned. Where did that leave him?

At length he set off northward. Last night his senses had warned him of the attack. This morning they told him to continue travelling the way he'd originally been bound.

He decided to keep his trust in them.

THE WAILING of death-dirges resounded in many of Yellfennie's homes that morning. During the night some fifteen towns-folk—ranging in age from a babe still in its cradle, to Old Cam Todger, the miller's grandfather—had been slain. The deaths had been particularly gruesome and no one could escape the sense of impending doom. It hung over the town like a funeral pall, close and stifling.

The townsfolk wandered the streets, bewildered by last night's events and confused about what the future might. One man had woken to find his wife butchered beside him—her body cold, the bed-clothes stiff with her blood—and he'd never stirred. What defense was there against an enemy who crept into your very home and slew your family while you slept?

Then a cry went up from the harbour and the townsfolk saw the grim red and yellow sails of a Saramand snake-ship coming to port, its decks bristling with the spears and axes of the yellow-haired raiders.

ABOARD THE Saramand craft *Traal-heim,* Hrolff Stemmensson glared shoreward, anger turning his ruddy cheeks a darker red. He gripped the haft of his great war axe with knuckle-white fingers and gave the order to land. Somewhere on these shores hid his son's slayer. A thrall's child Skeld might have been, but he'd had the blood of Hrolff Stemmensson in his veins as well. By the Skyfather, he'd teach these frail Islanders what it meant to slay his son.

FURTHER NORTH, the dyorn Galag gathered still more storm-kin and sent them out in ever-widening sweeps, searching for any Summerborn, but particularly seeking the two who'd escaped the stormkin's net last night.

It baffled him. He'd had them—of that he was sure. They'd been so close that he could have almost reached out and licked them. But then they'd vanished as though they'd never been, having left not a trace, not a spoor, not a scent for a direwolf to follow. But baffled though he was, impossible as the task had become, Galag knew that he still had to find them, and find them soon. If the Captain Fergun was to return at this moment...

Galag shook his head. He'd be wiser to keep his mind on the task at hand so that when Fergun *did* return, he'd have two heads on stakes to show the Captain. Not failure.

ABOARD *THE* *Ardweir*, Harper Wren breakfasted with his two guests and Captain Ander. The harper refrained from asking if Puretongue had any further thoughts on the dream he'd shared the previous night; while Puretongue, for his part, remained withdrawn. But if Wren and the tree-wizard had little to say, Deren more than made up for their lack of conversation. He plied the captain with a hundred questions about *The Ardweir*, her home berth, the voyages he'd captained and whatever else came to the young man's mind. Ander answered with good nature and the meal ended with him promising Deren a turn at the wheel.

Meeting Deren's glittering eye, Puretongue smiled.

The blessing of youth, he thought. To be able to set worry and grief aside with such ease—even if only temporarily. The dhruide was glad to see a smile on his young companion's face. He wished it could remain there.

FURTHER NORTH still, the old priest Penhallow stood amongst the great longstones of Pelamas Henge. He was the priest of a faith older than the hills of the Green Isles, a faith that stemmed from a time when there was no need for faith. A hoary old man, his hair and beard were as grey as the stones of the henge, and the silence in his taw was as deep as the dwystaw—the green silence of the Isles.

Penhallow was worried. He knew Puretongue was coming, but what of the others? He gazed south, his deepsight searching through a bewildering cloud of minds for those that came. At length, he sighed.

He turned his thoughts inward, conserving strength for the days to come. His skin coarsened as he stood there, taking on the texture of stone. His blood flowed earthy slow now, and still. When the wind came down from the hills to touch him, his long hair did not move against his breast.

AND IN Ardmeyn, the ice hand of Everwinter swept the land. It was the cold that was born in Damadar, the Mocker's realm, the snow and ice winds of the far north where the summer never came, brought to Ardmeyn by the Captain Fergun who followed his master's bidding with a cold, certain will.

Unlike the bloodthirsty skes and other stormkin, he felt little emotion. When he seemed angry—as he had been with the dyorn Galag—his anger was merely a tool. Frightened, the dyorn was capable of achieving more. It was that simple. What Fergun knew mostly was boredom. He had only one goal in life—besides the raising of his lord Lothan as the master of all creatures—and that was to find the slayers of his brothers: Dwar who had died in the dragon wars, and Stest whose body had never been found, but who must be dead. If he still lived, Fergun would have sensed the dark clot that was Stest's taw wherever it might be.

But for the moment his own goals had to wait while he raised the Everwinter in Ardmeyn, burying the Summerlord's last hope under sheets of ice and snow. Frosts and storm-giants bent the weather to Fergun's will, bringing the raging winds of Damadar to gentle Ardmeyn, covering her green hills in a shroud of white.

In caves and hollowed buarrows beneath the mantle of the storms, strange beings huddled for warmth against the unnatural weather. Dark-skinned beings dressed in furs and leather wrappings clutched flint knives to their breasts, gathering up pelts for warmth and building peat fires in their small hearths. And slender beings with fine-boned faces and hair like autumn woods, deep-eyed and pale-skinned, raised their own magical warmths in their halls of hill and stone. But strive though they might, these folk were the last survivors of waning races and they were no match for the strength of Lothan's Field Captain Fergun.

And so, while the hidden folk of Ardmeyn shivered in their holdings, Fergun stalked above ground, grinding their world under a weight of cold. He searched for some trace of the Summerlord, and wondered why no messengers had come from Galag with word that the Summerborn in Wenys Hollow were slain.

Tenth

"SEE IF ANY REMAIN alive in the main building," Tarn said, "and kill any you find."

Carrie cried out in protest, but all that came out of her shapechanged throat was a plaintive whimper. The skes who was Tarn turned to regard her with a strange look. Carrie felt the hackles of her neck-fur rise up as she met that cold gaze. Though she knew it was Tarn, and that they wore these shapes for safety's sake...on Tarn the disguise seemed too real. It was as though he'd *become* a skes, in mind as well as body. She knew strange desires herself—wolfish desires—but so far she'd kept them from gaining an upper hand. The fact that the two of them seemed so real was the measure of their success. She knew that. But the knowledge did little to ease her steadily growing fear.

The past day and night were still too fresh in her memory—and the danger wasn't over yet. She shuddered to recall their meeting with the stormkin last night. There were so many of the creatures with their bloodied talons and pitiless eyes. And then there was Tarn, fitting in with them as he did now, though that feeling could have been due to their fellow travellers.

They were in the company of another direwolf and three frosts, and the air was chilled because of the elementals. Carrie could see her own breath, but the thick direwolf pelt kept her warm.

Just now they were reaching the outbuildings of a farm holding north of Yellfennie. The farm was on the lower slope of a long hill. Its fields, neatly fenced and squared with fieldstone, made a patchwork view that rolled out to the coast road. Beyond that was the sea.

Tarn took his gaze from Carrie.

"Well?" he asked the frosts. "Why do you tarry?"

He used the guttural tongue of the stormkin, his voice low and sibilant. A stranger's voice.

Carrie bit back any further protest. When the other direwolf sniffed at her with suspicion, she turned to the creature, a low growl rumbling deep in her chest. She kept her gaze to the ground so that it would not see the unwolfish cast of her eyes. The wolf backed away from her and she turned to face Tarn once more, wishing for the hundredth time that he'd given her a shape with a throat that could shape words.

The frosts shambled off, hoarfrost crackling under their angular limbs and discolouring the ground. Tarn waited until the other direwolf had followed them, and then he met Carrie's gaze.

"There's no one there," he said, his voice quiet. "But even if there were..."

He shook his head, putting a hand to his temple.

"There's no one there," he repeated.

Carrie padded closer. She bumped his knee, wanting to be able to ask if she could help but knowing she couldn't, not trapped in this shape she wore. She thought Tarn acted confused, when he wasn't taking the part he played too much to heart. She understood somewhat. The direwolf shape she wore kept trying to twist her own thinking, at times leaving her grasping for coherence through a labyrinth of unnatural thoughts—unnatural for her, at any rate. A direwolf had a simple mind yet still it was hard not to lose herself in it. She couldn't imagine how dark and twisting a skes's mind must be.

Tarn pushed her muzzle from his leg.

"Never show concern," he said. "Not when they—" He motioned to the frosts. "—are near enough to see."

Then he stalked off, back stiff with anger.

Carrie stared after him, fear gripping her. Oh, Dath. Was she losing him to his stormkin shape? What were they doing here anyway? Once through the net last night, why hadn't they simply fled on their own?

For a moment she considered leaving Tarn and doing just that. She could find a hiding place and wait for the Turpens to come along with their wagon. But when she considered it, she knew it wouldn't work. Her only welcome from the tinkers would be a volley of arrows. They would see a direwolf, not her, and she needed Tarn to change her back because she didn't know the spell herself.

She hurried after him.

TARN HADN'T lied. There was no one alive on the farm, because they'd all been slain the night before. The bodies lay scattered across the courtyard. They had been killed by stormkin and they hadn't died easily. Carrie couldn't look at them—she'd already seen too much death. The other direwolf settled down beside the body of a young child and began to feed. Carrie's stomach lurched. She moved to Tarn's side, following him into the farmhouse.

They made a tour of the building—Tarn silent in his skes form while Carrie's claws clicked on the stone floors. Why were they here? she wondered. Then Tarn paused by a window to stare at the carnage outside. Ice glistened on stone walls and the barn, on the dirt of the courtyard. The frosts moved slowly away, heading towards a grouping of outbuildings higher up on the hill. The direwolf in the courtyard left its feeding and trotted off to join the frosts.

Leaning on the sill, Tarn took a deep breath to steady himself. When he was sure the stormkin were far enough away, he spoke a word and regained his own shape. He seemed smaller than ever at that moment, his thin features pinched and weary. Turning to Carrie, he took the direwolf shape from her, then slid down on the floor to lean against the wall.

Carrie stood there for long moment, savouring the pleasure of being in her own body. Then the cold hit her and she began to shiver. She joined Tarn on the floor by the wall and touched his arm. He looked up, his eyes his own once more—deep and warm, but exhausted .

"What are we doing here?" she asked, finally able to speak her worries aloud. "Why haven't we fled?"

"We can't. Galag—that's the leader's name—hasn't sent anyone north yet. If we were to leave , our departure would give us away."

"Then when can we go?"

"I don't know. Soon. I think he'll spread the net north by noon. We can go then."

He rubbed his eyes with his knuckles.

"Tarn, are you alright?"

He nodded. "It's the shape. Sometimes it fights with me and I can feel myself being drawn into keeping it. On one hand I'm myself, but at the same time I'm the skes San Ko, and his shape begins to feel too real."

"Then let's forget these shapes. I hate mine. The other wolf—did you see him? Eating the...the..."

Carrie's stomach lurched again as she remembered.

Tarn sighed. "We can't give them up, Carrie. The stormkin would be after us before we a got a mile. This way's our only chance."

"Then can you at least give me a shape like yours?"

"Can you use a skes blade?"

"No."

"Can you step so that you are almost invisible?"

"No, but—"

Tarn shook his head. "No one questions a direwolf. They are simply beasts. But as a skes—you wouldn't last a moment. You can't use the blade, you haven't the walk, the stance, the language."

"How come you can?"

Thinking of how well he fit in, Carrie's worries returned.

"Many of the dhruide studies are similar to those of the skes and dyorn. The approach is different, certainly. My studies were based on healing and maintaining the balance that holds the world together, while theirs is based on the pain and torment of other beings. Dhruide studies are much longer, but the end result—the ability to use the power of our taws—is the same. We're lucky I took up the use of the sword or we'd never have gotten as far as we have."

"That's right," Carrie said. "I've never heard of a dhruide with a sword until I met you."

"Most use a staff," Tarn conceded.

"Why did you choose a sword?"

"Well, I *do* have a staff as well," Tarn began, then he hesitated. A red flush crept up his neck. "Vanity," he added. "A sword seemed more dashing than a long piece of wood."

"Well, it *is* more dashing," she said, "and certainly—"

"Whisht."

Tarn leapt to his feet. His shape swirled into that of the skes San Ko. He spoke another word and Carrie became a direwolf once more. She growled in protest, but Tarn knelt by her.

"Quiet," he said. The skes voice accented his words again. "There's a dyorn coming. Pray that we shapechanged before he was close enough to sense my green magic."

He stood again and swept from the room, a silent dark shape with the wooden sheath of an assassin's sword on his back. As he stalked down the hall with Carrie padding at his heels he berated himself for the unforgivable lapse in judgment. He'd needed to break from the skes mind, yes, but to do it now had been the height of foolishness. If the approaching dyorn had sensed it …Fairlord, the stormkin would be on to them so quickly…

At the use of Hafarl's title, a strange uneasiness touched Tarn. The dark side of his mind fell back from the name. Then his lips twisted into a snarl and the skes mind swept over him once more. By the time he stepped out of the farmhouse his eyes were as cold as any stormkin born in Damadar.

"You!" the dyorn called out to him. It was a stranger—not the one named Galag who had sent them to this farm earlier today. "Why are you still here?"

Tarn said nothing as the dyorn approached him. His black hood was low over his brow. His cold eyes studied the dyorn without blinking.

"I sensed a…troubling," he said when they were finally face to face.

"As did I," the dyorn said. "Like a magic being worked—a Summerborn magic. Curious. You'd almost think—"

Tarn's hand was at his belt. As the dyorn spoke, he unclipped a throwing star and flicked it up with a quick motion of his wrist. It caught the creature in the throat just as it was shaping a blade in its own hand.

The dyorn toppled to the ground. Tarn rolled the dead creature onto its back with his foot, giving it a contemptuous look. He retrieved and cleaned his throwing star. He sensed Carrie move away from him as he studied his handiwork. Turning, he strode in the direction that the frosts had taken, not bothering to see if she followed or not.

The ground was frozen underfoot. Tarn's soft-soled boots crunched brittle grass. He worried what trouble the discovery of the slain dyorn might bring, then the thought slipped away. The dark power coursed through him and he found that he really didn't care. He wasn't a skes. No, he was something more deadly than skes or dyorn or any creature of the Icelord. Let *them* beware, not him.

Carrie growled at his side, breaking into the turn his thoughts had taken. Looking down, he read a question in her eyes. A dark rage took him for a moment—that anyone should dare to question *him*! Then he smiled with tight lips.

"It knew us for what we are," he said.

For what they were? No, for what she was, and he had been.

Carrie looked away from him, troubled by the coldness in his eyes. She was unhappy with the return of his dark temperament, but trapped in the shape of a direwolf again, there was nothing she could do about it. Tiny warning prickles went through her, , setting her heart to quicken its tempo. She remembered the fears Tarn had shared with her moments ago.

On the one hand I'm myself, but at the same time I'm the skes San Ko, and his shape begins to feel too real.

It felt that way to her, too, but what could she do?

THEIR PATROL dragged on throughout the morning. The other dire-wolf kept its distance from Carrie, watching her with a suspicious gaze. The frosts strode ahead, Tarn behind them. They came upon three more small holdings—two deserted, one with its owners dead. As they left the last place, a dyorn dropped from the sky and took its man-like shape on the road in front of them. Carrie's hackles rose but Tarn regarded the newcomer without expression.

"You are?" the dyorn asked.

"San Ko," Tarn replied.

"I am Whulrg, of Daduth's kin, with word from Galag. One of our kinsmen was slain in the area of your patrol. Have you come across any sign of the Green Ones?"

"None living."

Green Ones. Summerborn.

The dyorn nodded. "We fear they've escaped our net and gone north. Galag bids you send your frosts into the hills while you follow the road with the wolves. We meet tonight at the High Walk by the mouth of the Tooming. Do you know the place?"

"I know it."

Whulrg nodded. "Good. We will see you there tonight."

His shape became a brief dark glimmer, then black wings beat at the air and a black bird was skyborn once more, winging south. Tarn gave the frosts their orders. He watched them until the crest of the nearest hill hid their angular shapes, then he turned to the direwolves. One moment he stood motionless, the next his sword whispered from its sheath and the true direwolf lay gutted on the road. Tarn cleaned his blade on its fur and stood, his cold gaze lifted to meet Carrie's shocked eyes.

"Now we go north," he said.

Carrie shuddered at the tone of his voice. A small whine escaped her throat. Tarn fingered the sharpened edge of his curved blade, his eyes blazing under his hood. He nudged the direwolf with a toe.

"Would you be happier if we left that thing alive so that it could run to Galag and lead them back to us? They'll kill us if they have to, but they'd rather take us breathing. They mean to have a little sport with us before they turn us over to the Captain. Would you prefer that, Carrie?"

Numbly, she shook her head. Her throat was tight with fear. Had she been able to speak, her voice would have escaped her.

"Then we go north," Tarn said. "And we keep our disguises until we're far enough away to break free of the hunt. Do you agree?"

Carrie gave a slow nod. Under the thick mat of direwolf fur, her skin felt hot. With her gaze locked on Tarn's, her thoughts spun.

"Then come," Tarn said.

Turning, he strode off, his soft-soled boots soundless now on the frozen dirt of the coast road. Mournfully, Carrie followed. She kept her head low. Her tail drooped between her legs. With the skes mind so much in control of Tarn, she was almost as afraid of him as she was the pursuing stormkin.

Twelfth

BENJAMEN, THE PEDDLER TOLD himself, you're mad as a hare and there's no longer a smidgeon of doubt about it. What in Dath's name was he *doing* here?

Here was a thicket of young trembling aspens on a hill north of Yellfennie. Taking cheese and bread from his pack, he made himself comfortable. The quiet of his surroundings belied the nightmare journey of the morning just past and he kept a close watch as he rested and ate.

He'd tramped north all morning, following the coast road, but not walking on it. A couple of hours into his journey he'd come to a familiar rise; but when he reached the crest to look below— where Yellfennie should have been drowsing peacefully in the coastal sunshine— he saw instead a town fighting for its life. The sharp blade of war had come to Yellfennie in the shape of the yellow-haired Saramand.

Their snake-ship was in the harbour—a yellow and red splotch amidst the blue-brown of the inlet waters. Flames licked their way along Fisher's Mart into Yellfennie's main square. He could hear the distant clash of sword and axe, could make out the tiny battling figures moving from street to street. The Yellfennians, unused to war, were losing their struggle.

Benjamen had touched the knife at his belt. For one wild moment he'd been ready to go down below to lend what aid he could, even when he'd known that victory was impossible. He'd stood poised on the hilltop, trembling with anger. Stormkin abroad, snake-lovers raiding...was there never to be peace in the Green Isles again? But then he'd taken his hand from the hilt of his knife and lowered himself to the ground. Reason had prevailed. There'd been little that one man could have done to help. He would have been just one more victim of the Saramand's blades.

Crouching there, he'd searched for a new plan. He'd hoped for a refuge in Yellfennie, but now...what was the next town? Keddlenowe. In the mouth of the Tooming River under the shadow of the High Walk on its northern shore. And how far was it? Twenty-five, thirty miles? A long day's walk at the very least, and this day was half gone— and that was reckoning the journey as following the coast road, a route he couldn't take. Not with stormkin abroad and danger waiting at every step.

Under the aspens he reconsidered this mad flight north, but realized he had little choice except to see it through. He had goods that had a market here in the north. There was nothing left for him in the south. But with the Saramand striking this far north and stormkin stalking their prey...

Benjamen shook his head.

Lothan's minions were still out there. They'd tried to kill him once—the why and wherefore were irrelevant at the moment—and it was only luck and whatever fighting skills he possessed that had kept him alive so far. He'd seen stormkin from time to time this morning, but always in the distance. Let them keep their distance.

He scratched his chin. So far he'd been lucky. But there were many of them and it was only a matter of time before they spotted him. Another night was fast approaching.

That gave him pause. According to the old tales, stormkin were night creatures. If so, then what were they doing abroad now? Either the old tales were wrong, or something was driving them out into daylight.

But—and here was a good thought—perhaps that accounted for his success at avoiding them so far today. Perhaps their senses weren't so finely tuned in the daylight, allowing him to get this far unde-tected. When the night came he'd best be hidden away so well that not even his own shadow could find him.

He finished his meal and stood, slipping down the hill, keeping the undergrowth between Yellfennie and himself. He watched the way ahead and didn't breathe easier until the hill was behind him and Yellfennie was out of sight. He could still hear the faint sound of fighting, but it was muted now and the fear of imminent discover faded a little. Now if only he could avoid the stormkin as easily as the embattled town.

BY LATE afternoon he was well on his way. The stormkin were numer-ous, and although he had succeeded in keeping himself out of their clutches, their numbers appeared to be growing. A sinking feeling told him he might be nearing their main encampment. An old ped-dler with a knife didn't seem like much to pit against Dath knew how many creatures that might be waiting for him. But still he continued, trusting that his luck would hold.

The farms he'd passed so far—always from a distance—had all looked deserted. Once he'd dared to sneak in close, coming to stand in one farm's courtyard. The dead homesteaders he found there unsettled his stomach. As quickly as he could, he'd fled the place, but it was a long time before the stink of death left his nostrils. With every breath there was a faint aftertaste with a subsequent churning in his stomach.

A little while later he topped another hill, this one commanding a long view of the coast road running both south and northeast. He followed its twists and turns with his gaze, then almost directly below himself, he spotted stormkin. A figure in black, a pair of direwolves, and some angular man-shaped beings that seemed to be made of ice. He flattened himself against the rocks on his vantage point just as he caught the flicker of black wings in the sky. Lying still, hardly daring to breathe, he watched the winged shape drop from the air to greet the stormkin he'd first seen. It became a man—or at least it wore a man-like shape—and approached the others.

The stormkin conversed amongst themselves, then the newcomer took to the sky once more, winging rapidly south. The black-cloaked figure sent the white creatures into the hills behind Benjamen, then turned to face the wolves. A moment later Benjamen rubbed his eyes, unable to believe what he'd seen.

The figure in black had drawn a silvery blade from the sheath on its back and slain one of the wolves. The other backed away from him and he spoke angrily to it before stalking off. The remaining wolf watched the killer go, then slowly followed, obviously uneasy.

Benjamen frowned and scratched at his chin as he tried to imagine a reason for what he'd just seen. Fighting amongst their own ranks? That could only be good. But the whole incident made him nervous. The extra sense that was his built-in warning system told him that what he'd seen was not what it looked like. Unfortunately, it told him no more than that.

He watched the two stormkin proceed at an easy pace along the coast road. When a hill hid them from his sight, he checked his back-trail. The ice creatures were in the hills to the west, but angling north. Above, the sky was empty except for a scattering of puffy clouds that looked too innocent for a day such as this. Drawing a deep breath, he left his hiding place and scurried down the slope. He hurried past the dead direwolf and found cover across the road in the gorse that grew in a tangle all the way to the rocky drop-off down to the waves of the Channel Sea. Keeping to this scant cover, watching for the creatures that had fared on ahead, he continued his own way north.

NIGHTFALL FOUND the peddler very near Keddlenowe. He made himself a burrow in the woods that covered the lower hills near the Tooming. Deadwood dragged over a fallen tree and covered with branches made a rough hiding place. He then spent a good fifteen minutes erasing all signs of his presence, finishing with a sprinkle of banewolf powder along his trail to kill any scent that might have lingered. When he was done, he crawled into his makeshift camp and ate a cold dinner. Considering what the night may bring, he didn't dare light a fire.

He'd passed the figure in black and the direwolf a few hours before dusk. Since then he'd seen neither sight nor sound of any stormkin. It was his hope that either they weren't ranging this far north, or that he was well enough out of their way that they'd miss him even if they did pass by. Tomorrow he'd be in Keddlenowe—assuming it still stood. If it didn't, if either the raiders or the stormkin had taken it, he wasn't sure what he'd do next. Return south? Go on? What was there after Keddlenowe? Homesteads and wilderness until Leithaven. And if it had fallen as well?

Benjamen sighed. Then his breath caught in his throat.

There. His inner senses cut through his thoughts like a sharp pain. That feeling again. Like last night

He sniffed at the air and the wind brought the strong odour of direwolf to him. Heartbeat thudding in his chest, he loosened his knife in its sheath. He felt trapped. Leaving his pack in his hidey-hole, he eased out from between the boughs as soundlessly as he could.

How many were there? One wolf at least, and if last night was anything to go by, probably a couple more. And he sensed something else...something so sly that he was only aware of its presence by a strange absence of life where it walked.

He remembered the figure in black he'd seen earlier in the day and his blood went cold. Without questioning how he knew, he was sure that the same mysterious being was stalking him now . The knife he held in a suddenly sweaty hand seemed like a joke when he remembered the speed and ease with which the figure had killed the direwolf.

Benjamen wiped his brow. He tried to merge into the tree trunk as he hid behind it. His knife held out in front of him, he waited for the attack he knew must come.

Thirteenth

CARRIE'S KEEN NOSTRILS CAUGHT the scent first. She lifted her muzzle into the wind, tasting the night air. The wind shifted, turned on itself, and then she had it: Man scent. Not the foul odour of stormkin that was almost all she'd smelled for the past day, but man scent. And in it was something else...a deepness...a warmth...an echo of the silence of Wenys Hollow...

She looked ahead to where Tarn had stopped, his eyes narrowed, cold. In the instant their gazes met, she knew that her worst fears had come to pass. Tarn was now more skes than human , and he meant to kill the man. How she knew or why he would, she couldn't say, but his intention was as clear to her as if it was her own.

"No!" she meant to cry out, but all that came from her shapechanged throat was an ugly growl. Anger rose in her to meet the frost in Tarn's eyes.

She leapt at him, meaning only to knock him down, but the dire-wolf's instincts took over and she went for his throat. Tarn's eyes flashed. His hand swept down, blade-less, and struck her hard across the brow. Stunned, she dropped to the ground. Then Tarn melted into the shadows without a sound.

Carrie lay, head spinning, then she lunged to her feet and raced in the direction of the man scent. She broke into a glade and saw them both—the flicker of shadow that was Tarn in his skes guise and the man by the tree with a long knife held in his hand. A growl rumbled in her chest. She saw Tarn pause in mid-motion and turn towards her. His sword appeared in his hand. She crouched low, to the side, then charged; but before she could reach him he stumbled. His sword fell from limp fingers.

Carrie came to an abrupt halt. For one long moment she stared at the knife in Tarn's shoulder. The coldness was finally gone from his eyes, leaving behind the familiar warmth she'd come to know, but it was shadowed with pain. Then she turned to meet the man's attack. He stopped short when she faced him. Growls still rumbled in her chest and she paced slowly forward. The man backed away before her advance, waiting for an opening. His hands opened and closed and she knew he was wishing for a weapon.

A voice, Carrie thought. If she had a voice there'd be no need to fight. But she couldn't expect the stranger to understand that.

She shrunk from the thought of attacking, but could see no other course open to her. It was fight or flee, leaving Tarn behind to die. If she could just get the swanmage to give them back their proper shapes, perhaps they could reason with the man. But with things the way there were...

She had no other choice. Daring a quick glance behind, she saw Tarn on his knees. He'd drawn the dagger from his shoulder and was using his hand to staunch the flow of blood. His pale face lifted to meet her gaze. She could hear him muttering under his breath and strained to hear what he was saying, but suddenly the man was upon her.

The force of his attack sent them rolling across the ground. He wrapped his legs around her torso and got a two-handed grip on her throat. Her fangs slashed the air beside his face as her legs fought for purchase. Her claws, propelled by her powerful leg muscles, ripped at the leather of his coat and trousers. But the stranger hung grimly on, squeezing her throat with desperate panic.

Her chest hurt from the lack of air, but she heard Tarn call out and a familiar tingle ran through her body. She regained her own shape.

Taking advantage of the man's surprise, she wriggled out of his slackened grip. Rolling a few yards away, she collapsed, gasping for breath. The man stood, shaping a ward-sign with either hand. He took a step towards her.

"No!"

Tarn stood in his own shape, one hand clasped to his bleeding shoulder. He swayed on his feet. The man paused to study Tarn for a moment, then moved towards the wizard instead.

Tarn glanced at his sword. It was too far away and he was in no shape to use it anyway. Neither could he put a spell on the man. He didn't have the stranger's name.

He took a step back, stumbled to one knee. The man came closer, still wary, but more confident now. Tarn let his weakened taw rise and he searched the night. He spoke a name when he found what he was looking for and an owl lifted from a nearby tree to dive at the man's face.

The stranger lifted his hands to protect his eyes from the owl's talons. As he tried to fight off the bird, Tarn took the time to tear a strip of cloth from the bottom of his shirt and wrap it around his wound. It was clumsy work. He gritted his teeth from the pain, fumbling with the bandage as he held the cloth with his mouth and his free hand, trying to tie it. When he'd knotted it as best he could, he rose back to his feet, his sword heavy in his right hand. He called off the owl. The stranger backed away from him, eyes wide with surprise.

"Go away," Tarn told him. The words came out in a croak. "Don't make me take my sword to you."

"Oh, aye, lad," the stranger said as he bent to pick up a length of dead wood. "I'll go away so that you and your friends can hunt me later at your leisure. Do you take me for a complete fool? You can hardly keep your feet. I'll finish you here and now for I'm sick of scuttling about the countryside like a thief."

"We meant no harm—" Tarn began.

"Is that what you call coming at me with a sword?"

"There was a madness upon me. But I have it under—"

"Dath take us both. I'll tell you, lad. There may be some you can charm with honeyed words, but I'm not one of them."

Carrie had regained her breath while they were arguing. She rose, picked up her own makeshift club, and stole up behind the man. Just as he stepped in closer to attack Tarn, she let fly with her weapon, hitting the stranger on the side of the head. She hit him again as he was falling, then stared at his limp figure on the ground. The club fell from her hands.

"Oh, Dath!" she cried. "I've killed him. I didn't mean to…"

Her voice trailed off as she looked at Tarn and saw that he'd collapsed as well. She began to shiver, numbed with the shock of what she'd done. But then she lifted her hands to her bruised neck, remembered how the man had tried to kill her. She took a small step, then another, and kept going until she was kneeling beside Tarn. Was he dead, too? His shoulder was soaked with blood and his face was as white as the foams of the waves she heard falling against the shore in the distance.

"What can I do?" she asked, but there was no one to answer.

She cradled Tarn's head on her lap. He was still alive. She could feel his pulse and see a vein throbbing under the moon-mark on his brow.

"Tarn?"

His eyelids fluttered.

"Tarn?" she repeated.

"It was the knife," he said in a voice so low she had to bend her ear to his lips in order to hear him. "The darkness had me. I would have…killed the both of you…but the knife brought me back. The skes shape…don't let me take it again." He drew a ragged breath. "I'm too weak, Carrie. The strain of holding…our shapes…and the darkness…"

"What can I do to help?" she asked.

"Go on…to Pelamas…"

"I can't, Tarn. Not alone. I won't leave you."

"You *must*."

"Tell me how to help you," she insisted. "There must be a…a spell or something. I helped you before."

Tarn was silent for a long moment. When he spoke again, his voice was weaker than before.

"That was with the…power of Wenys. You don't have…training…
need training…to raise taw…heal…too late to teach you now…"

His head fell limply against her.

"Oh, Dath!" she cried. "Don't be dead. Please, don't be dead!"

She held him close and wasn't sure if the feeble stir of his life-
essence was real or born of her hope. He *wasn't* dead, she told herself.
But he would be soon unless she got him some help.

She tried to remember how it had worked in Wenys Hollow.
Raising the silence. It had been easy with Padhain to guide her and
the power of Wenys Hollow to make her strong. Tarn hadn't been
there to help her then either. If she gave him strength now, would it
even heal him? What if stormkin came upon them, drawn by the use
of green magic?

She glanced at where the stranger lay. What if he wasn't dead?
What if he regained consciousness and attacked her while she was in
a trance?

Stop it! she told herself and pushed the fears away.

First she had to raise her taw. Then, when the green silence was
around her, however feeble it might be, she would give its strengths to
Tarn. Perhaps it would be enough to help him. Perhaps—

She shook her head, stilling the babble of her thoughts. She needed
quiet to call up the silence.

She made herself breathe evenly and she hummed — an off-key version of the tune that had drawn her into the silence in Wenys Hollow.
Closing her eyes, she sensed a great distance opening out in front of
her. A feeling of peace stole over her, close and warm. From the distance came a murmur of sound…breakers on the shore that became
the drumming of hooves. She heard breathy winds and the sound of
reeds being lipped, pipes fluting softly. And a stringed sound, like that
made by a harp. The groan of stone turning deep underearth joined
the song. The crackle of a fire rose up in her memory and became a
part of the music as well.

After awhile, she sensed light coming from the distance, and the
sounds merged before fading into that solemn silence that was like
music. In the light she saw a stone, tall and weathered, standing high
on a hill. The stone had features, as though a master craftsman had

carved the semblance of a man into it—a man of unearthly beauty. And then it *was* a man she saw, a living, breathing man. Except there were ivory horns sprouting from his brow and his eyes…his eyes…

She fell into the depth of his gaze.

His eyes were like the blaze of autumn woods in full colour, a thousand mingled shades swirling and gleaming. The small horns rose from his brow to become the many-tined antlers of a stag. His face seemed familiar. Where had she seen it before? And the eyes…

Then she knew.

"Tarn," she said in a soft voice. The eyes like leaves were Tarn's eyes. "You're Tarn."

"No."

The voice was breathy, wind-like, but earthy-deep and hoary, too.

Carrie frowned. "Then who..?"

"My mother named my Hafarl."

"Haf-Hafarl?"

The Summerlord? Oh, Dath! The Summerlord!

"But how can that—" she began.

"Daughter, there is no time to explain. My brother's minions seek me everywhere. I am Hafarl, called the Summerlord, yes. But this is neither the time nor the place to answer the riddles that plague you. I need your help. Will you come to me—in Ardmeyn, on Taynbell Peak?"

"I…what about Tarn? And why me? And—"

"Your friend is healing as we speak. Carwyn, I need to know— will you help me?"

"But…why?"

"My blood stirs in your veins. Is kinship not reason enough?"

Carrie found it hard to concentrate. The vision—if that was what this was—seemed more real than the nighted forest where Tarn lay hurt and her body was crouched beside him . Was she still there, or here, or where? It was all too confusing. But at the same time, this moment felt very familiar, as though it was a part of her, and had always been a part of her.

"I…I'll help," she said at last. "That is, I *would* help, but what can I do? I'm just…me. You—you're a god."

The eyes smiled. "Not I. But their blood runs in me, as mine does in you. Does that make you a goddess?"

"No." She shook her head to emphasize the word. "But—never mind. I'll help you."

Seeing the peace in him—it was haunted by the threat presented by his brother, but still there like a deep shining—how could she refuse?

"Will you take me to Ardmeyn now?" she asked.

"No. It is too soon. First you must meet with the one-eyed boy and the dhruide Puretongue at Pelamas Henge. Then you must come—the three of you. As swiftly as you can. I can bring you part of the way of Pelamas, but you must complete the journey on your own. I've been present in this world too long as it is and I can feel the stormkin gathering on my trail. The length and breadth of the Isles, those who seek me have sensed my presence here."

When he said that, Carrie could hear—far off still, but coming closer—the sound that she'd come to know too well. It was the sound of the stormkin as they hunted. Fear skittered up her spine.

"What about Tarn?" she asked. "You said the three of us—a dhruide, a one-eyed boy, and me. What happens to Tarn?"

The Summerlord sighed, a long, sad sigh that shook Carrie's heart.

"He will come or not of his own choosing," he said. "There is something that troubles him, Carwyn. It lies deep in his soul and not even I can read the riddle of his desire. The weavers weave and tell no one where the threads fit on their loom. Now ready yourself. Take a tight hold of the swanmage and we will go."

"What about him?" Carrie asked, pointing to where the stranger lay. "Is he dead? And if he's not, what if the stormkin find him here?"

The peddler lives and I will see to his safety. But we must hurry now, Carwyn. Be strong."

His eyes became a swirl of autumn leaves, blown by a sudden wind, spinning and twisting in a swirl of bright colours. A deepness enfolded Carrie into its heart and she held tightly onto Tarn as a dizzying sense of motion took hold of them.

At first she thought they were falling—but the deepness still enveloped them in its safety and kept her panic at bay with its peace. The silence that had filled her with the coming of the Summerlord became a wash of sound once more. Music of unearthly instruments vied with the music of nature. The sound of waves and a harp. The sound of a flute and the wind. It rose into a rich crescendo, deep and stirring, and then—

It was all gone. They were no longer moving. The music faded. She could feel something solid under them once more.

Opening her eyes, she found they were on a cliff overlooking the sea. Tarn's head was still on her lap. His face had a touch of colour now and the lines of pain were smoothed away. She looked up and around, wondering where they were.

Here you will be safe. It was the Summerlord's voice. It seemed to speak directly in her head. *For awhile at least.*

Carrie looked around. "Where are you? Where are *we?*"

In Umbria—north of Leithaven. I must leave you now.

"But what about this Taynbell Peak? Can't you just take me there with you?"

No, you must go the henge in Pelamas while I must hasten away and lead the hounds of Lothan on a merry chase. If not, they will find you and we will be undone.

"But…"

Carwyn. If I tell you more, it will make it more dangerous for both of us. Be strong and trust me. We will meet again on Taynbell Peak—this the weavers have woven. Here you are safe and you can rest. Sleep, and in the morning the swanmage will be strong enough to take you on to Pelamas. Have him teach you how to raise and use your silence. And ask him about names.

Carrie could feel the unseen presence withdrawing.

"Hafarl!" she cried.

But there was no reply. Her eyelids suddenly grew too heavy for her to keep her eyes open. Weary beyond belief, she stretched out on the grass beside Tarn and was asleep as soon as her head touched the ground.

Fourteenth

ALAG HOWLED. THE DIREWOLVES answered with their own eerie cries. Frosts chittered and clicked icy limbs together. The skes stood silent, dark laughter gleaming in their eyes.

The Summerlord.

Here. Near. In reach.

They made for the hill where Carrie, Tarn and Benjamen were gatheredhidden, then shifted their course as the Summerlord's hated scent led them off to the north. The direwolves loped ahead of the slower frosts and traal. The skes had already left both behind, flitting ahead, silent and deadly. And the skyborn dyorn forced power into their dark winged shapes, beat the leather membranes as hard as they could, raced for the kill.

The Summerlord fled before them.

They could feel him close. And weak. Ever since his staff had broken, he was always weak. Weak, but sly enough to lose them time and again. But tonight they had him. They could already taste his cursed blood.

But still the Summerlord stayed ahead.

He swerved again, north of Leithaven, turning west into the Berwin Mountains in central Umbria. The stormkin followed, a howling pack. Dyorn and skes, with the others trailing far behind now.

And then he was gone.

The stormkin paused on the moors near the Berwin Mountains. Dyorn dropped from the sky. Skes searched the barren ground. They found a trail—a hint of a footstep, there a broken twig, here a twist of gorse that had recently felt the weight of a hoof. But then the trail faded. When the direwolves finally arrived, they followed the scent farther until they, too, lost the trail. They milled about, whining and uncomfortable. By the time the frosts arrived, the ground crackling with ice at their approach, Galag was in a foul mood.

He cursed Hafarl, cursed the stormkin, cursed himself. And he prayed that the Captain Fergun was too busy in Ardmeyn to have become aware of this latest failure on his part.

THE CAPTAIN lifted his head, breathing deep the icy air that now frosted the green hills of Ardmeyn. At the moment when Carrie raised the Summerlord with her taw, he felt a sudden emptiness in the land around him. With finely attuned senses, he searched Ardmeyn, unable to put his finger on what had troubled him. Something was amiss—he knew that—but...

And then he understood .

That sense of the Summerlord's presence that had tempered the very air of Ardmeyn was gone. Hafarl had fled south once more.

Fergun prepared to follow. But first he sent out a final questing thought, only to find that the presence was back as though it had never left. It was all around him, a rush of summer smells carried on the icy winds, and Fergun was no closer to finding the Summerlord than he had ever been.

A vague uneasiness touched him.

Was Hafarl actually trapped in Ardmeyn, or was there some other reason that he kept Fergun here, away from his troops in the south?

The smell of the Summerlord was all around, heady and strong. Fergun felt he was only moments from finally capturing him. But he'd felt that way ever since he'd come to Ardmeyn. If this was a trick, if there were deeds a-foot in the southern isles that needed his attention...

Those Summerborn that Galag had been ordered to capture. Why had there been no word of them yet?

AT THE height of the night, Puretongue lifted his head and stared southwest from the railing of *The Ardweir.* Deren could sense the dhruide's tenseness like a cord stretched taut between them.

"Puretongue?" he asked.

"Can you feel it?" the dhruide replied. "He is abroad. In Umbria."

"Who is abroad?"

Puretongue gave him a curious look,

"Why, the Summerlord, lad."

"No, I..." Deren began, but then he felt it, too, a strange disquiet entered his soul.

In his cabin, Wren let his fingers fall from his harp. He cocked his head and a slow smile spread over his features. He touched the strings again and the sense of wonder he'd felt became a wondrous melody that he caught on the strings of his harp and sent winging back into the night air.

PENHALLOW FELT it, too.

The old priest stirred from his stone-shape and gazed into the starred sky. He felt the Summerlord stirring. He felt, as well, the fine webs of the weavers drawing closer, binding, finishing off the tapestried tale that had begun so many longyears before.

"How will it end?" he asked the night air. "Weavers, what end to your threads foresee?"

But the night held its own counsel, and the weavers, if they heard, held theirs.

Penhallow sighed and found again the solace of stone thoughts, but that peace was long in coming.

IT WAS morning when Benjamen woke from a night of strange dreams. There had been a sense of...deepness in his dreams, as though he'd slept in the presence of some holy thing. But sitting up, he remembered the night. He rubbed the bumps on his head and that started him wondering about those he'd fought last night.

First they'd been stormkin—of that he was sure. But then the direwolf had become a red-haired girl and the other in his black cloak had become...a man, he supposed, but a powerful man, for all his wounds. A wizard, more likely.

Which was their true semblance? And why was he still alive?

There was no trace of either one of them except for his own knife and a strange sword that lay discarded on the ground. The sword had a two-handed haft, the single blade merging into the hilt without a guard. He hefted it, delighted with its balance. *This* was a weapon. Sheathing his knife, he felt a measure of confidence return. He sat with the sword across his knees. Let the stormkin come for him now. Let them come at him while he was armed with a weapon that might have been forged by the erlkin themselves. Then he paused and listened to the world waking around him, listening with his inner ears as well as his outer.

It was still. So still that it took him a moment to realize what was missing.

The stormkin.

The evil sense of their presence was gone as though the sun had washed it away as easily as the night. But though Benjamen was happy that they were gone—*seemingly* gone, he warned himself—he still felt uneasy. What was the old saying? Something about the lull before a storm.

The problem with such old sayings was that they were invariably based on some piece of truth.

LONG TOM was awake before the dawn. Kinn heard him moving and got up from his own bed. In a companionable silence father and son harnessed the horses and readied the wagon for travel. By the time they were done, Meg and Fenne had breakfast ready.

"It's a fine day for a journey," Long Tom said around a mouthful of cornbread.

Meg gave him a worried look.

"Will we find them?" she asked.

"Oh, aye. How could we not? We'll find them and still be in Heatherby in time for the Long Fair."

But, Long Tom added to himself, would they find them alive?

He kept a cheerful smile on his face. Worry was foremost in all their minds, but he wouldn't be the one to give it a voice. He pictured Carrie's innocent face, the thin-lipped determination that had been there when she'd left. Oh, Ballan help the ones that might have harmed her.

"Time we were going," he said, pouring the remainder of his tea over the fire. "Here's the sun getting higher by the minute and the road waiting, and what do we do? Laze about the fire like a pack of lairdy-lords."

Fifteen minutes later they left Wenys Hollow behind and were on the coast road, heading north to Yellfennie.

Fifteenth

ARN WAS SILENT FOR a long while after Carrie finished relating the events of the previous night. He stared off into unseen distances, his clouded brow reflecting the trouble of his thoughts. Around them, dawn grew into day. The sun lifted high into a cloudless sky. It beat upon the hills, summer-strong, and glinted on the white-capped waves that fell against the rocks far below.

Carrie tried to respect his silence, but she was puzzled. His strange mood worked on her until finally she had to speak.

"What's wrong?"

He turned to face her and she withered under the bitter look in his eyes.

"What's wrong?" he replied. "Fairlord! *I'm* what's wrong. Where I thought I was strong, I was weak. I've broken the very tenets of my dhruide teachings by letting my shapechanging control me. I let the dark taw of the skes seduce me and that should never, *never* have happened. How can I trust myself now? My control's no better than a novice's. And with all I know."

"But you were tired, Tarn. You've driven yourself too hard over the past few days."

"How would *you* know?" he asked. "*What* do you know?"

"I—"

Tarn wouldn't listen.

"I was sent to help you," he said, "but you've saved my life three times now. What does that tell you? It tells me that I'm useless. I'm the one who studied and trained for years, but *you* meet the Summerlord. He speaks with *you*. He even tells you that I should train you." The small mage gave a harsh laugh. "Shall I train you how to take shapes that leech your control from you? Shall I show you the dark reflection that's in each of us?"

"But, Tarn—"

"And in that final stage of your journey—when you leave for Taynbell Peak—he tells you that I won't even be going with you. 'Thank you very much, Tarn. You've done your bit, now run along like a good lad.'"

"It's not that way at all," Carrie said. "He said you'd come or not at your own choosing. *Your* choosing."

Tarn shook his head. "You don't understand. You've been dragged into this. Powers are waking in you that you've never even thought of wanting. Magic comes to you like water scooped up in a cup, whether you want it or not. It wasn't that way for me. I was nothing until Puretongue found me. I worked hard to learn, to become what I am. His teachings showed me options I never knew existed. His magics gave me a purpose. But now—when a time has become that I *can* be useful—I'm put aside for someone like you who doesn't give a damn about any of it."

"That's not fair!" Carrie cried. "I never asked for my family to die. I never asked to be hunted up and down the Isles or to be caught up in a war between gods. And you're right—I didn't want to learn about… about magic or any of it, but I don't seem to have been given much choice, have I? Whether I want to or not, I *have* to go on now, following you and the Summerlord, because if I don't, I'm going to die."

Her eyes glistened with unshed tears.

"What right do you have to feel sorry for yourself?" she went on. "You—you don't even know what being hurt *is*. You're so wrapped up in yourself, in your own importance, that you can't even see another person's grief."

Now it was Tarn's turn to be flustered. "I—"

She cut him off, stabbing a finger in the air between them. "You asked me what I know, well, it's very little. But I have come to understand a few things. This struggle involves *all* of us. It's not some stage for a mummer's play, set up for you to show everyone how smart and powerful you are. Real people are dying and all you seem to care about is whether or not you're important in this struggle.

"Dath! If I had my way you could take my place and I'd get down on my hands and knees in thanks that it wasn't my part to play anymore. But it doesn't work that way. Whoever made the choices has already made them. All we can do is try, and do our part and hope the whole thing works out before we all die. We..."

Her voice trailed off. She rubbed her knuckles into her eyes and an overpowering sadness washed through her. She saw her parents dead again, her home in flames, the yellow-haired Saramand grinning with their bloody axes...

"Dath damn you!" she cried. She stood and faced him, arms akimbo, eyes blazing. "You...you're no better than the stormkin yourself. Why don't you crawl back into whatever hole you came from and leave the world to people who care about it?"

As she said the last words she put her hand over her mouth. Tarn's eyes went flat and hard. The muscles in his face tightened and his moon-mark flashed with a sudden inner light.

"You're right," he said in a quiet voice. "I'm everything you've said and worse."

Carrie felt awful. She put out her hand to try to comfort him, to erase the harshness of what she'd just said.

"I didn't really mean that," she told him. "Honestly, Tarn. It—it's just that I've lost so much and...and I care about what happens...to you, to me, to the world..."

He brushed her hand away.

"No," he said, his voice gone hard. "You *are* right. But useless though I might be in the greater struggle, I can still do this: The Summerlord's power strengthens me. Before I'm nearly killed again, I'll make sure you get to Pelamas Henge."

His words struck Carrie like so many blows.

"Tarn," she said. "Don't be like this. I said I was sorry."

He gathered his taw and spoke a name, then the unicorn was in front of her, leaf-hued eyes flashing, longhorn bright and deadly pointing up from his brow. He pawed the ground, then knelt for her to mount. Carrie hesitated. She backed away from the angry white shape.

"Everything's black and white for you, isn't it?" she asked. "And one mistake, any mistake, should be punished as sternly as possible."

The unicorn merely waited.

"Then take me to Pelamas," she said, "and see if you can erase your hurts by yourself. See if you don't want a friend when your stupid anger and self-importance beats down on you without any respite, and there's no one there to help you ease the pain."

She mounted and clutched a handful of mane. The white hooves gouged the earth and sent clods flying as the unicorn leapt away. Carrie gasped and tightened her grip. The wind whipped the mane into her face and the speed of their passage tore a cry from her lips. The drumming of the hooves against the hills echoed Tarn's anger until she felt it thick and choking around her. It pounded her skull and the faster they sped, the more it grew.

At last she closed her eyes. Bending her face down against Tarn's neck, she concentrated on keeping her grip and not falling off. In her heart, another sorrow swelled to join the sadness that seemed to have found a permanent home inside her.

"It doesn't have to be like this," she cried into Tarn's ear.

But if the unicorn heard her, he ignored her, just as he ignored everything except for the driving anger that gave him his wild speed and the endurance he needed for this mad flight north.

Sixteenth

THE TURPENS' WAGON CLATTERED along the coast road, uphill and down. By mid-morning there were well north of Wenys Hollow and making good time. Long Tom kept their speed at a fast walk. Now that they were travelling, with the road unwinding under the horses' hooves, he felt his tensions ease. The tightness left his shoulders and the smile on his lips was more natural, with only a hint of worry in his eyes. For how could he frown with the sun high, the sky blue, and the land so open and free around them?

The road was good for that. It made all men equal. The same dust that rose from a lord's carriage followed the creaking wheels of a tinker's wagon. It hung from rich robes as well as from motley cloaks and jackets. It covered gilded shoes as well as old tinker boots. And to those who wended the roadways of the Green Isles, it would always be so.

So Long Tom laughed and the miles fell behind them. He teased Megan and demanded a tune from the children perched up on the wagon's swaying roof. Kinn played a march, keeping time with the wagon's clatter, Fenne pounded away on a rounded goatskin drum, and the music and laughter trailed along behind the wagon in a ragged tatter of sound.

But when they reached the hills near Yellfennie, their uneasiness returned. The instruments were put away. As they neared the crest of each hill, Kinn or Fenne would run ahead and scout the way. When they saw the smoke rising from where the town should be, Long Tom brought the wagon to a halt and silently handed the reins to Megan. Loosening the tinker blades in their sheaths at his belt, he walked on ahead, his features set in a tight mask.

When he returned his face was pale and grim.

"Raiders," he said. "They've got one ship a-harbour and the town's burning."

"Oh, Tom," Megan said. "What if Carrie's there?"

The tinker shook his head. "She wouldn't be that much of a fool. She'd avoid towns like she would the plague."

"Do you think she's still safe, Dad?" Fenne asked.

"Oh, aye, lass. At least as safe as any of us can be in times like these."

But there were others in Yellfennie who weren't safe at all. Long Tom's heart went out to them, but he hardened himself to the cold facts. There was a shipload of Saramand below and they were too few to be able to help anyone. There was nothing they could do for the Yellfennians except pray.

He plucked at the hilts of his knives, a slow dark anger moving in him. They had to leave the Yellfennians to their fate, but he didn't have to like it. Wordlessly, he led the wagon from the road.

Now they fared by ways that only the tinkers knew—hidden tracks that cut through wilds that a wagon could travel, though none but a tinker would guess that they existed. Long Tom and Fenne walked ahead, testing the way. One false turn and they could easily crack the wagon's axle, or lose a wheel to soft ground or some hidden burrows; and though they cut a long way off their road by travelling across the land, they lost hours as they struggled with the slow going.

Kinn scouted to the east, watching the approaches from Yellfennie. From time to time he returned to the wagon to report his findings, then just as silently as he'd come, he'd be off again—bow strung in his hand, one arrow between his fingers, the rest in the quiver that hung from his shoulder.

When they reached the coast road again, they were miles north-west of Yellfennie. It was mid-afternoon. They took the horses from their braces, letting them graze and rest while the family ate a cold meal.

"We were lucky at Yellfennie, bypassing trouble the way we did," Long Tom said, "but how much longer will this luck last? Broom and heather! I half expected the hills to be crawling with stormkin."

"If Carrie's gone north," Megan said, "they'll have followed."

Long Tom nodded. "Aye. But how far ahead are they? Carrie and Tarn have two days' lead, but if Carrie's alone and hiding, she'll not be travelling fast nor far. We could run into those creatures at any moment."

"Have you given a thought as to what we'll do when we *do* run into them?"

Long Tom gave his wife a bleak look. "Aye, Meg, and it's not heartening the thought is. But what can we do? What if Carrie's lying hurt somewhere—hid from the Mocker's crew, perhaps, but too hurt to travel? Should we leave off our search for fear of stormkin?"

"No. But she could be anywhere and I'm afraid for us—as you should be."

"And you think I'm not?" Long Tom frowned. "But perhaps you're right, Meg. Perhaps I should go on alone and not let you and the children chance the danger."

"I'm not asking that."

Megan shot a glance to her children and saw the protest on their faces. Ah, and did they think she'd let their father go on alone, without her, without them?

"We'll travel together," she said. "But Tom, we've been pushing the horses hard and if we wear them out, we could well run smack into a pack of stormkin and have no means of escape. And then who'd help Carrie? It's slower we should be going."

"We'll be careful," Long Tom promised. "But the time for speed's not passed yet. They've two days lead on us and the horses have grown fat from those same two days of idleness. We'll be safe for awhile yet."

THEY NEARED the woods by Keddlenowe as the day ended. The horses plodded in their harnesses, heads drooping and weary. Megan was alone in the wagon. Long Tom and Fenne walked on either side and Kinn was afield, scouting. When they heard the sudden trill of a lark's call, Fenne disappeared into the high grass to the left of the wagon. Long Tom called a half and walked a little farther before stopping. He rested his hands on his belt near the hilts of his knives.

For long moments he scanned the road ahead and the undergrowth to either side. Then he heard the crackle of movement in the brush and a stranger stepped down onto the road. He was a grizzled old man, tall and broad-shouldered, dressed in browns and greys with a peddler's pack on his back. In his hand he held a sheathed sword.

"Tom?"

"Aye, Meg. I see it."

The weapon was a twin to the ones that the stormkin were said to use—a strange, sleek blade, unlike the plain hilted straight swords common to the Isles. Long Tom glanced behind the man and saw Kinn rising from the brush, arrow cocked to his cheek. The lark's call had been his.

"Well-met, stranger," Long Tom said. "It's emptier than the winter barrens this road's been for more miles than I care to remember."

The stranger nodded. There was a wariness in his eyes.

"True enough," he said. "There's few honest folk abroad in times like these."

Long Tom bristled. "Meaning?"

"Meaning there are things abroad that should never be—slaying and killing. And they wear many shapes—some very innocent in seeming."

"Aye," Long Tom said. "But there are still ways to tell them from true folk. By their weapons, is one."

The stranger stiffened. Long Tom saw his fingers whiten around the sheathed blade.

"The sword's not mine," he said. "Or perhaps I should say, it *wasn't* mine. Until I won it in combat."

Long Tom watched the man's fingers inch their way up the sheath until they held the sword by the hilt. Now it would take but a flick of the stranger's wrist and the sheath would fly free, baring the blade for use.

"There's an arrow aimed at your back," Long Tom said in a conversational voice, "and another at your side."

He gave the stranger time to glance sideways to where Fenne stood, arrow notched. Kinn offered up a deliberate cough.

"Why don't you lay that sword of yours down on this fine road," Long Tom continued, "and we can talk about what's abroad and where you won such a weapon."

The stranger paled, then laid the sword down with obvious reluctance.

"Perhaps you are when you seem," he said, his gaze never leaving Long Tom's face. "The others would have slain me out of hand."

"What others?"

"Stormkin." The stranger spoke the word with loathing. "What do you think, man? Or are you blind? The Saramand are viking, oh yes, but there are worse than them abroad. They attack quick as thought. They can take any shape..."

Long Tom nodded. "We've run into one or two ourselves. But is that all you've seen on the road? No one else? And what about that sword?"

"The sword's part of a strange tale." The stranger sighed. "Look, you have me outnumbered and weary as I am, I'm in no mood to either flee or fight. If you want to trade tales, can we do it over a cup of something hot?"

Long Tom considered it. "Leave that knife in your belt beside the sword, aye, and your pack as well, and then move away from them."

The stranger did as he was told. When he was a good distance from the weapons and pack, Long Tom stepped over and picked them up.

"Kinn!" he called past the stranger. "Is there level ground where you are?"

"Aye, Dad. You can bring the wagon up along those elms where the bank dips."

"Then give your mum a hand with the wagon." Long Tom returned his attention back to his captive. "It's time we were bedded down for the night anyway. Now if you'll stay nice and quiet until we have the camp settled and a fire going, I can promise you tea and a meal. Other than that…well, let's wait until you've told your tale."

The stranger shrugged and stood aside as the wagon clattered by him. Fenne's arrowhead never left the target that was the small of his back.

"CARRIE," MEGAN breathed when the stranger had finished his tale. "He's talking about Carrie and Tarn. It *must* have been them."

"Aye," Long Tom agreed. "Except from what you've told us, Benjamen, they've changed a bit in the days since we last saw them. At last Carrie has. The other—this wizard Tarn—well, we don't actually know him. Broom and heather! The first time we saw him was when we were camped just outside of Codswill. It was early morning and…"

Benjamen sipped his tea as Long Tom told him all of what befallen his family since they'd first encountered Carrie in Codswill. He looked from face to face in the firelight, eyes watchful, his inner senses studying them.

"Why are you so concerned with this Carrie?" he asked when Long Tom was done. "You've known her—what? A week at the most?"

Long Tom regarded the peddler thoughtfully.

"Because she has no one else," he said at last. "What if it was my own Fenne that was in the same trouble? Wouldn't I want folks to do right by her? Ballan, man. Are you so hardhearted yourself?"

"No," Benjamen said. "But I was curious. There are few folk who would do so much for a stranger, whether in these troubled times when there are hundreds of homeless orphans and refugees about, or not."

"But we're tinkers," Long Tom said, as though that should explain everything. "She asked for guesting and could she travel with us, and we agreed. After that, how could we *not* help?"

Benjamen nodded, remembering his own encounters with other tinkers. Their hospitality was legendary on the road, and once they'd given their protection to someone, it wasn't withdrawn without very good cause.

"And you're going north now?" he asked.

"As far as need be. Tomorrow we cross the Tooming at the ferry in Keddlenowe, unless...do you know how things stand in the town? Have the Saramand struck it yet?"

"Not that I know. But I've spent most of the day wandering these woods, trying to come to grips with what I should do. I have an... inner guidance, as it were. It bids me go north, for all that reason tells me not to. There's nothing left for me in the south, true enough— not with the Saramand everywhere—and north there might be more stormkin, but I sense hope in the north as well. It's hard to know what to do."

He shrugged, then fixed Long Tom with a keen, questioning stare.

"Do you trust me yet?" he asked.

"I..."

Long Tom looked away from him to where Megan sat. She nodded her acceptance of the peddler.

"I trust you well enough," he said. "Why?"

"If you'll have me, I'd like to travel north with you. I can lend a hand in case of trouble and—at least for me—it'll be safer than going in alone. What do you say?"

Long Tom was one to trust his feelings. He thought for a moment, then grinned and thrust out a hand.

"Aye," he said. "Broom and heather, I say *yes*."

Seventeenth

$\mathcal{I}$T WAS MID-AFTERNOON WHEN *The Ardweir* passed through the strait between Ffoy in north Kellmidden and the Inverisles to sail west into Becks Bay. Puretongue called Deren from his studies and together they stood at the railing, looking north to Ardmeyn. Deren squinted. The deepsight of his studies was still on him and the glimmer-white land seemed to shine with an inner light. He felt the cold as though he stood on its frozen shores—a deep, numbing cold that bit to the bone. He turned to Puretongue with a question in his eye.

"No," the dhruide said in a soft voice. "It wasn't always so. That is the Everwinter, Deren, come to Ardmeyn. Lothan's power. The green hills are white with the Mocker's strength and somewhere amongst them, the Summerlord hides and waits."

"How big is Ardmeyn?" Deren asked.

"As big as North and South Gwendellan combined."

"And it's all..?"

Puretongue nodded. "Aye. The Everwinter lies over it all."

Staring at the frozen land that disappeared into the far horizon, Deren shivered.

"Over it all?" he repeated. "Lothan has *that* much power?"

"That and more."

"And we're supposed to stop him?" Deren asked.

He thought of the miserable progress he was making with his studies. The Everwinter's cold reached across the water, chilling him, numbing hope. He thought of Lothan and what they had to stop him: An old dhruide and a one-eyed boy. The priest Penhallow and a harper. What kind of an army was that? What kind of power? Not much at all compared to the Icelord and his stormkin.

"We'll never stop him," he said.

"We can try," Puretongue told him. "The weavers weave and who knows what pieces have yet to be played? We have to keep up our hope—above all else. The Summerlord still lives and the weavers are still weaving. The end is not yet here, for all that it seems to lie so close at hand."

"But the Summerlord's helpless—you've told me that without his staff of power, he can't do anything. And what have we to offer?"

Fire crackled in the dhruide's eyes.

"There is still power in these Isles," he said. "We have Penhallow in Pelamas and the Summerborn that Tarn brings north. Strength builds upon strength. Don't make Lothan's mistake and think us completely helpless."

"But—"

"And remember Wren's vision—Taynbell Peak and the stone with its strange symbol. The henge on that peak is the heart of Ardmeyn. I see the end coming to us then. Whether or not we'll be successful, I can't say, but it *will* end there. The Summerlord has yet to make his final play. Our task is to survive—and see that the others survive— until we all reach Taynbell and bring this to a close ."

Deren made no reply. He looked north and sighed. There was an iron strength in his companion, a will that would not admit defeat. But against a being that controlled something like the Everwinter, it may not be enough.

Deren's empty socket began to ache and he turned away, leaving Puretongue at the rail while he returned to mid-ship. There he sat crosslegged on the deck, out of the way of the sailors, and closed his eye. He worked at raising his taw, trying to still the clamour of his mind's inner conversation. But each time the silence rose up, an icy shiver pierced his soul and he lost his taw to a confused fear.

"**ARE YOU** sure?" Wren asked.

Twilight hung its grey cloak on *The Ardweir*. Its sails were pale ghost-clouds that hung loosely now that the wind had dropped. Sailors clambered in the rigging, furling the great sheets. The moon rose from behind the dark landmass that was Kellmidden, yellow and watchful.

"The time for speed has come," Puretongue replied, "and we can go more quickly in winged shapes."

"What about Deren?"

Hearing his name, Deren started. Nervous fear thundered in him. Dath! He looked down at his body, wondering if he'd ever be the same again. What if he only shapechanged part way? What if he lost his shape in the air and plummeted to his death?

"I will lend him what strength he needs," Puretongue said. "Thank you for your help, Harper Wren. Look to meet us again in Pelamas. If we're gone before you arrive..." He shrugged, showing his weariness. "We will speak again when I've returned from Ardmeyn."

Wren shook his head. "You're using up strength that you'll need in Ardmeyn. Hafarl's staff! Wait another day or two and you'll be there, rested and strong."

"Two days will be too late," Puretongue said. "Last night the Summerlord walked the Isles and I could tell he was weakening. Tarn draws near to Pelamas with a darkness welling up inside him—" He cut the words off. "We must be there as soon as possible." He turned away from the harper. "Deren, are you ready?"

Deren swallowed. "I...I suppose so."

"Then raise your taw, lad, and we'll be off. There are many leagues still to cover between the henge and this ship."

Deren nodded. He drew up the memory of the silence that he'd finally gathered that afternoon and let it cloak his fears and confusion. The Everwinter's cold reached out from Ardmeyn to touch his taw, but he pushed it away. His eye glittered in the moonlight.

The dhruide spoke a word and Deren felt himself change. A tingle ran through him, followed by an explosion of sensations. His body compacted and grew light as bones hollowed, skin feathered, weight fell away. He could feel Puretongue's presence in his mind, augmenting his taw with a bright gold power. The dhruide filled him with strength and the knowledge of how to use this new shape.

Come, he heard Puretongue say in his mind.

Fear was gone. He flexed unfamiliar muscles and his body lifted from the deck of *The Ardweir*. A rush of heady confidence filled him. Flight. Effortless flight. Strength and speed. It was all there as the night air rushed through his feathers.

Come, Puretongue repeated.

Deren followed the dhruide and passed him in a mad flutter of exhilaration, while on the deck of *The Ardweir* below, Wren watched the two hawks disappear into the darkness. When he turned from the rail, he found the ship's crew standing about, a numb mingling of fear and wonder in their eyes. Then there was a shout from the foredeck.

"Wind's rising!"

The moment passed. The men leapt to their tasks as Captain Ander shouted his orders. The white sails were unfurled and gathered in the wind, billowing out. *The Ardweir* inched forward, mustering speed as the wind grew stronger. Wren remained on the deck for awhile longer, staring into the darkness. Then he retired to his cabin. He held his harp for long quiet moments before he finally tested its tuning and began to play.

NEAR MIDNIGHT, long leagues south of *The Ardweir*, two hawks dropped from the night skies. Puretongue gave Deren his own shape back, and took his own. He paced away from his companion, shoulders bent, eyes grim. The nearer they drew to Pelamas, the greater his fears became. He could feel Tarn in his mind as though his prentice stood before him. A shadow had grown over Tarn's taw. He was changing—changed.

Puretongue remembered the great magic he'd sensed loose in Dathen when he was on the other side of the Channel Sa and knew it now to have been Tarn's dragoning. The very winds breathed tales of his magics now—stealth and death and the waking of things better not woken—and Tarn's names were woven in amidst them all. Tarn. Gald-meir. Swanmage. Another image rose in the dhruide's mind, bringing a mixture of anger and sadness to him. He saw Tarn as the skes San Ko.

"Puretongue?"

The dhruide turned slowly to face his young ward. Deren's features were still flushed from the wonder of his flight. His one eye gleamed with the memory of strong wings in the night air.

"Aye, lad?"

"What's wrong? Why have we stopped?"

Puretongue smiled. "For you, Deren. Do you still feel the feathers cloaking you? The strong thrust of your limbs riding the wind?"

Deren grinned. "You know, I do! That's why I'm asking why we're standing here when we could be up there."

"And *that* is why we *are* here. Walk about, Deren. Feel the earth against your feet, remember the feel of your own body. The hawk's shape isn't yours—you're only borrowing it. When we were riding the wind, you began to grow too hawk-like. You began to forget who you are."

He shook his head at the troubled look that rose in Deren's eye.

"No, no," he added. "It's not your fault. This is only your first shapechanging and though you learn your lessons well, you don't have the strength yet to stay too long in another creature's shape."

As he spoke, he again saw Tarn as a skes. Beside his prentice loped a direwolf. The Summerborn. All unknowing of magical skills, that Summerborn was stronger in its new shape than Tarn was in his—and Tarn was trained. Puretongue's anger grew again.

"Will it always be like that?"

The vision faded and Puretongue regarded Deren.

"No," he said. "As you gain in strength and become familiar with the use of your taw, you will gain mastery over the shapes you borrow. But that doesn't come in a matter of weeks. Work hard and study, and then it will come."

If the weavers left them time. If…

Puretongue looked inside himself, searching for another vision of Tarn. He saw a flash of white hooves and a small figure clutching a white mane. The Summerborn. And Tarn—changing, changed.

"Come, Deren," he said in a brusque voice.

He raised Deren's taw himself, raised his own, and spoke the names they needed. Grey-brown wings cut the air once more as the two hawks winged through the night skies.

SOUTH AND west they went.

Through Ffoy's highlands and wooded hills into Wickenfirlie and the foothills of the Ramshorn Mountains. The moon set. The stars wheeled across the sky in their slow, stately dance, unconcerned with the events enacted under their heights. Steadily, the two hawks winged, riding the wind when they could, rising to catch an updraft, dropped again.

South and east.

Deren flew as though each stroke of his wings was his first moment of flight. He never wearied at the wonder of it all. He felt, more than saw, the land unwind below them. A wild laughter sang in his heart and washed the last dregs of his bitterness away. The pain wasn't gone. But the need to avenge the deaths of his family and friends was no longer so strong. He lost himself to a hundred new sensations and when he remembered that the shape was only borrowed, he felt no sadness knowing it would soon be gone. Instead, it increased his need to learn, to study harder.

South and west.

Puretongue winged, grim with worry. For him, the night brooded. The sky seemed to tense and flex, as though it too understood that the struggle was drawing to a close, one way or another. Time was slipping away. The weavers wove. Yet there was still so much to understand. The riddle that was Wren's dream. And Tarn…

Time and again he let his deepsight rise to show him visions of his prentice. He saw the angry tilt of the long white horn, the pounding anger of the hooves as they tore the sod, the sad anger that welled in Tarn's soul. He saw the Summerborn for what she was—no more than a girl, red hair streaming behind her as she clung desperately to the unicorn's mane, legs clamped vise-like to its sweat-stained sides. Her thoughts were a whirling pattern of stranger memories. The past few days spun and churned inside her, trailing behind the pair in ragged streams, like her hair.

Puretongue followed that trail of memories and saw a darkness growing further south. Stormkin were gathering. They were slaying any with the Summerlord's blood in them. Dyorn and skes. Elemental frosts. Steadily, they moved north. Direwolves. Lumbering traals. And along the coasts—like a mocking shadow of the stormkin—the Saramand were raiding. Fishing thorpe and town fell under their axes. The red and yellow sails of the snake prowed ships were everywhere.

The Summerlord was gone and chaos raced to fill the places where his protection had lain. Puretongue's heart ached with grief. North was the Everwinter. South lay devastation and the ruin of war. And the army moved northward. A disorganized stream of Lothan's minions. Slaying. Laying to waste. And the Saramand—their coming so timely to Lothan's needs.

Puretongue shut the visions from his mind. He was weary of death, weary of this struggle. But it was too late for him to turn from it. What the folk of the Green Isles lost, he lost. And had lost a hundred times over.

For a moment his thoughts went trailing back over the centuries to a time he could never forget. Was this how he must pay for what he had been then? His soul rebelled as he remembered, and he closed those memories away. The time for soul-searching was long gone. Only this last struggle remained.

THEY REACHED Pelamas Henge a few hours before dawn. Dropping down amongst the tall longstones on weary wings, they regained their shapes. Deren lay on the grass, quietly remembering the joy of their long flight. When he turned at last to look at Puretongue, the old dhruide was standing a few feet away, head bowed. He breathed deep and long, then slowly straightened. The taw of the henge replenished him and he drank deeply of its green silence.

Deren looked away, around the henge. The stones towered above them, dark and forbidding. He thought he saw one of them move and he shut his eye. A shiver went through him. When he looked again, he saw that what he had mistaken for a stone stirring was an old man in a grey cloak who now approached them.

"Puretongue," the stranger said.

The dhruide turned slowly.

"Well-met, Penhallow," he said. "How do the days of reckoning treat you?"

Penhallow sighed. "Poorly. The land is uneasy. Winter is every-where—but mostly in the spirits of our people. The weavers weave."

"Aye," Puretongue said. "And will there never be an ending to it?"

"Pray not. Let this struggle end, but should the weavers leave their loom..."

"Perhaps," Puretongue said, "the world would be the better for it. Perhaps the world *should* die. Perhaps we should give ourselves over and let the Horner Lord gather a new people to these Isles—a people who know nothing of the waging of war."

Penhallow shook his head. "He did—and more than once. The Tus. The erlkin. And what became of them? Puretongue, this is not you speaking."

"No. It is my weariness. My sorrow."

They stood awhile in silence, as still as the stones around them. Deren remained where he lay, feeling a little uneasy in the presence of these two grim old men. He wondered if he should introduce himself, then shivered again. At the moment, he'd rather they just forget that he existed.

"The Oracle?" Puretongue asked suddenly.

Penhallow shrugged. "There is little new. Did you speak with Harper Wren?"

"Aye."

"Then I have nothing new to tell you. What of your search?"

"It went poorly—worse than poorly. The Summerborn fall under the blades of the stormkin—they kill even those with but a tiny breath of the green silence in them…" Puretongue shook his head, then glanced at Deren. "Oh, lad. Forgive my lapse in manners. Penhallow, this is Deren Merewuth. I found him in Gullysbrow—after the Saramand had paid the place a visit. He has come to help us as he can."

Deren scrambled to his feet.

"Pleased to meet you, sir," he said, trying to hide his nervousness.

Penhallow smiled, his teeth flashing white in the darkness.

"And I you, lad." He thrust out his hand. "I thank you for coming."

Deren shook hands with the priest and was startled by the firmness of the old man's grip. A flush crept up his neck as Penhallow continued to smile.

"I—I don't really know what I can do," he said. "but I'll try whatever you ask."

"We could not ask for more. And you shouldn't belittle yourself, Deren Merewuth. The High Lord has touched you. You will give much."

Deren shot Puretongue a puzzled look.

"Cernunnos is the High Lord," Puretongue explained. "He fathered the Summerlord. Remember that symbol Wren showed us? Remember the vision?"

"Yes, but—"

"You will climb Taynbell Peak to see that stone," Penhallow said. "The Oracle has shown us that."

"But what—what will I do there?"

The two old men regarded each other.

"I wish I knew," Puretongue said after a long moment. "By the Staff, I wish I knew."

Deren was about to ask another question when both Puretongue and the priest turned away from him. The dawn was a hint of grey in the east now, but the two men looked south. A chill went up Deren's spine. He looked from the dhruide to Penhallow, trying to learn what was happening from their grim features. But shadows still cloaked their faces.

"He comes now," Penhallow said.

"Aye. Filled with darkness."

"Shall we..?"

"No," Puretongue said. "Wait for me here. I will go out to them alone."

The dhruide seemed to shrink in stature. His shoulders hunched once more as though he bore a great weight upon them. Slowly he walked out of the henge and into the woods on the slope beyond.

Eighteenth

I T WAS AN OLD wood, thick with ancient oak and ash, birch and berry, elder, thorn and pine. In each tree, Puretongue saw the tenets and symbols of dhruidry, the secrets and truths unravelling before his eyes. He walked and remembered. Around him, leaf tongues whispered and murmured, green against the grey-brown bark, riddling the Lessons of Tree-Wizardry upon which he'd founded his teachings so many longyears ago.

Now, as he did much of late, he found his thoughts delving deeper into the past. It occurred more and more often as the weavers wove this struggle to its close. And remembering, he told himself that in reparation for the evils he had once done, at least he'd left this behind: The Lessons of the Trees, the voices of the forests that explained the earth's wisdom, the moon's mystery, the sun's sharp light. His legacy reflected in the ancient forests that were still scattered in small pockets here and there throughout the Isles. They were gardens of the world's heart. Where the First Men left their stoneworks, he set clues in leaf and branch and root to unravel those same riddles.

The woods opened up into a glade before him. There the grey of morning had drawn the night away, lighting the glade while deepening the shadows in the surrounding forests. A lone menhir stood in the center of the glade, tall and grey as the sky above, draped with moss and trailing vines.

Puretongue approached the stone and laid his veined hands upon it. He took a deep breath and let the longstone's power course through him, strengthening his taw, deepening his silence. It quickened the flow of his blood and laid his bitterness to rest. He was still tired, but not too tired to finish what must be done. The journey to Ardmeyn remained, and the heights of Taynbell Peak. Then he could rest.

He stepped back from the stone, sensing movement in the woods across the glade. He looked up, his sky-blue eyes shining with an inner light, and waited, tall and calm. The unicorn paced into the glade, pausing when it saw him. The girl on its back slid to the ground where she collapsed in a heap, her hair a spill of red against the green sward. For long moments the beast and dhruide regarded each other. Then the unicorn's form shimmered and Tarn stood in its place. He staggered once, drew strength from the proximity of the longstone, and straightened to meet the old dhruide's gaze.

"Tarn," Puretongue said softly.

His taw reached out, but his prentice's mind was closed to his touch. A shadow lay upon it. Puretongue remembered his vision—changing, changed—and a rush of helpless despair went through him.

"Hello, Puretongue," Tarn said finally.

The dhruide took a step forward, then paused. Something lay between them now—a darkness. A shadow. He knew that if he moved any closer, Tarn would turn and be gone.

"I've tried to be what you wanted," Tarn said, "but somehow it just didn't work out. I never lost...my pride, I suppose. When I took the skes shape—did you know that I failed a basic tenet of your teachings, Puretongue? The skes shape—it has a soul of its own and it's taken root inside me. It's still there, growing. It's dark—cold and dark. I think it started when I took a dragon's shape, and then I did too much, too soon, too quickly—all without resting properly, without being ready. But it's inside me now, that damnable skes soul, and it's growing stronger all the time."

"Tarn..."

"You know, I suffered under the Saramand's rule in Tallifold. I played the buffoon and fool for them while I watched them destroy something I loved. But I was waiting for your summons and had to stand idly by. Then, when the word finally came, I went to Codswill and found *her*." He nodded to Carrie. "She didn't even want to come. But I brought her through the stormkin's net all the same. I brought her here to you as you asked. But why do you need her?

"You trained me. Couldn't I have done instead? Look at her. She's weak. She's untrained. She doesn't even want her magics. But she's the one you and the Summerlord want."

"Why wouldn't she be weak?" Puretongue asked. "You've been drawing on her strength the whole of your mad flight north."

"I…"

Revulsion crossed Tarn's features and the moon-mark on his brow flickered with the light of his inner anger. He didn't want to believe it, but when he looked at Carrie, he realized it was true.

A tremor went through him. When he looked back at Puretongue, his eyes filled with tears.

"I could say that it was the skes soul," he said, "the growing darkness inside me that made me do it. But I think it was more than that. I've been flawed all along."

"No, Tarn. That's not—"

"I'd have given the Summerlord my soul if he'd asked, but he just ignores me. And now I see why."

"He doesn't want your soul, Tarn," Puretongue said.

By the Staff! he thought. How could he stop this? Tarn was killing himself.

"Then what *does* he want?"

"Peace."

"Well, I hope he finds it." Tarn looked away, bitterness cloaking his words. "I know I never will." His gaze met the dhruide's again. "Did you know I almost thought that I could be Summerborn myself? A shade of a dead silkie told me that. His name was Padhain. I almost believed him, too, but now…"

"You *are* Summerborn," Puretongue said.

"No."

"You are. It can't be denied. Truth is."

"I…" Tarn shook his head. "How come you never told me this before? How could you keep that from me?"

"Because of your pride," the dhruide said, his voice weary. "And because if I told you that, there were other things I would have to tell you as well."

"Like what?"

"My name. Your mother's name."

Anger blazed in Tarn's eyes. "You *knew*? All this time you knew and you never told me? Why? Tell me why—Puretongue, Master Dhruide, Founder, or whatever else you might call yourself? *Why?*"

"*You* could call me father."

Tarn's pale features went ashen.

"No," he said in a fierce voice. "No. Tell me that's not true."

"Would it be such an evil thing?"

Tarn said nothing for a long moment. His legs gave way and he knelt in the grass, head bowed.

"If," he began, his voice quiet now. "If you'd told me years ago—in Tallifold, even in Avalarn—no, it wouldn't have been an evil thing at all. But to leave me wondering all this time…If I could have known you were my father, then I—*How* could you have kept it from me?" He looked up, eyes streaming. "How?"

Puretongue sighed. The weight of past evils rose up from across the longyears to settle on his shoulders.

"Because it was too late then," he said, "just as it is too late now."

Tarn rubbed his sleeve across his eyes. Looking away, his gaze fell on Carrie. Her face was strained and pale from her ordeal, but still peaceful where she lay unconscious beside him. He reached over and pushed a strand of red hair from her brow, then looked up again.

"No more riddles," he said. "Please, just tell it to me now."

"Will you hear me through? Will you hear it from beginning to end and withhold your judgment until I'm done?"

"Who am I to judge you?" Tarn asked. But he nodded agreement.

Puretongue walked to within an arm's reach of him, then lowered himself down to sit cross-legged on the grass. The morning sun poured into the glade now. For Puretongue, it was as though his entire life was focused in this moment. He looked around the glade and every blade of grass, every leaf of every tree, stood out in sharp detail. When his gaze rested on Tarn again, he sighed and began.

"In the long ago, my name was Stest. I say *was* because the being I was then, I no longer am today. That much I *have* done with my life. I was a Field Captain of Lothan's—one of his three Captains—but I was something else as well. I was flawed as a stormkin, for something in me grew sickened with the Icelord's ways, and with the evils I did in his name. But despair as I might, I saw no way to be free of him. Who could I turn to, where could I hide? Who would trust one of Lothan's Captains? Who would believe his change of heart?

"It might have remained so to this day. I might have been the Captain in Ardmeyn instead of my brother Fergun. Whatever set me apart from my blood-kin is still a mystery to me.

"We were raised the same, our father and mother were the same. There were three of us: Fergun, who lives; Dwar, who I...who I slew in the dragonwars; and myself. But I was different. Where, how, why, doesn't matter anymore. I can only thank the High Lord that I was allowed the chance to change.

"My chance came in the guise of a woman. Her name was Tarasen and she saw through the shape I wore, saw through to the strange seeker of peace who lived in the skin of a Captain, and she drew me forth. I met her in the last days of the dragonwars. Because of her I killed my brother. Because of her I became what I am today. Because of Tarasen. Does her name mean anything to you?"

Tarn was so numb that he could only shake his head.

"She was the Summerlord's daughter. She helped me hide from Lothan's wrath. I disappeared—or rather, Stest disappeared—and no one knew what had become of him, or who slew Dwar. Only she and I.

"She gave me the name Puretongue and we were wed. Our years together were long and happy, for I learned to cloak my dark soul in the bright cloths of dhruidry. I learned to raise a taw of light instead of shadow, learned the green silence like music, and understanding what I had learned, I worked to share it with others.

"I founded the schools of dhruidry to set seekers upon the road I had taken, though I beset the way with mysteries and clues, for believe this, Tarn. Such studies *must* be cloaked in riddles. Unless one studies and works and strives hard for a thing, it means little when gained. It is as much the search for wisdom that makes one wise, as the wisdom itself. But I lose my tale.

"Tarasen and I lived long and well together until the time came—twenty-five years ago—when Tarasen bore me a son. In all those years we had no child, whether by her will, or the weaving of the weavers, who can say? I think at first we were unprepared for the responsibility of raising a child, but once our work in the Isles was done...

"We had laid the patterns to hold the places of power together, and then left the Lessons of the Trees for those who would seek after them. We did much and were weary of the doing.

"With our task complete, perhaps she knew we were now ready to create life, rather than to merely catalogue and protect it. Or perhaps she foresaw her own death and wished to leave a trace of her blood in the world. There is no one alive who can answer that now.

"But she gave birth to a son and we named him Tarn—'For what else will his taw be,' she asked me, 'but deep and still and strong as his grandsire's silence?' She bore you and a month later Fergun came to our home in Avalarn, drawn there by the birth of a deep green silence. He slew her, though not before she wounded him sorely and drove him off. I was in Pelamas Henge when this happened, called there by Penhallow who had sensed the approach of a great disturbance to the Isles. Can you already see the bitter irony?"

Unable to speak, Tarn shook his head.

"The disturbance he sensed," Puretongue said, "was Fergun's arrival in the Isles."

The dhruide fell silent, his gaze turned inward for long moments before he finally continued with his story.

"The moment your mother died, Tarn, I worked a great magic and returned to Avalarn. But I was too late. Her life left her—it fled as I held her in my arms. After that—forgive me if you can, Tarn—I could not bear the sight of you. You reminded me too much of her. I looked at you and thought that if you'd never been born, Fergun would never have been drawn to her. We would have been childless—but she would have lived.

"It was unforgivable, I know. But my grief was too great, and it pushed out any ability I might have had to be a good father. Instead, I brought you to Tallifold and fostered you with an old couple while I fled across the Grey Sea to the mainland, seeking comfort for my sorrow.

"That was the second last evil I have ever done, Tarn, and it weighs on my soul. It is a burden that will never be lifted.

"The last evil I did was never telling you the truth of who you are.

"For see. I returned at length, remorseful over my selfish deeds. I went to the home of that old couple, but new folk lived there now. Your foster parents had died while I was gone, leaving you to become one more orphaned urchin running wild in the streets. But I found you and though I could not bring myself to tell you who I was—I trained you as best I could. I knew you had power in you—that of your mother, bright and fair; and that of my own Cup in blood, dark, but powerful as well. I knew you must not come into it unschooled.

"But then this new trouble arose. Hafarl's staff was destroyed and Lothan went on the march again. I had to leave you—hoping I had trained you well enough—so that I could help Tarasen's sire. I...I am not infallible, Tarn. In some matters, I am not even wise. All of this I should have told you long ago. No, more than that. I should never have deserted you in the first place."

Puretongue fell silent. Tarn's mouth was dry, his tongue thick in his mouth. He didn't want to believe what he'd heard, but the truth of the dhruide's tale could not be denied. In Puretongue's green silences, that truth lay open for him to examine.

He swallowed hard.

"Why" he asked, finding his voice at last. "I don't understand. *Why* couldn't you tell me?"

Puretongue regarded him with sorrow.

"What?" he asked. "Tell you that you are Lothan's kin? That a Captain's blood runs in your veins? I thought it better that you never knew. Better it remained a thing hidden, and that with my death it would become a thing forgotten forever.

"What good does it do you to know this? The stormkin are a blight upon the world. How do you gain by learning that there is kinship between such abominations and yourself? They are unnatural.

Do you see the Summerlord fostering race upon race of creatures upon the world so that he can use them to gain power over his brother the Icelord, or his sister, the Mistress of the Seas? Hafarl had only one child and she...she is dead now. And never, *never* did he use her as Lothan used his sons. So I ask you, what good does it do for you to know this?"

"Nothing, perhaps," Tarn said. "But it might have allowed me to understand things better. Myself. You."

"Tarn, please—"

"No, I'm not angry. I just wanted to be useful, Puretongue. That's all I ever wanted. I didn't always want to be the young novice, the messenger, the one to fetch those who would do the deeds while I have to stand idly by and watch. It wasn't for glory and pride alone—though I'll admit to a shameful abundance of both. It was to have a place in the world where it otherwise seemed I had none. And what better place for a mage than in the workings of magics, great and small? And what better time than now?

"But I've been denied that, and now I think I know why. This thing inside me that I called a skes soul—it didn't come from a mismanagement of shapechanging. It was there all along, wasn't it? In my blood. I may be a swanmage, but I'm a darkmage, too."

"No, Tarn. That's not how it is. I understand now that it's the choices we make that define who we are—not our blood. For aren't Lothan and Hafarl themselves brothers, set apart from each other by the choices they have made?"

"Don't try to ease the pain...Father."

Puretongue sighed. How often had he wanted to hear that word from Tarn's lips? But never this way, not with such bitterness. The dhruide breached the distance between them with his taw to show Tarn the vision Harper Wren had shared. In silence, Tarn let the images spell through his mind. Then just as quietly, he stood, raising his own taw.

"I believe the rune of moon/flight is you," Puretongue said.

Tarn shook his head. "It could just as easily be *you*."

He crossed over to the longstone and leaned against it to draw on its power. When the green silence hummed strong inside him, he began to shape a new sword. He called its elements from the forest around them, from the depths of the earth underfoot—drew wood and metal forth until a curved sword and its wooden sheath lay in his hands. He strapped it on his back and returned to where Carrie lay. He knelt beside her and gently kissed her brow. Under his lips, he felt her unconsciousness slide into healing sleep.

"Go strongly," he said to the dhruide, his father, "and may you have your peace when all of this is done."

"Tarn," Puretongue tried again. "The rune must symbolize you. You've not been left out of shunted aside. Believe it."

"I can't. Not after what the Summerlord told Carrie. But I'll still do what I can."

"You'll come with us?"

"No. You may have exorcised the darkness from your own soul, Father, but I still have my own demons. I wouldn't be much help on your journey north and besides…Carrie and I, we're not exactly on friendly terms anymore."

His gaze left Carrie's face and returned to the dhruide.

"Tell her I'm sorry," he said. "Can you do that for me?"

Puretongue bit back any further argument and nodded, but he'd never felt so helpless before.

"I have to go now," Tarn said.

He let his replenished taw flood him and spoke a name. His form shimmered, darkened, and then where he'd knelt in his own shape was the skes San Ko. He stood and bowed to his father.

"No!" Puretongue cried. "Not *that* shape."

"How better to lose my demon, father? Think well of me, if you can. And I—for my part—forgive you for what you've done."

"Tarn!"

But neither Puretongue's cry, nor the raising of his power to hold his son, were quick enough. The skes melted into the woods and simply vanished. The dhruide cast his mind out in a desperate net, but it came back empty. He tried, again and again, but finally, he bowed his head and wept.

A long time later, he was able to gather Carrie's limp form in his arms and begin the walk back to Pelamas Henge.

Nineteenth

ARRIE AWOKE FEELING CLOSED in. She remembered the wild ride north, the argument with Tarn, but everything else seemed fuzzy. There'd been no time for anything except hanging on, legs clamped to the unicorn's sides, her fingers knotted in its mane. But now...

She lifted her head to look around. She was lying on a sweet-scented pallet in a small room. Its furnishing were austere—the pallet, a table and a chair by a small round window, and a hearth in one corner with a pile of animal skins on the stones in front of it. Then she felt someone's presence and turned to see a boy standing by the door. He was dressed in clean cotton trousers and a leather jerkin. A tousle of brown hair framed a pleasant face. Her gaze focused on the patch over his left eye.

"The one-eyed boy," she murmured, then caught herself. "Oh, I'm sorry. I didn't mean to—that is..."

But the boy smiled. "That's alright. I'm hardly used to the loss of the damned thing myself. My name's Deren."

"I'm Carwyn Lorweir, but you can call me Carrie."

"Then I will."

"Where are we?" she asked. "Is this Pelamas Henge? And where's Tarn?"

She could sense that he was nowhere near, though when she reached out with her taw, she tasted power and many who wielded it nearby.

"One question at a time," Deren said. "This is the henge—or at least the priests' rath that lies near it. As for your friend, I'm not sure where he is. Puretongue only brought *you* out of the woods, and he didn't say that anyone else had been there. In fact, he hasn't said much since you've arrived."

"Where is he? Can I talk to him?"

Deren shook his head. "He's in council with Penhallow and the others."

"But..."

She didn't bother to finish. It was obvious that she'd learn more when this Puretongue was ready to tell her, and not until then. She sighed and found a more comfortable position against the headboard. The bed was hard, but after the discomfort of the road, it felt soft as down. And it was strange to have the walls around her after having been out in the wilds for so long. The air felt so still.

"Can you tell me what's going on now?" she asked.

"Little enough," Deren said. He pulled the chair from the window and sat down closer to the bed. "But I'll tell you what I know— what Puretongue's told me. And this harper named Wren."

"I WAS NEVER meant to be a father, Penhallow."

Puretongue regarded his friend from the length of the long chamber and began to pace anew. Penhallow sighed and took a sip of mulled ale, thinking over Puretongue's strange confession. He had known the dhruide longer than anyone, but had never guessed at the man's origins. He'd never even thought to question them. It simply seemed that there had always been a Puretongue.

He waited until Puretongue had paced the length of the room a few more times, and then he spoke.

"Come and sit," he said. "Pacing won't help you and your son does what he must. Can you do less?"

Puretongue finally took a seat across from the priest and stretched his long legs towards the hearth. He frowned.

"The weavers weave," he muttered, "and I wish I could see what end they've woven."

"And what if *they* haven't seen it yet?"

Ruthin, another of the priests of Pelamas, asked this. He appeared to be older than either Penhallow or the dhruide, but unlike them, his blood was mortal and he was only eighty-seven years of age. To either side of him, also clothed in the brown-grey robes of the priesthood, stood another man and a woman. The man was Anearn; the woman Katha. Together, the five made up the inner council of Pelamas Henge's priesthood.

"Oh, they've seen it, Ruthin," Puretongue said. "They just keep it hidden from us. It irks me to work so blindly. This vision of Wren's—"

"And of many others," Anearn added. "Myself included."

"Aye. This vision. Can we trust it?"

"What else do we have?" Penhallow asked. "I'd be curious if this Carwyn girl has had a similar one. Is she awake yet?"

Puretongue nodded. "She's talking with Deren. But leave her aside for the moment. First we have to make a decision."

"Are you so undecided?" Katha asked.

"I..." Puretongue gave a helpless shrug. "In a hundred hundred years I've not been so undecided. I believe we must go to Taynbell Peak—only why? What is the riddle of the stone and its symbols? Until I spoke with my...my son, I thought I had it all clear in my mind. But now I'm no longer certain. With what he's doing..."

"You must forget Tarn," Penhallow said. "At least for now."

"How can I? I forgot him once and look what happened."

"You grief blinds you to—"

"My grief? Fairlord! It Tarasen was alive to see what I've done to her memory..."

The dhruide's eyes were bleak with sorrow, but he caught himself and sat straighter.

"Yet you've the right of it, Penhallow," he said. "I must put aside my personal grief. I will go to Taynbell Peak with Deren and Carrie and we will see what will betide."

"Now I must protest," Penhallow said. "You must take others. Those who've had the same vision. Anearn, and Wren and—"

"There's no time to wait for him, and Anearn is needed here."

"Some of the younger priests then," Ruthin said.

"Where are they?" Puretongue asked. "I've seen few around the rath."

"Some are in Traws," Penhallow said, "taking Pelamas' part in the council of kings. Others look after the steady stream of refugees. Still more repair the damage done to the coastal longstones by the Saramand. We can call back as many as you need."

"There's no time for that either," Puretongue said.

"I agree with Puretongue," Katha said. "The vision showed the three of them faring to Taynbell. If we accept the vision as true, then we must do as it showed us. What will be done, apparently, will be done by a few."

They all fell quiet then, considering their own thoughts.

What will be done...

The *what* was an unanswered riddle, and upon it hinged the fate of the Isles. If they failed, the Everwinter would soon begin its march into the south.

"But are we the right few?" Puretongue finally asked.

He was thinking of Tarn and the rune of moon/flight.

No one answered him, though they all knew his thoughts.

"The girl should be brought into the henge before you go," Penhallow said. "There is something about her...a power...a mystery that needs riddling as well."

"That is the Summerlord's blood in her," Puretongue said. "But I agree that she should see the henge before we go—if for nothing else than to replenish her taw." He stood. "I'll see if she and Deren are ready."

The others stood as he left the room.

"He pushes himself too hard," Katha said. "He punishes himself for things he should let lie."

Penhallow nodded, the concern plain in his eyes. "But can we stop him? What would you have me do? Forbid him to go when he's the strongest of us all?"

Katha shook her head. She slipped her hands into the sleeves of her robe.

"No," she said at last. "But we should pray for him."

CARRIE FOLLOWED Deren and the old dhruide out to the henge. Puretongue had related his conversations with Tarn, and the girl mulled it over now, feeling uncomfortable. Tarn. Poor Tarn. And he'd said he was sorry. Dath on high! Why couldn't he have told her himself—and sooner? To think of all he'd done for her...to think of him alone now, confronting Dath knew what...

And from what Puretongue had said, he'd damned himself. He'd taken the skes shape again and gone into the wilds.

She remembered the anger and hard words that they'd used the last time they'd spoken. Words were such gossamer things, but once spoken, they gained weight and couldn't be taken back. She couldn't stand the idea that she'd said too much and helped to push him away. Into the darkness. Into the wilds. Alone.

"What about Hafarl's staff?" she asked Puretongue, trying to take her mind from Tarn. "What good is going to Taynbell if the Summerlord still needs his staff, and we can't give it to him?"

"I don't know," the dhruide replied. "If I did, if I had that staff in my hand...the riddling would be done."

She had more questions but all of them fled as they reached the henge. All she could do was stare at the immense stoneworks. Longstones five times her height towered into the sky, with others balanced on top of them. They made a great circle of triad stones, two longstones supporting a third, around and around the henge. And those dolmen were so immense. Who had placed them here and for what reason?

She raised her taw and reach out with it, knowing a small pang of sadness as she remembered Tarn showing her how to do it. The henge crackled with power. The song of the green silence like music washed away recriminations and doubt. The silence sang in her. She drew a deep breath to steady herself, then stepped between two dolmen, crossing the inner circle to where four robed figures stood waiting for them.

The sky was graying into dusk. Long shadows webbed the stones. Nervousness returned as she stood in front of the figures with Deren and Puretongue on either side of her. She reached out with her taw again, this time to touch the silences of the four robed priests. Their calm met her and her shaken nerves were calmed in turn.

"Well-met, Summerborn," Penhallow said, beginning the formal welcome. "You stand in your grandsire's hallow and we stand with you. We greet you as friends and kin. Drink of the silence that you may go strong into the world. Make your peace, Summerborn, as we stand upon the brink of day and night. Here in the grey realm of your grandsire, speak or be silent as you will. But the Oracle will answer all the same."

Carrie looked from face to face. The solemn features of the priests reflected their inner peace. The ritual words burned in her mind, taking the shape of league-high topaz runes. Every cell in her body vibrated to a hidden music, to something deeper that the deep quiet that hung over the henge. Then she stepped forward, as Puretongue had told her to earlier, and knelt. She laid her head against the rough swell of the kingstone at the center of the henge—its heartstone, the focus of its power. From all around came the sudden sound of thundering hooves, drumming the green backs of the hills—a sound that was steady and clear.

High, keening music filled the henge—like fiddling or piping, or that joyful mingling of the two. Carrie thought of Kinn Turpen and his mastery over bow and fiddle. Then there was a sound like harping and she pictured Fenne with her brother, plucking the notes on her cittern. She saw old Long Tom standing behind them with Megan on his arm, their feet tapping to the drum-sound that still echoed its rhythm. Then the tinkers were gone.

She saw the dead silkie's face…Padhain…glimmer-pale and wet with sea foam. Then those features merged into another face that was Tarn's, but not Tarn's. That was stone, but not stone. That spoke. The voice grew clear above the music, singing a voiceless song that spiraled through her. It touched her very essence so that her heart beat in time to the throb of the drumming, her blood coursing through her veins like the liquid notes of fiddles and pipes. It touched the heart of her own green silence and went spinning through the dawn to encircle the henge.

And then the Summerlord was there.

For one long moment his face hung in the air beyond the king-stone. His eyes were like the autumn leaves of the stonewood tree, shining with a wild gleam that yearned for freedom.

Then it was gone.

He was gone.

"Go in peace," Penhallow said.

"By earth," Anearn said

"By sun," Ruthin said.

"By moon," Katha said.

Their voices echoed and rang in the henge, twisting together to form one voice. Puretongue called up a rune and freed it into the air.

"We will come to you," he said.

Silence fell upon the henge. A silence unlike the deep quiet of a taw. It was a natural silence, filled with insect sound and wind sound and the breathing of the seven who were present. Carrie drew back from the kingstone. There was a deepness in her taw now that made her tremble, a strength that seemed to have no end.

"What...what does...what did it mean?" she asked.

"It means we go," Puretongue said. "Tonight. We go to Ardmeyn where the Everwinter lies and seek the heights of Taynbell Peak."

"Was he really here?"

"Aye, Carwyn. You called him; the Oracle showed him to us."

Carrie reached her hand out to Deren and he clasped it. His eye was wide with wonder, but for all his awe he squeezed her hand and offered what comfort he could. For Carrie felt like bolting. She wanted to run and run, to hide someplace where she could never be found— not by stormkin, by the Summerlord, by anyone. The enormity of the power that had touched her left her shaken.

"We were told," Katha said, "that there could be hope. 'Let the Summerlord's staff be restored. Let magics swell across the Green Isles once more. Let silence speak and the oldest tune of all will mend all our hurts.'" She turned to Carrie. "And see? Magic *does* swell. Silence has spoken—not once, but several times. Now there is only the staff."

"In Ardmeyn," Penhallow said, then he translated the name from the old tongue to the common. "'The Land of Ever Stone.' That is where the staff is. How can it be otherwise? You have but to find it, Carwyn Lorweir."

They were all mad, Carrie realized. *She* was supposed to find it? When all of Lothan's armies had already looked for it and the Summerlord in that same land? After it had been broken and its pieces scattered? How could she find them all?

Panic edged into her, for all the calmness that the henge offered, for all the power with which it had filled her. But Deren's hand was a firm anchor to reality. They were both a part of this thing, and she wouldn't have to go alone. Frightened though she was to the depths of her soul, she found some comfort in that. She held onto Deren's hand as though to lose contact with him was to lose that part of her that was herself, that part that wasn't caught up in otherworldly magics.

"I'll help you," Deren said.

At that moment, he shared her fears and understood exactly what she felt. He remembered Gullysbrow and his loneliness. Puretongue had been there for him. He would do the same for her.

"I'll help you," he repeated.

"You already have," she said.

∼⌢⌢∼

A FEW HOURS later they left Pelamas Henge—three hawks winging their way north to where the Everwinter raged. They went swiftly and sure, traveling faster than true hawks might, and though game was plenty in the woods and hills below, never once did they stop to hunt. Something in Ardmeyn—perhaps the stone on Taynbell Peak, Carrie thought—drew them straight as an arrow's flight.

Twentieth

HE TINKERS SPENT THE night in the woods near Keddlenowe, arriving at the town well before noon the following day. They found the streets crowded with folk of every manner and description. There were merchants and farmers and smiths, hawkers and goodwives, and prentices running errands for their masters. But for the most part, they were simple fisherfolk come from their crofts and holdings that rimmed the coasts from Yellfennie and northward to Leithaven, seeking refuge from the Saramand. The town guard had their hands full keeping order in such a gathering.

Long Tom steered the wagon through the crowded streets. As they inched their way towards the ferry, they heard a thousand gossips and rumours. The Saramand had taken the whole of the coasts of Cermyn and were moving inland. They attacked croft as well as town, fishing boat as well as merchant ships. The Cermyn lords had overthrown their king, tired of waiting for his protection. There were plagues in Fairnland—as sure sign of Dath's wrath, speak his name in praise.

And it that news wasn't bad enough—believe only the half of it— there was a darker undercurrent to which the tinkers and Benjamen listened with special concern. The world was ending, some said, for they'd seen death's reapers riding the hills—packs of giant wolves and manlike creatures that had known no mortal mother. Others told how the dhruides in Kellmidden were hosting a great army to attack the gathering of the kings in Traws. Mysterious Ardmeyn was covered with ice and snow—Dath's judgment against the strange land that refused to honour him. The Saramand had hired assassins to slay key figures in the towns and villages so that the folk would have no leaders to rally around. Babes were slain in their cradles, the hills had become evil, death rode the night winds...and on and on it went.

"It's madness," Long Tom muttered, listening to an old hag tell how dhruides had slain her neighbors—husband, wife and two children—then raised them from the dead to attack her. She'd been forced to flee to Keddlenowe with only her life, leaving cot and belongings behind.

"And it'll grow worse," Benjamen said. "They're frightened. They've met stormkin and can't understand what they've seen, so they tell these tales. They fear that Dath is punishing them for their sins. They..." He sighed and shook his head. "Who knows what they think. The world's turned so topsy-turvy I don't much know which way's up myself."

Long Tom nodded. "Where's that damned ferry?"

"Turn left up there by that smithy," Benjamen said. He looked out across the crowds, down the long street. "How far is Pelamas now?"

Megan answered him. "It's twelve-days easy faring to the Dales of Heatherby—that's with stops and all. Pelamas is another few days past that, but through hilly land."

"So a fortnight, then," Benjamen said. "But sooner, perhaps, if we buy another team. Then we can switch horses through the day and save—what? Half a week?"

Long Tom frowned. "Perhaps. If we could afford another team. And the horses would still need rest, and so would we. And we'll be looking for Carrie and Tarn along the way."

"They've reached Pelamas," Benjamen said. He answered the question in Long Tom's eyes with a shrug. "I can...feel it."

Long Tom regarded him for a long, considering moment before he nodded.

"Fair enough," he said. "Then we'll aim ourselves straight for Pelamas."

They reached the ferry as they spoke. While Long Tom bartered for their passage, Benjamen made enquiries for horse dealers across the river. When he rejoined the tinkers, he had the names of two men who lived in Fletten on the far side of the Tooming.

"I'll cover the cost," he said.

Long Tom accepted his generosity with gratitude. He had less in the way of trading goods at the moment than he did in the way of labour—mending and fixing and what not. But there was no time for such work now. They had to travel, and travel quickly. If Carrie and her wizard really *had* already reached Pelamas—

Broom and heather! He shook his head. For them to have gone all that distance, while the wagon had taken a day and a half to travel from Wenys Hollow to Keddlenowe...

"Wizardry," Benjamen said when Long Tom mentioned it to him. "Wizardry pure, though not so simple, I should think."

They waited an hour for the ferry to unload, then another twenty minutes while their wagon and a dozen or so other folk crowded on board with their horses and goods. But at last they were moving across the Tooming, the slow water sluggish against the ferry-barge's wide prow.

"It's too bad one of us isn't a wizard," Long Tom said to Benjamen as they watched Keddlenowe recede.

The peddler nodded. He looked ahead and watched the opposite bank approach. There were folk milling about on the docks there—refugees and other homeless folk. Their baggage was piled around them, their faces gaunt and strained with worry. Where was there room for them all?

And that was part of the problem, he thought. Rather than everyone banding together against the common foe, the Islanders let the Saramand cut them down village by village. *Then* they banded together, in their hopelessness and loss. When it was too late.

His gaze fell on a brown-robed man who was helping a woman with five children huddled around her skirts. The man looked up and when their gazes met, Benjamen had a thought.

"Go ahead to that first horse-trader," he told Long Tom, "and I'll meet you there."

The tinker gave him a quizzical look.

"There's a man I must talk to before we go," Benjamen explained. "The one in the brown robe—over there."

Long Tom glanced over. "Do you know him?"

"No."

"But then..?"

"It's about wizardry," Benjamen said.

Then the ferry-barge came to dock and he vaulted over its rail to stride off across the docks.

Long Tom started to call after him but the ferryman interrupted.

"Hey, you! Tinker! Move your wagon. There'll be time enough to daydream when you're ashore, but we've got work to do here. Now move it, man!"

Long Tom bit back a retort and spoke the horses into motion.

BENJAMEN WAITED until the man in the brown rove had finished comforting the woman and her children before he approached.

The man regarded him curiously. He gave Benjamen a weary smile. Calling a final reminder to the woman to keep her heart strong, he walked over to meet the peddler.

"Father," Benjamen said. "I must talk to you. I need your help."

"There are many who need help in times such as these," the man began, then he paused.

His eyes widened. Benjamen felt something brush across his thoughts and his own inner senses leapt out to greet this strange intrusion.

"I thought," the man said, "that all those with the green silence in them were dead or had fled. But your taw is strong, and here you are..."

Benjamen shook his head, not understanding what the man was talking about.

"I know you're a dhruide," he said. "A priest of Pelamas, and—"

The man cut him off. "Not so loud—not around here. If they know what I am, they'll never accept my help. Come, let us walk in the town and find a quiet place to speak. My name's Temen—and yours?"

"Benjamen. I'm a peddler."

"Well, Benjamen," Temen said in a soft voice, "surely you've heard the rumours and fears running on either side of the Tooming. My people do what we can, but the coming of the stormkin and their dark magics have shadowed folks' regard for us." He sighed. "But still, we do our best . Perhaps we use Dath's name, but we keep the High Lord strong in our hearts all the while."

Benjamen nodded, feeling more and more out of his depth. They walked in silence, and he began to have second thoughts. When they came to a town square, Temen led him to an out-of-the-way corner by a well and they sat down on the gently worn wall around it.

"Tell me how I can help," Temen said.

Benjamen took a moment to gather his thoughts. Although the town bordered on both sides of the Tooming, the river divided Cermyn from Umbria. So the south bank of the town was Keddlenowe, while the north was Fletten. Since the refugees were fleeing into Cermyn, Fletten was quieter. Benjamen watched the townsfolk go about their business. They were withdrawn for the most part, keeping to themselves, and the gossip stones—where a dozen goodwives could normally be found passing the time of day—were empty except for themselves.

The peddler sighed and began to speak. He kept his tale as simple as possible, and the priest listened without interrupting. Only when Benjamen was finished did Temen speak, and then it was to ask the same question that Benjamen had asked Long Tom.

"Why do you go? What is the maid to you?"

Benjamen shrugged. "Surely, father, you can understand why we want to help her."

"Yes, but if it's help you're offering, the folk here have much need of it. There is no need for you to go as far as Pelamas. So I ask again, why? What can you hope to accomplish? With such forces in motion— stormkin and their Icelord—what can you do?"

Benjamen looked for an answer. He saw then that it was the tinkers' need to help Carrie, not his. *He* wanted to strike back at the stormkin. He didn't want to be like the folk he'd seen back at the docks, fleeing danger, hoping that if they fled far enough, it would pass them by. But the forces ranked against them were vast and far beyond the strengths of a peddler and a family of tinkers.

When he thought—*really* thought—about what they were doing, a cold dark fear filled him. His courage went skittering into a dim corner of his mind, cowering there until he took a deep breath and forced it out once more. They might be able to do little against the Saramand and the strange creatures of the Icelord, but they would do what they could.

His gaze rose to meet Temen's and he found the priest watching him with sympathetic eyes.

"I..." Benjamen began. "We must..."

Temen shook his head. "There is no need for you to explain further, Benjamen. You sent your thoughts to me, and I see now what truly lies in your heart. I needed to learn that before I showed you this."

He drew a rough map of Umbria and Kellmidden in the dirt near the well, marking the coast road. Along it, at intervals, he made small X's.

"Have you followed the road north before?" he asked.

Benjamen nodded.

"Then you have seen the stone markers—small longstones, or sometimes, cairns along the way? Good. These are holy places, filled with power—the same power that resides in your taw, your inner silence. Do you know of what I speak?"

"I think so. I call them my 'inner senses.' They warn me of things or...I don't quite know how to put it. Sometimes they tell me things that I should do."

"Exactly," the priest said. "Those inner senses are the voice of your taw, and you taw is a reflection of the dwystaw, the deep green silence that lies at the heart of the Green Isles, which in turn is a reflection of the High Lord's soul—from which all magical power stems. To learn its use well requires study—not a few hours, but *years*. If you want to utilize your inner strengths to their fullest potential, I would recommend that you remain in Pelamas when you get there and study with my brothers."

"But I need something now."

"Yes. And I will give you something. Have you followed me so far?"

Benjamen nodded.

Temen smiled. "It's not so hard to learn, this thing that I mean to show you. But it will be wearying. Do you remember how your taw reached out to me on the dock?"

"I remember a feeling of…reaching out, yes. But I don't know how I did it."

"I will come back to that in a moment. Now what you will do when you travel is reach out with your taw and augment the horses' strengths with your own. They will go much farther, much more quickly, and without tiring from it. *You* will bear the brunt of the weariness. And that is where the holy places I have marked come in."

Benjamen followed Temen's finger as the priest pointed out the X's on the makeshift map.

"There, in those places, you can replenish the strengths you've used. The holy places are like reservoirs of power and anyone with the knowledge, and with the green silence of their taw, can draw on those reserves. It will still be difficult for you. There is not a great deal of power left in those stones now. Once, it was said, they were powerful enough to open doors into other worlds; but if that was so, the knowledge of such use is long gone. What you need to know at the moment is that you can't let yourself be stretched too thin, for there is only so much the stones can do for you. But they can help, *and* be used—even by one untrained as you."

Benjamen swallowed, wondering why he'd ever thought of talking to the priest in the first place. But then he remembered the stormkin coming for him that night, and he thought of the many folk who hadn't been as lucky as he had been, who hadn't been able to fight them off. His resolve hardened.

"And the…the reaching out?" he asked.

"Do it like so."

Suddenly Benjamen felt the priest's taw reach inside him. He drew back in fear, then tried to relax. He'd come looking for wizardly help. Should he turn coward now when the impossible was offered?

He concentrated on what Temen was showing him. When the priest withdrew from his mind, Benjamen reached out—tentatively, hesitant about this new ability. But there was something there, something that could be used. His taw. He pictured it in his mind as one of his own hands, fingered and thumbed, a little gnarled, the veins prominent, reaching out, until...

"I did it," he said, staring at Temen with a big grin.

"So you did. But take care to ease into the minds of your horses. They will be skittish and if you're not careful, you could run them from the road. And remember as well, they will still need to rest—and so will you. *Real* rest. But the reservoir stones will help."

Benjamen nodded, still delighted with his new skill . It was so simple. Why had he never seen it before?

Temen stood.

"I must go now," he said. "There's still much to do here. Give my greetings to Penhallow when you reach Pelamas Henge. He is our high priest."

"Thank you," Benjamen said, standing as well.

"For what? For showing you a part of yourself?" Temen smiled. "Do what you can to end this madness, and that will be thanks enough, Benjamen. Travel safely."

He turned and crossed the square, returning to the docks. Benjamen watched him go for long, thoughtful moments, then hurried off to where Long Tom would be waiting. He saw the wagon outside the horse-dealer's inn. Long Tom met him at the door. The tinker's face was a study of frustration.

"They want the world," he complained, "delivered up them on a silver platter. Broom and heather! Come hear their prices."

"There's no need," Benjamen said. "I've got something better than an extra team."

Then he explained what the priest had told him.

"Oh, aye?" Long Tom said, unable to hide the doubt from his voice. But then he grinned. "Well, why shouldn't we have our own magic, eh? Let's be off. We've wasted enough time in this place."

He called a word to Megan and she shook out the reins. Fenne and Kinn retreated into the wagon, making room for Benjamen and their father on the driver's seat. As the wagon clattered off, Megan turned to her husband.

"Well?" she asked. "What now?"

"Benjamen here," Long Tom said, "has found us some magic so we don't need the extra horses. Don't ask him to explain as it'll only make your head go dizzy as it did mine, but we'll be as much as flying all the way to the henge."

Megan sighed and gave the peddler a glance. He winked back at her.

"What did I do to deserve this?" she asked no one in particular. "Wasn't one of them bad enough? Now I've got two babes in the bodies of men. Bah!"

But she smiled back at the peddler.

They soon left the town behind, taking the High Walk that led from Fletten to the coast road.

BENJAMEN FELT rather than saw the wagon lurch to a stop. He bit back a gasp and opened his eyes. His every muscle ached and his vision blurred. The noon meal rumbled in his stomach.

"Where..?" he got out in a croak.

Long Tom's arm was around his shoulders.

"We've come to the first of those stones you talked about," the tinker said in a quiet voice. He studied Benjamen's pinched white features. "Ballan, man. You're pushing it too hard. Ease back a bit."

Benjamen shook his head. Even that small movement seemed an effort.

"No," he said. "I'm fine. It's just...harder than I thought it would be."

His head ached as though a blacksmith was using it for an anvil.

"Have we...have we come far?" he added.

"Far and fast," Long Tom assured him. "And look at the horses. They're as fresh as when we left camp this morning."

He could feel the peddler trembling under his arm.

"Benjamen," he said. "Are you all right?"

"The stone. Help me to...to the stone."

Long Tom jumped to the ground. Easing Benjamen from the seat, he half-carried him to the stone and helped the peddler lean against it. Then he stood back, shaking his head.

This was a stone like hundreds, up and down the roads of the Green Isles. Were they all places of power?

Perhaps, perhaps not, he thought. But *this* one certainly was.

Benjamen's breathing evened out and his cheeks regained a healthy flush.

Long Tom shook his head again and returned to the wagon. The horses *did* seem fresh for all the long miles they'd traveled today. At this rate—Ballan! They'd be in Wickenfirlie before week's end. If Benjamen could keep it up until then. Long Tom frowned. They needed to reach Pelamas Henge as quickly as possible, but was it worth the use of magic to do so? He wondered, too, whether the use of magic would draw stormkin to them. Didn't like call to like? Power, then, to power?

A heavy sigh escaped him. He didn't want to think of confronting a pack of stormkin without Tarn's help. When he looked over to Benjamen, the peddler was standing, though he still leaned on the stone.

"It's a marvel," Benjamen said in a stronger voice. "It really does work. You know, when all this is said and done, perhaps I'll take that priest's advice and see what I might learn staying on in Pelamas."

"Are you well?" Long Tom asked.

"I'm better. I've still an ache in my head, but even that's fading. Let's rest here an hour or so and then go on. Dath, but I'm hungry."

Long Tom smiled.

"I'll get a fire going," he said.

Twenty-First

FERGUN STARED ABOUT THE empty barrow. Things were not going well. The Summerlord's essence persisted in floating just beyond his reach like some will-o'-the-wisp—present, but never tangible. So now, with his legions scouring above ground, he brought his own search down into the hidden halls and holdings of the erlkin and Tus, the remnants of those races who had once ruled the Green Isles, from north to south and east to west.

They fled before him. Many died, but many more escaped. Some fled above ground and died of exposure, or were slain by his prowling stormkin. Others went deeper into the hidden earth ways. And though Fergun continued his search through their smoky halls of earth and stone, he knew it was futile. These ragged folk had nothing. Their power was a weak and fragile memory. He could taste the Summerlord—Hafarl was that close—but Fergun knew he wouldn't find him in these dark, underground places.

Still , he couldn't remain idle, and neither could his troops. The stormkin he'd brought to Ardmeyn grew restless, and without the searches and patrols he sent them upon, they would have turned on each other long ago. But until word came from Galag, he had to keep them here—here, where the Summerlord's presence was strongest, for all that the Everwinter gripped the island from shore to shore.

He knew the end was approaching quickly now. The weavers wove their threads in an ever-tightening spiral. It would be soon. He could feel it coming in the land, in the sky, and in his own dark heart. Let the priests of Kellmidden raise the last of their broken powers. How could they hope to be strong when the very source of their strength, the Summerlord, was no more than a refugee himself?

The priests would persevere. They would struggle on even when the Everwinter came down from Ardmeyn and buried them in a storm of ice and snow such as the Isles had never seen. And then they would die and the Isles would be green no more. They would be White Isles and—heart and soul—they would belong to Lothan, a twin holding to the ice realm of Damadar.

But first they must bring the Summerlord to bay. While he lived, hope lived, and that was dangerous to all Lothan planned.

How Hafarl found the strength to stay just beyond their clutches, Fergun couldn't begin to guess. His power was halved, and halved again with the loss of Meynbos, his stonewood staff. He fought a losing battle. Soon Lothan would come down from Damadar himself to oversee his brother's final defeat. And then Fergun, the last of the Captains, would have a kingdom of his own to rule, though it be in the Icelord's name. The White Isles would be *his*.

Fergun smiled without humour. He knew it wouldn't end there, not when he knew the winter that stormed so bleakly in his lord's cold heart. Lothan would bring the Everwinter across the Grey Sea next, to strike into the homeland of the Saramand and beyond. There was no end to his appetite. In time, he would strike against his sister's realm as well and Morennen's rule, the great seas themselves, would lie frozen .

But first there was the Summerlord. It always came back to him. Why did Hafarl wait? Where would he make his final stand? If he waited for the miserly few Summerborn that still breathed, then he would wait forever. He would wait, hiding in some icy hole in Ardmeyn until Fergun dragged him forth and delivered him to Lothan. For those last few Summerborn would soon be dead. Galag would be bringing him their heads.

Soon now.

Galag would come.

But why did he take so long?

THEY CAME with the night that followed Puretongue's departure from Pelamas Henge, a horde of stormkin. Skes and dyorn, frost giants, traals, direwolves and frosts. They were drawn by the stink of green magic and the Summerborn. Hoarfrost grew thick around the henge. In the rath where the priests lived, the wood creaked and groaned, the stone foundations cracked. The priests sallied forth to meet them, their laws bright and glimmering in the darkness, their power a deadly thing.

But there were too many stormkin. Galag led them, howling and screaming, in a great wave that could not be stopped. The priests did their best. They pushed them back, here, for a moment, there, for another, but in the end it was a flood that could not be stemmed.

The priests were cut off from the henge. Skes blades flashed silver in the moonlight and the blood of the High Lord's priests sprayed the ground. Their flesh froze at the touch of the frosts. Dyorn spells cancelled their own. Frost giants and traals crushed them. Direwolves ravaged them. And the priests, who were powerful, but not many, fell.

The younger priests died first. They were newer to their strength and knew peace better than war, knew shapes of gentleness better than shapes that could deal death.

Then the older ones fell.

Ruthin was torn apart by direwolves, the silver blade of a slain skes sprouting from his back as he lashed about.

Anearn took the shape of a great bear, but his magics killed only a half of the frosts that attacked him. A great stone traal took the brunt of the priests ebbing power, then squeezed the life from him while the direwolves tore at his flesh.

And Katha, gentle Katha...she died, too. Galag himself tore her heart from her breast and threw it high into the air, caught it and swallowed it while it was still beating.

Then only Penhallow remained.

Compared to Puretongue, he was young, but he was still older than any living man. His heart broke as he saw his children fall, one by one. Then rage gave him the strength to work a final great magic. He wore the dragonshape, the shape that the stormkin feared above all others. But though he killed great numbers of them, even that shape was not enough.

The horde tore him to pieces.

At length silence lay across the rath of the priests of Pelamas, a silence that was broken only by the crack of bones as the direwolves fed. Galag gathered his army. Some he left to guard the henge that they were unable to enter. But they would stop others from taking advantage of its strengths. Others he sent on the trail of a Summerborn with the scent of a skes. That trail led east and north. The remainder he gathered around himself for the final journey into Ardmeyn where Fergun waited for them, where the Summerlord hid, to which the last of the Summerborn had fled.

They left the ruin of the rath behind them and fared north. When they came to villages and farm holdings in Wickenfirlie, they paused long enough to kill, and then kill some more, before faring onward. Umbria had felt their sting. Now Kellmidden knew the cruel hand of Lothan's army as they squeezed the life from its people.

And all the while, the weavers wove.

Part Three:

Finishing the Cloth

Seasons they change while cold blood is raining
I had been waiting beyond the years...

—Robin Williamson,
from "The Circle is Unbroken"

First

THEY FARED ACROSS WICKENFIRLIE, Puretongue, Deren and Carrie, three brown-grey hawks in Kellmidden's clear skies. The green hills and dales unwound below them. The contours of the land changed slowly, from the low, outriding foothills that rimmed the Ramshorn Mountains into the flatter lowlands that bordered either bank of the Narrow. The small dots of shepherds' cots and lonely steadings swelled into the clusters of stone and wood buildings that made up Kellmidden's northernmost towns.

By noon they were over the Werewood, a strange dark old forest that crouched for twenty leagues along both banks of the Narrow. Puretongue called a halt there and made them rest in their own shapes for a few hours. He did it not so much to conserve their strength—for the power of Pelamas still coursed through each of them—but to remind his novice companions that they were mortal man and woman, not creatures of the air. The dhruide knew all too well what the prolonged use of a borrowed shape could do those new to their magics.

"But I spent longer as a direwolf," Carrie complained.

"Aye," Puretongue replied.

He thought of his Tarn, and how much his son had known of shapes and shaping. And now the young swanmage was changing...changed.

"So you did, Carrie," he went on. "But we'll rest here all the same."

Carrie sighed when she saw that the dhruide wouldn't be swayed. But then she thought of Tarn as well.

Tarn as the skes San Ko. Tarn whose eyes had gone cold...who changed...who would have killed the peddler...who'd struck her...

All that was true, but at the same time there was an emptiness inside her that Tarn's companionship had filled. She was surprised at how much she missed him. And knowing that he was in danger...

But their paths had split and there was nothing she could do now except carry on and fret under Puretongue's stern silence.

"It's hard," she whispered to Deren who was sitting beside her. "He treats us like little children."

"And to him," Deren said, "are we much more than that?"

Carrie followed his gaze to where the dhruide stood hunched against a tree, his shoulders stooped. He stared into invisible distances deep within himself. The oak towering over him was old, very old, but he seemed older still.

"All the spells and magics," Deren added. "What do we really know of them?"

"Little enough, I suppose. But still..."

"I know. It's hard." Deren laid his hand on her arm. "But don't forget, Carrie. He's not so different from us in one way. He's lost someone, too."

"Tarn?"

Deren nodded.

They flew above the Werewood all that long afternoon, resting on the south bank of the Narrow late in the day. After an hour or so, Puretongue spoke new names and they were in the air again, feathered once more as they crossed the strait—three snow owls with wings gleaming white in the light of the sinking sun. They sped north, flying high as the wind, and the far shores of Ardmeyn grew near with the dusk.

Frost glinted on the beaches, and in the twilight they saw the endless fields of ice and snow spreading north for as far as their keen eyes could see. The air grew sharp with the cold. The winds bit deep. The cold entered bone-marrow and heart, chilling, relentless, unforgiving.

Carrie's will drained away and she had to fight to continue. It wasn't the cold or the wind that worked against her, but the sheer immensity of the power ranged against them. Seeing the Everwinter upon Ardmeyn, the endless white hills, there seemed to be no point in going on. This was what they were up against? A power that could lay waste to an entire land?

Fergun's presence, his power, sucked the will out of her.

If she'd had tongue and throat to shape words, she would have cried out her protest to Puretongue. But she could neither protest nor be comforted while Ardmeyn, frozen Ardmeyn, drew ever nearer. The Captain's presence thickened in the air. Carrie choked on his power. The Everwinter stole her strength. She saw Deren faltering as well. But Puretongue flew on, borne by the iron of his will, and they could only follow.

And then they were struck from another quarter.

Agony cut across Carrie's taw. Her inner silence rang with the cries of dead and dying. She dropped from the sky, her soul shaken by the discharge of power that rocked her senses. Shuddering, she fought to regain control. She lifted skyward, but the terror grew only stronger. The steady sweep of her wings faltered again, and the cold waste that was Ardmeyn came rushing up at her.

She fought to control her fall. Her wings lost their shape, misted, grew solid, lost their shape once more. She fell the last dozen feet in her own body. Her head was filled with images of Pelamas Henge and its rath nearby. She saw the priests dying and the stormkin, their presence was like an icy hand clutching her heart as they slew, and slew...

Carrie!

Puretongue's mental cry cut through her confusion like a sharp knife, drawing her back from the vision that had become too real. She drew a long, laboured and rasping breath, spreading her arms as though they were still wings, and struck a towering drift. The snow seemed to reach out and drag her into its cold embrace. She choked on it, breathing in a mouthful. Darkness welled up in front of her eyes—a swirling that had no end. Then she was clawing her way to the surface of the drift.

She looked around to find the others. Deren was hunched over in the snow, cradling his arm. And Puretongue…the dhruide lay in the snow like a small stick figure, broken and black against the white ground Then he lifted his head and she saw the tears freezing on his cheeks, and she knew there were frozen tears on her own.

"Puretongue?" she whispered. "What…what was that? I feel so empty…"

But she didn't need an answer. She already knew. The vision returned to her—the priests dying, the stormkin howling their victory.

Puretongue pulled himself erect and shuddered. He opened his mouth to speak, but the words caught in his throat.

"Puretongue?" Carrie cried.

Panic made her voice brittle.

"Dead," he said. His eyes were bleak, unseeing, his voice a husky rasp. "All dead. Penhallow, Katha…all of them dead!"

The dhruide lashed out blindly in his anger. Deren fell under the onslaught of the tree-wizard's grief. It seared Carrie's taw, but something inside her rose up to confront it—something strong and steadying. It sang the silence that was like music, deep and slow, stately and calm. When it touched Puretongue, his eyes cleared and he gave her a strange look. His anger drained away and he was ashamed.

"That power…" he said with wonder in his voice.

He stared at Carrie and for a moment he looked into eyes deeper and older than his own. There were a hundred autumn shades in that gaze, blinding him, binding him. He tore his gaze away, stumbling to where Deren lay, and held the boy's face in his hands.

"I…I'm alright," Deren mumbled.

"I never meant…." Puretongue began.

His gaze returned to Carrie, wanting to explain to both of them, and saw that she was changed again. The power that had been in her, that had calmed him, was gone. He saw only the girl, thin and shivering in the cold, watching him with frightened eyes.

"Fairlord," Puretongue murmured and shaped the Sign of Horns.

He helped Deren to his feet and reached out to Carrie, drawing them both to him. His heart drummed a quick tattoo as he relived the past few moments. He'd almost killed them both with his blind anger—he *would* have killed them, except for that sudden strength of Carrie's, strength and calm that was an unyielding power one moment, gone the next.

Holding her against him, he could feel her trembling. Deren was shivering, too. They needed new shapes, fur against the cold. Taynbell was still a good distance away and—

He paused, stiffening.

Deren and Carrie drew away from him, fear tensing in their eyes. Then they saw that the dhruide wasn't renewing his mad attack on them. He was listening and his old features grew older still, heavy and deep-lined with worry and sorrow.

"So soon?" he said.

"What is it?" Deren asked.

"Fergun," Puretongue replied. His voice was cold and hard now. "The Captain has discovered our presence and is coming for us."

For a long moment the dhruide felt only helplessness. Sorrow washed through him. For the folk of Pelamas, his friends...Penhallow. All of them gone. For Tarn, driven away. For Deren and Carrie who must go on alone. Then he drew on the depths of his taw and took the raw power he needed from his inner silence.

Fergun was coming.

His brother Fergun.

But he would find something other than Summerborn waiting for him.

He turned to his young companions.

"I will give you names," he said. "Names to take fur shapes and feathered. You must go on alone. I will confront Fergun and follow if I can."

"But—" Deren began.

"It's too late for anything else, Deren. Listen to these names. Remember them. But above all, remember your own name, your own shape. Lose that and, Everwinter or no, you'll have lost to the Icelord."

Puretongue regarded the two of them, reading the fear and confusion in their faces. Then Deren straightened his back and stepped forward.

"Give us the names," he said.

His one eye gleamed with the strength of his will. His bruised arm hung at his side, the pain ignored. Puretongue smiled to hear the iron in his young ward's voice. Who would have guessed that he'd find one such as Deren when he went searching for the Summerlord in Gwendellan? But the weavers wove, and the threads drew tighter, day by day.

He gave them the names for the shapes they would need—of fur, white wolf and arctic bear; of feather, hawk and snow owl; and one shape of water, a seal's, in case they would need it in this frozen realm. He laid a hand on each of their brows and sensed their pulses quicken.

"The High Lord be with you," he murmured, shaping the Sign of Horns. "Now go. Taynbell lies north and east of here. Even in this waster, you won't mistake it."

Deren and Carrie stepped back and eyed each other. When Deren nodded, Carrie raised her taw and hesitantly spoke a name. For a moment her form held, then it shimmered, furred, and a white wolf watched Deren and the dhruide.

"I'll miss you," Deren said. "You gave me back my life in Gullysbrow—not just by healing my body, but by healing the hurt inside me. For that, for the green silence you showed me..."

"You talk as though we're parting forever," Puretongue said in a soft voice.

Tears froze in Deren's eye.

"Folk like you," he said, his voice husky, "they come but once into the lives of folk like me. But strange though my life's become, I don't regret a day that was spent with you."

"Deren..."

"We'll go now. I'll take care of Carrie as best I can, as she'll do for me. We'll go on to Taynbell Peak, though what we'll do when we get there..."

He shrugged helplessly, then stepped forward to embrace the dhruide.

"You'll be alright?" he asked as he stepped back.

Puretongue nodded. He lifted his head. His clear blue eyes sparkled bird-bright. He appeared to gain in stature, growing from a slender, brittle twig of an old man into a tree of power. A tree-wizard. A dhruide.

"Then we'll go," Deren said.

He closed his eye, brows furrowing, and raised his taw. It responded swift and easily now. He spoke one of the names Puretongue had given them.

"Go with light," the tree-wizard said. "Moon and Horn be with you."

The two wolves nodded white-furred heads, then departed. The slender one that was Carrie held her pace to that of the one-eyed wolf beside her who favoured one paw. Puretongue watched them go with a heavy heart.

He didn't like sending them on alone. Not with Deren's power blossoming with such promise. Not with the riddle of Carrie's strange reservoirs of strength still unanswered. And they would need him on this last leg of the trek to Taynbell. But Fergun was coming. Lothan's Captain was coming. He had to be stopped here—without Deren and Carrie near to die with him if he should fail.

"Come then, brother," he said in a quiet voice. "It's time the weavers wove the end of our tale."

FURTHER NORTH, Fergun heard him.

Night lay thick around the Captain, a black-cloaked figure standing stark against the white, drinking down darkness. But the darkness was in his soul for the night skies were thick with stars and their light set the frozen hills to gleaming. Ice and snow and frost, league upon league, for as far as the eye could see. The darkness that lay inside was more to his liking.

He had felt the priests of Pelamas die, and he had smiled. Until in the middle of that sending from afar, another vision had come into his mind. Summerborn. Here in Ardmeyn. Summerborn and something else. Something that challenged him.

His smile widened into a grin.

He raised his dark taw, savouring the rush of power that filled him. He took a shape—a shape of winged ice—and called three dyorn to rise and follow him. They lifted into the air and their deepsight reached out across the frozen wastes to find the one that challenged him.

He was alone now, his Summerborn companions fled, leaving him to face them by himself. A dhruide. He wore an eagle's shape in the crisp night air above Ardmeyn and winged north to meet them.

Over frozen hills and frost-withered hills, he came.

They beat their dark wings, slow and steady in the frosty air, and went to meet him. Laughter trailed along behind them.

They did not intend to deny the tree-wizard a death at their talons.

Second

T HE TURPENS' WAGON RATTLED down the coast road. The horses, strengthened by Benjamen's newly-learned magics, were still strong and seemed prepared to travel forever, for all that a long day was behind them and the night had come. The miles disappeared under hoof and wheel, and now they were no more than half the distance to Leithaven, having left the High Walk and the Tooming River far behind. Benjamen sat white-faced between Megan and Long Tom, his eyes firmly shut, his brow wrinkled in concentration. He was beyond weary, for all that they stopped at the longstones and cairns along the way to replenish his depleting strengths.

When the shadows of the roadside trees grew long and dark, Long Tom sighed and spoke: "It's getting late, Benjamen. Time we were resting for the night."

"A bit further," the peddler replied through clenched teeth. He opened his eyes. "Surely there's enough light?"

"Oh, aye. And we could drive through the whole of the night, too, were it the light alone that concerned us. The stars'll be bright and the road's in good repair. It's ourselves that I'm worrying about. And you, man. Broom and heather! You need to give it a rest."

"You've done enough for one day," Megan added in a gentle voice.

Benjamen nodded in agreement. He was about to speak, but then his eyes rolled wildly in his head. He clutched the railing with a viselike grip. Whatever he'd been about to say choked in his throat.

"Ballan!" Long Tom cried.

He began to pass the reins to Megan so that he could give the peddler a hand when the horses went mad. They reared in their harnesses, then broke into a run. The wagon tilted askew. Long Tom hauled back on the reins with one hand while he scrambled for the brake with his other. Benjamen fell forward and would have dropped under the horses' hooves if Megan hadn't grabbed him by the shirt and pulled him back. Long Tom put his weight on the brake lever and sawed back on the reins. The wagon rocked back and forth as it sped down the road. The horses fought Long Tom's control and he knew that to save the wagon he had to act quickly.

"Take the reins!" he cried to Megan.

She propped the peddler up in his seat and called to the children. Kinn grabbed Benjamen by the scruff of his shirt and held tight while his mother took the reins. Long Tom whipped a knife from his belt and slashed at the horses' harnesses, leaping onto the back of the leftmost one when the leather gave way. Still bound together, they bore him far ahead of the wagon, mouths frothing, sides heaving, hooves pounding the road below.

Behind, Megan fought the brake lever now and was able to stop the wagon as it slewed towards the side of the road. It dipped against a small incline on the roadside, then was brought up short against a stand of gnarled hawthorn brush. She lost her grip and went flying into the bushes, arms held up in front of her face to save her eyes from the sharp branches. She landed, stunned but relatively unhurt, the breath knocked from her.

"Mum!"

Fenne dropped from the wagon and ran to her mother.

"I'll live, lass, praise the heather luck for it's not left me yet."

She sat up gingerly, shaking her head. Her forearms were scratched and raw.

"But your dad?" she asked. "And the others?"

They looked back at the wagon. Benjamen had taken a crack on the head and Kinn was propping him up in the seat again. They heard the clop of hooves and saw Long Tom coming down the road, leading the horses back. The animals were still skittish and the tinker's knuckles were white with the force needed to hold them quiet.

"Tom?"

"They'll be fine, Meg—at least I hope they will."

He tied them to the rear of the wagon and began rubbing them down with handfuls of grass, speaking soothingly all the while.

"They fought me for a hundred yards, then gave up the fight so quickly I was nearly thrown from my perch."

"What happened, Dad?" Fenne asked.

Long Tom shrugged and looked over to where Fenne was leading her mother back to the wagon. The tinker dropped his handful of grass and ran to them when he saw Megan.

"Broom and heather! Are you hurt?"

He took her in his arms, horses and wagon forgotten.

"They're scratches, Tom, and no more."

"Thank the heather for that."

"Aye. Fenne can put some salve on them and they'll heal quickly enough. But how's the peddler?"

"He's coming around," Kinn called over to them.

He gathered Benjamen in his arms and laid him down in the grass by the roadside as the other tinkers gathered around him.

"That's a nasty crack he's taken," Long Tom said. He knelt by the peddler. "How're you feeling, old man?"

Benjamen's eyelids fluttered. When he opened his eyes there was such anguish in them that Long Tom drew back.

"Dead," the peddler said. "They're all dead. I...I felt them die... each one of them..."

"Who's dead, man?"

A cold hand of fear brushed Long Tom's spine. Oh Carrie, he thought. Don't be gone now, just when we're coming for you.

"The...the priests of Pelamas..."

"And Carrie?" Long Tom demanded.

Benjamen started at the tinker's rough tone of voice.

"What of Carrie?" Megan asked, her voice gentler. "And her wee wizard?"

"They...she's gone."

"Dead?"

"No." Benjamen frowned, trying to concentrate. "They've gone on...into winter."

"The Everwinter," Long Tom said, remembering the talk in Keddlenowe. "They've gone into Ardmeyn. Damn! How can we ever hope to catch up with them when they've wizardry to spell them wherever they want?"

He stood up and looked away to the north, brow lined with thought.

"What now, Dad?" Kinn asked.

"We go on," Long Tom replied. "Ballan, what else can we do? But we'll camp here for the night."

"I'M SORRY," Benjamen began later.

They were sitting around the campfire. Long Tom and Kinn were mending the cut harness, planning how they'd pull the wagon back onto the road in the morning. The peddler had a white bandage around his head. Megan's cuts had all been cleaned and rubbed with morningmoon, and the various bumps and bruises of the rest of the family had been looked after.

"It wasn't your fault, man," Long Tom said. "But I've been thinking. Tomorrow—let's leave the travelling to natural means. It'll be slower going, but safer, too. That's my thought."

Benjamen shook his head, wincing at the ache that the motion sent through him.

"I'm prepared now," he said. "If it...if something like it should happen again, I know enough now to cut off my contact with the horses."

"I don't know..."

"Long Tom, what else can we do? Do you want to plod along and be too late to help anyone?"

"I'm beginning to wonder what use we'll be anyway," the tinker replied.

"You're thinking of giving up?"

"No." Long Tom frowned. "But they're always one step ahead of us, and Ballan! Their steps…they're like a league to an honest man's pace."

Megan put a hand on his knee. Setting aside the harness he was working on, he drew her close.

"What do you think, Meg?" he asked. "What should we do?"

"Go on," she replied. "And if…if they use their wizardry, it seems that we can only use what magic we've got to keep up as best we're able."

"I'll keep a close watch," Benjamen added. "Believe me. But we've got to go on. We're not much, maybe not compared to the stormkin and all their power—but I feel we'll be needed still."

Long Tom frowned, but finally nodded.

"Aye," he said. "I suppose so."

He was thinking of the power ranged against them. But he had the same feeling. They would be needed; they *were* needed. Still, seeing Megan hurt—no matter that they were only scratches—reminded him all too much of the danger into which he was leading his family. What had happened today had only been the result of some kind of aftershock—some wizardly reaching across the miles to touch them. What would they do when they faced the stormkin face-to-face? What then? But Megan and the children would never let themselves be left behind and knew he knew he had to go on.

He hugged Megan again, then went back to working on the harnesses. Kinn set aside his now-finished piece and went into the wagon, motioning Fenne to follow. A few moments later, as Long Tom worked on the leather, he heard the plunk of Kinn tuning his strings and the sound of the bow drawing a long note from the fiddle. Long Tom smiled at Megan as the pair of them returned to the fire. Kinn woke an old dance tune while Fenne's cittern dropped a waterfall of accompanying notes behind the melody.

There was always this, Long Tom thought. No matter the danger, we travel together.

He returned to his task, his fingers fairly flying over the leather as he braided the straps back together, one booted foot tapping rhythm on a stone by the fire.

Aye, they had this. And no matter what else came, they would always have these moments to remember.

They would go on. For Carrie was somewhere ahead and she needed them. She had no family except for them. So they'd go ahead, and bedamned to anyone who stood in their way.

Third

WHEN TARN ESCAPED FROM Puretongue, he let the forest swallow his skes shape, determined to escape the confusion inside him by running it into exhaustion. But Puretongue's revelations rose time and time again, swirling through his head, leaving his thoughts to spin helplessly in an endless circle.

Puretongue—the dhruide. The Founder of Tree Wizardry.

How could he be the lost Captain Stest?

How could he be Tarn's own father?

He ran harder, legs pounding the ground in a very un-skes-like fashion, eyes staring blindly into unseen distances, until he finally tripped over a deadfall and went sprawling. Brought up short, he lay on the ground and stared up into the interweave of the forest's canopy.

He should have told me before, Tarn thought. He had no right to keep the knowledge from me—not when he knew how badly I needed to know.

Puretongue.

His father.

As the Icelord was Puretongue's father.

Which made Lothan his own grandfather.

Tarn shivered as the full implication of that sunk in. It meant that the skes mind he'd sensed growing inside was not a result of the lost control over his shapechanging. It was worse. The skes mind was a part of him, a part of his tainted blood. Balanced, perhaps, by his mother's blood, but the taint was still there.

He tried to imagine her. Tarasen, the Summerlord's daughter. Was she honey-haired, or dark like himself? Was she tall or short? What would she have thought of him, her son with his tainted blood? Would she still have loved him? She'd loved Puretongue, for all the secret of his own dark lineage. But Puretongue was strong, while Tarn was flawed.

He raised his taw to find the cracks in his silence and found a web-work of shadow threads that led to a deeper darkness far inside him. He followed those threads to their source and the darkness closed around him, stilling the silence that was like music. All warmth fled. Cold frosted his heart. The shadow he'd named San Ko rose dark and strong. For a long moment Tarn hovered on a brink, caught between darkness and light, deep warmth and cold power.

He tried to fight the pull of the dark other-mind , but the shadows fell over him in waves until he lost himself in their blackness. His autumn leaf eyes darkened, their warmth fled. He stared out at the world with cold, dark eyes and the change was complete. The skes San Ko stood and drew his dark taw around himself like a cloak. The sun that came through the leaves above bothered his eyes so he took himself to the forest's deepest shadowed places, moving liquidly amongst them, a shadow himself.

The weight of the sword on his back, the sword in its lacquered wooden sheath, comforted him. Dimly he remembered that he'd been someone else once.

But there are many shapes, said the darkness inside. No matter what shape you were born to, no matter how many shapes you have worn, in the end you are only the shape that you wear now.

So he was a skes. San Ko. And his blade was unblooded.

That brought him up short.

He whispered the sword from its sheath and stared thoughtfully at the curved length of its blade. Unblooded. He imagined the sword cutting flesh, the blood-runnel red with blood.

That must be done, the darkness told him, and then the blade had to be named. You are now a shadow of Lothan. But you are incomplete. Your blade is unblooded. Unnamed. It shames you.

San Ko sat on his heels, the sword laid across his knees. He listened to that voice, his fingers wrapped around the sword's hilt.

Nameless. And it must be blooded. Whose blood would it drink first?

The reply came hissing up from the depths of the darkness inside him.

Summerborn, it said. It must taste the blood of the Summerborn.

San Ko nodded. Amber and gold glimmers rippled through his taw, but he blackened them. He heard a faint distant drumming, but he ignored it. His senses were wire-taut. He could feel the forest draw in around him, the trees closing, the leaves blanketing him. He held his hand out in front of his eyes, looking for a tell-tale tremble. There was none.

Then suddenly he was on his feet, blade whirling in shining arcs as he fenced with the air. His limbs blurred as he pushed himself to the limits of his skill, then demanded more. He went into a roll, came up striking, side-stepped, his sword weaving an intricate pattern, in front of, behind, on either side of himself. Only when all of his attention was narrowed to concentrate solely on what he was doing did he pause. The sword flashed once more as he sheathed it.

Unblooded. Nameless

As the hilt clicked against the wooden end of the sheath, he bowed his head, his arms limp at his sides. He drew his taw around him again—dark and shadowed.

He would go north.

Through the night he sped. He wore many shapes as he moved across Wickenfirlie. Dark-winged and quick, he rode the winds north of the Ramshorn Mountains. Across the moors and low-backed hills, he was a black unicorn running arrow-straight, the sunlight gleaming on his ebony flanks, black hooves cutting the earth. Then he was a frost with the hoarfrost crackling under every step. A black swan winging soundlessly through the night skies.

He spun and shimmered through the shapes, naming and wearing a bewildering array of fabulous beings and beasts, taking shapes for the simple sake of taking them. Fed by the dark power of his skes taw, there was no cost—except that each shape drew him farther away from the being he had once been.

As morning greyed the sky, he was a skes again, gliding north on soundless feet, the weight of a nameless sword on his back. The dark taw spoke to him as he travelled—cajoling, sibilant, unceasing. And he listened. The voice told him of the honour of the skes, how they were the elite of the stormkin, Lothan's beloved. Winter was in their souls and for that the Icelord loved them best of all. And for one who came before him with the blood of true Summerborn naming his blade— what would be denied him?

He came to a menhir standing tall and alone on its hill. The sunlight gleamed on its grey height and for a moment San Ko thought he heard a voice in the stone call out to him, but his dark taw spoke louder and then he was no longer certain that he'd heard anything. He gave the longstone a wide berth and hurried on.

Afternoon shredded into dusk. Uneasiness crawled through San Ko as the twilight deepened. He paused to look back the way he'd come. The long hills appeared empty for league upon league. No one was following him, but the sensation that there was something just put of sight, watching him, remained. The voice in his dark taw grew louder once more. He silenced it, suddenly irritated. Then he listened to the deep quiet that followed and heard the unseen distances speak.

The dusk was deep now, blackening into night. Not really sure why he was doing it, San Ko opened himself to the distance. He let his deepsight reach across the leagues. His spirit read the voices that the wind carried. His uneasiness grew. He sensed a great golden power, rich and earthy, beset by shadows. Cold shadows. Stormkin.

Revulsion spread through him until he remembered.

He was a skes. *He* was a stormkin.

Then his legs buckled under him and he fell to his knees. He bowed his head until it touched the ground and let his mind fill with the vision that his deepsight brought him.

It came from Pelamas Henge, across the long leagues he'd travelled. He saw the priests die near their henge, felt them die as though he wore their bodies, felt the glee of the stormkin as they slew and slew and slew again, and it sickened him. He quivered and trembled, his body flickering from shape to shape. With each priest's death, a deeper despair knifed through him. He moaned and the skes shape returned to him.

Superimposed upon the vision of the dying priests came another vision—a future, a weaving of the weavers that had still to happen. He saw the skes San Ko grow tall and terrible with his power, vying with Lothan's Captain for the position at the Icelord's right hand. Each of them worked a deed more foul than the other's to win Lothan's approval. San Ko saw himself killing a wizened greybeard and a one-eyed boy, then take a red-haired girl and tear her living heart from her breast to offer it to the Icelord, bloody and still beating. He saw Lothan's mocking grin and—

San Ko screamed. He tore at the ground with his hands and a long inhuman wail tore from his throat. He ripped the hood from his head and rolled his face against the rough earth. His salt tears mingled with the dirt, muddying his face. Streaked and marked, he lifted his head to stare at the sky.

"No!" he cried.

He drew his sword from its sheath and broke the blade across his knee. He shattered the lacquered sheath against a granite outcrop.

The first vision was real. The priests of Pelamas were dead. That could not be changed. But the other...

San Ko called a name into the air and his skes shape fell from him. Small and trembling, Tarn Galdmeir huddled on the hilltop. His breath came in ragged gasps.

Dead, he thought. They're all dead—Puretongue's friends, the Summerlord's kin. Dead. And Puretongue himself? Was he dead, too?

Tarn knew the answer as soon as he asked himself the question. North. Puretongue had gone north with Carrie and the one-eyed boy. While Tarn had given himself over to the dark half of his soul, they'd gone into the Everwinter to fight the Icelord. While he'd worried over his own importance, wallowing in self-pity, they'd gone on.

He shuddered as the past few days returned to him. Something pulsed on his brow and he lifted a hand to his mud-streaked forehead. His moon-mark was warm to the touch. Did that mean the darkness inside him was gone? Was he free of it, the threat ended?

No, that was a child's hope. It was part of him. It had been born to him and would never be gone. All he could do was bind it, and take care that it never broke loose again.

He sat quietly for a long while and slowly his trembling stopped. Warmth returned to his icy limbs, fired by the deepening of his taw. He began to sing, slowly, softly. His voice was thin and weak still. But as his green silence rose to greet the music, his voice deepened, and then he tapped a power that lay in the hills themselves. It was an echo of the dwystaw, the deepsilence of the Isles. It cocooned him with warmth and his voice carried far from the hill where he sat—a bittersweet sound that held all his heartache in its notes.

The green silence that was like music built more strongly under his voice, colouring its strength, deepening its magic. The taw of the hills, hoary and old, mingled with his own. The last remnants of his preoccupation with his own importance stripped away with that music. From the pit of his despair he found an echo of the old joy—the joy of his taw deepening with its green silence, of spells used for the sake of healing and growth. His eyes shone with an inner light, their shadows banished as they flickered and gleamed. His moon-mark pulsed.

Then in the magic of the moment, he heard a far-off sound that came closer until it slipped into his inner music. Harping. He recognized the tune for one that was well-known in Kellmidden—a road-wending tune, the kind that tinkers and travelling folk might play around their campfire.

Tarn stood. After a long moment of indecision, he spoke a name into the night air. His body compacted, feathered, and in swan shape he winged northward. The hills shone in the starlight, reflecting the calm silence of the stone that was their backbone. Then he saw the fire on a neighbouring hill, its light flickering on a shadowed figure. A menhir towered over both the harper and the fire.

Tarn made his way to the hill, dropping from the sky with his wings spread wide. The harper's eyes widened as he watched the swan shape shimmer to become Tarn. He drew a thick chord from the bass strings of his instrument, then let his hands fall to his lap. The two men regarded each other over the fire until the harper finally spoke.

"I was told nothing evil could enter the space a longstone guards," he said. "So welcome, traveller."

A shadow crossed Tarn's eyes. Nothing evil, he thought. This small sacred space needed a new guardian. But all he said was, "Thank you."

The harper set his instrument aside and motioned to a pot of herb tea that was sitting on a small stone by the fire. When Tarn nodded, he poured a cup brim-full and handed it to him. Tarn cupped his hands around its warmth and sipped.

"My name is Wren Briarsen," the harper said. "I'm bound for Pelamas Henge. And you? Was it your voice I heard a few moments ago?"

"I was...singing." Tarn's voice was low. "My name's Tarn."

"Puretongue's apprentice?" Wren asked.

And son, Tarn might have added, but he only nodded.

"We travelled together—from South Gwendellan," Wren said. "I'm on my way to meet him in Pelamas now. Have you come from the south? Did you pass through Pelamas and see him?"

"I saw him," Tarn said.

The vision he'd seen earlier burned in his mind again. His head filled with the cold-hearted stormkin at their deathwork, and he shuddered.

"Lothan's creatures are in Pelamas," he said. "They...there is no one left alive there now except for stormkin."

The harper shaped the Sign of Horns at the mention of the Icelord's name. Then his hand faltered, eyes widening again.

"None...alive?"

Tarn shook his head. The harper's eyes went bleak in the firelight. His face was suddenly drawn and pale.

"We're undone," he said.

"Three went north," Tarn said. "Carrie, my fa—Puretongue, and a one-eyed boy."

"Deren," Wren named him.

The harper dropped his gaze to the fire and for long moments they sat there, watching the flames, listening to the crackle of the wood as it burned. A soft wind murmured a doleful lament across the hills, suiting their mood. When Tarn shifted his position, Wren looked up again.

"What can they hope to do?" he asked. "Three of them against the Everwinter. It's madness."

Tarn sighed. A great weight settled on him.

"I don't know," he said. "But I mean to find out."

"Is that wise?" Wren asked. "You'll only be throwing your life away with theirs."

"What else can I do? Sit here and wait to see what happens?"

"No, but—"

"If the Everwinter comes, it comes." Tarn stared north as he spoke. "I won't see everything overrun by Lothan and his creatures without trying to do *something*."

He heard an echo of Carrie's voice in what he was saying, and the weight he bore grew heavier. He should have gone with her. Puretongue has asked him to; she had asked him to. How could he have refused them?

Wren nodded in slow agreement. "You're right. We have to do whatever we can. So you'll go north and I'll continue my journey to Pelamas."

"Now who's talking foolish? The priests are gone. Dead. All of them. There are only stormkin there now."

"What else would you have me do? I sing of magic; I can't work it. I can't take on magic shapes and go to Ardmeyn with you. So I'll go on to Pelamas. I'll give the priests a decent burial. When the Everwinter comes, it'll have to look for me there."

"But the stormkin…"

"I'll avoid them as I can."

Their gazes met and held until Tarn shrugged. He had no hold over the harper, just as the harper had no hold over him. Each to his own madness. For when the Everwinter came, what did it matter where either one was waiting?

Tarn set his cup down by the fire and stood.

"Then good luck to you, Harper Wren. The Fairlord's luck."

"And to you," Wren said.

He watched his guest's form shimmer and then the swan was there once more, lifting its white wings into the night air. Wren craned his neck to watch the swan disappear. When it was lost to his sight, he returned his gaze to the fire.

Penhallow, he thought. All of the priests. Dead.

Tears wet his cheeks.

The oldest and wisest were gone now and their like the world would not see again.

The world.

It would be a frozen world with the weight of the Everwinter upon its fair dales.

He took his harp onto his lap once more. Touching the strings, he drew a series of mournful chords from it. Then he began an old lament and poured all of his grief into the tune's sparse notes.

Fourth

URETONGUE CURSED THE WEAVERS' weaving.

Fergun and three dyorn were on his trail and he led them as far as he could from Carrie and Deren. Below him, Ardmeyn grew wilder with every sweep of his broad eagle wings. The Everwinter froze the pulse of the land, killing the summer with its ice, frosting all hope.

And the stormkin drew nearer.

Brother, he thought to himself. Blood of my blood.

I hate him, but can I kill him? Dwar has long been dead by my hand and the wound of that deed has never left my soul. I hated him as I hate Fergun, but we were still brothers. As are Fergun and I. How can I kill another brother?

A wood appeared under him—a thick forest, frozen and heavy with ice. He folded his wings, plummeting down, shifting shape as he dropped. He swept into the forest as a sparrow, his tiny wings taking him through the frozen foliage. Finally he found a perch on a broad pine bough and knew he could go no further. His flight must end here. He would need all his remaining strength for the fiercing to come.

The power of Fergun's presence fell upon the wood. Iced trees withered. Small creatures squealed in their dens and burrows. The wood shrieked as the remaining birds rose in a confused flock. Puretongue joined them, gathering the last ebbs of his weary taw as he rose.

He thought of Tarn...and of Tarasen. Tarn with the skes shadow eating into his soul. Tarasen slain, her bright eyes dimmed and glassy. The cold earth covering her. And Penhallow—dead now, too. So many Summerborn slain.

He tapped the deep wells of silence inside him for the strength to finish this last battle. A thousand tiny spells, webbing the whole of the Isles, dissolved as he released the part of his taw that maintained them. In Fairnland, a cairn held together by his magic crumbled. In Cermyn, a traal woke, freed at last from his stony prison. In Umbria, the shades of dead kings stirred in the Berwin Mountains. In Kellmidden, a Wild Hunt was freed from Dergwyth Wood and rode the dawn skies, its hounds baying, its riders led by a horned woodlord. In Gwendellan, a longstone cracked in the Gnarlwood, its power fading until it was lost.

For through the years Puretongue had walked the length and breadth of the Green Isles, mending the old broken stoneworks so that their powers returned, binding the small evils so that the Isles could be safe. But now he broke all those spells and bindings, calling the power back into himself.

Garnering that strength, he lost his sparrow shape, and then he was a squirrel racing along pine boughs, a rodent in the brush, a wren rising upward to break through the forest's upper foliage. Next he took the shape of a white dove. His deepest silences were tapped now. But still, he wasn't done. Delving even deeper inside, he drew up that echo he carried of the dwystaw that bound the Isles, the green deepsilence that was older than the erlkin, the Tus or the Dathenan.

The dawn was breaking. His dove-shape rose high in the morning air, white wings achingly bright as the sun caught them with its light. Fergun and his dyorn were waiting there for him.

The Captain wore a shape of winged ice—a cold, impossible shape drawn from Damadar's frozen wastes. The dyorn were paler reflections of his power, smaller shapes.

Puretongue darted higher still, garnering his strengths to their final depths. The power built up inside him until his soul burned with its potency. He loosed the names that bound the dyorn, stripping them to their essence—names that thrust so deeply inside them that their souls were wrenched from them and their bodies plummeted downward, shifting as they fell to return to the shapes they'd been born to.

Puretongue circled higher and the Captain followed. Fergun's power crackled in the air like quick, sharp thunder.

THE TWO wolves crouched in the shadow of a drift, whining, tails between their legs. One spoke a name inside its mind and then Carrie and Deren huddled together against the cold—a cold that iced their souls more than their frail bodies.

"Deren?" Carrie asked in a quavering voice. "What...what is it?"

They could sense the battle between the Captain and Puretongue as though it was being fought in their minds.

"I told him," Deren said, tears freezing on his cheek. "I told him we wouldn't see him again."

Carrie clutched him more closely, trying to find some comfort, to give some comfort. But all she could do was shiver. The deep cold cut through to their bones, pierced their souls, while the fiercing of the two wizards battered their inner senses.

"Oh, Deren," Carrie said as she tasted the Captain's fury and understood his strength. "We've got to help him."

Deren lifted her head, his fingers under her chin.

"How?" he asked, his single eye bleak.

THE DOVE and the ice-shape of the Captain jockeyed for position. Mist steamed as Puretongue withered Fergun's icy blasts with spells of flame. The dhruide dropped down, skimming the forest, his foe on his tail. He spoke a word and the trees lifted their branches to entangle Fergun. But the frozen limbs were brittle and thin, shattering under the Captain's own spells.

Puretongue swung upward again, weaving a strange path in the air that formed a rune of white fire, blinding and bright.

The Captain's shape mutated as he passed through it. His anger intensified. His power seemed to double.

Puretongue poured all his physical strength into his wings to escape Fergun's next attack.

BENJAMEN SAT *straight up, face beaded with sweat, eyes rolling. He stared north and distances dissolved. He watched the fiercing unfold; he felt the Captain like a cold shadow squeezing his soul, the dhruide as a warm grey mist that tried to ease the darkness. Benjamen's hands opened and closed at his sides. His face went white.*

"Benjamen?" Long Tom asked.

He left Kinn to finish the repair on the harnesses and strode over to the peddler.

"Man, what's wrong with you?"

Benjamen made no reply. He stared into the unseen distance, and bowed his head. He could watch no more of it.

PURETONGUE WASN'T quick enough. The Captain closed the distance between them, shaping claws of ice to grasp the dove in a grip of searing frost. They dropped from the sky. Then their minds met, locked, and merged.

The struggle was joined inside them as they continued to fall.

ABOVE THE *ice fields of Ardmeyn, shock pulled Tarn's swan shape from him and sent him spiraling down from the sky. He felt the fiercing of the two Captains as though it took place inside him. When he hit the snow, he went tumbling. It was a long moment before he could sit up, but then all he could do was kneel in the snow.*

"Puretongue!" he cried.

Blind fear for the dhruide went through him, sharp as a knife.

He must...he should...

He stretched out his arms, drew on the silences inside him, and named a shape that would take him to his father's side. But as he spoke the name, the snows whipped furiously around him and the ground buckled. Across Ardmeyn, the Everwinter grew stronger with every spell Fergun loosed.

"Father!" Tarn cried, but his voice couldn't cut through the winds.

They took the word from him, dispersing it in wide sweeps of ice and snow

Tarn bowed his head and wept.

⁂

ICE PIERCED Puretongue's soul. As Fergun's rage grew, so did his power, while the dhruide's strengths were used but not replenished. Once, had he not turned his back on the dark power, he could have met Fergun strength for strength, but that part of him was no longer his to command. He'd locked it away too deeply. Fergun's cold rage froze the names he tried to shape. The Captain lashed him without mercy, the whip of his strength battering the dhruide's soul as it tried to pierce Puretongue's defenses.

Their merged minds struck at one other, seeking position, better purchase. Each tried to weaken the other while bolstering their own defenses. And then, as their memories merged, they knew each others' secrets.

"No!" Fergun cried, seeing the truth revealed in Puretongue's mind.

The Captain went mad.

"Kin-Slayer!" he roared.

He attacked the dhruide with every strength at his command, but he was an instant too late.

Puretongue called up the power of the dwystaw, the power of the green deepsilence that bound the Green Isles, hidden until now behind the knowledge that he and Fergun were brothers. For a brief moment he tasted its potency. Then he let it go.

Power roared through the dhruide, firing his soul. It was too much for any one mind to bear. And joined to his brother, mind to mind, he knew that they would share one last thing in this world.

That knowledge brought him peace as they died between one breath and the next.

TARN STOOD in the snow-swept dawn, his face glistening with frozen tears. He lifted his gaze to stare into the greying skies, despair rooted in his strange eyes. Their many colours were muted, their brightness dimmed through his sorrow. He closed them and his father's features swam before him.

But Puretongue was gone.

Tarn's shoulders slumped.

What now? Puretongue had known what to do. What was left?

He thought of Carrie and the one-eyed boy. Deren. They were here, somewhere in the Everwinter that covered Ardmeyn.

"I'll find them," he said aloud. "I'll find them for you, father. I'll take them to Taynbell Peak as you would have. And if I die doing it, at least I'll be going to meet you again."

He spoke a name and his shape dissolved. Winged, he headed north, deepsight seeking some trace of the two he'd promised to help.

IN DEATH they regained their true shapes. The forest embraced their bodies as it had those of the dyorn that Puretongue had slain.

They landed in a tangle of limbs.

But while one Captain's face had become a mask of unfulfilled hatred, the other's was composed in the lines of a man who had found peace with himself.

"NO."

Deren murmured the word as Puretongue died. He looked into Carrie's tear-streaked face and thought his heart would break. Turning away, he stared off into the frozen wastes.

"He won't have died in vain," he said, his voice grim. "Come, Carrie. We've a journey to complete."

Carrie could only look at him. The mixture of sorrow and dread that lay across his features mirrored her own. But as she watched, determination settled over him.

"We're going on?" she said.

She saw Deren's mouth open to respond, but then her vision blurred.

Go on, said a voice inside her. You must go on. It was for you the dhruide died, for the last hope of the Green Isles that lies inside you. Would you have the silence that is like music be gone forever? Would you have the Everwinter be all?

"Carrie?" Deren asked, and the mist that blurred her sight was gone.

She met his eye and remembered her last sight of the dhruide, how she'd thought of him as embodying all that was fair and good about the Isles. He'd had strength, too. He'd been strength. While she...

"Carrie?"

"I'm not strong enough," she said, her voice so soft he almost missed what she said. "Don't you see? I'm not strong enough."

Deren held her, his arms gentle around her.

"None of us are," he said. "But we have to go on all the same. What else can we do now?"

Carrie laid her head against his shoulder to take a moment's comfort, then pulled back and nodded in agreement.

Fifth

EREN KNEW THEY WERE ill-equipped to survive the Everwinter in their own shapes, but he could delay no longer. His own thoughts were already entwined more and more with that of the wolf he wore. Hunger gnawed at his belly and every scent they crossed distracted him. But though Puretongue was gone, one of the dhruide's last lessons stood out sharply in the young prentice's mind: Untrained as they were, if they held a shape too long, they would become that shape forever.

Only it was so cold without the wolves' fur...

Deren shivered in anticipation of the change. He shot a glance at the sleek she-wolf trotting at his side. Her muzzle was crusted with frost and from time to time she stumbled with weariness. Deren fought back a new upsurge of wolf-thoughts as he tried to concentrate on finding them some shelter. A hollow, or a cave. If they could get a fire started and keep it going, they might have a chance.

When they came to a cleft in the snow-covered rocks, he left the route they were following to investigate. Carrie stayed by his side, unquestioning. The cleft, he discovered, was the beginning of a ravine that led northward. The wind funneled along its length, howling and tossing powdery snow in their faces. The wolves bent their heads down, threading their way around the drifts that wouldn't bear their weight.

Maybe a winged shape would be better, Deren thought, then dismissed the idea. The wind would blow them all the way back to Kellmidden. He padded on, gaze sweeping left and right as he searched for shelter.

He almost passed the cave's entrance. It was tucked away behind a fall of broken rocks rimmed with frost and snow, but he caught the black hole at just the right angle, and led them into its promised comfort. As soon as they rounded the rock fall, the wind lost its main thrust. Then they were in the cave.

Deren indicated to Carrie that she should go deeper before he called forth the names that would free their true shapes. He stumbled to his knees, weary beyond belief. A dull hammering began in his temples. He wanted to drop where he knelt. Turning, he saw Carrie stretched out on the cave floor, half-lost in the shadows. Her eyes were open, mirroring his pain, but she didn't have the energy to move. It was up to him.

He drew the tinker blade from his belt. Carrie had shared Long Tom's gift with him, so that they both had one. He used it to shred wood for kindling. The cave had that at least—no logs, but a plethora of sticks and branches. As he worked he tried not to think about what sort of creature would find this sort of den comfortable. Just so long as it didn't return.

But the cave had an air of disuse about it, and with the deep bite of the cold, and the wind still howling beyond its entrance, he was more concerned with getting a fire started. Even the wolf shapes had felt the sting of the Everwinter. They needed warmth now. If the smoke from their fire brought trouble, they'd have to face that moment when it came; but he couldn't imagine what sort of creature would be abroad in this foul weather.

The answer to that hissed in his mind.

Stormkin.

He shut the thought away.

Scraping flint against steel, he blew on the first glimmer of a spark. The shredded wood caught, and he added more fuel, estimating how much they had before they'd have to go looking for more. An hour perhaps?

When the fire was going, he helped Carrie over to take in its warmth. Then he twisted some of the longer twigs into a rough torch, lit it, and went exploring a little deeper in the cave. His head still pounded and he found the flickering of his makeshift torch's light hard to follow. Each flicker appeared to be timed to the throb in his temples, accentuating the pain. The cave ended after a sudden turn to the left. At the blank wall Deren gathered more sticks and some dried dung he found there. He returned to the front of the cave, satisfied now that they had only one direction from which to fear danger.

Carrie was sitting up when he got back. She huddled near the fire, so close to the flames that he was sure she'd singe her hair. She looked up at the sound of his footsteps. Her eyes were dull with pain. He dropped his burden within easy reach and sat across from her.

"I guess we should try bear shapes next," he said. "I don't know how fast they can go, but I've seen their pelts at the market in Gullysbrow. We'll be warmer, at least."

Carrie looked back into the fire.

"What's the use?" she asked.

Deren sat silent, not wanting to go through all the whys and wherefores again. His head ached too much to argue.

"Deren," Carrie went on. She looked up once more. "Think about it. I...I want to do something, but with this unnatural weather, it's... I don't know..."

"It's the Everwinter."

"Yes." Her voice was bitter. "And we're supposed to confront the creatures that control it. Dath! Tarn was right."

"In what?"

Carrie sighed. "He told me that I wasn't fit for this struggle, that my part should belong to someone trained to meet its challenge. I'm not trained. Dath! All I am is cold and hungry. And what will we do? March on until we collapse in the snow? Die in some other shape that the one we were born with?"

"But Puretongue was trained and—"

Deren broke off when he realized how stupid that argument was. Yes, Puretongue had been trained and look where that training had gotten him. The boy's chest grew tight with emotion whenever he thought of the dhruide. With him gone...

Carrie was right. What was the point?

But as Deren's hopes fell with hers, Carrie remembered the voice she'd heard when she was certain that she just couldn't continue. Puretongue was dead, it had said. But if his dying was to not be in vain, *they* had to go on and do what they could or else the whole of the Isles would meet the same fate as the dhruide.

The Summerlord had come to her. *He* thought they could do something. Shouldn't she trust him?

"Deren?" she said with a tremble in her voice.

She reached her hand out to him.

Deren added more wood to the fire, then moved over to sit beside her. They held each other close, words lost. Only the winds outside and the crackle of the fire broke the silence.

The throb in their temples dulled after awhile, leaving an ache that worsened only when they moved. Carrie laid her head against Deren's shoulder and he combed her hair with his fingers, wondering how they could sit here so peacefully when the whole world was falling apart around them.

Alone, he realized, each of them might have fallen prey to fears so strong that they would have simply laid down and waited for the stormkin to find them. Together, they bolstered each other's courage, see-sawing between comforter and the one in need of comfort.

"He's somewhere close," Carrie said suddenly.

"Who is?"

"Hafarl—the Summerlord. He's in Ardmeyn, hidden from the stormkin, waiting for us to do something. To save him, I suppose. I don't know how we're supposed to do that. I guess he's waiting for us to climb Taynbell Peak and whatever will happen, will happen there. But he's near. Close somewhere. I can feel him. Can you?"

Deren shook his head. "Just the cold."

"Under the cold," Carrie insisted. "He's near. If we can get to Taynbell Peak, you'll see."

Deren shrugged. He thought of Wren's vision, and Puretongue's interpretation of it. He and Carrie were needed. And a third person. There'd been three symbols on the stone. One for him, one for Carrie, and one for...this Tarn, he supposed. But tarn wasn't with them. And Puretongue was gone. Would the two of them be enough?"

"We'll have to be," Carrie said.

Deren moved away from her, startled.

"You had to be thinking of Tarn," she said. "Of what the two of us can do without him or Puretongue to help us. I felt you stiffen and...shared your thought, I guess."

Back and forth it went, Deren thought. One moment they were going and giving their all, in the next, one of the other was asking what the use of it was. And neither of them had an answer to that. He sighed, pulled Carrie close again, but she moved away. For a moment he was hurt, then he saw the look on her face. His fingers closed around the hilt of his tinker blade as he scrambled to his feet.

"What is it?" he asked.

Carrie shook her head, wincing at the pain the movement brought.

"Something...some*one* is coming. I can feel someone close to us."

Deren moved to the entrance of the cave and peered out. The cave's mouth was sheltered from the wind, but beyond the rock fall, it sent ice and snow whirling in white sheets across the ravine. He stood there, undecided. The hilt of the knife felt good in his hand; but remembering the vision of Pelamas, he knew it'd do little against stormkin.

What should they do? Make a break for it? Take a shape? What shape would be best?

His head ached as he fought to think clearly. He wasn't cut out to be a leader, but with Carrie looking to him for guidance, he had to think of *something*. She had her own knife in hand, but was holding it awkwardly. He knew she didn't know what to do with it.

Deren made up his mind.

"We've got to—" he began, then froze.

They both heard the groan of stone moving against stone. Carrie moved closer to him as he peered out the entrance. Then Deren realized that the sound had come from behind them. He turned quickly, head spinning with the sudden movement. With the knife held out before him, cutting edge up for close fighting, he took a couple of steps into the cave, then froze again. His deepsight cut through the shadows at the back of the cave. Beside him, Carrie gasped as she too saw the strangers.

There were three of them—small men, not one of them standing as tall as Carrie, with dark skin and jet-black hair. They wore fur leggings and tunics, and fur cloaks, and each of them held a rude bow, arrows notched and drawn back, feathered ends at their swarthy cheeks. They moved aside and two more filled the back of the cave.

Deren hesitated, not sure what to make of them. He held a name on the tip of his tongue, but wasn't sure he could say it, that they could shapechange and be gone quickly enough. But two knives against three drawn bows weren't very good odds. He tensed, ready to push Carrie aside and at least give her a chance to break free while he attacked. Then one of the two latecomers stepped forward. He wore a torc of beaten copper around his neck and held his hands open before him in a peaceful gesture.

"Knew ye'd come," he said. "Mearddha told't, read t' bones. 'Green-blooded warmhearts,' she said."

He looked Deren and Carrie over, brown eyes shining. His voice was heavily accented, but if they concentrated, they could understand him. He pushed aside the bow of the man nearest to him.

"Bid ye welcome, Summerborn," he said.

Deren wasn't sure what was happening. The threat appeared to be gone, for all three bowmen had lowered their weapons and they wore grins that stretched from ear to ear. The speaker's phrasing fell oddly on Deren's ears, but—

"Tus," Carrie murmured. "They're Tus, Deren."

"Aye," the man with the copper torc said. "We be Tus. T'People. An' ye be Summerborn, Urth be moon-sure. Mearddha sent us—long journey underhill, 'Be coming,' she said. 'Fetch 'em quick an' bring t' deep holding.' Ye be safe now."

"They want us to go with them," Carrie said

Deren nodded. He'd caught that much as well, but he felt uneasy.

"Come wi' us, aye," the Tus said. "Urth take ye t' safe holding. T'peat burns hot, aye, an' dark cold's a distant thing."

Pushing back the ache that still pulsed in her temples, Carrie raised her taw. Her deepsight had cut through the shadows, now her taw reached for the strangers' spirits. She smiled as she met their thoughts. They were old, deep earthy thoughts that held only warmth and kindness for them.

"Thank you for coming," she said to them.

She touched Deren's arm, motioning him to put his knife away.

Deren nodded, willing to give her the lead since she seemed to know what she was doing. He sheathed the tinker blade and took Carrie's hand, forcing a smile to his lips.

Legends come to life, he thought, regarding the Tus. But then, so were the stormkin.

"How did you know we'd be here?" he asked.

"Smelled ye, we did. Good clean smell—not stormkin." Urth's crooked fingers shaped the Sign of Horns. "Not Mocker's stink. Mearddha said ye'd be near, so we looked, deep an' far underhill. Smelled ye here."

He stepped back, motioning behind him where the back of the cave now opened into a tunnel.

"Ye come," he said. "Meet Mearddha. She knew ye'd come." He tapped his finger on his chest, over his heart. "Woodmother she be. Kens moon-magic an' reads t'bones. Erlkin she be."

"Erlkin?" Carrie breathed.

Something warm stirred inside her.

Here was the worth of magic, she thought. If there were horrible things like the stormkin, then there had to be erlkin and Tus, too. Of all the stories she'd heard when she was growing up, she loved the ones about the kowrie folk the most.

"Aye, erlkin," Urth said, grinning. "We live deepdown now— erlkin an' t'People. Hide from t'winter. Ye'll come see?"

Carrie and Deren looked at each other. Her sense of rightness spread to him and the warmth that filled him made his smile more natural.

"Come?" Deren said. "Oh, yes. We'll come."

Hand in hand, they followed Urth into the tunnel. The other Tus took up the rear. They heard the rock rumble shut and then the Everwinter didn't seem to exist anymore. They moved now through the veins of the earth, deep underground.

Sixth

URTH LED THEM ALONG the hidden roads of the Tus, down into the heart of the earth until after a long journey they came out in a cavern that was almost a hundred feet long, forty feet wide, and very warm. Peat fires burned in rudely made hearths. The smoke drained through hollow up-drafts so that there was little smoke in the cavern itself. Here and there, carved bowls were set out. Inside them was a liquid that gave off light—not a bright light; more like twilight in a deep wood. Furs were scattered on the stones around the hearths and folk were gathered in small groups upon them. Most were the swarthy Tus, though here and there were folk of a different race—tall figures in comparison to the diminutive Tus.

They were the erlkin, the wooderls of legend. Their hair was long and golden, braided for the most part, and they were slender and thin-featured. Under their furred Tus cloaks, glimpses of green and rust cloth showed through— embroidered with gold threads that glimmered in the dim light. They all appeared young, but there was oldness in their eyes. Age, and an aura of mystery.

Deren and Carrie stood for long moments at the entrance to the cavern, taking it all in and savouring the warmth. It washed over them, driving the cold from their bones, the ice from their hearts. Their escorts, except for Urth, left them there, hurrying off to their own clan-hearths.

Urth touched Carrie's arm.

"Come," he said. "Fire's a-burning an' root-broth's waiting for ye."

Under the curious gazes of the clan-folk, he led them across the cavern to where a tall erlkin woman awaited them, her golden braids spilling down to her waist. She lifted one of the bowls of light as they approached.

"Moon-water," Urth explained in reply to Carrie's question. "Erlkin magic. But t's faded an' pale now. Need t' moon t' grow bright again."

The waiting erlkin held up the bowl to each of their faces when they reached Carrieher. S,theyhe searched their features in its pale light, then smiled and returned the bowl to its place by the hearth.

"I bid you welcome, Summerborn," she said, "for Summerborn you surely are."

Carrie and Deren stood awkwardly in front of her, not really sure what was expected of them. They were each waiting for the other to say something first.

"Be cold an' hungry," Urth said to the woman. He turned to his guests. "Sit. Urth will bring ye broth."

He ushered them to places on the furs by the fire and spooned broth into three roughly-hewn bowls. Deren nodded his thanks when one of them was thrust into his hands. He looked into it, a little uneasy about the unfamiliar vegetables that floated there , then raised his eye to regard the erlkin.

"You're Mearddha?" he asked.

"I am indeed. And what shall I call you?"

"Deren. Deren Merewuth. And this is Carrie—ah, Carwyn..."

"Lorweir," Carrie finished for him.

Mearddha smiled. "The sea and moon come underhill," she said. At their blank looks, she added, "Your names. In the old tongue 'mere' means 'sea' and 'lor' means 'moon.'"

"Moon?" Carrie repeated. She was thinking of the moon-mark on Tarn's brow.

"Yes," Mearddha said. "You both have erlkin names—Merewuth and Lorweir. Old names. But your blood—*that* is older still. It's Summerlord blood. I almost gave up hope of your coming. I felt the Captain die—he and the dhruide, alike and yet so unlike each other. Then I sensed your journey through the Everwinter, so I sent Urth to find you and bring you here."

"What do you mean 'alike but unalike'?" Deren asked. "How could Puretongue be like the Captain?"

"Did you not sense it in that last moment? Their kinship?"

Deren shot a quick glance to Carrie, but she shook her head.

"Tell us," Deren demanded. "What did you sense?"

Mearddha sighed. "I thought it strange," she said, "but it answered many riddles, for—"

She broke off seeing Urth frown.

"Let 'em eat," he said. "Let 'em grow warm. Time enow for tale-telling later."

He sat cross-legged beside Deren and began to eat, spooning up his broth with obvious relish. Deren and Carrie exchanged glances. They were both burning with questions.

"Urth is right," Mearddha said. "We have waited a long time for you to come. To wait a little longer to talk is no great thing. Eat and rest—then we will exchange tales. You've no need to fear the winter's bite. We are deeper underhill than even the Everwinter may pierce."

Deren shrugged. The little while he'd spent with Puretongue had taught him to wait for answers.

Puretongue...

Thinking of the dhruide, a grim bleakness tightened his features. He glanced at Carrie again. She was spooning up her broth, questions forgotten. Watching her eat, his own belly rumbled with hunger.

So they ate, and the thin soup with its unfamiliar vegetables tasted far better than it looked. Afterward, though they wanted to talk, the combination of warmth and full stomachs soon had them both drifting off on the furs, oblivious to everything around them.

"Be so young," Urth said, regarding the sleeping features of their guest.

"I hope not *too* young," Mearddha said. "But their taws—especially the girl's—are strong. And they are all we have."

"Aye. Be all we have."

THEY WERE never sure how long they slept, for it was hard to keep track without the sun to track across the sky by day, or the moon and stars at night; and neither the Tus nor the erlkin seemed overly concerned with measuring it. When they woke, Urth and Mearddha were there with some of the other Tus—elders or chiefs of some sort, Deren decided, for they all had torcs similar to Urth's and they carried themselves with a certain air of authority.

Over a second meal they listened to what Mearddha had to say about Puretongue. Deren set his bowl aside, unable to finish his soup. He felt like he had a rock in the pit of his stomach.

When Mearddha was done, no one spoke for a long moment. Deren and Carrie wrestled with the new information, each trying to come to grips with it in their own way.

It wasn't so hard for Carrie. She hadn't known Puretongue very well, and she felt a surge of admiration for the wizard, knowing he'd been able to rise so high above his evil past. Her awe for him was strengthened by these new revelations.

Deren had a harder time of it. He remembered Puretongue telling him how there was seldom such a clear-cut definition between black and white as there was in this present time. And that might be true, he thought, but what did it mean when the most beloved of the forces of good proved to be one of Lothan's sons? What did it mean for the other stormkin? Was there hope for them, too? Instead of trying to destroy the stormkin, shouldn't he be trying to convince them of the injustice of their ways?

"There is always hope," Mearddha said when he put the question to her, "but at the present time, the lines have been drawn. If any of the stormkin meant to join us, they are long overdue. Many and many of our folk have been slain by Lothan's armies. Would you have us come out of hiding to talk to them, only to be slain in turn?"

Deren shook his head. "No, no. Not at all. It's just that…I'm confused. I can't believe that Puretongue was ever one of them. He was so…peaceful…"

Except for the iron in his eyes, Deren remembered. And it was the evil done by the stormkin that had put the grimness there, wasn't it?

"Can you help us?" Carrie asked. "Is there some underground route that could bring us close to Taynbell Peak?"

"There is," Mearddha replied, "but the time has not yet come for that journey. There are only two of you The stone on Taynbell has three runes. We must wait for the one who is still to come."

"You mean Tarn," Carrie said. "But he's not coming. He…"

She looked to Deren for help. Briefly, Deren related what they'd heard of what had happened between Tarn and Puretongue, and how the swanmage had left Pelamas in skes shape.

"Bad news," Drow said. He was a squint-eyed Tus, old and wrinkled, so thin that his furs hung voluminously upon his bony frame. "If t'swanmage be gone, Mocker's won."

Around the hearth, Tus fingers shaped the Sign of Horns.

"He will come," Mearddha said.

Carrie looked at her. "How…how can you be so sure?"

"T'bones," Urth said. "She read t'bones—three t' come, they said. Like t'runes on the peak."

Mearddha nodded. From a pouch at her belt, she drew a handful of bone discs. They gleamed yellow and pale in the dim light as the erlkin tossed them up and down on her palm. The pouch at her belt held still more and they clicked together whenever she moved.

"Glory-bones," the erlkin said, her voice holding reverence. "They have the power to peer between the threads the weavers weave—at times."

Carrie watched the discs go up and down with the motion of Mearddha's hand. Her taw came bubbling up inside her, warm and singing with the silence that was like music.

"Would you see them do their work?" Mearddha asked.

Without waiting for a reply, she let the bone discs spill from her hands to fall upon the furs by her knee.

Carrie watched them turn over and over slowly, as though they fell through honey rather than through air. Her taw was strong inside her. Her deepsight pierced the gaps between the falling discs and she gasped. She saw a fleck of sky, clouds streaking it, and high above them, a white swan winging. Then the bones touched the fur and the vision was gone.

"Tarn," she said. "Where is he?"

Tarn! her heart cried. And not in skes shape. The clean lines of the swan burned in her memory.

"You saw him?" Mearddha asked.

"Just for a moment. I...I *did* see him. *Is* he coming? Where is he?"

Mearddha sighed. "He comes—that is all I can see. And here..." She motioned to the scattering of bones discs. "Here I see the same."

Carrie followed the movement of the erlkin's hand. Whatever Mearddha saw in that pattern of discs wasn't there for her to see. But the vision—no matter how brief—*that* she had seen.

"You see nothing now?" Mearddha asked.

Carrie shook her head.

"But that you saw even as much as you did..." The erlkin smiled. "Truly you are close to the Summerlord, Carwyn. And you, Deren? Did you see aught?"

"Nothing." Deren's disappointment was obvious. "But what do we do now? How do we join him?"

"For now you can only wait."

"Wait? But we don't have time to wait."

"Time must be made," Mearddha said, her voice firm. "Without the swanmage, there is nothing you can do except throw your lives away."

"But..." Deren turned to Carrie.

"Stay with us," Urth said. "Be safe here."

"The Everwinter grows no worse," Mearddha added. "With the Captain dead, there is no one to lead the stormkin. When the swanmage has come, *then* you should go to Taynbell."

"And if...if he doesn't come?" Deren asked.

He kept his gaze from Carrie, staring firmly at the erlkin woodmother.

"He will come."

"I saw him, Deren," Carrie said. "In swan shape. The darkness was gone from him."

Deren shook his head. The urgency that had driven them north, that had led to Puretongue's death—where had it gone? Was he the only one who still felt it?

"If I went on," he said to Carrie, "would you come with me?"

"I..."

Carrie looked from Deren to their hosts. Their disapproval was obvious, but she read something deeper in Deren's question. Like her, he'd lost everything. They had only each other. She was all that remained of the familiar, sane world for him, and he was the same for her. They might have Hafarl's blood in them—but they saw each other as ordinary people, no matter what anyone else saw.

"Yes," she said. "If you want to do, Deren, I'll come with you."

Deren sighed. Their gazes met. Slowly he reached over and took her hand in his own.

"I had to know," he said. "With everything so strange around us..."

"I know," Carrie told him.

They were each other's strength.

Turning to their hosts, Deren managed to find a weary smile to give them.

"It's not that I don't appreciate all you've done for us so far," he said. He thought of the Everwinter's bitter cold and how they'd still be fighting to survive its fury if it hadn't been for the arrival of Urth and the other Tus. "It's just that I'm...we're not used to all of this. For us it's...stories come to life."

"We all understand the burden you bear," Mearddha said. "Could we do it, we would willingly take your place. We, too, have lost our loved ones and our land—we who had already lost so much. And now our last haven is stolen from us. There is not one of us here today who hasn't lost kin in this struggle with the mad Lord of Winter. But the weavers wove you into the struggle. Stay with us now and gather strength. We will see to your comfort until the final step must be taken."

"How will you know what that is?" Deren asked.

"The glory-bones bid you to wait now," she said. "When it is time, they will bid you go. It is not just your friend Tarn that we must wait for, but for a certain moment as well. If you go now..."

"Ye doom us all," Urth said.

Deren nodded, feeling uncomfortable under their scrutiny. The sense of urgency didn't leave him, but he realized as well that he'd have to wait. Without Puretongue to guide them, they had to take what help they could find.

Carrie squeezed his hand.

"We'll stay," he said.

"And thank you," Carrie added. "Without your help, we'd be lost now."

Mearddha reached out and laid her hand over Carrie and Deren's clasped grip.

"It is little enough we do," she said.

Seventh

BENJAMEN AND THE TURPENS came in sight of Pelamas Henge at mid-afternoon of their twelfth day out of Keddlenowe. They topped the last of the rounded foothills of the Ramshorn Mountains and looked down to where the great henge stones stood dark in the afternoon light. Harried and ragged from their journey, they paused at the hilltop. Dark circles rimmed their eyes and a pinched weariness palled their features. The peddler was in the worst shape.

Long Tom looked away from the henge to regard Benjamen. The peddler sat like a broken man, hunched forward in his seat, hands gripping his knees, face white. The tinker wiped Benjamen's brow and sighed.

"It's not long now," he said.

Ballan, who'd have thought they could make it so far, so fast? They wouldn't have done it without Benjamen's wizardry—but that wizardry had cost the peddler dearly. This past day there'd been no cairns or longstones to replenish his depleted strength. Only empty hilltops and wooded valleys.

"Go on," Benjamen had said at their noon stop earlier in the day, so weak he couldn't stand. "I...I can feel the henge from here. It's giving me strength."

But they'd both known he was lying.

Now they were here. Long Tom looked away from his friend to study the way they must go. Squinting, he could make out tiny figures moving around the ruins of what must have been buildings. Were they Saramand? Or stormkin?

Long Tom frowned. They couldn't turn back now, but the land below had a ravaged look, and he hesitated to lead his family down there. Beyond the henge stones he saw a long mound of freshly-turned earth that reminded him of a barrow. Then he remembered. The priests were all dead, slain by the stormkin. So who *was* that below?

Long Tom sighed, knowing there was only one way to find out.

"Fenne!" he called. "Kinn! Ready your weapons."

The two young tinkers scrambled to the roof of the wagon where they strung their bows and readied their arrows for easy access. Beside Long Tom, Megan strung her own bow, her features grim. Benjamen didn't move.

Long Tom shook out the reins and called the horses into motion. His tongue felt like it was stuck to the roof of his mouth. He and Benjamen should go on alone, he thought, but glancing at Megan he knew he'd never win that old argument. They were coming with him to the end of the journey and that was that. It was up to him to see them all safely through. He had a moment to consider going so boldly down the hill, but it was too late to reconsider. Their arrival had been noticed.

But all the tinkers' war-like preparations were unnecessary. The only folk that came to meet their wagon were a half-dozen or so grief-stricken priests, drab in their simple brown robes. Benjamen looked up when Long Tom brought the wagon to a halt. Then he called out, his voice no more than a croak.

"Teh-Temen?"

One priest left the others to step closer to Benjamen's side of the wagon. His sorrowful gaze searched the peddler's face.

"Benjamen, was it?" he said. "Is it you?"

The peddler nodded wearily. "How did you manage to get here before us?"

"A horse with a single rider can make better time than a wagon. I had need for haste because…" The priest's voice broke. "You…do you know of the attack?"

Benjamen shuddered.

"I saw it," he said, and the memory flooded his mind again. "I saw them all die…in a vision. And later…"

Another shudder ran through him.

"Puretongue," Temen said. "His name was Puretongue and he was the Founder of Dhruidry. He killed the Captain, but he died doing it."

"Then it's over?" Long Tom asked.

"I wish it was. But I'm afraid it's just the beginning of the end." Temen stepped back from the wagon and looked away to the north. "The stormkin are gathering in Ardmeyn now, looking for the Summerlord. I'm afraid it won't be long before they find him."

Ardmeyn, Long Tom thought. Where Carrie was.

"How far?" he began to ask, then shook his head.

First they had to see to Benjamen and regain their strengths. Then they could begin the final leg of their journey—a journey that felt like it grew longer each time they neared its supposed end.

"Our friend needs help," he said to the priest. "Does the henge have the same power as the stones along the coast road?"

Temen nodded. "There is enough power stored in those stones to make the road-stones seem like mere drops of water in a vast ocean. But without an elder—without Penhallow, the chief priest…" Emotion clouded his voice again. "It would be dangerous for him to draw on the henge's power alone, and no one here is trained to control it. But there is a small menhir in the woods nearby, and we will take him to it. Make your camp where you will, and we will see to your friend."

Long Tom and Megan exchanged glances, then with a shrug, Long Tom nodded. Priests helped Benjamen and led him stumbling off into the woods while the tinkers busied themselves with setting up their camp and seeing to the welfare of the horses. But when the small familiar tasks were done, Long Tom felt at loose ends. He left his family by the wagon and wandered aimlessly among the ruined buildings that had fallen under the stormkin's attack.

Priests worked here and there—removing charred timbers, sweeping debris from around the foundations, and making a start on rebuilding the stone walls. Near the henge they had already begun to raise supports for a new building; wooden beams were thrusting out of the blackened stone foundation like the bare limbs of wintered trees.

Winter, Long Tom thought, and that reminded him of the Everwinter. Carrie was there in its grasp as Lothan's storms laid waste to Ardmeyn. There, where the Summerlord was hiding and stormkin scoured the land, looking for him.

Long Tom left the priests to their work. Later he would help them. Now he was restless, and needed to walk his thoughts away.

After awhile he found himself near the great henge of Pelamas. He stared up at the tall triad stones and remembered what the priest Temen had said about their power. He could almost feel something himself. A presence. A strength.

His gaze shifted to the barrow where the slain priests had been buried. Seeing a cloaked figure kneeling beside the raw earth, he walked over.

The man was so wrapped in his grief that he remained oblivious to Long Tom's presence. A harp case stood on the ground beside him, its drawstrings tightly fastened. Long Tom sat on his heels beside the harper, keeping silent in respect for the man's sorrow. They remained like that for a long time before the harper finally looked up. Long Tom met his gaze and felt himself drawn into eyes that had seen too much sorrow.

"He told me," the harper said, "but I didn't believe him. How could it be possible? How could Penhallow and all the priests be dead? But when I came...when I came I saw them. Those damned stormkin. They were still here and my blood froze. For two days I hid, watching, yearning to lay those holy men in the soil, but unable to do a thing. The others came...the other priests who weren't here when the doom fell upon Pelamas, and we all waited together.

"And then...when the stormkin finally went north...we came down and did what we could for the dead." He touched the raw earth with a trembling hand. "Now here they lie. Returned to the bosom of the Earthmother. And what is left to do now but wait for the Everwinter to come finish us? I sit here and mourn, but there's no end to my grief. It's not only these priests—it's the whole of the Isles."

He shook his head. "I should have gone north with him. He told me there'd be nothing here."

"Who told you?" Long Tom asked.

"Puretongue's prentice—Tarn."

Tarn. The name raced through Long Tom's mind. The small wizard was still alive.

"Was there a girl with him?" he asked. "A red-haired girl named Carrie?"

The harper shook his head. "He was alone. But he told me of the girl. She went north with Puretongue and Deren...just the three of them. Three of them against the Everwinter. Now the priests tell me that Puretongue is dead, too, so those children are alone in Ardmeyn with the Icelord's stormkin."

Long Tom shaped the Sign of Horns and his own hopes failed again.

Silence fell between the two men and lengthened, then Long Tom drew himself up from his brooding to study the harper once more.

"Long Tom Turpen's my name, friend. What do they call you?"

"Wren."

"And you're a harper?"

"Yes."

Long Tom said nothing for a long moment. The harper's features were drawn tight with sorrow, and that look of hopelessness he wore was becoming too familiar a sight to suit the tinker. Too many folk were withdrawing into themselves, letting their sorrows sour them, letting their fear of the Saramand and stormkin rule them. Oh, these were dire times, no mistaking them, but if a man didn't fight the hopelessness, then his enemy had the battle half-won.

"You should play that harp," Long Tom said. "Play out your sorrow on its strings."

Wren faced him, his eyes bitter. "I can't. How can I play when... when..."

His gaze returned to the barrow.

"Play their passage to the Otherworld," the tinker said. "That is what my folk do. We lose our sorrow in music and dance. Not to forget, so much as to make the burden of our sorrow less heavy. So play a lament for those dead priests now. Play that the hills and sky will know your sorrow and it doesn't stay trapped inside you. Or if you can't do that, then look around you. Broom and heather! The priests who remain are working to rebuild, but their hearts have lost hope. Their faith falters. Play for them—for their grief— if not for yourself."

"I..."

Wren faltered as he tried to explain why he couldn't play. The music he harped came from a belief in the old ways, in the Fairlord and Moonmother, and the Horned Man of the Wilds, He felt forsaken. They were all forsaken. How could the gods allow Lothan's stormkin to slay the holiest of the Isles? Either the gods no longer cared, or they were gone, as the Summerlord was gone, as hope was gone. What was the use in searching for any of it?

But then something stirred inside him.

Hope, he thought. A man could keep hope, couldn't he, even when all else was lost?

Uncertain, he reached for his harpcase and loosed its ties. Emotions played across his features as he drew the old instrument forth. He stared at it for long moments, then touched the strings, one after the other, to check their tuning. The sweet notes carried no further than a few yards. He looked up at the tinker, a question in his eyes.

Long Tom smiled and urged him on.

Bowing his head so that his red-gold hair fell across the harp, Wren began to play.

He drew an old lament from the strings—a simple melody with no accompanying chords. Then inspiration grew out of his grief. His eyes took on a far-off look and the harping swelled. It tore at Long Tom's heart with an aching beauty. At first it seemed to only increase his sorrow, but then under his grief he sensed a small white-winged wonder growing. Hope, frail and tender. He looked up and away to where the priests worked. One by one they laid down their tools to listen. Long Tom watched the wonder come to them, saw it lighten their sorrow with that small promise of hope that the tinker had recognized as well.

Long Tom rose and left Wren to his music. The harper's gaze lifted and in his eyes Long Tom saw that the dark edge of Wren's grief had grown less keen. He smiled at the harper, a weary smile, and returned to where his family was waiting for him.

THAT NIGHT they all gathered around the tinkers' campfire. Benjamen sat propped up against a wheel of the wagon, his features still strained, though somewhat healthier. The tinkers made room for the priests who numbered no more than fifteen. They were all who had managed to return to Pelamas so far.

Long Tom had cooked up a huge pot of stew when he came back from speaking to the harper, leaving Megan to brew the tea in a collection of small pots and pans. When the meal was done, the two older Turpens sat with Benjamen and two of the priests—Temen and a black-haired, gaunt-cheeked man named Yanun.

In time, Fenne brought out her cittern and a small tin whistle. She began an air on the whistle that Kinn joined in on with his fiddle. Beneath the melody, Wren laid rich harp chords and the magic of the music grew in the night air. Around the fire, faces lost their hard edges and tentative smiles gleamed in the firelight. The other priests drew near, sitting in a quiet circle around the tinkers' fire.

"We should never have forgotten," Temen said when the tune ended. "We wore our sorrow in such tightly-wrapped lengths that we only brought more grief to ourselves. We should not forget the horror that has befallen us, but neither should we simply remember and be no more. We will rebuild the rath of Pelamas as it was first built: With joy and hope. And we will learn again the faith we once knew."

"That is how Penhallow would have wished it to be," Yanun said.

Temen nodded. "And when the stormkin return, we'll meet them as a strong folk, not as broken-hearted ones."

Long Tom thought of Carrie as the two men spoke. She and Deren were alone in Ardmeyn where the stormkin ruled now. Had Tarn found them? Were they even still alive?

He sighed heavily and tried to let the music fill him. The morning would come soon enough and they would continue their journey then. And when would it end? Who could tell?

Megan snuggled closer to him and he sighed again.

Soon, he thought, as Kinn and Fenne began a new tune. Ballan, let it all end soon.

Eighth

HE STORMKIN GATHERED IN the hills that fell under the shadow of Taynbell Peak. They had come from the length and breadth of Ardmeyn, and from across the Narrow. The dyorn Galag stood at the head of the throng. Behind him lay a jumble of broken longstones—a henge that had been destroyed by the Captain in his search for Hafarl. Against one jagged rock, skes bound an erlkin prisoner and the stormkin grew quiet to watch what was about to unfold.

Galag stood silent and grim, long after he'd gained their attention. His thoughts were ugly. Who would have thought it? The Captain dead—killed by his own brother, who had turned from the darkness and so damned himself. Now Galag was in control, but he took no joy from it. His success was no better than Fergun's had been, and soon the Icelord would demand reckoning.

For a week or more he'd scoured the frozen hills of Ardmeyn, seeking the source of that ever-present hint of the Summerlord's presence. For he *was* here. Nearby. There was no doubt of it. But unlike Fergun, Galag knew his limits. He'd continued the search for as long as he could, but now the skes grew restless. The dyorn demanded blood—he could feel the need in his own gut. The direwolves needed fresh meat. He could no longer hold them.

At first he'd found Tus and erlkin for them, dragged them from their hidden holds and killed them. But that supply of living meat had dwindled until now they could find nothing. He knew that some Tus and erlkin survived, but they were hidden as well as the Summerlord—if not better. He could at least sense Hafarl's presence, knew that he was still in Ardmeyn. Those others had fled this frost-bound isle, he reckoned. Fled to the south.

So now blood was needed for the stormkin, and the Summerlord for Lothan, and then they could all go south again to finish the slaughter.

Galag turned to the skes that stood by their prisoner.

"Kill it," he said.

A silver skes blade flashed and the erlkin's blood stained the snow red. The stormkin howled—a piercing skree that echoed and rang across the hills. Direwolves moved forward to lick the red snow, but Galag kicked them away. He spoke words that manifested as dark runes and hovered in the frosty air.

The direwolves fled, whining. Galag knelt in the snow and, peering at the pool of freezing blood, he spoke another word. This one hung in the air, then slowly descended to dissolve into the blood. The pool iced over, its mirrored surface reflecting Galag's face as he grinned into it. He traced a finger along its edge and spoke another word.

His own reflected features shimmered into a whirl of dark mists that spun into the Icelord's cold features. Lothan was white as frost, with eyes deep with the dark of long polar night.

"Why do you trouble me, dyorn?" the image asked.

Galag leaned closer and opened his mind to the probe of Lothan's thoughts. He laid bare the events of the past weeks, of Fergun's death and the name of his slayer, of his lack of success continuing Fergun's work. He waited for his master to finish his probe before sitting back, his eyes still caught in Lothan's dark gaze.

"Stest!" the Icelord said. "I never thought him dead, but for him to have turned to the light..." He frowned, then shook his head. "But he is dead now. And Fergun..."

His eyes cut deep into Galag's mind.

"What do you want of me?" he demanded.

The reproach in his voice was deadly and Galag trembled. Behind him the stormkin moaned and laid their faces in the snow, all except for the skes whose eyes grew only more hooded than before.

"Master..." Galag began, then his voice gave way.

The Icelord sighed and the sound was like the howl of a winter wind.

"I will come," he said then. "I will come and finish this thing myself. Cry it to the winds, dyorn, that my brother hears it. Lothan comes!"

His voice held such menace that even the skes averted their faces.

Galag bowed his head in acquiescence. Teeth chattering with fear, he spoke the closing word and the pool misted, cleared to the red of blood once more. When he stood, his eyes were bleak. He faced the gathered stormkin with a grim set to his features.

"You heard!" he cried, covering his own fear with harshness.

"Lothan speaks through Galag," one of the dyorn answered. "His will be done."

The stormkin scattered and their cries rang though Ardmeyn.

"Lothan comes! Lothan comes! Rise if you dare, Hafarl, Lord of Nothing. Lothan comes!"

IN DAMADAR, the Ice Realm, Lothan rose from his throne and paced half the length of his hall. Rage iced his gaze so that servants scrambled for the relative safety that lay beyond his sight. The Icelord turned to face the throne. The sword imbedded in its stonework glittered mockingly back at him.

"How can they not yet have him?" he asked the weapon. "I broke his damned staff, broke his power. How could he still escape? I was meant to arrive in triumph, not go into battle myself."

The whole of Damadar trembled as he raged. Veins of ice rippled into dire runes under his anger. Frost, already thick, deepened the length and breadth of his realm. He stared at the sword. Yaljoryon. The Deathreaper. The great iron sword that was his power as much as Hafarl's staff had been his.

He returned to the throne and put his hand on the hilt, drawing the long blade from the stone.

"I will find him!" he cried. "I will find him and finish this myself!"

His realm moaned under the thunder of his voice.

AND IN a hidden place, the Summerlord heard. And hearing, stirred.

Now, he thought, his voice weary with the weight of so many slain in this struggle. Now, weavers, your threads near their end.

Upon Taynbell Peak, the snow and frost turned to water and ran from its heights. In the midst of the stone circle at the crest of the crag, the air turned warm; and for all that the Everwinter's' winds howled outside their perimeter, the grass grew thick and green between the stones.

"Come to me, my kin!" the Summerlord cried. "Harshly have you been used, but now it ends. Come, my kin. Gather to me!"

Ninth

FOR A WEEK AND more Tarn searched Ardmeyn.

He fought the stormy rule of the Everwinter in many shapes, replenishing his taw at the few secret places of power untainted by the stormkin. In the first few days, the Everwinter blew him far to the north and he spent a long while working his way back to the hills around Taynbell Peak, and then further south.

As he searched for some trace of Carrie and Deren, he was often in danger of the stormkin sensing his Summerblood. Time and again, black-winged dyorn lifted into the air, troubled by the hint of his presence; and then Tarn had to flee far and fast, returning hours later to begin his own search anew. A litany ran through his thoughts as he flew high above Ardmeyn, his deepsight sweeping the land below.

Too late…too late…too late…

That was his deepest fear, that he had fought the battle inside himself and won it too late to do Carrie or Deren any good. And when his thoughts turned to Puretongue—it was still so hard to think of his teacher as being his father—his grief knew no bounds.

The rune of moon/flight is you, the dhruide had said at their parting. *You'll come with us, then? The rune is you.*

Was it him? If any might have known, it was Puretongue, but his father was dead and now he was...

Too late...too late...too late...

But he would *not* be too late, Tarn vowed.

He cut the Everwinter's winds with bright wings. He padded in furred shape across the frozen wastes. He found the secret holdings of the Tus and erlkin. In them he discovered the remains of those slain by the stormkin, their bones scattered, the teeth marks of direwolves on shredded jerkins and trousers. Shuddering, he would break aboveground, thankful that the remains did not belong to Carrie or Deren, but heartbroken that such pitiful remnants of the old great races were reduced to being butchered by his grandsire's ice-hearted creatures.

Too late...too late...too late...

It was night again. The sky was black above him, the ground below, a frost white. The cold bit to his bones, sapping his strength, stealing his inner warmth. He drifted downward, lost his feathered shape to draw the warmth of fur around him, but the cold ground sucked at his feet, tearing the skin from the pads of his paws. He bit back a cry of pain and changed shape once more. Wearily, his wings fought the bitter ice winds. They battered him across the sky and he struggled to stay aloft, all the time searching. But nowhere could he find a trace of them. Carrie and Deren. There was nothing but the ice and the polar cold.

Too late...too late...too late...

Grey touched the eastern skies, but the rising sun brought no relief. It reflected off the ice and snow, blinding him. His wings faltered, the cold numbing his over-strained muscles. His taw was weakened and in desperate need of replenishing. And then in his confusion, as the cold bit deep and he floundered in his winged shape, he heard a babble of voices.

Stormkin voices, echoing in his mind.

Darkness reached out to touch him—a darkness that was deeper that any he'd experienced before. It was like the shadowed side of his taw, only older, stronger, fiercer.

Lothan, he thought.

He fought the winds with renewed fury. Lothan was coming and he was too late. Carrie and Deren were lost to him and he was left to face the Icelord on his own.

Too late…too late…too late…

He refused to accept it.

He beat his wings harder, trying to lift above the wind. He drew on the last vestiges of his power to set his feeble strength against the power of Lothan's darkness as it continued to seep into his soul.

And then it came. Like a murmur. Like a great form turning in its sleep. A hill rousing. A forest stirring. A deepness upon the world.

The silence like music cut across the wailing and howling of the stormkin's babble, stilling it. Tarn's pulse drummed to its ancient rhythm. He turned his face westward, with the sun at his back, and winged towards Taynbell Peak. The music chimed inside him. His strange eyes were alight with an inner glow.

Hafarl was stirring. The Summerlord. His other grandsire.

He was calling and Tarn could do nothing but answer and go to meet him. If they were all that remained, then they would face Lothan together, grandsire and grandson.

I'm not too late, Tarn told himself. I won't be. I can't be.

He was nearing the peak. He could see it in the distance, a great cloud of steam rising from it, fogging the sky. Tarn's Summerblood quickened. He felt stronger now, and he bent his weary muscles to attain more speed. The peak drew nearer still. Now he could see tendrils of darkness veining the steam. Then he was inside it. After days of bitter cold, the heat felt like an oven around him, burning the frost from his feathers. He flew faster still. Dark thoughts lapped at his mind but he kept them from binding him with deft side-steps of his own thoughts.

Then he was through the mist and dropping from the sky, aiming for the henge that topped Taynbell Peak.

The air whistled through his head feathers. He dropped lower still, until the stones of the henge were all around him. He landed on the ground, marvelling at the green of summer, here in the midst of the Everwinter. The tall dolmen of Taynbell's henge rose grey and grim, massive and solemn in the warm air. The sound of hoofbeats twinned his heartbeat.

Tarn took his own shape and fell to his knees from weariness. His palms were torn and swollen from frostbite. His feet ached in his boots. Every muscle protested the rough treatment he'd given them and begged to be left in peace. But he stumbled to his feet to look around the henge. Where was the Summerlord?

Too late…too late…too late…

The insidious chorus continued to throb inside him, but he refused to believe it. The summer was here. It made the blood hum in his veins, echoing the rhythm that quickened in the air.

Beyond the longstones, the grey mist was webbed with more dark veins than when he had arrived. He turned from it to look for the stone Puretongue had shown him—the stone with the runes. The riddle stone that would unlock the mystery of what he was supposed to do.

The grass grew thick inside the henge. The longstones had moss on their inner sides. Briars and roses twisted around the kingstone. And then Tarn spied it. It was not a stone—or at least not *only* a stone, not anymore—but the runes were still there. He stepped forward and traced each rune with his finger. Wonder deepened in his eyes, for the stone that Puretongue had shown him had grown, and now it was a tree. No more than a sapling pushing up out of the stone, true, but a tree nevertheless. Its stone branches twisted everywhichway, and on each twig leaves blossomed—tiny leaves, webbed with veins. Leaves the colour of Tarn's eyes.

Leaves of the stonewood tree.

"Meynbos," Tarn murmured in awe.

Here was Hafarl's staff of stonewood, growing anew. Under his touch he could feel its growth accelerate, as if his blood flowed from his fingers and into the stonewood, strengthening it.

He looked beyond the longstones again. The mists were still darkening there as Lothan's power grew. The Icelord was very close now.

"Hafarl!" Tarn cried. "Summerlord! Where are you?"

At the sound of his cry, the drumming rhythm inside the henge increased in volume. The stonewood tree continued to grow, but Tarn was alone— and alone, he didn't know what to do. Now it seemed that Lothan's dark thoughts were slipping into the henge, whispering in his mind, binding him with their lies. He shook his head, trying to clear his thoughts.

Too late…too late…too late…

Again the litany ran through him.

"No," he said, but with less assurance.

Where was the Summerlord? Why did he delay?

Tarn felt the rhythm inside the henge slipping away from him. Its green silence developed cracks and Lothan's thoughts gained stronger footholds.

Blood calls to blood, the Icelord said, speaking directly into Tarn's mind. *I recognize you, kinsman. You are mine.*

Tarn shook his head. But Lothan's thoughts continued to batter him. He fell to his knees, cradling his face against the rough stone of the wondrous tree.

You are mine!

"No."

Mine!

"No!"

"MINE!"

The last word was spoken aloud—a roar that seemed to come from all directions.

Tarn fell away from the tree as darkness swelled around him. He felt the touch of a cloak on his face—a touch of icy cloth, polar threads. He scrambled away from its touch and backed up against the kingstone, mouthing curses that caught in his throat. The rose briars tore at his clothes and skin as he stared into the darkness. Frost settled on his limbs. Ice caked his face. His blood grew thick and frozen. And in the darkness, he saw a white cloak flutter in the cold wind. His gaze met the Icelord's. Lothan's eyes were a flickering, cold blue.

Tarn tried to call up one last spell—a name to change his shape and flee—but the magic wouldn't pass his frozen lips. The cold numbed his thoughts and stole away his will. His taw became a distant will-o'-the-wisp that was lost in the shadows. Songspells were gone. Strength failed. Nothing remained but the hard features of the Icelord and his voice that cut like a winter wind.

"Too late," the Mocker said, echoing the terrible litany that Tarn had fought so long to silence. "You were always too late, grandson. Now you are mine, body and soul."

The small swanmage tried to shake his head but Lothan's bond held him fast. He tumbled over onto his side, face buried in the frozen grass, and the darkness swallowed him.

Tenth

"HE TIME HAS COME."

Mearddha lifted her head as she spoke, her gold eyes shining in the cavern's pale light. At the other clan-hearths, erlkin dropped the tasks at hand to stare into unseen distances, searching for the source of the feeling that rushed through them.

"He is stirring," Mearddha said. "The Summerlord—can you feel him?"

Understanding spread among the Tus and wonder touched their swarthy faces. Urth, who was sitting beside Deren, nudged him, his lips pulled in a wide grin. Carrie looked from face to face and sensed the beginning of a new fear rise up inside her. She'd waited for this moment for so long...hours drifting into days and never a word. She'd almost begun to forget why they were here, for in the cavern she was part of a family again—she who had lost her own twice: Once her blood kin, and then the Turpens. But while she hoped the Turpens were still alive, they were far away at the moment.

Deren and she had become part of Urth's clan-hearth. The Tus had lost his own family to the stormkin, so although his clan-hearth had only two hearthkin before she and Deren had arrived—Mearddha and himself—now it numbered four. It was a new thing for the Tus—clan-hearths of mixed races. But Carrie had fit right into her new life. She'd forged for provender with Urth and Deren, learned erlkin wisdoms from Mearddha, spent long hours around the clan-hearth, wrapped in furs and drinking spiced tea. That was when the old ways were explained, and best of all to Carrie's mind, tales were told.

From both Mearddha and Urth she learned more about the powers that stirred inside her. She learned that there was peace in their magic as well as war, joy as much as sorrow. Waning though the powers of the Tus and erlkin might be, they were still born to spells and the old ways of the Moon Mother and Horned Lord. So Carrie, whose first plunge into magic had been the shock of the stormkin, now had the chance to learn something about the old wisdoms that were the foundation of what stirred inside her.

She didn't forget why they were in Ardmeyn; but having been told that they must wait, she simply waited. Sometimes she thought of Tarn. As time passed, he seemed more like a character in some tale than a person she had known; though still she felt an emptiness that his presence had filled. That was because he'd been the one to wake her taw, Mearddha had explained.

Carrie thought of the Turpens as well—and less often, she thought of her own family. She knew that locked behind those memories of pain and ruin and the red swords of the Saramand had been another life, one that held its own warmth and fullness, but that life seemed to belong to someone else.

In this new world, she was Summerborn, and Hafarl called...

"Can you feel him?" Mearddha repeated.

Carrie felt the Everwinter chill her blood, and she imagined stormkin leering from the shadows beyond the clan-hearths—distorted goblin faces hiding from the light. She didn't want to go anywhere. When she left the cavern, the horrors would begin all over again. So she tried to ignore the bright wonder in Deren's eye, Urth's grin, Mearddha's solemn hope.

"No," she said. "I don't feel anything..."

But she did feel it. Something besides fear was stirring inside her. It was the echo of a great shape waking, deep as the earth's bones. A hill moving, and the drum of hooves upon it sent her blood pounding through her veins. If stone could speak, if forests could pull up their roots to walk…it would feel like this. The deep silence of the taw of the Isles washed over and she realized that the Summerlord had finally come. His voice was inside her—that same presence that had come to her once before to ask for her help. It was speaking inside her.

But I didn't understand what you meant, she said to him. *I really didn't know.*

Were it simply for myself, the Summerlord said, *I would not ask this of you. But my brother will rob the Isles of life if we don't move against him now.*

But I'm afraid.

We are all afraid.

Carrie shook her head. The power throbbed inside her. The glow of the Summerlord's presence was in her every pore—a shining music that thrilled her, yet terrorized her. She trembled like a leaf, hands opening and closing on her lap. Then she finally took the power the Summerlord offered her, took it and used it to seal away his presence, to still the thunder he'd woken in her veins.

Silence deepened inside her and she opened her eyes. The others were giving her strange looks, questions plain in their eyes. Folk drifted over from the other clan-hearths and Carrie wished she could disappear into one of the tiny cracks that rilled the cavern's floor. She wanted to get away from everything—the watching eyes, the presence inside her…

"T'peak," Urth said. He pulled her to her feet. "Waiting's over and time's come t'be goin'. Swift an' now."

Without waiting to see if she'd follow, he hurried for the cavern's entrance, Deren at his heels. Carrie watched their receding backs, and felt the weight of the crowd's gaze upon her. Mearddha took her by the arm and steered her after the others.

"Finish it," she said. "Finish it and you'll be free."

Finish it? Carrie thought. She wasn't sure she could. And what did being free mean? Free of what?

She listened to the quiet, wondering where the Summerlord was now that she'd shut him from her mind. Was he at the peak, waiting for them?

Mearddha took her by the shoulders, her hands gentle, and looked into her eyes.

"What is it, child?" she asked.

"I can't do it," Carrie told her. "I just can't. I'm too afraid."

"You *can* do it. Carwyn, you must."

"It's too great a responsibility. I'm not strong enough."

Mearddha sighed. "Then share your load. Deren is with you. Why do you think he came all this way? Just to watch? Let him help you with your burden."

Carrie remembered that moment of sharing her spirit with Tarn and wasn't sure she could do it again. It left her feeling too exposed, too bare.

"I've read the glory-bones," Mearddha said, "and they still say that you are all three bound to do this thing—Deren, Tarn and you. You've come this far, Carwyn. Surely you can finish the journey?"

"But..."

"Whisht." Mearddha kissed her on the brow and gave her a quick hug. "Go, Carwyn. Go and do what must be done. The riddles will all unravel on Taynbell Peak and you will understand why the Summerlord trusted this task to you."

"You *know* this?"

"I believe it."

Carrie stepped back from the erlkin. The stillness inside her seemed endless now—not the silence that came when she raised her taw, but an emptiness. Why did it have to be her? she wanted to ask, but the words wouldn't take shape in her mouth.

"The Moon's own luck be with you, Carwyn," Mearddha said.

Then Deren and Urth were at her side again, asking why she was dawdling. She shook her head, trying to answer, but they each gripped her by an arm and led her off. They sped through the tunnels, and it was all she could do just to keep up. Her fears and doubts remained unspoken. The emptiness grew bleaker inside her and her stomach churned, bringing a sour taste to her mouth. And on they hurried, through long corridors and up, always up.

"Here!" Urth cried, and they came to a halt.

The Tus set his hands to a stone wall, veined with seams of quartz and ore.

"Here be t'way t' Peak."

Carrie leaned weakly against another wall, hands clutching her sides. Urth said a word and touched the stone, his fingers shaping the Sign of Horns. Under his touch, the whole wall moved aside with a heavy grinding groan to reveal another tunnel. It was dark inside that tunnel, as were all the tunnels outside the cavern. Urth had used the magic of the Tus to see by, while Carrie and Deren had used their deepsight. Using that keener sight now, Carrie looked up the new tunnel, then shrank back against the further wall.

"I can't do it," she said.

She could feel Lothan's presence in that new tunnel. Lothan's power. The shadows roiled and churned in its darkness. Tendrils crept out and encircled Carrie's feet, crawling up her legs, oozing like slugs along her flesh. She screamed, flailing her arms, trying to shake them off. Urth stared at her, not seeing anything. Deren, whose taw wasn't as developed as hers, saw nothing either, though he felt an uncomfortable tingle along his spine. He caught her arms to stop her from hurting herself.

"Carrie!" he cried. "There's nothing here."

"They're on me! All over me!"

Deren held her more tightly and lifted her up in his arms.

"Lead on," he told Urth. "I'll follow with her."

Urth looked at Carrie as though she'd gone mad. He could see nothing on her and though he was beginning to feel Lothan's presence now as well, it was still a distant thing. Frowning, he turned and led the way up a spiralling tunnel that cut through the rock and would eventually lead them into the henge on top of the peak.

Deren tried to comfort Carrie while hurrying after Urth. She grew still in his arms, but her eyes rolled wildly. She brushed weakly at the tendrils, shrank back from the walls where they dripped from the rock. She tried to close herself to their touch; but the higher they went, the darker Lothan's shadow grew, the stronger the unseen tendrils.

Deren began to sense something of what Carrie saw, and his skin crawled with revulsion. But he remembered an old healer who'd saved his life and give him purpose—the old healer who'd turned out to be the Founder of Dhruidry, and with Puretongue as an example, he forced himself to go on.

"Fight it, Carrie," he murmured in her ear. "Fight it. That's why we're here."

She knew that. But Lothan's shadow was slithering its way into her soul. Its alien presence sucked at her strength, and the cold...

Deren trembled under weight, his breath coming in rasps. They breathed the frosty air of the Everwinter now—all three of them. Its cold cut to their bones. Frost rimmed their noses and mouths.

No further, Carrie pleaded silently. Please.

The cold ate at her soul. The darkness sucked her strength. And inside her there was only the waste, the emptiness.

"Here!" Urth cried.

He stumbled forward and spoke an opening word. The stone cracked open and they fell into a place of bright light. It took them a few moments to realize that there was grass under them, and the stone that had opened was the kingstone of Taynbell Henge.

Carrie was the first to recover. She wriggled loose from Deren's grip and was brought up short by a tree that was carved from stone. She scrambled to her feet and as her eyes adjusted to the light, she saw it all.

Time moved terribly slowly. She saw the branches of the tree in front of her—stone branches, with stone leaves, beautifully carved—and then remembered Puretongue telling them of Hafarl's staff and the tree from which it had come.

This was it. A stonewood tree with its leaves the colour of the Summerlord's eyes. Of Tarn's eyes. And then she saw the swanmage lying huddled and covered with frost at the foot of the tree.

She meant to kneel beside him, but the Icelord's thoughts tore her gaze away until it rested on a grim man standing in the henge with his white cloak and polar-cold eyes.

Lothan. Icelord. Mocker.

Her soul shriveled inside her, iced and black with hoarfrost.

"Hafarl," she murmured through blue lips. Her summoning was pitiably feeble. "Hafarl..."

Surprise at their arrival died in Lothan's eyes and a mocking smile awoke on his thin lips as he regarded the three of them.

"Oh, he's not here, little Summerborn," he said. "And I doubt he'll be coming any time soon."

Carrie opened her mouth to say, "I know," then saw a rush of movement from the corner of her eyes. It was Urth and Deren attacking the Icelord, the one with his flint knife, the other with a tinker blade.

"Mortal weapons cannot hurt me," Lothan told them.

A small blizzard raged around the three struggling figures, then an inhuman howl of pain rang in the henge and the storm died as suddenly as it had sprung up. Deren fell senseless at Carrie's feet, his right arm and side encrusted with ice. Urth went flying across the henge. He struck a longstone with a dull crack of snapping bone and landed at its base, his head titled at an unnatural angle.

Lothan held his arm where Deren had struck him with the tinker blade. Black blood dripped between his fingers, hissing and smoking when it touched the air.

"Where did you get that blade?" he demanded. "Where did you get that cursed ice-bane metal?"

Carrie's legs couldn't hold her up any longer; she fell to her knees between Tarn and Deren. Her own tinker blade hung heavy at her waist. In a moment he would see it. In a moment they would all be dead.

She laid one hand on Deren's brow, the other on Tarn's. She could feel life stirring in them, present but faint. All the while, her gaze was frozen on the Icelord. He took a great black sword from where it hung at his side and drew it forth from its sheath. Yaljoryon, Carrie remembered Puretongue telling them on the trip north. That was Yaljoryon, the Deathreaper. It was the focus of Lothan's power as Hafarl's staff had been his. But where was the Summerlord? Where was his staff?

The answers came as her gaze locked on the rise of Lothan's sword. The tree behind her was the staff—would be the staff—and the Summerlord...she knew...oh, she *knew*. She remembered him speaking to her in the cavern of the Tus, the feeling that he was present.

Dath! He was inside her—hidden in her taw. And she'd sealed him away with his own power. Used it to trap him.

The black sword went high over the Icelord's head. Carrie bent her will to raise her taw. She took power from Tarn, from Deren. And sent it spiralling down inside her.

Awake! she cried, summoning him, and felt something stir.

The Summerlord's presence rushed through her and Tarn and Deren moved under her hands. Lothan's sword was at its peak. Arcane lights flickered along its black length, sparking with power. But there was power in the henge, too. Carrie's taw leapt in answer to it, drawing the Summerlord up and out of her. His spirit broke from hers, from where it had lain hidden inside her. His form took shape behind her, his antlers gleaming in the pale light, his hands gripping the branches of the stonewood tree.

I need power, he murmured in her mind. *I need time.*

Power there was—a roar and rush of it crackling inside the henge, leaping in bolts of pure energy from stone to stone, but the Summerlord had no focus for it.

Lothan saw him take shape behind Carrie—his hated brother, staffless, helpless. The great blade came roaring down to sweep Carrie out of the way, but Carrie was already in motion.

With a speed that surprised even her, she drew the tinker blade out of its sheath and lifted it to meet the thundering approach of Lothan's sword. It was a hopeless gesture. Deren stumbled to his feet at her side, blinded. Tarn was up too, dazed by the power that rocked the henge, still stunned from his own encounter with the Icelord. Then the two blades met. Yaljoryon struck the tinker blade, forged from a metal no tinker could name. Long Tom had called it erlkin metal. Lothan called it ice-bane.

The blades met with a clang.

Carrie was knocked to the ground by the impact. Her tinker blade should have snapped, but it held on for a long moment until Lothan's power slagged its metal. Instinctively she reached for power and cried out as the henge's unfocused strengths surged into her taw. She screamed louder as it tore through her, cutting her nerves raw, leaping to meet the Icelord's attack, arcing from stone to stone and from her to where Hafarl shaped his staff.

Lothan staggered back, surprised, even baffled at the resistance. He saw his brother clutching the stonewood tree, chanting, using the girl between them as his focus for the henge's power. The longstones were crumbling from the strain, but half-formed under Hafarl's hands, the tree was taking the shape of a new staff. The Summerlord sent out a summoning cry for he needed more power. Carrie crumpled to the ground as her taw was drained. The hengepower that had flowed through her was all gone. She lay as still as death with only a glimmer of faint life in her veins.

Lothan stepped forward, ignoring her now, Taljoryon raised once more. This time Tarn and Deren closed in to meet him. Lothan threw a word of power at Deren and the one-eyed boy fell near Carrie.

Then there was only Tarn.

"You are mine, grandson," Lothan said. "Step aside."

But the Icelord's hold on him had been broken by the touch of a cool hand and a sweet silence he'd shared once before. Now he saw the dead Tus, and grieved. He saw Deren, and grieved.

He knew the Summerlord needed time and he meant to buy it for him. He stood firm. But when he looked on Carrie lying so pale and still, when he remembered the deep warmth of her taw, his heart broke in his chest. The litany returned to him.

Too late...too late...too late...

"No!" he cried.

He lifted his hands against his grandsire, golden fires flickering between his fingers, and called up a deep magic, sought a name for it, named it.

Lothan's sword lowered. He faced his grandson, eyes barren of emotion, his own power reaching out. Tarn's magic died under the Icelord's attack. He replenished it as it failed, drawing deeper inside himself than he'd ever delved before. The shadowed side of his taw cried out to be used, but he saw his grandsire smile and he shook his head. He would only take what came from his Summerblood, only what he could find in the green silence that was like music.

Too late...too late...

His hair grew coarse and whitened. His skin withered as he aged. He fought, but every moment he stood against the Icelord took its toll. Dimly he could sense the henge trembling around them—not from the power he took, but from what the Summerlord took as he struggled to shape his staff.

A longstone tumbled over with a thundering crash. Then another. Stone shards whipped through the air. Tiny slivers struck Tarn's chest, his face, but he ignored the pain and the blood that ran in his eyes. He focused on his grandsire's face, his magic faltering.

Too late…too late…

No, he told the damned voice in his head. *Not too late. Only not enough.*

He was on his knees now, staring up into the Icelord's grim face. All humour had left those cold features, the mockery dying as he felt his grandson's strength. That strength was not enough to hurt him—not in the long run—but it delayed him for too long.

More longstones toppled, their ancient strength withering under the demands placed upon them.

Too late…too late…

Darkness welled up inside Tarn again.

"I tried, Carrie," he said in a broken voice. "Not…not for you…not just for you…but for…for all of us…"

Then he could no longer withstand the Icelord. He tumbled forward, one outstretched hand falling across Carrie's limp form, the other clutching at the grass. His black curls were grey and white now, his youthful face lined like an old man's, his young limbs hunched with age. Deep in his throat he moaned at the backlash of pain.

Then the frozen darkness came again and he knew no more.

Eleventh

A T EARLY DAWN, WHEN the east skies were just reddening, Benjamen rose screaming from his blankets. Long Tom leapt up from where he sat sleepless by the fire, twin blade winking in the pale light.

"Ballan!" he said. "What ails you—"

Then he saw the priests awaking in their camp, hands clutching their heads, cries of pain breaking from their lips.

"Are you all mad?" Long Tom cried.

"It's the henge!" Benjamen replied. He rose to clutch the tinker's arm. "We've got to get to the henge. The battle's begun and the Summerlord needs its strength."

"But—"

"Tom, it's now—now or never!"

Long Tom hesitated only a moment. Reading the look in Benjamen's eyes, he gave a quick nod.

"Then let's go," he said, "and see this through."

"No!"

Temen blocked their way. Other priests gathered around him. The first shock of terror in their eyes had dimmed to a pale understanding that Long Tom found more frightening. Their brown robes were drabber than ever in the early morning light, but their earnestness was hard and bright in the set of their shoulders, in the gleam of their eyes. They were afraid, he could tell—for the Summerlord, for the Isles—but they were more afraid of waking the power in Pelamas Henge without an elder on hand to avert the terrible destruction that could be unleashed.

"Fools," Benjamen said. "Can't you feel it? He needs that power. Without it he's doomed. We're *all* doomed."

Temen spread his hands out before him. "If you use that henge without an elder, you'll be doomed sooner rather than later."

The strain was plain on his features. But it was also plain that he would not be budged.

There were fifteen priests, Long Tom thought, and only he and Benjamen standing against them. The harper was present, but he had taken no side yet. Long Tom looked down at the knifes he still held in his hands. Behind him he could hear his family stirring. He knew that longbows would be strung, arrows notched. Three bows and as many arrows for the first volley. And before the priests could close in, there'd be another three arrows in the air.

"Move aside," Long Tom said.

"You doom us," one of the other priests protested.

"Broom and heather—we're already doomed. Now move!"

Still they hesitated. Long Tom heard the twang of a bowstring and an arrow stuck in the ground at Temen's feet, spitting up dirt on him. He leapt back.

That would be Fenne, Long Tom thought, who was developing the same lack of patience that her father had, Ballan bless her.

Shocked, the priests moved slowly out of the way.

"Please," Temen tried again.

He reached for Long Tom's arm, but his hand fell limply to his side as a tinker blade cut the air between them.

Long Tom and Benjamen ran through the priests. The other tinkers brought up their rear, moving slowly, back to the henge, watching the priests. The harper moved towards them, raising his hands as an arrow turned to point at his chest.

"I want to help," he said. "If I can."

Megan regarded him for a long moment, then gave him a brusque nod.

"Then go," she said.

She watched the faces of the priests, her heart pounding with fear for Tom. Life had been madness since they'd left Codswill and she wanted to see an end to it all now, but Ballan keep her Tom safe.

"WHAT CAN you do?" Long Tom asked the peddler when they were inside the henge.

Benjamen stared about himself. "I...I'm not sure..." His eyes held a haunted, helpless look. "Damn those priests. They could've helped."

"They've made their position plain," Long Tom said. "But we're the ones who came north, drawn by a thing to do. Now here it is to do—or do we join the priests?"

Long Tom looked at the tall longstones as he spoke and felt very small. They were so large—so *powerful*—this close up. Standing amongst them, all he could feel was awe.

"Let's do what must be done," he said quietly. "Tap their power, Benjamen. Like you did on the trip north with the cairns and stones. Tap it and send it to the Summerlord."

Benjamen nodded. He bit at his lip. Slowly he knelt in the grass, pushed his fingers deep into the sod.

"Tom?" he asked. "Can you...give me a little support? I...I'm afraid."

Long Tom looked at the tall stones again and shivered.

"Aye, Benjamen. I can do that."

He sheathed his knives and knelt at the peddler's side, putting an arm around Benjamen's trembling shoulders.

"May I help?"

They both started at the new voice. Long Tom's free hand stopped halfway to the hilt of one of his knives.

"Aye, Wren," he said. "It's welcome you'll be."

The harper knelt on Benjamen's other side. With the two men on either side of him, the peddler took a deep breath and closed his eyes.

He opened himself, as he had so many times on the road north, and his small taw trembled, then woke. The familiar sense of well-being touched him as the green silence swelled and grew strong. He tried to focus it towards the cry for help that had woken him, to send the power there, but it grew too strong and too quickly for him to control.

Both Long Tom and Wren sensed something stir inside the henge. Their gazes met over Benjamen's hunched form. Chills ran up and down their spines and their hair stood on end. Then they heard it—just a dim echo of what was resounding in wave upon wave through the peddler. Hooves on green sod. The swell of the green silence that was like music.

Power crackled from henge stone to henge stone, bathing the dolmen with a fiery light. The power burned through Benjamen's mind as he tried to channel it.

"Take it!" he cried to the Summerlord whose call still rang inside him.

He felt something like a great hand close around him. His breath died in his lungs and his head swam. Long Tom and Wren supported his suddenly limp body. A crack of sound like a great peal of thunder sounded directly overhead and then darkness fell over all three of them.

"TOM!" MEGAN cried, turning from the priests to look at the henge.

Her heart nearly stopped as she stared the stones. Fire licked across the dolmen, leaping from one to the other. She saw the three men huddled together. They grew hazy in her sight. As the peel of thunder echoed away, a brilliant flash of light exploded in the henge and suddenly all three were gone.

"Tom!" Megan cried again.

She threw aside her bow and ran for the henge. Kinn caught up to her just before she tried to pass between the burning stones. His cheeks ran with tears as he cradled his mother's face against his chest. He met his sister's gaze over Megan's shoulder and saw the bleak loss filling her eyes.

"Oh, Tom," Megan murmured into Kinn's shoulder. "Tom. Oh, Tom…"

But there was no Long Tom left to answer. In the henge where he'd knelt with Benjamen and the harper, there was only the grass, white in the reflected light as the stones continued to burn.

Kinn looked away, holding his mother as close as he could, his chest tight, his heart bursting with sorrow.

Twelfth

ON TAYNBELL PEAK, HAFARL bowed his antlered head. Grief swelled in him, dark and sharp-edged, as he saw them fall one by one, his kin, his allies, while Lothan prevailed, the great black sword in his hand, his strength increasing. The henge lay in ruins around them, the tall longstones broken and jagged, frost caked their surfaces, snow drifted deep around them.

Slowly, the Summerlord raised his head to face his brother.

He fixed his gaze on the Icelord. He could not look inside himself or his grief would break him. He could not look around the henge, to see it broken, to see the slain Tus covered with hoarfrost, to see the fates of the three who had held his hopes. If they had not come separately...

Had they come together there would have been time to raise the power, time to shape the staff anew, for in them he'd hidden the riddles of his hope, hidden them so that Lothan wouldn't suspect until it was too late.

Carrie had borne him in her green silence—carried him so secretly that even she had not known he was there. Deren had the knowledge given to him from Puretongue's lesson, and he was to be the balancing factor. Tarn carried that knowledge too, but he was to have been the catalyst, the power that was neither winter nor summer that would set the hope into motion. But Tarn had come alone, the others following and now it was too late.

Lothan grinned, a wide smile that was as cold as the heart of winter. He knew. He reveled in Hafarl's failure.

They stood, brother to brother, enemies. Hafarl's taw still sent forth the summoning call, but he knew now that its call was an empty hope, for who was left to answer it? He stood in the midst of ruin, in the heart of the Everwinter. The henge was gone, its power shattered and drained. But still Hafarl called, his strange gaze locked on his brother's.

And then, from Pelamas, the first and oldest of the henges, came an answer.

Power surged anew in the ruined henge on Taynbell Peak—a raw, wild power, unfocused but strong. Lothan staggered under its onslaught, but Hafarl stood firm and drew it to himself. One part of his mind was aware of three new presences in the henge—three bodies. One was a charred husk, the other two more stunned than hurt. He grieved anew at yet another ally slain—a mortal never meant to wield such power. But then…that the deaths of so many not be in vain…he drew taller and concentrated fully on the task at hand.

The stonewood tree bent into shape under the pressure of his fingers, forming a staff as he became a focus for all the power that came from Pelamas. It scorched him, tore wide rents in his soul, and burned lava-molten as it rushed through him.

And Hafarl, to whom the folk of the Green Isles prayed, prayed himself. He prayed to the Moon and the Horned Hill-Lord, his own dame and sire, as he faced his brother again. Meynbos was in his hands now, reformed and ready.

TARN OPENED his eyes and found himself floating in a sea of cold darkness. He sensed that he was not alone, and the pain that had sent him floundering into unconsciousness was gone. All that remained was a stiffness in his mind, and an emptiness deep inside him.

He drew up his taw and his deepsight pierced the darkness. Reaching out, his hand closed on Carrie's. She stirred under his touch, and woke. His other hand clasped Deren's, and Deren, too, stirred.

The limbo of ice and darkness broke. They saw the Green Isles unfolding below them, as though they regarded them from a great height. First they saw Taynbell Peak where their bodies and the bodies of others lay crumpled under the ever-growing drifts of wind-torn snow. Two mighty figures faced each other there, two silences locked in the greatest fiercing of all.

Then their view widened. Now it seemed that the Isles themselves were unwinding below them. The works of the ancients leapt out at them — henges and solitary menhir, hilltop cairns and ruined towers, old road that traced the paths of leys, the moonroads that joined each place of the ancients, bound them in a riddle that...

...unraveled.

They saw it then, that the leys bound the ancient places and that they were placed to mark the power lines of the earth's strengths. The lines twisted and swirled through the Green Isles, and as their view broadened still more, they saw that the lines reached out to bind all the world with their pattern.

And then the three of them knew.

They watched a thing revealed in the ancient stoneworks and the leys, a wonder that was older than the ancients themselves had ever been. The stones spoke, the first voices of the world spoke with the silence that is like music. Mountains moaned, the hills sighed and the long dance of a hidden mystery reawoke for them, deep in their spirits like the blade of a sharp tune, echoing like hoofbeats, drumming a rhythm that only waited for a melody.

The leys outlined the shape of a harp, a great harp that patterned the world. The stoneworks were the wells of its power, the leys connected them, one to the other. And from that harp came the first murmur of the oldest tune of all, the song of stone and rock that upheld the world, the song that came before growth and growing, hoary and old—the dwystaw of the world, a harpstrength of silent music that was skirling and wild, thrumming with birth, keening with sharp wonder, exultant with a mystery of joy for which there could be no name.

They saw it and their hearts grew still with peace.

Deren raised himself from bruised depths to smile.

Carrie's heart swelled with a joy that not even the Icelord could quell.

Tarn was struck numb, humbled, his awe shining in his leafy eyes.

It must not fail, *he said at last, his voice an echoing murmur in Carrie and Deren's minds.*

For in that harp shape of the world's deep silence, they saw the balance that held the world together, that joined opposites, how the opposites existed to keep the very balance.

Lothan meant to break it.

It must not fail, *Tarn repeated.*

He tightened his grip on Carrie and Deren's hands. His taw trembled as it filled with the deep peace, as the three of them joined their taws to focus that power of the world's heart into the Summerlord where he stood on Taynbell Peak.

HAFARL BOWED his head as the power flowed into him. The strength of Pelamas Henge had reshaped his staff, but the worldstrength of silent music that filled him now would end the battle. When he lifted his head once more, his eyes brimmed with peace.

"Understand," he urged his brother, opening his heart to him, reaching out with his taw to share the wisdom.

Lothan roused himself and shook his head. Mouthing a rune of great power, he leapt forward and struck out with his sword. Rage crackled like blue fire in his eyes. His power roared cold and dark. His anger drummed like an avalanche of monstrous ice. The great black sword came whistling down and Hafarl's staff jumped up to meet it.

For a long moment they were locked in that position, power crackling between their weapons. Then Hafarl's strength doubled as he loosed the final powers he'd been holding back—the last whispers of his taw which were all that had kept him from succumbing to the Everwinter and Lothan's might. The staff glowed amber-gold and hummed in his hands. Lothan faltered, but could no longer retreat. The connection between the weapons held him fast. Yaljoryon began to crack along the length of its black blade. The tiny veins spread and widened.

With a clap like thunder, the sword snapped in two. Lothan fell to his knees, staring at the pieces of the ruined weapon, the broken blade on the grass, the hilt in his hand. Hafarl stood above him, staff upraised, his many-coloured eyes flickering with emotion.

"Peace," he said in a soft voice. "Let there be peace between us."

"*Never.* Kill me now or I swear I'll return to kill you."

"Brother..."

Lothan snarled and struck out with the jagged piece of the sword that protruded from the hilt. Hafarl's staff swept down, striking his arm with a sharp cracking sound. Again they faced each other. Yuljoryon's hilt lay on the ground beside the other half of the blade. Around them, more and more of the grass was showing through the snow. The air grew warmer, clouding with mist.

Lothan clutched his arm—cut once with an ice-bane blade, now broken by his brother's staff. His eyes were those of a trapped creature—unforgiving, desperate, afraid.

Hafarl sighed. His own emotions told him to kill this monster that was his brother, but he knew the balance must be maintained. Summer and winter, each to follow the other in the circle of seasons. But the winters would not be so harsh now—not for many a year.

"Then go," he told Lothan.

He lowered his staff so that it touched the Icelord's pale brow and spoke a rune of power. At that touch, Lothan was gone, returned to Damadar to brood and plot and plan again. Now *he* was the one without a focus for his power. But Hafarl had no intention of taking his brother's rule away from him. He touched each of the broken pieces of Yaljoryon, and they too were returned to the Icelord's realm.

Turning, Hafarl strode to the edge of the peak. He stared out across the Everwinter that still lay across Ardmeyn.

"Begone!" he cried in a voice like thunder.

Power rippled from him to flow from the peak. Stormkin fought to escape the heat as the Everwinter died around them. Drawing deep on the worldstrength, Hafarl gazed further across the Isles, at the warring of the Saramand.

"Begone!" he cried again.

To the raiders, it was as though their Skyfather spoke from the clouds and they trembled. Warchiefs broke their blades at their priests' bidding and spoke of peace.

Then Hafarl knelt on the ground. Pressing his forehead against his staff, he wept.

Thirteenth

ARRIE WAS THE FIRST to lift her head. The power of the worldstrength had healed her body, but nothing could heal the scars in her mind. She stood, head reeling, and looked around. The henge was ruined, its longstones all toppled and broken. She saw the horned Summerlord, head bowed and weeping. The ice and snow were gone. Underfoot she saw green grass and the briars around the king-stone—which was all that remained upright in the henge—flowered with roses.

Beside her, Tarn stirred. When he turned to face her, she stepped back in shock. She knew him by his features, by his strangely coloured eyes, but he was an old man now, white-haired and wrinkled. He looked like—

"Puretongue!" Deren cried.

But then Deren looked closer. This man was beardless and his eyes...

"He was my father," Tarn said, his voice soft. He stumbled to his feet and took a step towards Carrie. "Carrie, I—"

He broke off when she shivered and backed away from him. She remembered it all, everything that had happened; but inside her, where the silence that was like music had hummed, there was only emptiness again. The power was no longer there.

"It's gone," she said. "After all the horrors, now when...when I know how good it can be...when the shadows aren't there...I... it's..."

"Carrie," Tarn said. "It doesn't have to be this way."

She turned from him and saw the still forms of Long Tom and Wren.

"Oh, Dath!" she cried and ran to the tinker's side. "Don't be dead, oh, don't be!"

The tinker stirred under her touch, opened his eyes and she threw her arms around him.

"Carrie," Tarn tried a third time.

She turned to look at him. "No more. It's finished for me. Whatever magic I had is gone and I don't want it back. I just want to be normal again. I've done what I had to do—I've been used until I'm all used up. My part's done, so leave me alone ."

She knew that the swanmage was not part of her future—that he never could be. The magic had brought terror, but there'd been a promise of peace in it, now that the struggle was done. She regretted its loss, but not enough to search it out again.

"You still have your taw," Tarn said. "It can be reawakened."

"I just want to put it all behind me," she replied. "I'm sorry, Tarn. I know it wasn't really your fault—any of this—but I just want to go back to the wagon and live with Turpens. I'm not magic. I never really was, no matter what's awake or asleep inside of me."

As she spoke, she helped Long Tom sit up. The tinker stared around with a numb expression, unable to understand where he was. Tarn nodded in reply to her, hands clenched at his side.

"I understand," he said.

But he didn't. His own taw still thrummed with the wild joy of the vision they'd shared. He knew her magics weren't gone—only hidden again. But he also saw that for her, they might just as well have never woken in the first place.

The Summerlord rose suddenly and turned towards them, his cheeks glistening.

"So much sorrow," he said. "And for what? The weavers weave and the world is much as it was—though there are so many more dead now. So much life and wonder has fled."

He walked over to Carrie and helped her to her feet, then raised the tinker to his. Wren stood to one side. Long Tom stared down at Benjamen's charred corpse and in his mind the Summerlord's words echoed.

So many dead...

Grief burned in him, stark and grim.

"My family," he said. "Are they safe?"

"They live," Hafarl said, "but they grieve for you. I will return you to them in Pelamas. I will send all who would go."

He lifted his staff and looked around. Wren stepped closer to Long Tom and Carrie. Tarn looked away, his expression unreadable. When the Summerlord's gaze came to rest on Deren, Deren slowly shook his head.

"Then it will be the three of you," the Summerlord said. "Return to Pelamas and take up the reins of your life once more. I give you thanks—such heartfelt thanks as you cannot imagine—but what are words amidst such pain? Raise a cairn for this one, your friend who died and gave so much that the Isles could be free of the Everwinter."

And to Carrie, he added silently, *Daughter, will you ever forgive me?*

Carrie started as the words rang in her head. She looked up to meet the Summerlord's sad gaze. He had paid far more than any of them, she realized. And was paying for it still. What he had done, he had done not for himself, but for the whole of the Isles, but that didn't make the weight of the burden he carried any less.

So many dead...

"I do," she said.

A brief, sad smile touched the Summerlord's lips, then he spoke a rune and a golden haze settled over Carrie, Long Tom and Wren. When it faded, they were gone, along with Benjamen's body. The Summerlord's gaze turned to Deren once more.

"Where would you go?" he asked.

Deren looked up to the Summerlord.

"I want to return Urth's body to his kin," he said, "and then I want to learn more. I have nothing to return to."

"So you want to continue your prenticeship?"

Deren nodded. He remembered Puretongue and his lower lip trembled. A small hand clasped his shoulder from behind.

"I'll teach you," Tarn said, when Deren turned around. "If you'll have me."

The face was Puretongue's, and it wasn't. Mostly it was the eyes, eyes like the Summerlord's, eyes like the leaves of the stonewood tree. He gave Tarn a shy smile and Tarn squeezed his shoulder.

"Then I will go," Hafarl said. "There is much to set a-right. Deren...Tarn, my grandson...farewell."

TARN AND Deren stood alone amidst the ruin of the henge. They were quiet for a long time before Deren finally spoke.

"When will we begin the lessons?" he asked.

Tarn looked away. He remembered a young street singer asking a greybeard that same question once, long ago in the streets of Tallifold. They were both gone now—the old man and the boy he'd been.

He turned to Deren, the memory still thick in him.

"We have already begun," he said.